Grace and Disgrace

Kayne Milhomme

For Jayson and Michael

Contents

Prelude

It was rare for a man to be walking in these mountains alone. For a dead man to be doing so was remarkable.

The moon shifted behind silvered clouds, dousing the dead man in shadow. From high among the emerald mountains he came, using ancient footpaths to guide his way. The clannish roads led him to an isolated valley of lush growth where an enduring population survived among the wilderness. Such mundane details did not interest the dead man. Only his destination.

The dead man forded a mountain river two miles from a village, his trousers pinned above his knees to avoid getting wet. The water was cold and clear and moved at a whispering pace. The dead man could have been a mere shadow, so little did he disturb the olden flow. He regained dry land at the settling stone where the villagers came daily to claim their ration of water.

The path to the village was well marked from here. The moon was now in full flight behind the scattered clouds, the sky black and the stars filling its exposed depths like the remnants of a crushed diamond, their pattern ancient and bright.

The course was steep and would be treacherous in such conditions. Only the tremulous glow of the village was visible, a scattered dust below. Such was the distance that it seemed he could cradle the glowing embers upon the palm of his hand and send them swirling into the night.

The dead man was weak, the disease slowly ravaging his body. Breathing was difficult with his rattling lungs. Reaching into his haversack, the man broke off a piece of bread and moistened it in the river. He chewed upon it slowly. For several minutes he looked into the darkness below, lost in contemplations that bore profoundly upon him. Occasionally his thoughts were broken by fits of deep coughing that left him gasping for breath. At length the moon alit from behind the slumbering clouds, the way made clear once again. With a patient step, he moved on.

The dead man was dying, a seemingly ironic state of affairs. But in truth, the foregone conclusion of his nearing demise was the very reason for his return to this place. Death itself, draped in black and bearing a gleaming scythe, was his inspiration.

Never before had he strayed from the rules of a confidence game. Yet poignantly, in the midst of his most elaborate con of all, he had been forced to procure an amendment. There was no purpose in taking the prize for himself, after all. He would be dead. It would have to be passed on, but in a style of his making. With a twist.

He trusted that those who he eventually sent invitations to would accept, for nothing promoted chaos into an endeavor more assuredly than the simple inclusion of people. People with diminutive concerns, apprehensions of contrived importance in their own minds. Trials and tribulations and other laughable complications. Foolish, contrite distractions.

The dead man hoped they would prove obstructive to one another. He had no intention of letting this be easy. Not with such a rich reward at stake. But there was a long time to wait before any of that occurred, and he turned his attention back to his current endeavor.

An old church rose above the gnarled trees, its bell tower stabbing at the moon like a spear. As he approached, the tower's jagged finger dug deeper into the night sky's luminescent heart, the protrusion finally piercing through the moon entirely to merge with the starlit canvas.

The remains of the small church were more or less intact, the single desolate building appearing as lonely and windblown as a treeless island. It was a simple stone edifice, able to house no more than a room for worshipping. It had been years since he had last seen it, but everything looked the same.

The dead man stepped through the front entrance, a vacant archway that had not seen a door in over a century. A small chamber with gaping windows and leaning pews awaited him, cluttered and smelling heavily of mildew. Rubble and debris were scattered across the floor, a lone moonbeam highlighting their mundane existence.

Assorted tools, wooden ladders, and rough-hewn scaffolding clustered at the center of the opposite wall, shadowed evidence of more recent and orderly endeavors. Canvas bundles were carefully situated in wooden crates.

The work had begun.

But it was the moonbeam itself that caught the dead man's eye, his weakened heart skipping a beat at the spectacle. Hues of cobalt, burgundy, and dark green swirled together into riotous patterns, bringing to mind the promise of sapphires, rubies, and emeralds where the fantastical light spread across the floor. And enclosed within the darker radiance a softer tone drifted down like a collection of glittering snowflakes, gifting all that they kissed with a frosted white light.

His gaze shifted upwards towards the stars, dazzling in their splendor.

Yes, he decided, this new confidence game would do very nicely.

Arrival

March, 1902

The man in the fashionably short frock coat walked with a slight limp under the evening shadows of Cross Street. With every other step, a click, sharp and metallic, resounded off the clapboard buildings surrounding him. A handsomely formed mahogany cane, silver tipped, was the cause, the thin apparatus gripped tightly to lend support to his left side. He stood erect, as if to contradict the conclusion that his unbending leg should collapse under the weight of his body. Nobler still was his ability to keep his left arm from shaking as it transferred the brunt of his weight to the cane.

If one at first considered him lessened by imperfection, that observer would think again upon viewing his nonchalant countenance. Dark eyes like soft coal stared from beneath a slim brow from which a thin-ridged, rather neat nose protruded. Cheeks deepened under the shadow of a wide-brimmed top hat, the chin prominent and clean-shaven. Forty-one years in the making, it was an experienced face, not without its share of misgiving and sorrow.

It had been nine years since Jack Tuohay had walked the meandering streets and crooked alleys of Boston, and much had changed in that time. But one thing inevitably had not—he was once again late for an appointment. The faded, silver clasp-watch in his right palm announced as much, ticking nearly in time with the click of Tuohay's cane. The smell of the sea was sharp and thick, the wail of the gulls outperforming the animated banter of two poverty-stricken youths, evidently drunk, lounging aimlessly on the corner of Fifth and Center streets as Tuohay passed by. The buildings rose above him shoulder to shoulder, hiding the view of the harbor. Many were on blocks, reminiscent of a time when the shallows of this part of the city, the "Neck" as it had been called, were regularly swept under the frothing sea. At that time the crabgrass had shared space with the cobblestone, and instead of trade buildings and shops, docks and warehouses had filled the landscape. But that time was long ago.

The building of interest came into view just as the electric lights flared to life above him. Jack Tuohay eyed the tall sentry-like posts with distaste. The soft aura of the gaslight with its shadowy embrace had been replaced by the crisp and utterly unnatural incandescent Edison bulbs, casting their white and artificial haze upon everything in their grasp. The unnatural light cut the darkness to ribbons where the gaslight had been kinder to it, allowing the darkness to dissolve into a coherent embrace with the light. Perhaps the man was not a progressive. He certainly was not among the throng of people who clamored into the newly glowing electric streets when they had first come into vogue. And for his taste, there was something to be said for shadows. Progress allowed less room for such things.

Tuohay stopped at the base of the landing and looked up the small flight of wooden steps to a maple porch. Above it, shutters were closed, save on the third floor where a single window perched in the darkness unspoiled by the electric streetlights, which seemed to avoid the place. A sign above the front door indicated the building as 'The Offices of McBarronThayer'.

Pulling three folded pieces of paper from his pocket, Tuohay checked the contents.

> The Western Union Telegraph Company
> RECEIVED at Harrington Hotel   845 AM.
> Meeting set up at law firm of McBarronThayer, 25 Center Street. 5 PM. Ring bell on arrival. Interview in Loft Room. Telegram sent to John too. He will be there. He has questions, of course. So do I.
>
> Eliza.

> The Western Union Telegraph Company
> RECEIVED at Harrington Hotel   855 AM.
> I just noticed the emblem on your original telegram. District Inspector 2nd Class. At least the ten years in Belfast were not wasted.
>
> Eliza.

The Western Union Telegraph Company
RECEIVED at Harrington Hotel 915 AM.
Telegram received from Eliza this morning. She
wires "Meeting set up at law firm of
McBarronThayer, 25 Center Street. 5 PM. Ring bell
on arrival. Interview in Loft Room. " Will meet
you there. Just like the old Sleuthhound days.

John Eldredge

With a practiced step he ascended the porch and exchanged the silver pocket watch from his pocket with the telegrams. The working of the minute gears chirped like a lonely cricket, incessant and unchanging. He was still late, of course, as confirmed by the slim hand that had barely budged from the "2" since his last glance. He snapped the case shut with a flick of his wrist and deposited the watch into his coat pocket. His eyes fell upon the door, and for a moment a chill flickered in his chest. Coughing slightly, he raised his hand towards a thin rope indicating the house bell, but a voice called out behind him.

"Jack!" A thick man hustled down the walkway and onto the stairs, his hand pressing his bowler cap safely to his skull.

Tuohay watched the approach with a measured smile. "Mr. Eldredge. You have not changed a bit." Tuohay removed his top hat and bowed slightly at the arrival of his friend.

John Eldredge, forty, with a deceptively childlike face and bulbous blue eyes, was short of breath. Slowly he nodded, his pudgy frame jiggling. He was informally dressed, still the daytime attire, dark waistcoat and tweed breeches the color of molasses. The points of his highly starched shirt were pressed into wings, and a loose ascot, its token white jewel embedded at the bottom, hung somewhat askew at his rounded belly.

"Jack Tuohay," said Eldredge happily, offering a hand that was accepted with enthusiasm. His voice dropped to a whisper as his face crinkled with curiosity. "So it takes the possible discovery of a lost artifact to bring you back to Boston after all these years?"

"Not just any artifact," Tuohay corrected, "the Templar Diamond."

"The Templar Diamond," Eldredge asserted. "Disappeared from St. Peter's Cathedral in Belfast six years ago." He took a moment to wipe the beads of sweat from his forehead. "But that's not all that brings you here."

"The priest's death, yes." Tuohay replied somberly. "Aiden Kearney was an old friend."

"I recall. We ran a few investigations for him years ago," said Eldredge. "I am sorry to hear of his death. But you are also here following a suspect from Belfast?"

"From across the ocean, yes. You and I have much to discuss, but the interview awaits."

"Of course," said Eldredge. He pushed open the door and stepped in. "Shall we?"

"Should we not ring?"

"Ah yes," Eldredge said. "I thought perhaps you were already making your way in." He tugged on a small rope hanging from a brass loop. No ring was discernable. Waiting a few moments, Eldredge tried again. Again no ring was forthcoming, or any sign of welcome from within.

"No matter, the offices are empty save our interviewee." Tuohay reached into the inside pocket of his coat and produced an envelope. "Before we go on—this was sent to me anonymously several months ago." Tuohay handed it to Eldredge. "Are you still working with codes?"

"On occasion."

"Good. This letter is a peculiar invitation, as you will see. Regardless of the rather outlandish content, there is at least a grain of legitimacy to be found within. I also have a hunch that it is encoded." Tuohay stepped past Eldredge into the hall beyond the door. He was peering into the gloom as he spoke. "I must admit, I was not certain you would accept my request for help on this case."

"What's a decade between friends?" Eldredge murmured, flushing slightly. He followed Tuohay inside. "Besides, I have been in want of some excitement. Generating population and agricultural statistics for the government does not exactly stimulate the senses. Neither does writing telegram and pocket codexes, despite what one may believe. To be frank, the idea of working on another Sleuthhound Case is tantalizing."

"This endeavor will be far more involved than any of our amateur cases," warned Tuohay, facing his companion. "I am still working for the RIC and as a liaison for Scotland Yard, as well as consulting with the Boston authorities."

"You have become important in the last ten years," Eldredge remarked, only half-kidding. "So how has your time been with the Royal Irish Constabulary? I hear Belfast is…tense."

"Belfast is a booming industrial city," Tuohay replied, his attention drawn down the hall as he spoke, "mostly known for its remarkable shipyards. I will tell you this—there are floating wonders along the city's emerald shores the likes few have seen. To a visitor, it must seem as if Belfast believes it can conquer the very sea with the elegant monstrosities it is erecting." Tuohay's eyes lit with dry humor. "But there is still a place for a man such as me as well, especially in my old stomping grounds of Ardoyne. Action abounds."

"Indeed. I would love to hear about it."

"We must catch up later, old boy. For now, the present." Tuohay patted Eldredge on the shoulder. "You are officially deputized, along with Eliza, for this investigation."

"Miss Wilding." Eldredge smiled, his voice reminiscent. "It will be good to work with her again. So you can do that? Assign any partner to an official case, just as the mood suits you?"

"No one has told me otherwise. At least not yet." Tuohay winked. "Come along."

Tuohay focused on the entrance hall. Dark pine stretched across the floor, the pitted boards gleaming from countless polishes. A heavy Persian rug hugged the far corner of the room where the staircase began, a steep and narrow affair. The walls of the room were of similar make and demeanor, but were burgeoned with pictures and paraphernalia—announcements for the South Catholic glee club abutted a call for volunteers at Saint Elizabeth's, "to be paid by the hour with the adoration of His Grace". Beside this was a daguerreotype of the 1892 Champion Boston Beaneaters, the hero slugger, Hugh Duffy, center front.

"Do you remember their 1891 season?" Eldredge asked, following Tuohay's gaze. "It was the last before you left Boston.

We took Eliza to one of the final games, a whopper. The only thing missing was Hugh Duffy—he was still with the Reds."

"Of course. When it comes to Eliza my memory is intact, as I am sure is yours, even after a decade. I am looking forward to seeing her again."

A silence followed Tuohay's words. "So, let us speak of Sara Conall. All of this conversation about ourselves, and yet we are late to the very meeting that I requested."

"Before that…" Eldredge peered at the envelope Tuohay had handed him. "If I may?"

"We are already tardy for the interview. I assume she is waiting?"

"I assume so," Eldredge shrugged. "But she can wait just a moment more, no?" He looked at the envelope with a longing gaze. "You mentioned a code ….?"

Tuohay sighed. "As you will."

Eldredge opened the envelope with care and unfolded the document, scanning it quickly. The paper was as black as night on both sides, the script in flowing silver. A white border contained two winged serpents beautifully drawn in gold. The creatures were in circuitous pursuit of each other, bending around opposite corners of the border with fangs bared.

"Rag paper," Eldredge commented, rubbing the material between his thumb and forefinger. "Soaked with ink, it would seem." It was soft to the touch, but left no trace of ink on his fingers.

AN INVITATION TO THE CHASE

February, 1896
Dear Mr. Jack Tuohay,
I hope you will allow this unforeseen intrusion on your time. This correspondence is presented with humility and no intention to mislead. It is, plainly stated, an INVITATION. You of course have heard of the Star of Bethlehem, otherwise known as the Templar Diamond.

I, the writer of this correspondence, am at fault for the recent dramatic theft of the diamond. As I am sure will come to light, there was a company of three individuals responsible for its disappearance. I was one.

You should be receiving this invitation almost six years after the crime. I am certain the diamond will not yet have surfaced. Thus, this letter is the cue that the chase to recover the great Star has begun.

To explain, I am dying. The entire enterprise of stealing the diamond was an elaborate confidence trick that even my two partners were not aware of. For that reason, I alone now know the location of the diamond.

Because of my failing health, I have decided to change the rules of the game and share the diamond's whereabouts to anyone clever enough to properly listen. I am enclosing information to that effect. For me, it has always been about the chase, and not the prize. Therefore I am honored to now share that experience with you.

However, know this. You are not the only recipient of an invitation, for what measure of game would that make? And be aware—the other beneficiaries may be out for more than just riches. They may be out for blood.

Your information is as follows:

> A man named Kip Crippen will sail for Boston, America, in late February of 1902. He will be searching for the diamond.

Do with this information as you please, but I implore you to seriously consider it.
You were chosen for a reason.

I welcome you, in advance, to the chase.

Your Friend in Sympathy

Eldredge folded it up, following the original creases. "I have never seen anything quite like it. You are sure it is authentic and not a hoax?"

"That is my inclination, but truth be told, I am in the process of figuring that out right now, old boy."

"Who has analyzed the letter so far?"

"Inspectors at the RIC in Belfast, who I shared it with. And a copy was furnished for Scotland Yard by the RIC."

"Is there consensus on the existence of a code?"

"No. Simply a hunch on my part."

Eldredge swelled with a look of importance. "I will take a closer look at it tonight. Is this why you are in search of Kip Crippen?"

"The primary reason, but we will speak of the details later," said Tuohay. "For now, let's focus on the interview." He peered up an adjacent staircase. "Eliza's telegram said to meet Miss Conall in the loft. That would be upstairs, I presume."

"Ten years as a constable in Belfast has taught you much," Eldredge said with a sidelong glance at Tuohay.

"District Inspector, 2nd class, to be specific," Tuohay corrected.

"You could have been a doctor and avoided all of this, you know."

"Yes, but medical school was not for me, as you should recall. And so here I am. To the top, then?" Tuohay motioned for Eldredge to lead the way.

The pine steps groaned as the men began their climb.

"Miss Conall," Tuohay called, his voice rising up the stairs. They stopped for a moment to listen.

Eldredge shook his head. "No response. Odd." He cupped his hands around his mouth. "Miss Conall, are you up there?"

Following Eldredge, Tuohay took his cane in hand and used the wall on his left to support his weight. Alighting onto the second level, the two looked upon a single hallway. It was crammed with offices, a framework of order constructed around the chaos of articles, files, and other odds and ends accumulated through lawyerly interests.

Eldredge led the way to an adjacent staircase. "This one must lead up to the loft."

They ascended the stairs, at the crest of which a partial view of the gloom-ridden attic came into view. Open rafters hung threateningly low from the main joist, shadows hiding in the corners that the dying light could not reach. The fading breath of day entered through a broad window at the south of the room where an empty chair sat cockeyed from a neighboring desk. It was free of dust and appeared to be recently used. A scattering of papers littered the desk, a pair of wire rim glasses atop them. An open bottle of ginger beer stood stoically beside the papers.

Tuohay walked over to the desk with an unhurried step and raised the bottle to his nose. "Fresh. Recently opened." He set the bottle down and inhaled slowly through his nose. "Do you...?"

"Smell the lingering scent of tobacco? Yes."

"Spice tobacco. Perique."

"A brand of pipe tobacco, yes," Eldredge agreed.

Tuohay turned back to the desk. One of the papers revealed a title in eloquent cursive: *Essay for Admission. Adoration of the Magi in Religious Art: Restoration Practices of Oil on Canvas, Mural, and Stained Glass. Authored by Colin Allotrope of Great House, Trinitarians of Mary.*

Several of the pages beneath it had edit marks over the original writing. Tuohay made a mental note of the author's name.

"So, where is Miss Conall?" he inquired, his stare burning into room.

Eldredge bit his lip. "I cannot say. Do we have the correct time?"

As if in response to Eldredge's question, the watery trickle of an out-of-key piano drifted from below.

"What is through there?" Tuohay asked, striding over to the center of the attic where a small, nearly hidden door stood ajar. The piano reverberated with surprising clarity beyond it.

"Storage, I believe," Eldredge replied, stumbling after his tall companion. Despite his limp, Tuohay moved swiftly, his stiff leg orbiting from his hip fluidly for its condition. The thin tune grew louder as the door was pushed aside. Shadowed and strange shapes stood end upon end before the two men: old flower vases upon boxes upon desks without drawers, dusty cloth bags reduced to cheesecloth by hungry moths, old ice skates with rusty blades, faded portraits where only the artist's signature could clearly be made out. All of this clutter Tuohay passed by until he came to a vent at the north end of the room. The ballad rose in volume and texture from the vent as if from the trumpet horn of a phonograph.

"Strange," Tuohay remarked, peering at the dark vent. He turned to Eldredge. "Back down, I suppose. Let us see who our mysterious player is."

Several minutes later the two men were on the first floor again, the melody pulling them along like a current. Tuohay led the march, his eyes riveted on the small doorway leading into an apparent drawing room. A plaque at the doorway displayed, "The Seymore M. Left Room" in brass lettering.

Stepping through, Tuohay immediately focused on the musician in the corner of the room. "Miss Conall?" he said.

The music died away as the young woman playing the piano turned on the stool to face the two men. "I did not think you were coming. It is a quarter past the hour." Her voice was soft, the Celtic accent pronounced.

"Yes. Well, we decided to do some exploring first," Tuohay replied.

She cocked an eyebrow. "Northern Ireland? Ardoyne?"

"Remarkable," Tuohay said, his eyes widening with surprise. "Did you glean that from my accent?"

The woman laughed. "You were born and raised in Ardoyne as a young child, but sent to America by your mother for schooling. Spent most of your formidable years in Boston. Returned to Belfast to serve your homeland in the Royal Irish Constabulary for the last decade. Drawn to where the trouble is, it seems." She smiled softly. "No, it was not your accent that gave you away. My uncle Aiden told me about you before he died. You are Jack Tuohay."

"Yes," said Tuohay, comprehension crossing his face, "of course. How very foolish me. Father Kearney was your uncle. He was a remarkable man, if I may be so bold."

"A father figure?" she ventured. "Do not be surprised by my remark," she continued softly, the smile fading. "He was a father figure to many."

Silence spilled past her comment, and Eldredge made a small show of removing his hat. "Did you not hear us calling your name when we entered, Miss?"

"Sorry, no," she said, her thoughts seeming to rush to the present. "I was in the back courtyard waiting for the bell to ring. I see you took the liberty of letting yourselves in."

"Ah, yes." Eldredge blushed as he bowed. "That was my fault." Eldredge gathered himself. "I am Mr. John Eldredge, associate to this fine gentleman beside me. He recently returned from solving crimes in the darker sections of Belfast. We are at your service."

The young woman sat unmoving. "Darker sections of Belfast, you say? And where may they be, pray tell?"

"Wherever you like them to be," said Tuohay, "for the darkness exists in the hearts of men, not the streets they inhabit." He took a moment to visually collect Sara Conall. She bore her age well enough, which was mid-thirties by all accounts. A delicate countenance with sharp features and a slim neck were the most admirable qualities. Dark auburn hair was pulled into a tight knot at the back of her head with a few strays dangling in slim curls about her eyes. They were tired eyes, emerald green with more moss than gemstone. She wore a fitted bodice of plain white, the front skirt hovering dangerously just above the ankles. Slender hands rested on her lap, fingers tapping lightly, no ring or other jewelry visible.

"Miss Conall, did you perchance leave anything in the attic before your flight downstairs?" Tuohay asked.

Sara shot Tuohay a curious look. "I was not upstairs. To be clear, I am not overly familiar with this building. My late uncle's lawyers, Mr. McBarron and Mr. Thayer, generously suggested that I use it for this interview today, as it could afford privacy. They of course have been fully briefed in advance of this meeting."

Tuohay looked closely at Sara. "So, you are alone here?"

"I let myself in with the key and have only been to this room and the back courtyard."

"I see. The two lawyers, Mr. McBarron and Mr. Thayer, do they formally represent your interests?"

"With the recent death of my uncle, their representation has ceased save for certain kindnesses. They were *his* representatives."

"Certain kindnesses, you say. Such as?"

"Such as guidance regarding this interview. They still have an interest in information pertaining to their late client."

"Then why are they not present?"

"Mr. McBarron is both a very devout and very busy man, and despite his personal interest in the affair, it is no longer a professional concern. Mr. Thayer has actually stepped away from the practice, and only has a personal interest at this point as well." She looked down at her hands. "I hear the name of the firm is to be changed to McBarron and Associates, after nearly a century as McBarronThayer. I do not believe there is any love lost among the two men."

She raised her head. "Nonetheless, as I recall, your letter stated that you preferred to interview me unaccompanied about my late uncle. And so here we are."

Eldredge cleared his throat softly. "My lady, was that John Paine's *In Spring* that you were playing when we entered?"

"You know it?"

He smiled in satisfaction. "The first American symphony? Of course I know it."

"Eldredge here is quite the source of knowledge for the finer melodic achievements of the century," Tuohay added.

"Is that so? Then perhaps you know this."

Turning, she held her hands rigidly above the instrument as if waiting for the perfect moment to make contact, and then gently, almost invisibly, allowed her fingers to fall into a slow but beautifully flowing dance upon the thin keys. The lonesome melody filled the room like a weeping ghost, its cold arms shrouding the men with melancholy, transfixing them until its final refrain.

Sara set her hands upon her lap and regarded them patiently.

"*Easter Snow*," said Eldredge. His voice was soft with reverence. "You play it very well."

"From where I come, it is known as *While the Shepherd Watched His Flock*," she said, smiling quietly.

"So it is," said Tuohay.

The room grew dark, the last shred of day slipping from the windowpane into oblivion. Eldredge broke from his reverie to attend to it. A colorless light popped on, followed by a second, and Tuohay looked at the lamps Eldredge had ignited with distaste.

"You prefer the darkness?" Eldredge asked. "Truly you are not in opposition of such a wondrous device as a lamp that runs on electricity."

"They say the world will run on electricity someday," Sara remarked. "It is quite an astonishing thought."

Tuohay shook his head. "Indeed it is. Electricity will run the world, but what will run the electricity?" He procured a slim metal case from his pocket, tapped it once on his palm, and caught the black cigarette. Sliding the canister back into his pocket, he looked about and frowned. "Usually there is a live flame available at these late hours. Another inconvenience of the great electric light." Reaching into his back pocket, he retrieved a British match case and with deft fingers opened it, removed a match, and struck it. The cleft of his chin glowed orange as he raised the match to the cigarette in his lips. The aroma of cloves rose into the air.

"Medicinal or recreational?" Sara asked.

Tuohay gave Sara a sidelong glance. "Both, though I wonder at your interest."

"I think it is a fair question," she replied, a warm flicker in her eye.

"Indeed, Miss Conall. The mythical art of smoking, like many of the forbidden fruits of our society that appear fashionably continental, in reality becomes quite commonplace after a spell. Nothing intrigues a man more than that which is taboo, and nothing is more inadequate than finally experiencing the forbidden fruit and realizing it tastes no different than any other."

Sara was unimpressed. "You seem to be an overly opinionated man."

"A lame leg and defunct lungs force a necessity of careful thought upon me, which I occasionally delight in sharing with others." He took a drag on the cigarette. "I cannot fancy my pain away, Miss Conall. So I talk. Does it displease you?"

"No." Sara smoothed her dress with her hands. "But perhaps we should get to it."

"Of course." Tuohay motioned to Eldredge. "Three chairs, my good man. I am more than willing to assist you, of course."

"No need," Eldredge replied, sliding three chairs over from the unlit fireplace. They settled in, Tuohay turning his head with a slight groan. "John, please turn out at least one of those forsaken electric lights, if you will."

"Right." Eldredge extinguished one of the lamps as Miss Conall looked on with a questioning look.

Tuohay followed her gaze. "Mr. Eldredge is quite a capable man. He is not an errand boy, mind you. He will be an indispensable aid to my work here." He flicked the last of his cigarette into the cold hearth and leaned back in his chair, the expression on his face hidden by the thin shadow that accompanied the subtraction of the light. "And you have met Eliza, of course. The woman who set up this interview while I was sailing to Boston from across the sea."

"Is she why you left Boston for Belfast? A jilted romance?" Sara's smile was thin. "She was tense with excitement at the news of your return."

Tuohay appeared puzzled at Sara's remark. "Hardly. My abandonment was of an entirely different nature. I am surprised your uncle did not tell you of it." He exhaled softly, as if releasing the matter from his mind. "But to stay on topic, let us start with your relation to the deceased brothers."

"My uncles. Father Aiden Kearney and Uncle Rian Kearney."

"Yes."

"Are you here to investigate their deaths? Or are you here to find the Templar Diamond?"

Tuohay tapped his cane lightly against the floor. "And when, pray tell, did I mention the Templar Diamond?"

"You did not," said Sara, brushing an errant strand of hair from her eyes. "But Uncle Aiden did. *Surely* you know that, inspector. *Surely* that is the reason you have taken the trouble to come all the way across the ocean to speak with me. Because I have information that you want about the lost diamond."

Tuohay steepled his fingers. "Let me set the stage for you, Miss Conall. This week, I took a steamship across the Atlantic in pursuit of an alleged criminal named Kip Crippen. I am following him because it is possible that he is linked to the disappearance of the Templar Diamond, which occurred in Belfast in 1896."

Sara seemed to pay closer attention at the mention of Kip Crippen. "Go on, inspector."

"The diamond was mysteriously thieved while in transit from St. Peter's Cathedral to a safe house in the city. Stolen despite the fact that there were two decoy carriages—each with an impenetrable safe within—three safe house locations, a series of hand-picked, armed guards, and highly specialized personnel coordinating the efforts throughout the city. I should know," Tuohay added sourly, "I was on detail in the Gaeltacht Quarter when word reached us that the diamond had disappeared."

"That must have been embarrassing for the Constabulary," said Sara.

"More than you know," admitted Tuohay. "However, a few months ago, and nearly six years after the crime, your late uncle Father Kearney rekindled interest in the case when he claimed to have come across evidence about the diamond's disappearance. He did not specify how he came across it, but evidently he did so while gathering information for his appeal against the archbishop of Boston." Tuohay leaned his chin on his fingers. "It was me he initially contacted, by telegram. He wanted to tell someone he could trust that was in a position to help."

Sara's gaze narrowed. "Is that the only factor that brought you here? A correspondence from my uncle?"

"No." Tuohay nodded at Eldredge, who produced the letter and handed it to his curious neighbor. The silver ink glimmered in the firelight as Sara perused the contents. She handed it back with a thoughtful frown, but did not comment on it further.

"And now let me set the stage for *you*, Inspector Tuohay," she said. "As you are aware, my Uncle Aiden and his brother Rian were both found dead in their shared flat on Kneeland Street two months ago. It was ruled a double suicide, but I wonder at the pronouncement. Are they dead because of what Uncle Aiden discovered about the diamond? Are they dead because somehow it was exposed that he contacted the authorities across the sea by telegram? That he contacted *you*?"

Tuohay was silent for a moment. "I pray not."

"Praying is merely despair masked as hope," Sara scolded. "So let us speak plain. You are here to determine what, if anything, my uncle may have told me that can help you in your search for the diamond. As simple as that."

"The death of your uncles is prominent in my mind, but when skinned to the bone, yes," Tuohay acknowledged. "My official business is to locate the stolen diamond."

Sara sighed as if burdened by the confirmation. "Then let us start with that."

Trials and Tribulations

"I apologize if I appear short with you, gentleman," Sara began, smoothing her dress again with her hands. "But you must understand that my experiences in Boston have left me both wary and weary." Her Irish accent left even less distinction between the two words.

"There is no need to apologize," Eldredge said with a helpful smile.

"Both of you as well as your friend Eliza Wilding were once known as the Sleuthhound Club. Harvard and Radcliffe graduates moonlighting as…what would you call it? Consulting detectives?"

"It was an interesting diversion, yes," said Tuohay. "We ran the Sleuthhound club for a few years before I dropped out of medical school and entered the Boston constabularies, and a short span of years afterward that. Understand Miss Conall, it was twenty years ago and we were amateurs, at best."

"Yes, and twenty years ago Uncle Aiden hired you to help with his investigations," said Sara. "He used your information with his own to build his case against the archdiocese and the archbishop."

"He employed our skills on a few occasions," confirmed Eldredge, "and though we may have suspected his reasons, we were never *in the know* regarding his intentions. Most of our work was to perform interviews with parishioners that had claims against the Church. I think he came to us because we were discreet."

"He trusted you," Sara said, "and continued to, some twenty years later. That is why he telegraphed you, Inspector Tuohay." She stared at the two men as if to challenge her statement.

"Yes, he relied upon me," said Tuohay.

"You were among the very, *very* few that he trusted by the end," said Sara, her voice dropping to a whisper. She let the thought linger for a moment before straightening herself, forcing a pleasant smile across her face.

"So let us begin at the beginning—"

A loud rap at the front door echoed from the hallway.

"Are you expecting anyone?" Tuohay asked.

Sara's gaze narrowed. "No, are you?"

The three sat in wait as the room dropped into a silence. The second succession of knocking reverberated like a warning through the house.

"Perhaps I should get it," Eldredge offered. "My presence, of any, will raise the least amount of suspicion."

"None of us belong to this law firm," said Tuohay, "so I am afraid suspicion may be aroused regardless of who answers."

"It shall *not* be me." Sara's tone left little room for argument.

Tuohay began to rise, but Eldredge leapt up to block his path. "No, Jack. I can handle it."

Tuohay nodded in concession, his leg buckling slightly as he slid back into his chair. Eldredge left the room, and the sound of the front door opening was followed by a nasally, staccato voice.

"It's the *papers*," Sara hissed, her eyes widening. Tuohay confirmed his agreement with a concerned nod.

Eldredge's raised voice preceded the slamming of the front door, and several moments later he reappeared in the room. He quickly drew the curtains, causing Sara to raise a worried hand to her mouth.

"A journalist?"

"Yes, by the name of Mountain," said Eldredge, concern lining his voice. "He writes for the *Boston Evening Traveler*. He had a tip that an investigator from Scotland Yard was meeting with a client of McBarronThayer's tonight about the lost Templar Diamond, and wanted me to comment for the record."

"How in the blazes did he hear that?" Tuohay thundered. "Misinformed though it may be, it is close enough to the truth." He turned to Sara with a flash in his eyes. "Who have you told about this interview?"

"I should ask you the same, inspector," Sara snapped.

"A moment, please," said Eldredge. "Let us not reach for one another's throats. There is more than a fair share of people that are aware of this meeting, if I am not mistaken."

Tuohay nodded reluctantly. "True, old friend. The Boston authorities, for one."

"And Mr. McBarron and Mr. Thayer, and perhaps some of McBarron's staff," Sara added. "As well as my brother, Sean."

"And Eliza," said Eldredge.

"The point is valid," Tuohay said, raising his hand in surrender. "I apologize, Miss Conall. I should not have come at you like I did. It is not relevant at this moment *how* he heard, but simply that he did and is no doubt waiting somewhere nearby."

"I do not want to be publicly associated with this investigation," said Sara, lines of worry creasing her face. She turned to Eldredge. "You said nothing to the journalist?"

"Nothing that he can put in the paper," Eldredge replied with an embarrassed smile.

Sara did not appear soothed. "The papers have been unkind to my family over the years. *Very* unkind. Even with my uncles' recent death…I could not bear it."

"We will see to it that you remain nameless," Tuohay reassured her.

"Either we wait Mr. Mountain out or try to give him the slip," mused Eldredge, tapping the back of his chair with his knuckles.

"I am certain you will think of something," Sara said, a soft confidence returning to her voice. "But we are here for a reason. Let us get to that first."

Eldredge frowned. "But the journalist—"

"Let us at least share something meaningful so we have something to hide from him," Sara said, the corner of her lips curled into a small smile.

Eldredge returned to his seat as Tuohay took a long draw on his clove cigarette. Flicking the remainder into the cold hearth, he turned to Sara. "Am I to assume you have something meaningful to share, then?"

"I have two letters, the same as yours."

"Two?" Tuohay's curiosity was piqued.

Sara carefully removed two pieces of parchment from a purse at her feet. They were on folded black paper. She handed them to Tuohay, who opened them one at a time as Eldredge jostled over to look. The silver penmanship was unmistakable.

The letters were identical in script and design to Tuohay's letter, save for the salutations and the indented clues.

Dear Miss Sara Conall….

…Your information is as follows:

You uncle Aiden rightly took the archbishop to trial, but was ruined for it. Take comfort that unearthing the diamond will lead to the downfall of those your uncle opposed.

A man named Jack Tuohay will come to America in search of the diamond. He will find you. If you assist him, he will assist you in uncovering the truth.

Dear Father Aiden Kearney...

...Your information is as follows:

You seek redemption. A ray of light: your nemesis, Father Robert Donnelly of Plymouth, played a role in the crime of the Templar Diamond.

But it is evidence you need, not mere whisperings in silver lettering. Ask his former lover, she knows his secrets. She will help you, if you help her. Start with the codex.

Tuohay handed the letters back. "When did you receive these?"

"About five months ago," Sara replied, tucking them back into her purse. "Uncle Aiden gave me his for safekeeping after I told him that I had received one as well."

"What trial are the letters referring to?" Eldredge asked.

Looking up, Sara's green eyes were stark against the pale electric light. "My uncle discovered serious wrongdoing in the Church during his tenure as a priest," she replied, "but rather than being heeded, he was ignored. Over twenty years of service, he was jostled from parish to parish, and with each departure he took with him accusations against his brethren of nepotism, concubines, mismanagement of property, nonpayment of salary.... The list was as exhaustive as it was disturbing. At first he was careful in how he shared it, but by the end he was quite willing to make it entirely known to the public at large. The press referred to him as a rabble rouser, among other things. Eventually, it got to the point where the archbishop cast my uncle out for good by removing his priestly faculties, his very livelihood."

"And this led to a trial?" Eldredge prompted.

Sara smoothed her dress with steady hands. "Yes. Uncle Aiden took Archbishop Walsh to trial for recompense. Not an ecclesiastic trial. A trial in the public courts. Such a thing had never been done in Boston before. Perhaps all of America." Her gaze dropped to the floor. "The trial was a sensation in the press, but a disaster for my uncle. The defense attorneys destroyed my uncle's character with *lie after lie*. Prostitutes took the stand and claimed that Uncle Aiden had relations with them—they turned his *very claims* about corruption on him! *He* became the sinner in the eyes of the public, the transgressor." She laughed with unrestrained bitterness. "He was devastated by the loss of the trial... a shattered man, never again the same."

When she looked up, her face was flushed. "But what is it to you, anyhow? You ask about the trial, but it is merely periphery. What about the *diamond*, you are wondering. You are staring at me, waiting ever so patiently. How does my little story about Uncle Aiden tie into your *primary* concern?"

Tuohay and Eldredge waited expectantly for Sara's answer, but it was a question she put forth to Tuohay. "My invitation in silver ink said that you would find me, Inspector Tuohay, and you have. It goes on to say that if I assist you, you in turn will assist me. Is that true?"

"In any capacity possible, yes," Tuohay replied.

"Then let me say this." Sara's voice dropped to a near whisper. "Bregagh Road."

Eldredge expressed a puzzled frown. "Bregagh Road?"

"Bregagh Road, near Belfast," said Tuohay, his voice careful. "What about it?"

"It was close to my uncle's seminary," Sara replied.

"Yes, and?"

Sara leaned close to Tuohay. "You *know* he was a good man, inspector. You know that he was framed, mocked, ridiculed. Possibly *murdered*. The question is, how do I know that *you* are a good man? How do I know that you will right the wrong done to him, and not make this only about the diamond? How do I know that you are not simply a player in this strange game concocted by the black letters?'"

"Why do you ask this of me?"

"Why would I help you otherwise?" Sara replied.

"Promising trust is not the same as earning it," said Tuohay. "But I put forth my promise as a beginning."

She considered Tuohay's words for a moment and then spun on Eldredge with a charming smile—the kind of smile that could win a man to her side with little in the way of effort. "You asked about Bregagh Road, Mr. Eldredge. I will tell you of it."

"As you please," replied Eldredge, blushing slightly under Sara's emerald gaze.

"Many years ago when in seminary, my uncle spent time volunteering his services at a home for destitute children along Bregagh Road. I still remember when he first told me about it—I could not have been more than seven at the time. '*It is full of children like you, Sara*', he said. '*Only they are gravely ill in one manner or another, and are not long for this world.*' I remember my hand warm in his grasp that morning, and the smell of his cologne."

"He told me about a boy he met there," she continued. "'*Gregory was a young boy,*' he said, '*and as young boys go, he was heedless of danger. On a misty morning in a small village along Bregagh Road, he and his brother had a scrap as brothers do.*'"

Sara's voice had grown distant, as if to mark the vast expanse between present day and her childhood memory. "He told me that in their recklessness, young Gregory was pushed into the road by his older brother, who fell after him. '*The two of them barely had time to hear the carriage before it appeared out of the fog,*' he said, '*Gregory was hit and instantly crippled. Unable to walk, unable to write, barely able to take food*'.... When my uncle first saw Gregory at the children's home he was lying in a jagged little box, staring at the ceiling. Uncle Aiden spent many months with Gregory thereafter, and became close friends with him until God took the poor boy under his wing."

Sara's gaze returned to Tuohay and Eldredge. "I asked my uncle why he shared this miserable account of a crippled boy with me. And you, I am sure, are wondering the same about why I have shared it with you."

"I am," Eldredge confessed after a brief pause.

She looked at Tuohay's cane, and then at the inspector himself. "Because those of us who can walk must do so for those of us that cannot."

A long silence followed Sara's final words, so much so that Eldredge finally leaned forward and asked tentatively, "Are you concluded?"

"Yes," Sara responded. "I imagine a clever man like Mr. Tuohay can make use of what I have told you."

Eldredge appeared at a loss, but Tuohay's features remained guarded. Sara seemed to take no notice of their reaction as she stood to go. "I can make my own way out by the courtyard. An escort is waiting for me near the gate there, and will take care to hide me from any stray journalists that might be spying the grounds."

Eldredge stood and bowed awkwardly as Sara withdrew. Tuohay waited a moment before speaking, his voice stopping her cold. "It was thirty-one years ago."

"Was it, indeed?" she replied, her back to Tuohay.

Tuohay's voice dropped. "Tell me, Miss Conall, are you familiar with the name of Gregory's *brother*, the one who pushed him in front of the carriage and crippled him for life? I most assuredly believe that you must be."

"I am, in fact."

Tuohay regarded her for several long moments before speaking. "I am sincere in my desire to remedy whatever wrong was afflicted ·upon the late Father Kearney. Whether or not it is linked to the diamond, I will see to it that your uncle's killer, if one exists, is brought to justice."

Sara turned and contemplated him quietly, her gaze lingering on the cane at his side. Slowly, she walked back to Tuohay's chair. "There is a chill in the air tonight, inspector."

"Take my coat," said Tuohay, standing with a grimace and offering it to her. "Perhaps it will hide you from prying eyes, as well."

"Thank you." She turned to Eldredge. "Mr. Eldredge, if you would see me out?"

She departed the room without another word, Eldredge following her with a perplexed look on his face.

Tuohay settled back in his chair, listening to the sounds of the house. All was quiet save the fading footsteps of Sara and Eldredge in the back hall. Eldredge returned to the room with Tuohay's coat over his arm, his puzzled expression deepening as he handed it back. A worn-looking book was wrapped inside it.

"Sara had the most unusual response to me just as she was leaving, and this book— "

"Lower your voice, please."

"Hmm? But why? The journalist?" Eldredge peered at the curtained windows. "I highly doubt he can see within, never mind hear us."

"I maintain, it is important."

"If you insist," said Eldredge, his puzzled expression expanding. "As I was saying," he resumed in a softer tone, "upon her exit Sara removed a soft padding from the doorbell in the hallway. She said nothing of it, but it was evident that the doorbell was not meant to ring when we tried it. And then she handed me this book…which she took from behind a chair in the hall. She wrapped it in your coat and whispered that it was to be viewed in private. Specifically *not here*, at the law firm."

"Whispered, you say?"

"Yes, whispered. Like I am doing now." Far from a whisper, the irritation in his voice was growing.

"Anything else?"

"She also said that her uncle Sean will meet with at you at the Harrington Hotel after she speaks to him tonight." Eldredge scratched his jaw. "I am not sure how it happened, but it seems you have somehow gained her trust."

"I hope so."

"Curious, I say." Eldredge peered at the book in Tuohay's hand. "Will you review it now, or wait as she asked?"

"We shall wait." Tuohay was staring into the cold fireplace.

"Do you—did her testimony have anything of value for you? It was rather…*odd*."

"It is a beginning." Tuohay did not elaborate further, but changed the subject. "I will need you or Eliza to contact Sara's uncle regarding the time for the interview. But more importantly, I have a criminal to catch tomorrow. Would you like to take part?"

"Of course!" Eldredge proclaimed, but quickly dropped his voice again. "Who is it? This Kip Crippen individual you followed from Belfast?"

Tuohay presented an understanding smile. "Yes. I will impart more details when we reconvene tomorrow afternoon. The walls—I fear they have ears. And eyes."

Eldredge's own eyes widened. "What do you mean?" he hissed.

"Exactly what I said." Tuohay exhaled slowly and stood with a grimace. "Come."

The two men departed the room and walked down the dark hallway to the exit, Eldredge gripping his bowler hat with whitened knuckles. Tuohay pushed the front door open, inviting a cold breeze to brush past them. Raising his left hand to a ribbon of pale moonlight, he captured it in his palm like melted gold. The door clattered shut as they stepped onto the porch.

"The journalist is out there somewhere," Eldredge remarked. The two men stared into the darkness. Eldredge took a moment to extract a ring of keys from his pocket. Choosing the largest on the ring, he locked the front door. "Sara gave these to me when I walked her out," he said as way of explanation. He handed them to Tuohay. "They are Mr. Thayer's, the lawyer. But she asked that you return them to her Uncle Sean tomorrow."

The keys made a metallic clink as Tuohay dropped them into his coat. "I believe I will return them to Mr. Thayer himself," he said. He handed the book to Eldredge. "Shall we trade?"

"It appears to be a generic codebook." Eldredge accepted the book and raised it out of the shadows just enough to read the title. "An old copy of the Goldman's Cable Codex." He sounded slightly disappointed.

The two men alighted from the porch onto the walkway, eyeing the shadows warily.

"It may not be as banal you think."

Eldredge tucked it into his coat as he walked. "Is the codex linked to the letter? Perhaps the codex referred to in Aiden's letter?"

"Possibly."

Eldredge's interest was renewed. "I will examine your letter and the codex tonight."

"Good."

The men struck out onto the cobblestone footpath that was partnered with the road. "What was all that talk about the crippled brother, I wonder," Eldredge said as he navigated the cobbles. "Her entire interview…there was no correlation to the diamond whatsoever."

"It was a test of sorts."

"Test? What do you mean?"

Tuohay grew thoughtful. "Memories are like shadows, Eldredge. Light may cast them aside momentarily, but the darkness will not be refused forever. Not by a thousand candles, nor by a city of electric lights. It is always there, waiting for its time to return. And return it shall, despite any attempt to prevent it."

"Sorry?"

"An act of wickedness cannot be undone by a thousand subsequent acts of good. It stands on its own accord."

"I still do not follow."

"Her uncle's account about the two boys. Gregory, the younger brother, was pushed into the road by his older brother."

"Yes, yes. Though what that recollection has to do with anything is beyond me. And why did you make that remark about "thirty-one" years?"

"The account of the two brothers is one of my ties to her uncle, the deceased priest. It is the reason he contacted me in Belfast about his findings several months ago—and the reason he *first* contacted me for assistance so many years ago when we were in the Sleuthhound Club. Even then he knew me, and trusted me. And if Sara knows that, which she clearly does, it means she was told by him. But she needed to see it for herself before offering more…she needed to meet us, judge our intentions."

"Judge our intentions?" Eldredge peered up at his companion. "And what "tie" to her uncle are you referring to? What does Sara know of?"

"In her telling of the two brothers," Tuohay prompted.

"What of it?"

"After the accident but before sailing for America, the older brother went to confession. He admitted to the fledgling priest—young Father Kearney—that he *knew* the carriage was coming, that in the heat of the moment he *meant* for his younger brother to be struck. Sara failed to mention that in her telling, but she identified everything else correctly."

"Hold on a moment. How could you *possibly* know the details about the older brother's confession?" Eldredge was incredulous. "In fact, how could you know *anything* about him at all? The event took place years ago."

"Thirty-one years ago, to be precise."

Eldredge grew silent as the meaning dawned on him.

"Yes, old friend," Tuohay said, his voice a hoarse whisper, "the older brother responsible for crippling young Gregory was—is—*me.*"

An Important Passenger

The afternoon was as gray as a tombstone. A damp mist gnawed at the bones, impervious to all manner of cloaks and coats, furs, caps, scalding coffee, or Highland whiskey. Tuohay and Eldredge huddled beneath a lamppost dripping with nature's tears, the flame within the dewy globe coughing forth a spidery web of light.

Both men chewed on the rewarding end of burning tobacco; Tuohay, in the form of a pungent clove cigarette, Eldredge a squat, academic pipe. Anticipation hung in the air like a noose, full of warning and dire expectation.

"My nerves are a jumble," Eldredge cursed, frowning around his pipe, "being in close proximity with this fellow Kip Crippen and all."

"Rest easy, old chap," said Tuohay. "The Boston jacks are on it. They will have our man straight from the boat. We are just here to make sure they nab the right man."

"It must be the atmosphere. It betokens a sense of dread." Eldredge tapped the remainder of his pipe onto the ground as he peered uncertainly at his surroundings. A long row of warehouses stretching through the mist faced each like a ragged rugby line, graceless edifices the shape of coffins perched along the dock's edges. The pungent odors of salt, brine, and seaweed were heavy in the air.

"Fear not! Here comes our Jack-o-lantern to brighten the gloom," said Tuohay, a smile in his voice. Eldredge followed his gaze to a woman approaching along the dockside. She walked with a spirited confidence, her smile warming the two men far more than their artificial methods of smoke and coffee.

"I would recognize that saunter anywhere," said Eldredge. "I have not seen Eliza since she moved to New York six years ago. Where is she staying?"

"I understand that she still owns an apartment in Boston," said Tuohay. He stepped forward to greet the woman as she arrived at the lamppost, a fragrance of rose and lavender arriving with her. "Eliza."

"How's tricks, boys?" Eliza Wilding lifted the straw hat from her head, revealing an energetic, humored and exquisite face of forty years framed by loose burgundy curls.

Tuohay took her hand and bowed, a thin rivulet of water tricking from the brim of his hat. Eldredge appeared as one struck unawares, his breath on hold. His eyes followed Eliza's movements as she pulled the strap of a copper-beaded purse up her shoulder. A tight-fitting white shirt fitted with a silver brooch was tucked into an ornate black blouse of fine embroidery that ran to charcoal bicycle boots. Eliza's figure pressed rather too pleasantly against the Gibson Girl outfit and Eldredge smoothed his tie against his chest. He took his place beside Tuohay with a bow.

"It is good to see you," said Tuohay.

"Truly," added Eldredge.

"The old schoolboys," Eliza said, regarding each of them in turn. "Goodness, the pair of you added some gray to the temples."

"Too true," Tuohay replied. "But you look like the decade never passed. New York has been good to you."

"I would use a few different adjectives than *good* for New York," Eliza commented, "but it *has* been an experience."

"Your plays are on Broadway," Eldredge gushed, "and that is nothing to sneeze at. *Parlous* came to Boston, and it was just magnificent—"

"Thanks, Johnny," Eliza interrupted, "I appreciate it, I really do. But I'm here to get away from all that for a spell." She elbowed Tuohay playfully. "I couldn't refuse *Inspector* Tuohay's request for assistance, after all. Reading the telegram from the Royal Irish Constabulary gave me goose bumps."

Tuohay looked skeptical. "Goosebumps?"

"Hey. Things have been dry, alright? This was just what I needed." She sidled up to Tuohay. "An inspector in the Royal Irish Constabulary is one thing, but Scotland Yard? How did that happen?"

"Simply a consultant for the Yard. The case officially belongs to the RIC, but Scotland Yard is…interested, let us say."

"I am not surprised, considering how much the diamond is worth," said Eliza, "and the fact that it was stolen from British soil."

"It is all very exciting," Eldredge interjected, though he looked more queasy than exhilarated.

Tuohay flicked the remains of his clove cigarette onto the wet cobblestones. "Well, now that I have dragged you both from the drudgery of your everyday lives to the thrill of official police work, shall we proceed?"

"Let's have at it," said Eliza.

"Onward," said Eldredge, tugging bravely at his bowler cap, which released a stream of water past his face. "Ah, gads."

Tuohay pulled his collar up against the misting rain. "Follow me."

Stepping onto a narrow cobblestone lane bordered by rows of long, sea-bitten warehouses, Tuohay led his companions onto Long Wharf. It jutted out before them like the branches of an old, twisted New England oak, the interlocked docksides and warehouses a web of spindly subdivisions reaching into the misty sea.

Passing a lamplighter in the gloom, Tuohay nodded respectfully at the man representing a dying breed. They passed covered horse-carts bursting with crated goods, their owners flagging down dockhands for assistance. A surly looking group of black-capped sailors bearing canvas bags and nets materialized from the gray mists and bounded past with collective purpose.

Tuohay led the way down a narrow alley between warehouses. A series of planks marked an artificial crossing point between two docks, causing a temporary pause. With a nod to the others, Tuohay crossed the trembling planks with care and followed the ensuing alleyway to the wayside of a court. Eliza and Eldredge followed suit. At their right was a brick edifice displaying a weather-bitten sign: WINE, LIQUOR and CIGARS.

Standing under it was a stocky man in a gray trench coat and matching fedora. His ruddy complexion was complemented by a fiery red goatee and mutton chops stretching to the jaw line, completing the fashionably authoritative appearance. In his middling fifties, his stance was one of a steam engine ready to depart the station; a man in a hurry yet still tethered to his post. He looked up from the polished gold watch in his hand as Tuohay reached him.

"Good afternoon," Tuohay said. "Are you waiting for a ship to dock?"

"The Queen Victoria."

"Long live the Queen."

The two men shook hands. "Inspector Jack Tuohay," said Tuohay.

"Inspector Dennis Frost of the 4th precinct," Frost replied in a no-nonsense manner. "Your man will be disembarking in a few minutes."

"Is everyone in place?"

"Six constables linin' the docks with every conceivable exit covered. We could do without the blasted fog, though." He glanced at Eliza and Eldredge standing a few feet back. "These them?"

"Local partners assigned to me for the case," Tuohay confirmed.

Frost frowned in their general vicinity.

"What's with the sour look?" Eliza said, peering from under her sagging hat. "You got a problem work'n with dames?"

"Private citizens in general, actually," Frost scowled. "The docks usually ain't the safest of locations. And certainly not while a surveillance operation is in place. Even for members of the illustrious Sleuthhound club." He smiled at their look of surprise. "Aye, I did my research on you lot." He turned back to Tuohay. "You recruited members of a defunct *collegiate investigation club*?" The emphasis was not delivered in a kindly voice.

A smile flickered across Tuohay's face. "Inspector, I take full accountability for my partners."

Eliza crossed her arms. "*You* take full accountability? How about *I* take full accountability."

Frost shrugged. "It's your show."

"Thank you, inspector."

Frost checked his watch again. "So this man you're after, Kip Crippen. A confessed jewel thief. Sounds like a good fit, except for the fact that you're lookin' to collar him based on what—word of mouth? Do you really believe he can lead you to the lost diamond?"

"What I believe does not matter; what he can tell us does. We will see once we question him."

"*Interrogation* is the proper term for it." Frost struck a match against a light post and lit a snub-nosed cigarette.

"Call it what you will."

A flash of light appeared from a nearby rooftop, the small beacon quickly swallowed up by the thick fog. It reappeared in three successive blinks. Frost turned to the others. "There's the signal."

Eldredge tensed. "So what is the plan?"

"Your lot waits here," said Frost. "Not worth the bother of you gettin' in the way."

"If you think it is best," Eldredge said, a note of relief in his voice.

Frost smiled around his cigarette. "Don't worry. My men know this area like the back of their hands. We'll have Mr. Crippen in custody before he sets foot on the shore. Just sit tight."

With a tip of his hat, Frost departed. The embers of his cigarette disappeared into the fog like a fading star.

Eliza frowned at Tuohay. "We just wait, then?"

"Yes."

"Not quite as exciting as you promised."

"But exciting enough," Eldredge broke in, tapping the water from the brim of his hat. "We are here as observers, Eliza. I do not think our purpose is to tackle alleged criminals to the ground."

Eliza smirked. "Leave all the fun to the professionals, huh?"

The black canvas of a nearby wagon slapped in the wind, the cold gust shredding a portion of the fog into wispy vapors. Tuohay attempted to light a match, but after the third attempt gave up on the flawed operation.

Eldredge stepped forward with a burning match cupped in his hand, and Tuohay leaned in with his cigarette. "Good show, Eldredge."

"I am useful for more than numbers, you know."

Eliza plucked the burning cigarette from Tuohay's fingers and took a long draw. Coughing slightly, she handed it back. "So you have time to explain who this Crippen fellow is, and how he ties to the diamond?"

"He is believed to be one of three suspects in the crime."

"Why three?"

"Three crowns," said Tuohay. "A crown etched into each of the three glass-diamond decoys discovered in *each* of the three safes meant to house the Templar Diamond during its stay in Belfast. The three medieval crowns—all of which were slightly different in design—could be a ruse, but most of the analysts that have worked the case agree that the heist was coordinated by three individuals—

a master jeweler, a man on the inside, and a logistics coordinator. The crowns act as their collective signature, if you will."

"Braggarts too clever for their own good." Eliza twisted her mouth into a thoughtful frown. "So which one is Crippen supposed to be?"

"The master jeweler," replied Tuohay. "Kip Crippen grew up as an orphan at Sacredwood Priory in North Belfast. The priory was known for its emphasis on artistry, especially in colored and stained glass."

"I hope that's not the only evidence you have," Eliza remarked, exhaling smoke through the corner of her mouth.

"No, of course not," Tuohay replied. "Crippen showed promising gifts, but ran away from the orphanage as an adolescent and disappeared from the public eye for years. He resurfaced as a master craftsman working for the Ocean Steam Navigation Company, otherwise known as the White Star Line. Primarily a glassblower, he also dabbled in mechanical work with intricate skill—they had him working on their high end products ranging from chandeliers to navigation tools to personal wrist watches sold on the ships." Tuohay shrugged. "But that was his day job, as it turned out. His propensity for high-end jewel thievery, primarily from Protestant churches and rectories across the countryside, was uncovered by the RIC. By me, specifically. Once taken in, his skill—and *passion*—as a gem cutter was uncovered through interrogation. He was an exhibitionist at heart, an artist. He wanted his work to be recognized."

"Another braggart," Eliza scoffed. "Don't they know that the most successful criminals keep a tight lip?"

Tuohay nodded in agreement. "There are attention seekers in every field. He was unparalleled in the artistry of gem cutting, and several unsolved crimes fell into his lap, which he happily confessed to. He spilled information on his partners in exchange for an abbreviated sentence, and spent four years in the clink. He was out a year prior to the disappearance of the Templar Diamond."

"That is all very intriguing, but what about *hard* evidence?" Eldredge inquired.

"The deceased priest, Father Kearney, wired me at the RIC several months ago. He said that he had uncovered details about the Templar Diamond. His contact with me was close to the time that I received my anonymous invitation in silver ink, predicting that Kip Crippen would sail for America in search of the diamond."

Eldredge scratched his chin thoughtfully. "Not exactly hard evidence..."

"True. But Kip Crippen *did* sail for America, as predicted," said Tuohay.

"And Father Kearney is now dead under mysterious circumstances," added Eliza.

Tuohay took a drag of the clove cigarette. "It was enough of a concurrence for the RIC to give me leave to follow Crippen—on a faster ship than his, of course—to America. And for Scotland Yard to pay attention, *and* for the Boston authorities to cooperate. All in the hopes that if Crippen knows something about the diamond, he will sing."

"And now we wait?" Eliza eyed Tuohay's cigarette. "Those cloves are a horrid habit, Jack."

"And now," Tuohay paused, handing the cigarette back to Eliza, "we wait."

A shout in the distance grabbed their attention. It was followed by several others, echoing from the various mist-soaked alleyways. There was a sudden, sharp *crack*.

Eldredge's eyes widened. "Was that a gunshot?"

"Well, that was quick," Eliza quipped.

"Stay here," Tuohay ordered as he strode onto the road towards the sounds, his cane striking the ground with force.

"Like hell," said Eliza, jogging up next to him.

"Eliza, this could be dangerous."

"Tell me something I don't know."

Eldredge appeared beside them. "We are coming along, old friend." The tremor in his voice was less than convincing, but he put on a brave smile.

"Come on, then." Tuohay led them to a narrow alley crowded with discolored boxes and crates. The scent of the sea washed over them as the alley opened onto a seaside wharf, a pair of thirty-foot cutters lashed along its length. Iron rings and multi-hued buoys lay scattered on the jagged deck, joined by foot-snaring seaweed, rope, and the occasional moldy oar.

"Thick as pea soup," Eldredge commented, the renewed blanket of gray fog smothering the quay before them.

"Where're we going, Jack?" Eliza asked, stumbling as a rope squelched under her boot.

As if in response, a gigantic dual-stacked steamship emerged from the fog, gray vapors spilling down its barnacle-encrusted bow like the strands of a hag's mane. The massive ship rested between the tight confines of two protruding piers, the image not unlike a stiffened body trapped in an unyielding coffin. The deep clang of a bell broke from above the bow like a warning.

"Is that the ship Crippen was on?" Eldredge asked. "We cannot reach it from here." Isolated shouts rang out from the far wharf.

Tuohay stopped his advance. "Damn. Yes, it's the ship. We are on the wrong side of the waterway. How do we get over there?"

"Backtrack," said Eldredge.

"Give me a boost," Eliza demanded, stepping onto a rickety crate. The two men looked at her in confusion. "A boost up to the roof. Quickly."

"Right." Tuohay moved into position, and Eliza used the crook of his shoulder to step within reach of the warehouse crown. The roof was gently sloped and ran the full gamut of the wharf, stretching into the mist in either direction. Scrabbling with her hands and elbows, Eliza unceremoniously twisted up and over the ridge. On all fours, she peered back down at her partners. "I'll go to the other side. The piers bend around, and I should be able to see where they link up. Back in a jiff."

She stood and raced up the roof, the thump of her boots on the wood slates subsiding quickly. Tuohay and Eldredge stared up into the silent gray after her. Suddenly, a loud clap reverberated off the walls of the surrounding warehouses, followed by more shouts.

"Another shot! And it sounded close," Eldredge breathed, looking about in alarm. "In the same direction Eliza just went."

Tuohay swore under his breath. "Eliza!"

Silence persisted.

"Come on, John—" Tuohay was cut short by the sound of tramping feet from above. Eliza appeared and crouched at the edge of the roof.

"Quickly, head through there," she said, pointing to an adjacent warehouse with a faded sign reading *Agricultural Warehouse*. "It connects through an old merchant house, and there's an exit on the other side."

38

"Away from the steamship?" Tuohay asked.

"Yes, away from the steamship! He's on the run."

Tuohay broke into a limping stride down the wharf, reaching the dark entrance of the heavy brick warehouse referred by Eliza. A stout brass plate and its inscription of welcome were ignored as Tuohay limped past, his cane echoing off the wooden floor within. The interior was barn-like, intensified by the scent of stale hay, vegetables and horse dung. Tuohay and Eldredge entered a low row of make-shift hallways.

"Look there—banana crates!" Eldredge declared as he jogged beside Tuohay. He was pointing over the low wall to a pillar of crates nearly two stories high. "It reminds me of the statistics I ran on trade revenue in Boston last autumn. Technical abstracts from the import department were lacking, revealing an imperfection among the previous studies, including agriculture—"

"John."

Eldredge bit his tongue. "Right. I do tend to ramble when I am nervous."

"It would be something if your rambling at least made sense, old boy."

Tuohay shouldered a small door open and the pair stepped into an abandoned tea shop, facing the opposite side of the large warehouse. A small bar, rotting and covered in dust, was the only reminder of the once cozy affair. Tuohay clattered over to the heavy oak door and peered out its smudged window. Cursing, he rubbed the grit clear with his sleeve.

"What do you see?"

Tuohay pushed the door open with a grunt, a surge of seaside air greeting his effort. The two men exited onto an enclosed patio comprising the southeast corner of the building; above their heads the courtyard ceiling supported the upper stories; the adjacent walls were non-existent except for a few faded pillars supporting the ceiling, leading to the harbor. Directly ahead the water channel was clogged with three-mast schooners, their sails furled and anchors dropped. The unadorned masts appeared like a forest of winter pines rising from the mist.

Tuohay turned left. The deck stopped abruptly, dropping three feet into the harbor. A thicket of wood pilings protruded from the water like gravestones, the pier they once supported having long rotted away.

"There is a man out there!" Eldredge gasped.

"Kip Crippen," Tuohay breathed with a curse.

Crippen, a grizzled man in a short frock coat and wool hat, was crouched precariously on one of the wood posts protruding a foot above the brackish water. His shoulders hunched, he held a small object in his hand. Suddenly, he leapt to an adjacent piling, one foot catching the water and nearly toppling him into the harbor.

Eldredge shook his head in wonder. "How did he get out there?"

"More pertinent to us is where he is going," said Tuohay, pointing to a single-mast dinghy at the far end of the drowned coppice. Tuohay's brow furrowed with concern. "The posts make a path of stepping stones leading right to that boat."

"What do we do?"

Tuohay stepped to the edge of the platform just beyond the roof and peered up. Above him Eliza crouched on the roof, watching Crippen dance from one slick piling to the next.

"Do you see anything from up there?"

"Sure as night follows day," Eliza called down, pointing in the direction of Crippen. "Looks like your pal Inspector Frost is Johnny-on-the-spot."

A rowboat emerged onto the scene from beneath a nearby pier, a uniformed officer rowing from the center with undisciplined fury. At the bow of the rocking boat the bulky form of Frost loomed precariously in his trench coat.

"I do not recommend it, Mr. Crippen!" Frost's voice carried the length of the water to the onlookers. "You are outnumbered and outmatched."

"I have done nothing wrong!" Crippen shouted back, a thin cockney accent marking his words.

"You were told to stay put," Frost returned. "Do so now, and all will be well! We'll swing by nice an' easy."

"You are surrounded, Mr. Crippen," Tuohay joined in, cupping his hands around his mouth. "Do as the inspector says!"

"And who might *we* be?" Crippen shouted back, the growl in his voice as clear as if he had been standing right beside them.

"The RIC."

40

Crippen muttered something unintelligible at that and spun around to face the oncoming rowboat. It was less than thirty feet away in the water, but could not proceed into the maze of pilings. It careened into the obstacles like a cavalry charge converging onto pikes, nearly flinging Frost from the boat.

"Steady!" he roared back at the officer.

"You won't have me!" Crippen cried, aiming his pistol at Frost.

Tuohay pulled a Colt Derringer from his pocket, the metal slick with perspiration. Eldredge gasped as Tuohay's arm stretched full length, but Frost was faster. Despite his uncooperative position in the bow of the heaving boat, the Boston inspector was quick to draw. A single flare and ensuing crack from his pistol indicated the shot.

Crippen froze as if something had startled him. And then, as if contemplating the watery grave below, he crumpled forward and pitched headlong into the depths.

A heavy silence fell.

"Was he hit?" Eldredge cried out, his voice dry. "Oh God, was he hit?"

"Either that or he's a terrible diver," Eliza called back.

A thunder of commands issued forth from Frost. More officers appeared from the fringes of the piers, picking their way through various obstacles to get into available watercraft. Frost shouted at them to get over to his location as he tried to pull the boat through the pilings with his hands.

"Gads," Eldredge breathed, eyeing the rippling surface of the water Crippen had disappeared into. "Where did he go?"

"Down," said Tuohay.

"Jack." It was Eliza. She was pointing at a nearby dock running parallel to their own. "Rag men on the loose."

Tuohay turned to where she was pointing. A handful of eager, feral-looking men raced down the pier towards the officers, notepads in hand.

"Journalists," Eldredge groaned. "And I recognize that man Mountain among them. The visitor from the interview at Sara's house. He's there—the gaunt man in the olive trench coat."

Tuohay's frown deepened into a scowl. "Did you set up that interview with Sara Conall's uncle?" He returned his gun to the inside of his coat.

Eldredge blinked.

"Well, man? The doctor, Sean Kearney. Sara Conall's last living uncle, brother to the two dead men."

"Eliza set it up. She's the smooth talker, remember? This evening, at your hotel." Eldredge's bewilderment was etched across his face. "But… but what about Crippen? Is he not your main concern?"

"*Was*, old boy." Tuohay took a long, last gaze at the water where Frost and his officers were stumbling along the pilings. "Get working on that code book, Eldredge. It appears Mr. Kip Crippen will be of far less use than I had anticipated."

Promise of Menace

The bells of Notre Dame Academy rang through Copley Square, proclaiming the hour with harmonious authority. Tuohay looked up from his newspaper and frowned, his lips curling around his diminishing cigarette. The scent of clove lingered close. He reached into his pocket, extracted his silver watch, and flipped open the lid with his thumb.

"Seven o'clock," he murmured. He leaned back and finished his cigarette with a protracted draw, his eyes returning to the evening edition's headline.

Templar Diamond HIDDEN AWAY in Boston

Died with his boots on. Grim fate for Irish jewel thief on the run. Boston authorities gun him down in cold blood as he disembarks from steam liner.

Tuohay tossed the paper onto the table with a sigh.

It had been a long day, and with nothing good to show for it. Crippen—or his body— had not been discovered as of an hour ago, mystifying the police. Either he had escaped clean, or had sunk into the mire. It was anyone's guess which was the case.

The remaining time with Inspector Frost had been distasteful. Tuohay had received the report that Kip Crippen somehow knew of their trap, and sprung a surprise of his own by grabbing a nearby passenger and holding her hostage until he could break free.

One rumor was that he had received a message via Morse code aboard the steamship by a member of the press asking for an interview.

All in all, it was a messy affair. And more likely than not, the press would continue to dig, diverting precious resources from the imperative elements of the case. That would only complicate matters.

Tuohay exhaled softly. "Focus on the present endeavor," he reminded himself, gathering his thoughts.

The parlor of the Harrington Hotel was too bright for his liking, the furniture overly tasteful and rich. Tuohay had been forced to claim a table on the west side of the room where the electric lightning was less prevalent. A broken wall of newspapers obscured the evening readers, creating a virtual maze of paper and ink. Every paper carried a version of the Templar Diamond story.

"Well, Dr. Kearney, let us see what you have to offer," Tuohay murmured. He called for the waiter, a gangly youth who appeared more fit for the docks than a high-end hotel.

"Yes, sir?"

"There should be a gentleman by the name of Dr. Sean Kearney waiting in the lobby with an associate of mine. If you would be so kind as to show them to my table?"

"Of course. Is there anything else?"

"No." Tuohay waved the boy away and waited.

A nearby newspaper rustled as a reader at an adjacent table flipped through the pages. A moment later, a question emitted from behind the paper veil. "What do you intend to learn from Doctor Kearney?" Soft like velvet, Eliza's voice was a welcome reprieve for Tuohay from his thoughts. Hands gloved in white-lace held her paper in a relaxed manner.

"Doctor Sean Kearney is the sole surviving Kearney brother. He must know something." Tuohay took a draw of his cigarette. "Perhaps Aiden Kearney confided in Sean Kearney about his discoveries, or of danger afoot." He slipped his watch back into his pocket. "Keep an eye open for anything unusual during the interview."

"Not a problem," she replied, a smile in her voice. "I am ever the observer, especially when I am out of the way."

"To be continued," Tuohay murmured. His gaze had fallen to the approaching waiter with three individuals in tow. "Eldredge and the good doctor, but who is the young woman with them?" Tuohay stood as they reached the table.

The doctor was the first there. He had a robust face, merry-red and solid. It was draped by a curling silver beard and finely curved moustache, a strong argument for gentleman status. He waited, regarding Tuohay with intelligent eyes of faded green. His left hand rested at the upper left breast pocket of his tweed coat where an ebony pipe protruded with promised comfort.

The young woman took her seat gingerly, her large chestnut eyes absorbing the room like that of a curious child. In her middling twenties, she had an imperious face with high cheekbones and thin nose, the edges touched with red from the cold outside. Her lips were rouge, a deep crimson against the soft paleness of her skin, and her raven-black hair was gently pulled back into an intricate braid. Her fur-lined coat was a simple, faded affair, and did not match the regality of her natural appearance. She kept within its confines as if still warding off the cold.

Eldredge nodded to Tuohay in greeting as the men took their places at the table. Eldredge had a striped blue ascot on for the event, matched by a dark-hued blazer with a spot of dried mustard near the collar. "Jack, I would like to present Miss Mary Hart and Dr. Sean Kearney. The doctor is the brother of the late Father Aiden Kearney and of the late Rian Kearney." Turning, Eldredge reversed the introduction across the table. "This is Jack Tuohay, District Inspector 2nd Class of the Royal Irish Constabulary."

"Royal Irish Constabulary." Mary raised a thoughtful brow.

"Never heard of it," the doctor remarked.

Tuohay motioned to the waiter. "Whiskey and branch water, if you please. Mr. Kearney, Miss Hart?"

Kearney seemed to disapprove. "None for me, especially in the middling hours before dinner."

"I did not realize the time of day affected the taste of whiskey." Tuohay stretched his leg as his new companions watched him curiously. The pain had diminished with the administration of the cloves, but sitting for too long stiffened the joints, especially after the earlier activities that day.

"Gin," said Mary Hart, to the evident surprise of the doctor. She took no notice, her eyes resting upon Tuohay with curious defiance.

"She has been through quite a fix," the doctor offered, as if in explanation.

"We all have been," Mary replied softly, the challenge in her gaze fading.

Eldredge declined a drink and turned to Tuohay as the waiter departed with the orders. "As you are aware, Dr. Kearney has agreed to speak to us on behalf of his two deceased brothers."

"The evening headlines have me concerned," Dr. Kearney said pointedly. "We are not interested in publicity, inspector."

"Understood," said Tuohay. "Anything you tell us will be in the strictest of confidence. Now, if I may inquire about your professional life. Just a few details will suffice."

"I am a senior physician at the Boston City Hospital, where I specialize in the new field of prostatectomy surgery. I also practice asylum psychiatry in several of the lunacy wards near Boston, and I lead a small research lab utilizing fluoroscopy to research the capabilities of x-rays—it is quite the sensation in the medical field. I envision it telling us more about not just the inner workings of the body, but also of the mind."

"Fascinating," said Eldredge.

"Enough?" Doctor Kearney addressed Tuohay.

"Yes. I am a medical school dropout, myself."

"Is that so? Harvard? They have raised the admissions standards in the last twenty years, and done away with the apprenticeships."

Tuohay nodded. "I made it part of the way through the first year of the program, but it was not to be." He shrugged. "In any case—"

"Yes, yes. I would like to get to the point of this meeting."

"I am not too fond of formalities myself," said Tuohay, "and I appreciate your candid approach. But if I may—Miss Hart, would you care to tell me your connection to this affair? I admit, your name sounds vaguely familiar to me."

"There is more to this "affair", as you call it, than you realize," the doctor replied for her.

"That does not surprise me," said Tuohay. "Miss Hart?"

Further communication was held up by the appearance of the waiter with the drinks. An array of clinking glassware marked the transfer, after which the waiter removed himself from their vicinity.

Mary took a sip of her gin. "I am a streetwalker, Mr. Tuohay. A concubine, if you will."

Tuohay's gaze swept from Mary to the doctor.

"A prostitute, Jack," Eldredge said.

Tuohay cast a sidelong glance at his partner. "I am well aware of what a streetwalker is."

"Not... *too* familiar, though," Eldredge added tentatively.

Mary suppressed a smile at the exchange, but the doctor's frown deepened. "I was assured by my niece Sara that you and your staff are of the highest caliber, Inspector Tuohay. This is sensitive business we are here to discuss, and should not be trivialized with such…banter."

"Of course," said Tuohay, casting one last glance at Eldredge before continuing. "And you can be fully confident in our capabilities. Now, Miss Hart— "

"Mary, if it pleases you."

"Of course. Mary."

"Miss Hart is the more appropriate designation for the present," Dr. Kearney interrupted. "We must maintain a certain level of formality during the course of this interview."

Tuohay took an excruciatingly long sip of his whiskey before continuing. "Fine, then. As I was saying, Miss Hart—"

"Mary," the former concubine repeated, avoiding the doctor's gaze. A long silence lingered, and Tuohay made no motion to dispel the evident tension between the two newcomers.

Eldredge put on a brave smile. "Shall we just go with first names then? What do you say, Sean?" The doctor glared at Eldredge, who smoothed his ascot nervously in response. "Doctor Kearney it is. But you can call *me* John, if it pleases you." Another glower from the doctor had Eldredge clearing his throat. "Or simply Eldredge to keep it proper. *Mr.* Eldredge, I mean." Eldredge coughed. "Yes, yes. Mr. Eldredge is spot-on." His last words were a jumbled, trailing affair, matched by the overlapping creases his fingers made of his scrunched ascot.

Mary raised a delicate hand to her mouth and laughed. It was short and musical, shattering the nervous tension from her demeanor. She wiped her eyes once, her cheeks flushing. "I am sorry for the outburst," she said. "It is just that my emotions are… I am not quite myself at the moment. And the good doctor here is really just being noble. A protector of sorts." She looked down her glass.

Tuohay leaned back, new interest in his voice. "It is quite alright, Mary."

"Yes, to be expected," Eldredge added. "Such conversations have a way of pulling at the emotional strings, so to speak." Another long pause followed, and Eldredge waved the waiter down. "A tonic, if you would be so kind."

"You may as well get one for me as well," the doctor barked, tugging at his moustache. "And add some gin to that. When in Rome, as they say. Though we are far from such greatness here."

Mary set her hand gently on the doctor's arm. "Dr. Kearney, please. It is extraordinary, meeting here with these men, and exposing our truths. But the events we have been through are even more extraordinary, are they not? And Sara trusts these good gentlemen. She is a fine judge of character, after all."

"*I* will be the judge of character in this matter," the doctor replied, but his stance had visibly softened. He gave Tuohay a grudging nod. "Of course, I am aware that you knew my brother Aiden. That is the *only* reason we are here." Further speech was interrupted as the waiter delivered the drinks. Once the transaction was complete, the doctor pressed forward. "Sara gave you something last night? A book?"

"She did. A Goldman's Codex."

This seemed to comfort the doctor. "She trusts you, just as Aiden did."

"As she should," said Tuohay, but a sudden stiffness in his leg caused him to grit his teeth.

Kearney frowned. "Are you in pain, inspector? Is it your leg?" He peered under the table. "Perhaps you should have it examined."

"I am not in need of medical assistance at the moment," grimaced Tuohay, "so if we could just *move on*." He turned to Mary as the pain subsided. "Please, Mary, as swiftly as you can, tell Mr. Eldredge and myself why you are here with the good doctor."

"As I said, I am a streetwalker." She smiled to herself as if at some hidden secret, and seemed to be waiting for a second interruption, but none was forthcoming. Satisfied, she continued. "Nearly ten years ago, when I was seventeen, I began relations with a well-known priest named Father Robert Donnelly. It was the spring of 1892. *The spring of my content*, as I called it then." She smiled sadly. "He was my beau."

Eldredge coughed up a mouthful of tonic water, his eyes wide with surprise. "Excuse me," he dabbed at his ascot. "Are you referring to *the* Father Robert C. Donnelly of Plymouth? The polymath?"

"*The* Father Robert C. Donnelly," Mary confirmed.

"Take a hold of your senses," the doctor warned, watching Eldredge fidget with his collar.

"The man is a priest, a practicing physician, an expert herbalist, an accomplished architect, a well-known writer..." Eldredge shook his head. "I had the honor to attend a series of seminars he led on general astronomy, spectroscopy, and star mapping. He made the complex look simple. It was truly elegant."

"They call him Imhotep," Mary said, "after the ancient high priest of Egypt."

"Yes, Imhotep was a fabled expert in several fields of study," acknowledged Eldredge. "Fitting name. He even has a rather successful medicinal product, I believe. *Father Robert's Cough Elixir*. A likeness of his face is on the bottle, in fact."

"You speak of him as if his genius is an excuse for his vice," the doctor countered with a growl. "He works with as many poisons as he does antidotes, I would bet."

"All the more reason that Eldredge's concern is understandable," Mary said. Her voice held a note of fresh sorrow. "Robert is a powerful and important man. And it was more than relations that we shared, you see. We were...together."

Tuohay looked doubtful. "He was your *beau*. A priest. Excuse me, a *Renaissance Man*, who happens to be a priest."

"I told you there was more to this affair than you are aware, inspector," replied the doctor, tapping the table for emphasis.

"I have yet to see any sort of connection, however."

"You will." Mary took a sip of her gin. "In 1894 the late Father Aiden Kearney— the good doctor's brother—was assigned to Robert's, that is Father Donnelly's, parish in Plymouth. Aiden was rumored to be an agitator of sorts, a muckraker. A 'journalist priest', Robert called him, and not in a kindly manner." She ran her finger along the brim of her glass. "And my Robert had reason to be concerned. Before long, Father Aiden had found out about Robert's and my relationship. Aiden Kearney was always sticking his nose where it didn't belong."

"You cannot blame Aiden. It was *Father Donnelly* that was not playing by the rules," Eldredge pointed out.

"Sticking *his* nose where it didn't belong, you mean?" Mary winked at Eldredge. Eldredge reddened like a beet as the doctor's frown deepened.

"So—Father Kearney confronted Father Donnelly about the relationship?" Tuohay asked, edging the conversation along.

"He did, after collecting sufficient evidence," the doctor answered. "It was two years later, in 1896, when Aiden challenged Father Donnelly with his findings. The beginning of the end, as I have come to remember that time. You see, my brother did not look the other way when it came to dealing with impropriety. He *was* a journalist priest in that sense, but in the best sense of the meaning. Aiden opposed Father Donnelly's inexcusable practices, but it led to his *own* undoing."

"In what manner?" Tuohay asked.

"Unfortunately, the archdiocese, including the archbishop himself, did not take kindly to my brother's findings," said the doctor. "It was politically... troublesome for the church in Boston to have the reputation of a prominent priest like Father Donnelly tarnished. There were ways dealing with such indiscretions *internally*. Sweep them under the rug, as it were. But my brother would have none of it, and his persistence led to his persecution from within the confines of the Boston diocese itself."

"He would simply not shut his mouth," Mary said plainly, "so they figured out a way to shut it for him. Or thought they did."

Tuohay nodded in understanding. "Father Aiden Kearney's discoveries, if proved valid, would expose certain weaknesses in the leadership of the emerging Catholic church in Boston. Which would have not looked good to Rome."

"Yes," the doctor replied. "And *just* at the time that the Boston archbishop was under consideration for promotion by the pope. He would be the first man to be elevated to cardinalship in Boston, a great honor."

"And one of the first cardinals in America," Eldredge recalled. "The winter of 1897, I believe. The papers drummed up all kinds of excitement in the city about it. But the news was interrupted by even bigger news...news that the same archbishop was being taken to public court by a fallen priest—the very trial Sara told us about."

"Correct," confirmed the doctor. "My brother Aiden took Archbishop Walsh to trial, and the timing was no mistake. Shortly after the trial ended the cardinalship decision came from Rome."

"Of course," said Eldredge, "the timing makes sense. Archbishop Walsh was passed over by Rome—even though he was found innocent. Rome chose an archbishop in Baltimore for the cardinalship. Embarrassing for Boston."

"Father Kearney, rest his soul, caused mayhem with his claims, enough to tarnish the archbishop, enough to stop from him from attaining his highest aspiration," said Mary with sudden fervor. "Aiden Kearney was a driven man, a man of passion and virtue. A man who saw only right and wrong, despite the circumstances. He would not walk away from a fight, and it was a fight he made. It was about the church, sure. But it was about *him* as well. And because of him and his so-called noble actions, my Robert—Father Donnelly—pushed me away forever." She stared at the table as if ashamed to look up. "He was involved in the trial, and scarred by it. He was therefore part of the archbishop's embarrassment. The good doctor called that year the 'beginning of the end' for his brother....so it was the end for me and Father Donnelly."

The doctor did not challenge Mary's heartfelt comment, and Tuohay looked on in silent contemplation.

Eldredge cleared his throat. "I do apologize, Miss Hart, but I must ask: you had every reason to despise Father Aiden Kearney, did you not? He exposed your relationship with Father Robert Donnelly, which ended as a result, per your remark."

"Yes," said Mary. "You are right on both counts, Mr. Eldredge. I despised Father Kearney. And I am usually a fast learner, only..."

"Only what, Miss Hart?" Tuohay prompted.

"Only, my anger against Aiden Kearney blinded me to my Robert's shortcomings. I was not aware of the type of man 'the great' Imhotep, my Robert, really was, and how far he would be willing to go to save himself, and perhaps the archbishop, from further embarrassment." Her voice faltered. "He was a teacher to me, a companion, a lover. Yes, he always had the promise of severity about him, but never—never of menace."

Tuohay pressed gently. "What do you mean?"

"I..."

"What she means...," the doctor interrupted, but Mary quieted him with a gentle touch of her hand. She looked up with a firm gaze.

"What I mean, Mr. Tuohay, is that four years ago my beloved Robert...the acclaimed Father Donnelly...had me committed to a lunatic asylum."

An uneasy silence fell across the table.

"It was to keep me quiet," Mary continued. "I was committed shortly after the trial between Father Kearney and the archbishop ended. Directly after my testimony against Father Kearney, in fact." She laughed at the irony. "And there I languished, bound like an animal to my bed, probed and prodded like some kind of experiment. All the while I did exactly as they had asked all along." Mary's voice grew thick with emotion. "I would have gone mad if the good doctor did not get me out when he did." She closed her eyes as if to shut out the memories themselves.

"Egads," Eldredge whispered, his hand frozen above his drying ascot.

"What prompted you to get Miss Hart out of the asylum?" Tuohay asked the doctor.

"Not out, *transferred*," corrected Doctor Kearney. "I moved her from the asylum in Danvers to the hospital in Medfield, where I have some jurisdiction, and where Mary would receive proper care. They had her on crude preparations of morphine and heroin, and on additional nerve-seizing drugs. Hallucinates. Her recovery has been slow. Currently I have her on *Doctor Leven's Anti-Anxiety Number 9* and laudanum."

Mary extracted a small glass bottle of pills and a vial of crimson liquid from her purse. She rattled the pills with a remorseful smile. "I have them wherever I go. Whenever a bad dream threatens, I just swallow a pill and wash it down with a tincture of opium. Good night, Mary."

"The experience sounds dreadful," said Tuohay. "But certainly Mary is not the only patient to have ever been exposed to such medical practices. Why did you specifically move *her* from the hospital?"

Doctor Kearney leaned both elbows on the table and looked as if he was about make a very grave statement. "Miss Hart was a concubine for Father Donnelly, the very man, who along with the archbishop, destroyed my brother. And then Father Donnelly attempted to destroy *her* because she was proof of his transgressions. She had been his lover, and she knew the truth about how the trial was staged, of how she was forced to bear false witness against Aiden." Doctor Kearney's voice was as solemn as his graying temples. "I discovered through Aiden, before his untimely death, that Mary was a witness with information that could dismantle the leadership of the archdiocese of Boston. That she had been put into a lunacy asylum because her truths could destroy the very fabric of the men who had unjustly torn my brother Aiden's life to shreds. And that, Inspector Tuohay, was not an opportunity I was not about to pass up."

Tuohay nodded in understanding, but his expression was still one of perplexity. "Fine, yes. But I must ask the plain question. How, in any way, is this connected to the Templar Diamond?"

Mary expressed a nervous grin. "I can answer that."

All eyes turned to her as she continued in a wavering voice, "The information that you received from Father Kearney by telegram, before he died. The information that he said he had about the Templar Diamond..."

"Yes?" Tuohay prompted.

"And the codebook and the letter given to you by Sara..."

"Yes, yes. What of them?"

"Well, that information... the information about the stolen diamond... That's the information the doctor is referring to. That information came from me."

The Templar Diamond

A man in a gray trench coat appeared in the doorway of the hotel parlor. His frown was discernable under his heavy moustache as he scanned the room.

"It is Inspector Frost," murmured Tuohay, eyeing the gray-clad observer. "With blunt news on his tongue, I do not doubt."

All eyes turned from the table to the man in the doorway. It was silent for several moments until Mary's pills spilled on the table. "Sorry," she said, her cheeks flushing as she picked them up with a trembling hand.

The doctor turned to Tuohay, fire in his eyes. "Is he looking for you, inspector?" Even as the doctor asked, Inspector Frost caught sight of them among the forest of newspapers and strode in.

"Mary, are you alright?" Eldredge noticed her eyes widen. She was as pale as new fallen snow.

"I am fine." She raised the gin to her lips with a trembling hand.

Eldredge was incredulous. "Fine? You don't look fine—"

"Inspector Tuohay." Frost arrived at the table like a dark thundercloud, his presence looming over them. The scent of tobacco and rain followed him in. "Can we talk?"

"We will give you some privacy." The doctor's voice was as stiff as his movement as he helped Mary up and led her from the parlor. Frost watched them go before taking a seat.

"That was Mary Hart," he said in a gruff voice.

"You know her?"

"Right as rain I do. Tracked her down a few years back when investigating Father Aiden Kearney's affinity for streetwalkers. Discovered she was having relations with him. The prosecution put her on the stand against Kearney during the trial, along with two other harlots. Did him in at the trial, they did."

"Excuse me—you said she was having relations with Father Kearney. Did you mean to say Father Donnelly?"

"Kearney," Frost growled. "Don't you think I know what I'm talkin' about? *Kearney's* the one she was in bed with."

"I see. I must say, your presence seemed to put her ill at ease."

Frost shrugged. "I have that effect on people. What are you doing with her?"

"I am asking her and the doctor questions about Father Aiden Kearney as part of the investigation of the Templar diamond."

"I just told you what you need to know," said Frost. "Could have saved you time."

There was no further offer from Tuohay. Instead, he changed the subject. "You bring unpleasant tidings, I fear."

"Depends on your point of view."

"My point of view is that Kip Crippen needs to be healthy and alert so that I may interview him. I came a long way to see what he knows about the diamond."

"Then you are right, Inspector Tuohay. I bring unpleasant tidings. Mr. Crippen is dead."

Eldredge gasped. "Dead?"

"Still searching for the body, but there is no doubt on the issue. I'm a crack-shot, but even a blind man could have hit Crippen from where as I was standing. The bastard never came back up, and coppers were everywhere. No chance of him surfacing without notice. Won't be too long before we find the body."

"Bly me." Eldredge wiped his forehead with a cloth napkin.

"He had a gun, Tuohay. You saw it."

"I did," Tuohay confirmed. His voice was measured. "I assume there will be a full report?"

Frost chuckled. "Scream the house down, is that it? Send another dozen Cockney's from London to meddle in our affairs? Or is it the RIC?"

"The RIC has jurisdiction, though Scotland Yard is…present. Officially, the RIC must be included on all relevant updates to the case. Nothing more." Tuohay took a sip of his drink and frowned.

"What is it?" Frost demanded.

"Nothing." Tuohay took another long sip before putting the drink down. "Just *thinking*, inspector."

"Thinking? Action, Tuohay. That's how you get things done." Frost absently scratched at one of his muttonchops. "Will your boys back in Belfast be upset?"

"They will review the full report and make a recommendation from there. You were just doing your job, Inspector Frost."

Frost's eyes narrowed. "I never said I wasn't. Kip Crippen weren't no French pigeon."

"No, he was not." Tuohay pulled a silver flask from his coat pocket and poured some brandy into his glass. The scent was woody and sweet. "Is that all?"

"What are you up to here?"

"An interview, like I said."

Frost grunted. "And after this?"

"I plan on visiting Father Robert Donnelly in Plymouth. I have a few questions for him relating to the case." Tuohay smiled thinly. "I have nothing to hide, Inspector Frost. As the RIC promised the Boston brass, my whereabouts and a full report thereafter will be available."

"If you say so." Frost stood, his chair scraping against the floorboards. "I am sure we will see each other soon." He tipped his hat and exited the way he had come, his hands thrust in his pockets.

"Jack—" Eldredge began, but Tuohay held up his hand.

"Later." He swallowed the contents of his glass in one swig. A long silence followed until one of the newspapers nearby crackled audibly.

"Frost wants in on the Templar Diamond." The woman's voice, aimed at Tuohay, came from behind the previously raucous newspaper a table away.

"This is not the best time to discuss case details, Eliza," Tuohay replied. "The doctor and Miss Hart will be returning any moment."

Eliza set her paper on the table. "Inspector Frost is a hard-boiled case, and he's worming his way into this one."

"I am sure we have not seen the last of him," Tuohay agreed, drumming his fingers on the table. "It's to be expected, of course. We are on his turf."

Eliza scooted over to their table and leaned next to Eldredge. "Johnny, here's the codex back." She slipped a small, hardbound book with the title of 'Goldman's Cable Codex' in gold lettering to Eldredge. A pile of notes sat atop it.

"But I just gave it to you," Eldredge protested, a confused look on his face. "Did you have time to look at my analysis?"

"Hold a moment," said Tuohay, critically eyeing his two partners. "What is Eliza doing with the codebook?"

Eldredge shrugged. "I wanted her to review my analysis of it."

"Explain, please."

"I was eager to get to work after we got the codex from Sara at the interview, and I did some analysis on it and the letter late last night." Eldredge voice brimmed with excitement as he leaned forward. "As you know, there are many ways to encrypt or encode a letter."

"Of course," said Tuohay. "Book ciphers, running ciphers, code books."

"And the like, yes. Before us, we have a presumably encoded letter—an invitation, to be specific—and the means to decipher it, i.e. the code book. The assumption is that they are linked, as we were also shown Father Aiden Kearney's and Sara's invitations by Sara, and the priest's invitation mentioned a codex."

"Yes," said Tuohay impatiently.

Eldredge positioned the letter on the table. "So there is the letter."

AN INVITATION TO THE CHASE

February, 1896

Dear Mr. Jack Tuohay,

I hope you will allow this unforeseen intrusion on your time. This correspondence is presented with humility and no intention to mislead. It is, plainly stated, an **INVITATION.** *You of course have heard of the Star of Bethlehem, otherwise known as the Templar Diamond.*

I, the writer of this correspondence, am at fault for the recent dramatic theft of the diamond. As I am sure will come to light, there was a company of three individuals responsible for its disappearance. I was one.

You should be receiving this invitation almost six years after the crime. I am certain the diamond will not yet have surfaced. Thus, this letter is the cue that the chase to recover the great Star has begun.

To explain, I am dying. The entire enterprise of stealing the diamond was an elaborate confidence trick that even my two partners were not aware of. For that reason, I alone now know the location of the diamond.

Because of my failing health, I have decided to change the rules of the game and share the diamond's whereabouts to anyone clever enough to properly listen. I am enclosing information to that effect. For me, it has always been about the chase, and not the prize. Therefore I am honored to now share that experience with you.

However, know this. You are not the only recipient of an invitation, for what measure of game would that make? And be aware—the other beneficiaries may be out for more than just riches. They may be out for blood.

Your information is as follows:

> *A man named Kip Crippen will sail for Boston, America, in late February of 1902. He will be searching for the diamond.*

Do with this information as you please, but I implore you to seriously consider it.
You were chosen for a reason.

I welcome you, in advance, to the chase.

Your Friend in Sympathy

"And the codebook. First, look here." Eldredge opened the Codex to a random page and pressed his pudgy finger against the top portion.

166   THE GOLDMANS CABLE CODEX

Shiver,	At what rate can you charter a vessel to bring following cargo from — to this port?

Shook,	At what rate can you charter a vessel to bring following cargo from Boston to this port?
Shopkeep,	At what rate can you charter a vessel to bring following cargo to this port?
Shoplift,	At what time did she arrive?

"In a case such as this, each word represents a corresponding meaning. Either a phrase, as in the examples seen here, or a number, or even another word, as defined by the codex."

Tuohay nodded. "Yes, I know how codebooks work, John."

"Last night I spent nearly four hours analyzing each word in the letter as it corresponds to its analogous phrase, word, or number in the Goldman's Codex, and summarized them as best I could. There are three hundred and forty-two words in the letter. Fifty-five of those letters appear in the codex, with a corresponding partner. Those partners were made up of forty phrases, nine words, and six quantities. I was exhausted by the time I completed it, and could not locate a common theme among them.

"For example," he continued, unfolding one of the pages of parchment thrust into the codex, "here is the analysis I performed on the first paragraph of the letter. Each underlined term has an associate in the codex."

Dear Mr. _Jack_ Tuohay,
I hope you will allow this unforeseen _intrusion_ on your _time_. This _correspondence_ is presented with _humility_ and no _intention_ to _mislead_. It is, plainly stated, an _INVITATION_.

Jack→ summer
Intrusion→ do not think...
Time→ $48
Correspondence→ he has not done so
Humility→ A Happy New Year
Intention→ 7s, 4d sterling

Mislead→ is anyone ill?

Invitation→ in the event of...

Eldredge shrugged. "There was no common theme in my tired eyes, so I gave my full analysis and a copy of the letter to Eliza, along with the codex."

"Because John knows how observant we Radcliffe girls are," said Eliza with a smile. "He passed it to me after the shenanigans with Crippen."

"Just for a glance. Eliza *is* very observant." Eldredge returned her grin.

Eliza pointed at the letter.

"First question. Does this appear to either of you like the sort of letter that would be encoded with a codex?"

"No," Eldredge admitted. "Not without a double encryption or initial code, perhaps. It does not create a clear message for the receiver after decoding."

"How exactly did you obtain the letter?" Eliza asked Tuohay.

"I picked it up at the post in Belfast," said Tuohay. "The same way the others received theirs, as I understand it."

"Sure," said Eliza. "Nothing special there. So let's change our perspective for a minute. Goldman's Cable Codex is as common as dirt. It can be purchased for ten cents at any variety store. Even this older version is still available. So what makes this particular copy special?"

Both men shrugged.

"Well, there is the fact that there is a highly starched and folded handkerchief being used as a bookmark." Eliza opened the book to where a thin, white handkerchief was inserted.

"Yes, of course," Eldredge sighed. "I did not move it in case the location was meaningful."

"Page fifty-two and fifty-three," said Eliza. "There are markings on each page—a bordering sketch of strawberries. The handkerchief itself is Irish-linen, and so heavily starched that it's nearly as stiff as a board. And there are small designs of strawberries along its fringe as well."

"Useful for a book marker at first glance," remarked Eldredge, "but I did not pick up on the strawberries on the border of the page *and* the handkerchief."

"You must have been tired to miss that," Eliza teased. "Even so, there are no *obvious* clues. Strawberries, a handkerchief starched to the stiffness of a bookmark, and the pages it is marking."

"One of those *could* be a differentiator between this specific codex and one bought off the shelf," said Tuohay. "It that your thought?"

"Yes, there is that," said Eliza. "But the letter may include a clue as well."

Eldredge's eyebrows raised. "So the letter plays a role in finding the secret message, assuming there is one?"

"Yes." Eliza pointed at the letter. "Look there."

Tuohay and Eldredge peered closely to where Eliza's red nail pressed against the soft paper.

"*Your Friend in Sympathy*," Eldredge read. "It did strike me as an odd phrase."

Tuohay did not appear to be listening as he murmured to himself. "Sympathy… Could it be that simple?"

Eldredge frowned. "Could *what* be that simple?"

But at that moment, Eliza grabbed the book and slipped back to her table. Eldredge's scattered pages of analysis were left behind. "Miss Hart and the doctor return," she hissed. Reaching her table, she snapped her newspaper up.

Eldredge gathered his notes in a hurried fashion as Tuohay watched the pair approach. Turning to Eldredge, he said, "All of this talk reminds me—I need you to investigate a name."

"A name?" Eldredge whispered back, thrusting the notes under his chair.

"Colin Allotrope, an author on an essay for admission to seminary. The essay is called *Adoration of the Magi in Religious Art,* as I recall."

Eldredge thought for a moment. "That essay we spotted in the loft of the law firm?"

"That is the one."

"Adoration of the Magi," Eldredge murmured, "one of the most famous scenes in Christianity. I wonder what the relevance is—"

His question was cut short by a frown from Tuohay as Mary and the doctor arrived. The men stood.

Mary mustered a forced smile as she resumed her seat, followed by Tuohay and Eldredge. The doctor sat down heavily beside her, setting his leather briefcase at his feet.

"Inspector Frost detained us," Dr. Kearney commenced in a strained tone.

Tuohay leaned forward. "In what manner?"

"Asking questions about why we were meeting with you."

"And what did you tell him?" Tuohay asked.

"The truth, as far as it could go," said the doctor. "You are representing the Royal Irish Constabulary on a case that involves my deceased brother, to whom both I and Miss Hart have a connection."

"I see."

"I fear Inspector Frost's interference was difficult on Miss Hart."

"I am fine, truly," she protested.

"You will be as soon as the medicine begins to work," Dr. Kearney said in a firm tone. "You have the most difficult details to relay yet, and I need to be assured that your frail constitution can handle it."

"I took your damned medicine," Mary muttered. "What else do you want?" She flushed. "I'm sorry."

"Think nothing of it." The doctor turned his attention to Tuohay. "After our discussion, we presume you will act on our behalf to further investigate the wrongs against my brother Aiden. The wrongs that led to his and Rian's death. You owe him that much."

"Your refer to the double suicide."

"Yes, clearly," said the doctor. "You know of the details of their deaths, of course."

"Yes, yes," Tuohay replied, but there was a note of curiosity in his voice. "And I affirm that I will do my utmost to bring any wrongs against your brother to light. Now, what does Miss Hart have to share?"

Miss Hart frowned into her remaining gin. "Miss Dwyer."

Tuohay tapped his cane against the floor. "Miss Dwyer?"

"A concubine who was close to Miss Hart," said Dr. Kearney. "She was killed in cold blood last October, just four months ago. Two months before the suicide of my brothers."

"Killed?" Eldredge gasped.

The doctor ignored him. "Trauma to the head by a blunt weapon," he said. "She was under my care at the time, and so I was called to the scene. I was also present when she expired the next morning, and assisted with the post mortem."

Tuohay raised his cane onto his lap. "And how does she pertain to the recent events you have shared?"

Mary looked up, her stare glassy-eyed. "She was paid to lie on the stand at the archbishop's trial against Aiden Kearney, along with me and one other concubine."

Tuohay straightened in his seat. "Are you alright? You look unwell."

"It is the medication," the doctor replied. "She needed it, after being accosted by Frost." His tone bordered on defensive.

Mary smiled shyly. "One pill and a swallow of the good doctor's tincture, and I'm better." She leaned forward against the table. "Still want to hear what I have to say?"

"Of course," said Tuohay, though he appeared troubled by Mary's ability to focus.

The doctor cleared his throat. "Mary—"

"I'm fine," she snapped. Sitting up straight, she turned back to Tuohay. "Sorry." She blinked the daze from her eyes. "So—the trial. When word of the impending trial became known , there was…. a *reaction* from the Catholics of Boston. There were some in the church that were not going to let Aiden taint the archbishop with his filthy accusations. One night, about a month before the trial was to begin, I was approached by a man from the Boston police force. He claimed to be an inspector. He told me that I was going to testify against Father Kearney, and state *under oath* that Father Kearney frequented the house of prostitution on Hawkins Street where I had once worked. I was to state that I had relations with Father Kearney there on several occasions, and that he was known to take to the drink and grow violent at times. As the inspector put it, it was my Catholic duty to protect the Church from a lying, malicious scoundrel. But I saw it in another way. It was my opportunity to get revenge on Aiden Kearney, the man that had ruined my chance at a normal life. A *real* life."

"The inspector that met with you…he was Inspector Frost." Tuohay was eyeing Mary closely as he stated the name.

Mary's bottom lip trembled. "Yes. It was—it was him that forced me to take the stand and lie about Aiden Kearney."

Eldredge moaned. "Inspector Frost is a *criminal*?"

"Calm yourself, man." Tuohay knocked the table with his knuckles. "Mary. Who were the other concubines?"

Mary exhaled, gathering her thoughts. "Katherine Dwyer, who I already mentioned. She was eighteen at the time of the trial. And Susan Lovelace. She was twenty-one. They both falsely testified that they had taken up relations with Father Kearney, just as I did. And like me, they were promised money and protection by Inspector Frost. But both of them are dead now." A lump formed in Mary's throat, and she covered her mouth as a sob hurtled forth. Several patrons turned from their evening musings with raised brows.

Doctor Kearney leaned forward, his voice dropping to a harsh whisper. "I have reason to believe Mary is in danger. I did not want to bring her here for that reason, but I thought her story had to be told to someone... someone who can help us. And now the papers are running the story on the Templar Diamond, and the sudden appearance of Inspector Frost..." he shook his head. "It is attracting too much notice."

Eldredge turned to Mary. "Where are you staying? Are you in a safe residence?"

"We are not inclined to share specifics," Dr. Kearney replied. "Even with you. Suffice it to say she is in good hands."

"I am safe with Sara Conall," Mary confirmed. "Thank you for asking, Mr. Eldredge."

"We must keep quiet about such details," admonished Dr. Kearney.

"Your secret is safe with us," Tuohay assured them. He turned to the doctor. "Regarding the case—clearly you believe that the recent death of this second concubine, Miss Kathryn Dwyer, is connected to the trial, and to Miss Hart. That is why you believe Miss Hart is in danger?"

"Precisely so. It is a conspiracy," Dr. Kearney said, irritation still evident in his voice, "which is why we must take great care for our safety. In 1897, Inspector Frost was the man who carried out Father Donnelly's request to have Mary committed to an asylum shortly after she testified at the trial. *And* he is the man that Miss Katherine Dwyer was on her way to see when she was killed last October."

"Miss Dwyer was going to see Frost when she died? Do you have proof of this?"

The doctor shook his head. "No. That is where you come in, is it not?" He dropped his voice. "Though it is not proof, I *do* have Miss Kathryn Dwyer's statement to me the morning she expired. She told me in her dying moments that she was on her way to meet with Inspector Frost when she was attacked. That is how I know that he was involved in her death. She told me she was going to see him *per his request.*"

"Was there anyone else there when she told you this?"

"No, I am afraid not."

Eldredge spoke up. "If the trial was over three years ago, why was Miss Dwyer in contact with Inspector Frost as recently as October?"

"We had provided affidavits for an appeal," Mary replied. "Katy—Kathryn Dwyer—and I took part in providing the statements to lawyers at McBarronThayer for Father Kearney. I knew we had done wrong by him at the trial three years ago, which was made clear to me the day I was put in the asylum by Robert. I was locked away for three years before Aiden Kearney found me, stating that he had received a letter. A black letter with silver writing, and that it said I would help him. That I had evidence against my Robert."

"Father Donnelly," Eldredge interrupted.

"Yes, Father Robert Donnelly. I told him it was true. I had evidence hidden away."

"Did Aiden show you his silver-scripted letter?"

She nodded. "Yes."

"Did you recognize the writing? Anything at all about it?"

Mary shook her head. "Not at all. And neither did Aiden, from what he told me. Said the letter came straight out of the blue, like a message from God. I thought that was overstating it a little bit."

"It meant a lot to him," the doctor commented.

Mary continued, "As soon as I told him my intention to admit to the truth and reveal the evidence, he had his brother," she nodded in the direction of Doctor Kearney, "transfer me and Katy—Kathryn

Dwyer—from Danvers to Medfield, where his niece Sara, a nurse, could look after us."

"That is correct," the doctor affirmed.

"It was not difficult to get Katy to come along with me," Mary continued, "she had suffered as well over the three years. She and I provided the evidence and affidavits to Father Kearney's lawyers, Mr. McBarron and Mr. Thayer, to be used as part of the appeals process. The lawyers and Father Kearney were both enthusiastic by the prospect of a successful appeal, or at least a new trial." She shrugged as if not sure which approach they had been leaning towards.

"McBarron and Thayer, the lawyers for the original case," Tuohay said. "Was anyone else present during the affidavits?"

"Only Father Kearney."

"My brother and the two lawyers," confirmed the doctor. "They had won an appeal, but it never came to fruition."

"Because Father Aiden Kearney was dead by December, just over a month later," said Tuohay.

"Yes."

Mary turned to Doctor Kearney. "The evidence."

Doctor Kearney set his briefcase on the table and snapped the clasps open. "I kept this at the front desk when we first arrived. I wanted to meet you first before handing these over." He pulled a series of thin hardcover books from the case, bound together by twine. "These are second copies of the accounting books for the Plymouth parish during the years 1887 to 1898, all under Father Donnelly's tenure. They were confiscated by Aiden during his investigation, and given to me in October for safekeeping, just as he gave the Goldman's Codex to Sara. All of this originally came from Mary."

Mary smiled sheepishly. "I knew after the trial things were going to get rough with my Robert, so I stashed away some collateral just before they collared me. Didn't have time to do anything about it before I was stashed with the lunatics. Nobody listened to me after that."

Tuohay returned to the doctor's conversation thread. "So Father Kearney sensed he was in danger? Is that why he gave you the fiscal records, and the codex to Sara?"

"After the death of Kathryn Dwyer, he was certain of it." The doctor pushed the books across the table to Tuohay. "Perhaps they will be of use."

Eldredge turned to Tuohay. "I can review these, Jack."

Tuohay nodded, and Eldredge dragged the books to his spot at the table.

Doctor Kearney stared at Tuohay for a long moment. "So what will you do next, Inspector?"

Tuohay turned to Miss Hart. "I would like to know more about the evidence."

"I do not know any more than you do. I simply was aware of these things because Father Donnelly told me about them, and I told Father Kearney. It was because of me that he knew where to look."

"So what would *you* have us do next, Mary?"

Surprise registered in Mary's eyes at the question, but it quickly resolved into a hardened gaze. "I would have you find Katy Dwyer's killer. And those who drove Aiden and Edward Kearney to commit suicide. I would have you root out the bastards, and put them away for good, before anyone else is hurt. *That* is what I would have you do."

"Yes. But how so?"

"As I am sure you are already planning to do, start with Father Donnelly," she said. "And there is something in it for you as well. My Robert told me once that he was connected to the disappearance of the Templar Diamond. That it was hidden away from prying eyes. And that six years after the crime, when attention on the diamond had grown cold, the three responsible for stealing it would convene upon these shores to claim their prize. That there would be some kind of puzzle that would reveal to them where it waited— that there was a letter, and a codebook. What a fool he was, to whisper such secrets in my ear and then cast me into the abyss," she added, venom lacing her words. "But I *returned*."

"You told Father Kearney what Donnelly said. And he got the letter and the codebook."

"I may have hated Aiden Kearney for shattering my life with my Robert, which is what the trial did. But not as much as I hated Robert for casting me into the asylum." She finished her gin with a straight shot. "Yes, I shared Robert Donnelly's deepest, darkest secrets to his most hated enemy. And Aiden Kearney did just what I hoped he would—he snooped around, he found evidence, and he went to his lawyers and appealed his trial. It probably would have worked for him, and for me, if he didn't suddenly *die*."

She set the empty glass softly upon the table. "I suppose I didn't really answer your question."

"That will suffice," Tuohay replied.

The doctor slipped his timepiece from his pocket. "We should be going, Mary. I worry about Inspector Frost lurking about. No need for an additional encounter."

"Of course."

"Thank you, gentlemen." The doctor stood abruptly, followed by Tuohay and Eldredge. Mary stood last, clasping her coat tight about her. Her eyes lingered on Tuohay. "You will perform your duty to Aiden Kearney?"

"I came a long way to make things right, Miss Hart," Tuohay replied, "and I daresay I will not return to Belfast until it is done."

"Thank you."

"Thanks should not be forthcoming until there is a reason to give it."

Mary smiled softly. "All the same."

The doctor and Mary departed, the latter's gaze lingering on Tuohay from over her shoulder as she exited the parlor.

Tuohay and Eldredge resumed their seats, Eldredge whistling softly. "Gads, Jack. How will you get the truth out of Father Donnelly about the diamond? It sounds like he can tell you directly where it is!"

"Easy, old boy," said Tuohay. "As always, one step at a time. What do you make of the accounting books?"

"The books?" Eldredge shrugged with disinterest. "Looks like I have a lot of numbers to run through, if it's really necessary. I assume I am checking for fabrication?"

"It is imperative," said Tuohay. "Hard facts are what we need. Your statistics can be used?"

"Absolutely," said Eldredge, brightening. "I'll employ a new device learned through a friend of mine, Simon Newcomb. It will indicate any purposeful modifications."

"Sounds thrilling." Eliza set her paper down and joined them at their table, settling softly in a chair after some rustling with her dress. "Good thing *you're* the math genius."

68

"Nice try, Eliza," said Eldredge. "I have seen your aptitude with numbers up close, and it is nothing to sneeze at."

Eliza shrugged. "So I'm multi-talented. What of it?"

Tuohay stared thoughtfully at the door to the parlor. "Mary mentioned that there were three concubines that took the stand against Aiden Kearney. Herself and Kathryn Dwyer, and Susan Lovelace. I need information on Miss Lovelace, including how she died."

"On it," said Eliza. "And I'll get more detail on Kathryn Dwyer's killing as well."

"What about the letter?" said Eldredge, turning to Eliza. "What did you mean by *Sympathy*? We were speaking of it before the doctor and Mary returned."

"Right." Eliza pulled her lace gloves off and set them in her lap. "I used the sympathy method in one of my first plays, *L'invité secret*." Eliza's French accent sounded remarkably accurate. "Sympathique. Corrélation. Affinité."

Eldredge strained his memory. "I remember the play…a mystery set in a grand hotel near mineral springs. But I saw it years ago."

"Let me clarify, then," Tuohay offered. "Before a scientific explanation was brought forth, the term *sympathy* was used by the French chemist Nicolas Lemery to define the observable affinity between red-lead and vinegar, and quicklime and arsenic sulfide. Basic and acidic compositions, as it were."

"Encre sympathique," Eliza added, continuing with the proper inflection.

"Encre. Wait a moment…." Eldredge's voice trailed off. "Do you mean—"

Eliza smiled. "Invisible ink."

"In the code book?" Eldredge sounded doubtful. "But where? And with what medium?"

"I cannot answer *everything* for you, Johnny," Eliza replied. "Perhaps the presence of the pressed handkerchief means the book is to be pressed, allowing the medium to seep through the paper. It would work with arsenic sulfide, like in my play. Very little medium is needed, if I remember. The message, or messages, will appear on whichever pages they were scripted. I could sit on the book and test the theory. Or you could."

"Ha, indeed." Eldredge shook his head. "Did you ever actually perform any of these experiments, or just write about them?"

"What's the difference?"

Eldredge turned to Tuohay. "The book is evidence, I assume. Can we test Eliza's theory?"

"By having her sit on it?"

Eldredge shook his head. "No, no! I know several techniques—proper techniques—regarding invisible ink."

Tuohay nodded in agreement. "The method Eliza is talking about, mixing quicklime ink and arsenic sulfide, can be quite dangerous. There is a side reaction that creates a toxic gas—"

"I already tried it," Eliza said.

The two men looked at her in astonishment

"Don't worry, nothing terrible happened. But nothing good, either." She produced the book and slid it to Eldredge. "Must need a different method."

"Thankfully so," said Tuohay.

"It is not like the book would have burst into flames," Eliza said reproachfully.

"As a matter of fact, the chemicals you were referring to *are* actually combustible—" Tuohay caught Eliza's glare and cut himself short.

"Are we through?" Eliza asked.

"Yes."

"And the plans for tomorrow?"

"I will be interviewing Father Donnelly tomorrow in Plymouth," said Tuohay. "Leaving quite early."

"I am sorry I cannot join you for that," said Eliza, "I have tea with the production manager at the Boston Athenaeum. But I will be available shortly thereafter."

Tuohay nodded. "Excellent." He turned to Eldredge. "And you?"

"Heading to mum's in less than an hour, in fact," said Eldredge. "Dinner and such. But I will be back tomorrow morning at first light to join you for the trip to Plymouth."

Eliza leaned forward, her eyes on Tuohay. "And for the remainder of tonight? I may be heading out with some friends." She paused. "Well, actors. But they can be entertaining. You are welcome to join us."

"As enthralling as that sounds, I will have to pass." He took the codex from Eldredge and thumped it with a fist. "I must visit the dispensary, and then convert my hotel room into an operating workshop. I would like to give this a go, if I may."

Eliza smiled. "Just make sure to decode the message before you burn down the building, alright?"

"I have to concur," Eldredge added.

"Of course." Tuohay turned his gaze back to the book. "Mary mentioned that a *puzzle* would lead to the diamond… And I would not want to permanently char the one item possibly holding the clues."

Visitor

The pale candlelight flickered in the sudden breeze, stirring the shadows of Tuohay's hotel bedchamber. The moan of the wind tugged Tuohay from his dreamlike state until he finally woke, the darkness meeting his blurry vision. He leaned up and spit red into a china bowl on the floor, wiping his mouth with a handkerchief from the nightstand.

With a grunt he reached across his chest to the awaiting flask, his fingers shying away from the low-burning candle beside him. The metal of the flask felt unusually cold to the touch, but the liquor was strong with the welcome scent of Highland whiskey. Wetting his lips, he became aware of something unnatural in his surroundings. His eyes dug into the thick shadows.

The room remained silent, the inky blackness impenetrable. Inanimate objects breathed in the darkness beyond the candlelight, shivering and creaking in the language of the night. Decanters, cups, and bowls created a crumbling keep in the shadows of a nearby table, surrounded by a mass of invaders—a pair of alcohol burners, a pile of matches, thimbles of liquids, heaps of granular oddities, and other laboratory equipment.

Tuohay focused beyond these on a slight movement near the drapes.

"Who's there?" he demanded.

A dark form slid to the drapes, the clicking of boots upon the wood floor breaking the silence. A brief glint of moonlight followed the uninvited guest out the open window, exposing a splash of olive. Tuohay swung off the bed in pursuit.

"Stop!"

He landed on his lame leg and stumbled into the bureau. Grabbing his cane from atop the bureau he strode to the window and peered out. A deserted courtyard was within leaping distance and beyond that an iron gate separating the hotel grounds from the desolate road. Farther still were the south harbor and its multitude of warehouses.

Tuohay's breath caught in his throat as he limped to the table. The code book was there, closed. "I left it open," he whispered, his memory a jumble. "But the sickness came on so quick, I cannot be sure."

Tuohay grabbed his coat and pulled out his watch. It was nearly four in the morning.

Tuohay fell back on the bed and pressed the back of his hand against his forehead. He was in a cold sweat. His stomach twisted and a burning sensation rose into his throat. Grabbing the china bowl he vomited into it. He wiped his mouth, pushed the bowl away and closed his eyes. Dizziness swept over him as he fell into the bed again.

"It will pass," he said. "Come now, Jack. Easy." He lay with his arms over his face and his eyes closed, the world spinning beneath him.

He jolted up suddenly and wiped the cold sweat from his face. "Eliza." Sliding from the bed, he pulled on his trousers and shirt and grabbed his short frock coat. Taking his hat as he reached the door, he strode out painfully, his lame leg out of sync with the thud of the cane. The hotel was quiet at this time of night, the dim electric light of the lobby acting as his beacon from the hall. The bellman looked up from behind the desk and straightened his red cap into a presentable position.

"May I help you, sir?" he inquired, his thick Italian accent underscoring a slickly curled moustache and weathered bronze skin.

"The local booth, please. And quickly." Tuohay handed the man two nickels.

"Yes, of course. A candle, yes?"

"A candle? No, no. Just the key please."

"Here you are."

Tuohay took the key from the hand of the bellman and strode to a small recess in the east end of the lobby. Above the entrance an elegantly decorated sign read: 'Boston Telephone Service—Local Only'. Unlocking the glass-paneled door, Tuohay entered and sat down on a bench against the far wall. Residing on a small table to his left were a paper tablet, pen, and a silver candlestick-telephone. It was Swedish make. Pulling the highly polished receiver off the switchook, he held the cold metal to his ear and listened to the silence on the other end.

"Yes?"

"Hello, operator? I would like to be connected to Eliza Wilding of Number Four Province Court in Boston. It is quite urgent."

"One moment sir." The operator's voice gave way to a static-filled hiss. The hiss lasted a moment and diminished, returning again a moment later. The phone line hissed several times before the voice of the operator returned.

"There seems to be no answer, sir."

"Let it go a little longer," said Tuohay. He shook his head as Eliza's line continued to hiss. "Come on, Eliza." After a few more moments without an answer, Tuohay placed the receiver back onto the switchhook and returned to the hotel desk with the phone key in hand. "I need to get to Province Court right away."

The bellman mused for a moment. "The hotel automobile. Work for you, yes?"

"When can it be ready?"

"Right away. The fare at this hour is one dollar."

Tuohay gave the bellman a dollar and watched impatiently as the Italian called in a driver from the hotel phone. After a moment he turned back to Tuohay. "You will be picked up out front."

A cold drizzle blew against Tuohay's face as he stepped outside. Gathering his coat, he walked to the road and watched as a pearl gray fog rolled sluggishly towards him from the east. The finer tendrils of mist soared above his head, their gray fingers transparent under the nearby electric light. Suddenly a muffled roar broke the night's silence, and a yellow globe materialized from the darkness. The mist parted as the globe quickly approached, revealing itself as a dew-covered lantern latched to the front of a vibrating automobile. The garbled hum of the auto's metallic heart echoed in the night as the driver pulled up beside Tuohay.

It was a toboggan on wheels. Chocolate brown in color, the self-propelled carriage had four wheels, a skeletal metal frame, and a long seat for two. The driver, hunched on the right side of the vehicle, held the thin metal shifter firmly in place as his left hand grasped the rudder-like steering shaft. The engine rumbled from within an enclosed steel box situated directly behind the seat, and as Tuohay climbed up he could feel the mechanics vibrating beneath him. The driver, a surprisingly young man by the looks of him, was dressed in a short gray sports coat and a checkered baker boy cap. He nodded to Tuohay and wiped the rain from his glasses.

"Ever ride in a cah before, mack?" the youth asked, smiling roguishly.

"Kindly call me 'sir'."

"Please to meet yah, sir. I'm Ronald."

Tuohay squinted through the rain. "How old are you, Ronald?"

"Turn twelve tomorr'a, sir. How 'bout you?"

"Never mind, boy." Tuohay studied the youth. "Are you certain that you are capable of handling this thing?"

"Been do'n it for a full month now. Think I got her down pretty well."

"Splendid."

"It sure is, sir. Cuh've Dash Olds. Only four hundred of 'em on the road. You're a lucky fella to hop a ride in one."

"Is that so?" Tuohay pulled on his gloves. "Shall we?"

"You're in charge." The boy clamped the safety off with his right hand and thrust the gear shift forward. The auto jerked to the fore and nearly sent Tuohay tumbling off the seat. Grabbing the steering rod to save himself, Tuohay inadvertently yanked the control from the youth and the Olds twisted sharply onto the sidewalk. With lightning fast reflexes the boy grabbed the steering rod back and yanked it the opposite direction. The auto swerved to the left and bounced back onto the road with a thud. Righting their course, the young driver howled with laughter.

"Close 'un, sir! But we're on track now." The boy wrenched the steering rod to his chest, and the Olds squealed left into the fog bank. Tuohay cried out, expecting to see a brick wall materialize before them, but they passed through its gate, just barely visible in the concealing haze.

"How can you see anything in this fog?" Tuohay shouted above the rattle of the motor.

"Don't need to. I know this route by ha't."

Tuohay watched in sickened amazement as they slashed their way through the impenetrable pea soup, the light of the lantern dissolving into a gray nothingness mere inches ahead of the auto. "This is absurd."

"Oy?"

"Nothing. Concentrate on the road."

"Hold on, sir. 'Er's a rough patch com'n up."

"Hold on? To what?" Tuohay grabbed the finger-thin iron rail pressing against his left thigh. It was the only thing between him and the road below. The Olds suddenly began shuddering like an earthquake. Tuohay gritted his teeth against the vibration.

"We call this run the salt shak'a!" said the boy, his voice quivering.

"What in heaven's name are we driving over?" The ground had changed from cobblestone to treaded dirt to patchy grass. One of the wheels snatched a fallen branch that snapped apart in a spray of splinters.

"Short cut, sir," replied the boy, staring into the fog.

"Indeed," Tuohay muttered.

Several large stones blinked in and out of the haze as the auto sped past. The fog shrouded the scattered stones ominously, rows of ghostly soldiers lined up in perfect order. Tuohay watched with morbid curiosity as they continued past the strange sight until a realization struck him. "Are those....?"

"Oy. Tombstones. Don't worry 'bout them none, sir, I know where they be."

"We are in a graveyard," Tuohay stated matter-of-factly, his senses numb to any more surprises.

"There's a path through it, sir."

"I would hope so."

The rattling suddenly ceased, followed by the drawing back of the fog. The auto lurched left again, but this time Tuohay was ready. He held on to the rail firmly with one hand and his top hat with the other as a wide trolley road opened before them.

"Central Street. Nearly there, sir," the boy said, shifting down a gear as he made a smooth right turn.

Tuohay suddenly remembered the Derringer. It was back in his bedroom where he had left it in his hasty exit. "Kill the motor before we get to Province Court."

"Sir?"

"I would like to be as discreet as possible."

"Yes sir."

Tuohay recognized the area. A quiet gloom had settled over the buildings, but even as late as it was, a scattering of lights glowed from various windows. The street remained empty, however.

The boy slipped the gear shift into neutral and the motor stilled. Gliding silently with just the crunch of dirt under the wheels, they crept up to Province Court like some kind of strange horseless apparition. The boy pulled the brake and the car stopped with a squeak.

"That was quite memorable," said Tuohay, slipping a nickel into the boy's hand.

"Shall I wait, sir?"

"Yes." Tuohay eased himself off the vehicle, using the cane for support. "If I am not back in five minutes, get the authorities and bring them to Number Four Province Court, apartment D."

The boy appeared troubled. "The authorities? What for?"

"Kindly do as I say," said Tuohay, pressing four more nickels into the boy's palm. "If I return or give you the signal, you may go on your way."

The concerned look remained on the boy's face as he pocketed the money. "Yes, sir."

Tuohay departed the auto, the boy's eyes on his back. Avoiding the electric lamp at the corner of Province Court, Tuohay lingered in the shadows as he regarded the single-block, dead-end alley before him. A hub of entrepreneurship, the secluded back street was besieged with advertisement boards hanging from various heights of the surrounding buildings. Thick bold print called out available services by plumbers, carpenters, painters, grinders, concavers, woodworkers, and iron workers. The brick buildings housing the businesses stood side by side overlooking the thin street, their numerous windows acting as vantage points for eager merchants on the lookout for potential customers. But in the dead of night the ever-watchful businesses were off duty, allowing Tuohay to tread down the street unnoticed.

Stopping at a freshly painted door halfway down the alley, Tuohay tested the doorknob. It turned with a slight catch. A dark carpeted hallway waited. Following it, Tuohay passed two doors before stopping at the one marked 'D'. Pressing his ear to the door, he listened. The building hissed and groaned, the natural creaks of its inner workings indistinguishable from any potential human interference. The door was not locked, and Tuohay was soon inside Eliza's apartment, listening to the silence. He took in his immediate surroundings, the small parlor and adjacent kitchen barely visible through the moonlight of an adjacent window. His eyes fell upon the coat rack beside the door, causing him to pause for a moment. He left the apartment quickly, his cane sinking into the carpet. Stepping outside under the glow of the electric lamp, he waved to the boy in the auto.

"'You 'right, sir?" the boy called.

Tuohay signaled the affirmative with a tip of his hat and the boy waved back. The roar of the engine was a distant memory as the door to apartment D closed behind Tuohay again. Discovering a chair drowned in papers, he brushed them to the floor and set himself down with a slight groan. The chair was a sight more comfortable than the vibrating auto had been, but was still less than satisfactory. Resting his chin in his hands, Tuohay closed his eyes and waited.

The window was framed in burgundy when Tuohay was stirred awake by a door clattering shut. It was before sunrise. Stretching his leg with a grimace, Tuohay remained seated and ignored the pain as best he could. Soft footsteps became distinct in the hall. The footsteps stopped and the door opened. Eliza, draped in a long fur coat, stepped through yawning.

"Do you make it a practice to leave your flat unlocked?" asked Tuohay. Eliza started, her keys clattering to the floor.

"Jesus, Jack." Eliza stared at her friend. "Are you trying to frighten me to death?"

"There are far more efficient ways to dispatch of someone than fright," replied Tuohay.

Eliza bent down for her keys. Her cheeks were flushed, but she kept her composure as she straightened up. "I assume this is not a breakfast call."

"I am afraid not. You were out all night, I take it?"

Eliza stood facing Tuohay as if unsure of how to answer. Finally, she laughed and pulled her coat off. Casting a sidelong glance at him, she sank into an armchair. "I have a private life, you know."

"Point taken."

"In case it is not painfully obvious, I am a solitary woman who lives on her own. And as you may have guessed, my neighbors do not approve. Nor do my friends, or old classmates at Radcliffe, colleagues, strangers, you name it. First in New York, and now here."

Tuohay rubbed his eyes. "Breaking the mold, as they say."

"Is that what it's called?" A loose strand of hair fell across her eyes. "Jack, what are you doing here? And I don't think you want to hear what my imagination is coming up with."

"No, I do not suppose that I do," Tuohay admitted. "I apologize. I realize this is highly inappropriate."

Eliza smiled despite the concern in her eyes. "Yes it is. Now what is it about? You have me worried."

"I doubt that what I say next will dispel that notion." Tuohay paused. "I came here to make sure you were safe."

"And why is that?" Her tone was suddenly careful.

"There was an intruder in my room tonight—last night, that is. You get my meaning."

Eliza's eyes widened. "While you were *there*? Asleep?"

"Yes. But I woke up, to both his and my chagrin, I assure you."

"Did you get a clear look?"

"Not clear enough to positively identify him—or her. I gave chase but he escaped. I then came directly here, for I am certain if he was in a bother about me, he will not leave my closest colleagues alone."

"What about John?"

"Eldredge went straight to his mum's and is returning in the morning, so I am certain he is fine. However, now that I see that you are safe, I plan on checking his apartment."

"You are sure this intruder is connected to the case?"

"Coincidences, my dear Eliza."

Eliza frowned thoughtfully at her shoes, and as if an afterthought, slipped them off. "Right. *There are no coincidences.* Your favorite turn of phrase."

A gentle light filled the room as Eliza turned a gas lamp on, and Tuohay regarded her for a quiet moment. Her azure evening dress was slightly rumpled, the gold lace along the hem and sleeves gleaming in the new light. Her lipstick had been wiped clean save a few traces at the corners. Her hair, jauntily rouge, had been set into a rising swirl of interlaced braids, many of which had unraveled and now hung as wayward curls. A scent of lavender touched his senses softly.

"I have just now realized how truly scandalous it is that I am present here."

Eliza laughed again. "Good old Jack. Never one for social etiquette."

"So…you are well? Last night was…good? You have a friend? Or friends? A group of actors, you said?"

"Stick to what you are good at, Jack." She smiled softly. "But I appreciate your invented interest. I am well enough."

"You are… involved?"

Eliza rolled her eyes. "Gads, Jack."

"My apologies."

She curled her legs under her. "As luck has it, one of my plays is running at the Boston Athenaeum. I tend to spend time with the cast. Especially the understudies. They are the ones in the most need of guidance." Her eyes twinkled.

Tuohay shook his head. "Yes, of course. The *understudy*. I am sure he, whoever he may be, appreciates your guidance."

"And *that* is where I draw the line."

"As you should." Tuohay cast her a tired smile. "How about the work itself? It is being seen, then?"

"The new penname helps," she said. She took a small bow from her sitting position. "Presenting R. L. Wilding. As you know, we cannot have a woman writing dramas for the stage. Too fragile and all of that. R.L. Wilding is a presentation of strength, resolve, and depth. Everything expected of an artistic man."

"So who is your ghost writer? Do I know him?"

Eliza threw a pillow at Tuohay, who deflected it in midair.

"Quite the jester," she said.

"I picked up a few pointers across the sea." A sudden pain stiffened Tuohay's leg, and he rubbed it with a grimace. A slight wheeze followed his sentences. "My lack of rest appears to be catching up with me."

"Are you really surprised by that, in your state?"

"Very little surprises me." Tuohay reached into his pocket and pulled out a clove cigarette. Producing his lighter, he lit it and sighed as the pain slowly eased. "Tell me, have you ever ridden in an automobile? I just had the pleasure."

Eliza's face brightened. "You drove here?"

"I was driven here, rather, and am pleased to have the experience over with." Tuohay noticed her eyeing the cigarette and bent forward.

"What was it like?" She reached across her chair and took the offering. "You really ought to quit these," she remarked after a long drag.

"I believe my life was more at risk in the automobile than it was with the intruder."

Eliza cast him a crooked smile. "I'll bet." She handed the cigarette back.

Tuohay rubbed his temples. He could feel the beginnings of a headache setting in. "Would it be too much of an imposition if I asked to take a short rest here? I will be on my way to Plymouth in a few hours."

"Sorry, all booked up."

Tuohay eyed her skeptically. "In that case I should ask Eldredge if I could stay with him and his mother. A nice long rest in the country would do me well. Only a few days in and this case already seems to be wearing on my senses."

"From what John has told me, she is a very nice lady. I am sure you would be welcome there."

Tuohay chuckled. "Well, it is good to know that at least one house will take me in without protest."

"It is only because she does not know you very well."

Tuohay took a drag of his cigarette. The cloves tasted wet in his mouth. "You always did know how to cheer me up, Eliza."

The Lead

The horse-drawn carriage jostled along the Old Coast Road, the early New England spring framed in the smudged glass of the carriage window. Beyond the window stretched an affectionately pale landscape of green glens crowned with pleasant houses and quaint beach cottages, all sharing a view of the frolicking maiden that was the cold eastern sea. The window was slightly ajar, allowing in the slightest mixture of sea-air and early spring blossom. They had been at the road for several hours now, having passed by the rolling blue hills of Milton, the bustling shipyards of Quincy, the wildlife-rich marshes of Cohasset, the sheltered beaches of Scituate, and finally the mansions of Duxbury into Kingston.

It was just the two of them at the moment enjoying the hazy light of the late spring day as it filtered through the window in stark contrast to the dark interior of the carriage. Eldredge had been agape by Tuohay's tale of the intruder, and the two spoke at length of possible motives and identities for the culprit. The former discussion point ended clearly at the codex, but the latter was gray mystery, save the unlikely prospect of Kip Crippen.

The journey had been several hours of such conversation and wanderings of the imagination as both men peered out beyond their secluded transport. They were alone on the three o'clock horse-drawn to Plymouth, and by Tuohay's silver counter it was just after five. Despite the availability of two more popular routes, the Plymouth and Kingston Street railway out of the newly constructed South Station and the cheaper Number 6 trolley-to-ferry route embarking from North Quincy, the choice of the carriage had never been in doubt. It had been Tuohay's prerogative that they take the horse-drawn express. Eldredge had offered up a valiant but doomed argument for taking the railway, which would have been far more comfortable and expedient than their current vehicle, but Tuohay would have none of it.

"My dear friend," Eldredge had said as the two met outside the hotel, his eyes peering down the busy thoroughfare in the direction of the City Point railway station, "Plymouth is not exactly a short jaunt from Boston. The Plymouth and Kingston is a well-respected rail. It will get us there in a quarter of the time that an old horse-drawn can."

Tuohay leaned against his cane. "Why the rush?"

"It is not a matter of rushing," replied Eldredge. "It is a matter of *expediency*. Of *efficiency*. Would our time not be better spent at our destination than in transit?"

Tuohay produced a long-stemmed cigarette from his coat pocket and rolled it in his fingers. "Do you know anything about the Old Coast Road?" he asked.

"I have heard of it," shrugged Eldredge.

"It is the road that connects Boston to Plymouth."

"Well, there is also now a *railway* that connects Boston to Plymouth," said Eldredge.

"Let me get to the point," said Tuohay, wrinkling his nose at Eldredge's remark. "A road such as the Old Coast Road is like an old grandfather rich with lore. It is a painting of the times that were, times now being bypassed by mechanical steam engines and electric gadgetry." Tuohay lit his clove cigarette and held it in his fingers after an initial drag. "Imagine the Old Coast Road first as an Indian path, following the coast and skirting along the base of the great hills, crossing rivers and streams on its way. As time progresses and civilization forms, the roads are cleared and taverns appear for weary travelers to wet the dry gullet. Coach lines are established that run with dust rising from their wheels as their passengers gaze out upon the same sea that the Indian had gazed upon not so long before. But the passengers' eyes now fall on shipyards, inns, and cottages. It is more than just a shaky blur passing them by through the window of a fast-moving locomotive."

"You are no stranger to the locomotive," said Eldredge, regarding his friend skeptically. "And will take one again, I am certain."

"Allow me this one pleasure," Tuohay said, placing his clove cigarette in his mouth and tugging on his gloves. "Life is not meant to be economized. It is not meant to be passed through using the most direct route from A to B. Life is about observation. And one cannot observe if he is stuck in a cramped seat with life blurring by." He nodded at the approach of a horse-drawn carriage. "And that, my friend, is why we are *not* taking the railway today."

Body of police victim vanishes from the harbor

Questions abound about a cover-up. Foreign Intrigue suspected in Search for Templar Diamond. Boston Authorities deny taking orders from Scotland Yard.

Eldredge set the paper aside with a sigh. "At least *we* are not mentioned in the article."

"There is time yet," said Tuohay. "But we best keep our heads about us. We do not need the press following us about."

"Of course," acknowledged Eldredge. A thoughtful silence passed between them for a moment. "Jack, a question."

"Yes?"

"Do you believe Miss Hart? That she had an affair with Father Donnelly? That he had something to do with the theft of the diamond? The man is a pillar of society, an advisor to the archbishop himself. An expert physician. A Renaissance Man. Why resort to theft?"

"What could be more enticing to a man of genius than to put his gifts to the ultimate test? The Templar Diamond heist was no mere theft. It was a work of brilliance."

"So you believe Mary, then?"

"I believe there is truth to her words. But we will need more than belief to solve this case. Ah, speaking of which." Tuohay pulled a note from his jacket pocket and handed it to Eldredge, who procured a pair of wire-rim glasses in response. Setting them on the crook of his nose, he examined the note.

mnrwtcwagooxsevthzxeaoptxboevxhktyhwtasrsevthzxnvohgkhzrt
dcayelerzsbxmsifmxlfojhvhyreazqltrvdznxxiniagopsugrwtcjrxsfw
dxobsvytilstgkdefthqtthec

"Where did this come from?"

"It appeared in my coat pocket the night we interviewed Sara Conall. If you recall, she asked if she could wear my coat due to the chill. A somewhat odd request, since we were inside. She must have slipped this note in the pocket just before giving you my coat back, with the code book wrapped in it."

"Another code," Eldredge mused. He looked up at Tuohay. "Have you deciphered it?"

"No. Care to try?"

Eldredge accepted the challenge with a thoughtful frown. "More secrecy." He turned back to the code and studied it intently. Mumbling to himself, he took out a pencil and small, leather-bound notepad and began to make notes. The long silences were broken by bursts of 'ah ha' and 'yes, yes.' The scratch of the pencil did not cease, even when he was staring at the code, his eyes averted from the pad. Finally, Eldredge set the pencil down, leaving only the sound of the carriage wheels crunching along the dirt road.

Tuohay leaned forward. "Do you have it?"

Eldredge patted his forehead with a lavender handkerchief. "I do."

Tuohay glanced at his pocket watch. "Nine minutes, and we'll say forty-five seconds."

"You were timing me?"

Tuohay tapped Eldredge with the end of his cane. "Of course."

Eldredge handed the note to Tuohay. "It was quite a simple code, as you surely suspected. Though I got surprisingly fortunate in my attack on it. It's simplicity indicates that the codemaker was not well versed in the practice. A novice, really." He pointed to a few spots in the code. "From my review, I was fortunate to discover two recurring sets of letters. They are underlined, as you can see."

mn<u>rwtc</u>wagoox<u>sevthzx</u>eaoptxboevxhktyhwtasr<u>sevthzx</u>nvohgkhzrt dcayelerzsbxmsifmxlfojhvhyreazqltrvdznxxiniagopsu<u>grwtc</u>jrxsfw dxobsvytilstgkdefthqtthec

"Yes, I see them—'rwtc' and 'sevthzx'."

"This recurring pattern indicates that the key to the encryption is repeated. Therefore, it is not likely to be a random string, nor a long phrase, but a word that is repeated over and over again for the length of the message. Due to the fact that it is repeated, it happens to fall across the same plaintext a few times, giving us the necessary clues to solve it." Eldredge looked up at Tuohay. "Figure out the word, and you have figured out the key. Figure out the key, and you have figured out the message."

"You performed a letter count between the common terms?" The carriage shivered as it hit a large divot in the road, but both men ignored the brief interruption.

"Precisely. Since there are combinations of letters that are repeated in the coded message, it is likely that these are in actuality repeated *words* in the un-coded message, or plaintext. The fortunate circumstance of the words cropping up like this means that the key fell across them in the same manner, thus the encrypted version was also identical." Eldredge pointed at his notes. "There are twenty-eight letters between the coded letter combinations 'sevthzx', and one-hundred and five letters between the coded letter combinations 'rwtc'."

"I will take your word for it."

"Since the key is matched in an identical fashion with the matching code words, it must also fit perfectly *between* each code word. In terms of numbers, the key must be the length of the gap between the code words, or a factor of that gap."

"In the case of 'sevthzx', the key needs to be twenty-eight characters long, or a factor thereof. Is that what you mean?"

"Correct," Eldredge continued, his voice warm. It was clear he was in his element. "And with 'rwtc' it must either be one-hundred and five letters, or a factor thereof. Assuming there is one key, of course, we must find the common factor." Eldredge pointed to his scrawl on the note pad.

Factors of 105: 1, 3, 5, 7, 15, 21, 35, 105

Factors of 28: 1, 2, 4, 7, 14, and 28

Common factors: 1, 7

Keyword is 7 characters long

"Then some guess work began based on the facts in hand. The letter was given to you by Sara Conall, *fact*. Based on the condition of the paper, and the fading of the ink, I surmised it was not recently written—at least not as recently as a few days. Eliza is the expert on forensic graphology, but I picked up some basic skills."

"So not a fact, but a deduction. And we did not see Sara Conall plant the note in my coat pocket, so that is not technically a fact."

"Fair enough. Either way, I made the assumption this note may also be linked to the codex. But if so, where did it come from and who was its intended recipient? I realized that line of thinking was short sighted, so I took a different tact. What if the note actually *belonged* to Sara? Or what if it was written by her, and intended for you? What names would be associated with her? Or with us? Of course her late uncle came to mind."

"A reasonable assumption."

"One must start somewhere." Eldredge pointed to his notes. "Based on the little I know about Sara Conall and her late uncle, Father Aiden Kearney, I thought about mutual themes. What do the two individuals have in common? Would they pick a key along some kind of common theme? As novices, which seems plain, I thought a common theme likely. Nine times out of ten that is the way of it."

Ireland

Boston

Religion

Catholic

Kearney

Niece

Uncle

Priest

Truth

"Any one of those was simply a starting point. The key was likely seven letters, remember. I briefly tried the few on the list that were actually seven letters, such as Ireland and Kearney, but to no avail. Realizing the time commitment to continuing with this line of thought, I reflected. Were there any other quick ways to attack this—and one method came to mind. Father Aiden Kearney."

"Meaning?"

"Keeping in mind that I am trying simple solutions first, I made an assumption that this is a coded message *to* Sara, most likely from her deceased uncle. *That* is where I got fortunate—my assumption was correct. And as a letter, even a short one, it was possibly signed by him. I tried employing versions of his name to the last words of the letter, and—to my great astonishment—was successful."

Again Eldredge pointed at his notes. "I tried F.K, Father Kearney, Uncle Kearney, Uncle Aiden, and Aiden. The latter exposed the key."

Assumption: Last five letters in the message = Aiden

Plaintext (P): aiden
Ciphertext (C): tthec

aiden (P)→[C] tthec →key ?
(A) → [t] (resulting shift = 19) → 19 corresponds to key letter T
(I) → [t] (resulting shift = 11) → 11 corresponds to key letter L
(D) → [h] (resulting shift = 4) → 4 corresponds to key letter E
(E) → [e] (resulting shift = 0) → 0 corresponds to key letter A
(N) → [c] (resulting shift = 15) → 15 corresponds to key letter P

Key is seven letters
TLEAP _ _

TLEAP

_ _ TLEAP

LEAP _ _ T

EAP _ _ T L

AP _ _ TLE

P_ _ TLEA

APOSTLE is the key!!

A faint gleam of crimson sunlight filtered through the carriage window, dancing off of Eldredge's spectacles. "From there, I simply applied the key and deciphered the code."

Key: apostleapostle apostleapostle apostleapostle apostleapostle apostleapostl

Ciphertext: mnrwtcwagooxsevthzxeaoptxboevxhktyhwtasrsevthzxnvohgkhzrtdcayelerzsbx

Plaintext: mydearsarawehavethetwoaffidavitsandwemayhavethecrosssoontooiftheclaim

Key: eapostleapostleapostleapostleapostleapostleapostleapostleapostleap

Ciphertext: msifmxlfojhvhyreazqltrvdznxxiniagopsugrwtcjrxsfwdxobsvytilstgkdefthqtthec

Plaintext: istrueaboutdonnellysinvolvementmoveourdearfriendstomedfieldforsafetyaiden

My dear Sara,

We have the two affidavits, and we may have the Cross soon too if the claim is true about Donnelly's involvement. Move our dear friends to Medfield for safety.

Aiden

Tuohay rapped his cane against the floor. "Well done, old friend."

"It was nothing, really." Eldredge removed his spectacles and stared at them for a moment. "The affidavits in this note must be referring to those of the late Miss Dwyer and Miss Hart. The ones that were to be used during the appeal, and recorded by the lawyers of the late Father Kearney."

"McBarron and Thayer, yes. We will be visiting them. I need to see those affidavits."

"I expected as much," replied Eldredge. "And what is the Cross a reference to?"   Tuohay glanced out the window as if the distant landscape held what he was seeking. "The Templar diamond. The jewel has several names associated with it, among them the Star of Bethlehem, which is its most familiar name, and *Diamant de la Croix.*"

"Diamond of the Cross." Eldredge nodded in understanding. "It is clear from his message to Sara that Aiden Kearney believed there was a smart chance of danger about."

"Precisely. So as you can see, I have some pertinent questions to ask of our good friend Father Donnelly."

Eldredge returned his leather-bound notebook and pencil to his inside coat pocket. "Speaking of Father Donnelly, how did you get yourself an interview with him?"

The carriage ground to a halt. They had arrived in the ancestral home of the Pilgrims. Through the side window a great ivy-coated church was visible, the bell tower stretching above the rooftops of the surrounding seacoast town.

The door of the carriage swung open, ushering in the sharp smell of the sea and diverting the passengers' attention to the dirt-encrusted driver as he announced their arrival in Plymouth. Tuohay handed the man his bag.

"The interview with Father Donnelly," repeated Eldredge, "how did you obtain it?"

"I had the chief of the RIC clearly state the importance of the interview via telegram to the archbishop."

"To the archbishop?"

"We dabble with the upper crust now, old boy."

Eldredge exited the carriage, eyeing his partner with renewed respect. "You really have moved up in the world, Jack."

"From pawn to bishop, old boy. But still far from the most important piece on the board."

*

The door closed behind Tuohay quietly. He was in a large, richly furnished study with the curtains drawn. There were three sets of lavender drapes, one directly behind a desk, the other two adjacent to that at a diagonal, following the contour of the wall. A deeply polished floor rose to meet several strong backed chairs and along the walls numerous volumes of loose-leaf books rested in oaken shelves. Tuohay was well-read, but his eyes barely noticed the precious tomes.

To the right, a portrait hung above the fireplace, the handsome face of a young priest gazing through chestnut eyes. His black hair was combed back straight with the hint of Irish curls. Tuohay studied the portrait intently as he limped across the room. The scent of hickory was thick and sweet, but the evening fire gave little in the way of warmth. To Tuohay's left, a grandfather clock stood like an old sentinel beside a pair of closed pocket doors. The weights behind the glass hung low along the chains, gleaming in the firelight.

Father Robert C. Donnelly stood behind his great mahogany desk with his hands clasped behind his back. A black biretta sat atop his ancient white head and a matching black cassock with dark buttons extended down his lean frame to his ankles, blending him into the shadows. Tuohay noticed the gold insignia ring with a blood-red ruby on one hand, and a second gold ring with an emerald inset on the other. Both rings sparkled like colored stars in the low light.

"Welcome, Inspector Tuohay," he said, regarding Tuohay with paternal concern. "You are uncomfortable?"

"Every moment of my waking life," replied Tuohay, indicating his stiff leg as he leaned against his cane. "But one learns to live with it."

"Please, sit."

Tuohay took a seat, the wood unusually cold to the touch. Donnelly took a chair opposite him beside the hearth. "The proximity to the sea brings with it a desperate chill," said Donnelly, "one that seeps through the walls, clings to the wood, and holds tight." Despite the melting away of the shadows in the aura of the firelight, the crevices in the old priest's face created shadows of their own.

"I wish to thank you for granting me this time on such short notice," said Tuohay, leaning his cane on the side of the chair.

"Your telegram said it was of the highest urgency." Donnelly poured himself a drink from a glass decanter, his wizened hand steady. "Sherry?"

"Yes, thank you." Tuohay took a sip and felt the warm liquid run down the back of his throat.

"I do not typically grant interviews. That is what I have curates for. But, when the archbishop contacts me about meeting with an inspector from Scotland Yard, I comply."

"I appreciate it, Father," Tuohay responded. "Though I must clarify, I am with the Royal Irish Constabulary. District Inspector, 2nd Class. I am working on a case that Scotland Yard has interest in."

"Ah yes, that is right. The archbishop mentioned you to me." Donnelly arched an eyebrow. "It seems you are on probation?" Silence followed Donnelly's statement. "Does it surprise you that I know?"

"I was recently reinstated to the RIC," Tuohay acknowledged, "and am operating on probation with further review contingent on the outcome of this investigation."

"I see." Donnelly took a moment to regard Tuohay. "So what is the investigation about, inspector?"

"You know of the Star of Bethlehem, of course? The diamond, that is."

Donnelly smiled faintly. "The Templar Diamond. A 150-carat diamond the size of a man's fist. Breathtaking to behold, and priceless beyond mention. It was rumored to be formed from a single-faceted diamond. A possession of Rome, it was kept with the relics of Saint Antony in a reliquary for over three centuries. Most intriguing of all, it was rumored to be part of a larger, lost Templar treasure linked to the Copper Scrolls."

"And what do you know of its disappearance?"

"I was asked these same questions by the authorities several years ago, inspector."

"I beg your pardon, Father Donnelly. But if you do not mind sharing them again?"

"Of course," Donnelly said gently. "Six years ago the diamond was purposely separated from the relics in Rome to be sent on a holy circuit. The circuit included the Roqumaure in France, Whitefriar Church in Dublin, St. Peter's Cathedral in Belfast, and the Cathedral of the Holy Cross here in Boston. The latter visit was a bold plan of Rome's to lend credence and visibility to the emerging Catholic Church on this side of the Atlantic." Donnelly's lips pursed into a humble frown. "Alas, the diamond disappeared from St. Peter's Cathedral in Belfast, and the investigation—both that of the Church and that of the secular authorities—came up cold. It is true that I was one of the curates responsible for the logistics of transporting the treasure, but my part was performed through remote communications. I never actually *saw* the diamond. The details of the circuit were reviewed extensively by the Church and the authorities at the time."

Tuohay set the half-finished sherry down and picked up the leather-bound portfolio he had brought. With a practiced hand he rifled through the papers inside and brought forth a handful of documents. "The archbishop informed you of my purpose?"

"Only that you had questions about the Templar Diamond, and would be contacting me. Again, I must assume it is because I was involved in the logistics of its transfer to Boston."

"It is not that. In fact, I have already versed myself in those details."

"You have been reading the papers, then?" Donnelly pointed to a small stack by the hearth. "Today's papers are running articles rehashing old details about the theft in Belfast. All in connection to this shooting on the Boston wharves two days ago. Were you involved in that?"

"I would not rely on the papers for accuracy."

"Which is why I am asking you, inspector."

Tuohay regarded the man before him carefully. "Do you know a man named Kip Crippen?"

Donnelly gave it a moment's thought. "I am afraid not."

"He was a jewel thief from Belfast, one of the best in the business. I have reason to believe he was involved in the theft of the Star of Bethlehem, and followed him here to find out."

"Ah. Was he the man who was shot by the Boston authorities?"

"Unfortunately, yes."

"I see. Quite...fantastic. But it is all beyond me, as you can imagine. I wish I could help you, but there is very little I know."

"Are you familiar with a priest by the name of Father Aiden Kearney?"

Donnelly paused. "Yes, of course. The *fallen* priest, God rest his soul."

"Is it true that he accused you of insurance fraud? Of harboring a mistress?"

The priest's eyes narrowed. "And of many other things. He made many wild accusations, Inspector Tuohay. Against me and other established priests. Surely you are aware that he took the archbishop to civil court? A debauchery. Aiden Kearney, as brilliant as he may have been, was diseased in the head."

"Miss Mary Hart is willing to testify that you asked her to lie on the stand during Father Kearney's trial against the archbishop."

Donnelly's face remained unchanged. "So I have heard. But what does this have to do with the diamond?"

"If you will bear with me for a moment longer, Father."

Donnelly did not seem to relish the idea of continuing the interrogation, but he relented. "The truth is this, inspector. Miss Hart is being manipulated by Aiden Kearney's brother, Dr. Sean Kearney. The doctor removed her from a sanatorium as payment for helping Aiden, who wished to produce false testimony in support of an appeal of the trial against Archbishop Walsh."

Tuohay met Donnelly's gaze. "Did you ever visit Miss Hart while she was in the sanatorium?"

"Of course not. Why would I?"

"You are an accomplished physician, are you not?"

"I am a licensed medical practitioner," Donnelly allowed, "but my field is not psychiatry."

Tuohay's chest rumbled with what would have seemed to be laughter in any other circumstance. He took a handkerchief from his vest pocket and patted his lips. The handkerchief came away scarlet where it had touched his mouth. "Excuse me," he said, his voice hoarse.

Father Donnelly's paternal voice returned. "Inspector, please. You are ill. Let me take a look, or at the very least, refer you to someone."

"Thank you, but no. I have only one question more, and will be on my way."

"About the Templar Diamond? That was your original course, but none of your questions have had any import on it."

94

Tuohay cast a quick smile at Donnelly. "As it so happens, these questions *all* have import." The smile dissolved. "Did you receive a letter, recently or some time ago, that looked like this?"

Tuohay produced Sara and Aiden Kearney's silver-inked invitations, the black paper melting into the shadows so that the script seemed to float in the air, bounded by the golden serpents. Donnelly's reaction—the subtle difference in facial movement indicating surprise but not confusion—was the only answer Tuohay needed.

"Read them, if you please," Tuohay offered, sliding the two letters across to the priest. "You will better understand why I referenced Aiden Kearney in my questions to you."

Donnelly read the invitations carefully, the paper whispering under his fingers as he traced the ink with bony fingers. When he was done, he peered up at Tuohay with a humored frown. "Someone is playing an elaborate hoax."

"May I see your invitation, Father?"

"I am afraid I do not have it anymore," Donnelly replied. "The contents seemed absolutely absurd at the time, and became provender for the hearth after my first read."

"If I may, what did the letter say?"

Donnelly finished his sherry, setting the empty glass down. "In fact, it read nearly identical to these. The only real difference was what I suppose could be considered the 'clues' or information."

"And they were?"

Donnelly thought for a moment, but shook his head. "For the life of me, I cannot remember."

"I see," Tuohay replied.

Donnelly smiled fondly at Tuohay. "Is there anything else?"

"That will do, Father Donnelly. I appreciate the time you have taken." Tuohay glanced at the grandfather clock near the window. Frowning thoughtfully, he slipped his pocket watch out. "Speaking of time, you are aware that your clock is fifteen minutes fast?"

Father Donnelly smiled ruefully. "You are an observant man, Inspector Tuohay. Yes, I am quite aware."

"And why is that?"

"It was a practice of Abrams, my nephew." Donnelly indicated the stern painting over the fireplace. "That is a self-portrait he did when he was in Ireland. As you can see, he was a priest. But he was also a wonderful artist, like his brother." Donnelly seemed to drift back into a fond memory. "Such wonderful promise. Oil on canvass, wood working, stained glass, murals. He was a gifted boy."

"Sounds like he took after you, Father. A man of many talents."

Donnelly smiled soberly. "That was of his own accord. I call him nephew, and have all the love and affinity I would for my own kin, but he was adopted, to use the term loosely. He and his brother were orphans in a convent in Ireland, but their gifts were recognized at a young age by the nuns, and the Church became their official benefactors, and I his guardian. He spent time both here and in Ireland."

"I have heard of such practices," Tuohay said. "If I may, you said he 'was' a priest?"

"He passed on of complications of tuberculosis nearly six years ago, a very difficult loss. He was a frail boy, and even as a man was pale and lacking physical vigor. When he got sick in Ireland, he sailed back in an attempt to regain his health. I looked after him myself, up until his last days in the spring of '96." Donnelly's eyes had a distant look to them. "To the last moments, in fact."

The phrase caused Tuohay to pause. "Last moments?"

Donnelly contemplated his next words for a moment, the ghost of a smile passing across his lips as he did so. It was tinged with sadness. "I am a man that has mastered many skills, Inspector Tuohay. In the case of my nephew, I acted as his physician, his priest, and his mortician."

"Mortician?" Tuohay twisted his mouth into a perplexed frown. "You embalmed the body?"

"Yes." Donnelly acknowledged Tuohay's surprise with an appeasing nod. "Peculiar, I know. And I would be the first to concede that I have led an interesting, albeit rather extraordinary, life. I learned embalming during my short tenancy as a missionary in Haiti thirty years ago. Not from the Vodun sorcerers who practiced *zombi*, mind you," he added with a chuckle. "That would be frowned upon."

"Zombi. Dare I ask?"

"A term for the phenomenon of returning the dead to the world as mindless slaves," answered Donnelly, his voice devoid of mirth. "Supernatural beliefs are quite integral to their culture. It is fascinating, in truth. *Zombi* is the removal of the *ti-bon anj*, or the awareness and remembrance, from a persona, while retaining the functioning body, or the shell."

Tuohay frowned with distaste. "I see. Yes, I imagine that practice would be frowned upon."

"It would," Donnelly emphasized. "And yet it is my nature to inquire about such astonishing things—outlandish religious practices, ancient sorcery, magic. Not for application, for I am a devout Catholic, of course. But for insight. That may surprise you, coming from a priest, but there are many of us of the cloth who are philosophers at heart. We too want to learn from history, from nature, from science; to truly understand the beauty and purpose of God's universe, and some of us are willing to occasionally look beyond our own scripture for inspiration."

"That does surprise me," Tuohay admitted.

"But," Donnelly continued, pushing himself back from his desk, "I am rambling now." He pointed at the grandfather clock. "You are still interested, I presume?"

"I am."

"To answer your question, I have continued the admittedly sentimental practice of running the clock fifteen minutes fast in my nephew's honor. He did it with all of his time pieces—it was the way he assured he would be on time. He was creative, but not…punctual."

"I see." Tuohay gently snapped his watch shut. "I am sorry for your loss, father."

"Thank you." Father Donnelly smiled anew. "If I may ask one question of you?"

"Yes."

"By your own admission, you have come a very long way. In your own words, you are here in search of the Templar Diamond. Why were you asking questions about Aiden Kearney?"

"First, because he too received an invitation on black paper with silver writing. But more importantly, because Father Kearney then uncovered hard evidence about the Templar Diamond, and shared it with me. I intend to use that evidence to find the diamond, and finally collar the criminals responsible."

"And this evidence of Father Kearney's…are you sure he truly *uncovered* it?"

"Sorry?"

"Inspector Tuohay, are you certain it was not *always* in his possession? These…letters, or invitations, or whatever they are. They appear to me to be…well, a ruse of sorts. A game. And games are just that. They are not to be taken seriously."

Tuohay stood, leaning heavily on his cane. The pained expression on his face appeared to be from more than just his leg. "Whatever the case may be, I will root out the truth." He bowed stiffly. "Thank you for your time, Father Donnelly."

Departing without another word, he left the overwrought silence behind him.

*

The late-hour express carriage running the Old Coast Road to Boston rattled over a scattering of fallen branches, jostling the passengers as the storm blew fiercely without. The flickering lights of Plymouth faded behind a welcoming grove of dark oaks buffeting the wind to a near standstill. The two men inside the carriage sat across from each other just as they had on the reverse trip, their faces cloaked in shadow.

The crimson light of a match appeared suddenly, driving the shadows back by the width of a hand. Tuohay's face was revealed in the red glare, pale and fatigued.

"We should have stayed the night in Plymouth," Eldredge said as Tuohay lit his cigarette. The small cabin instantly filled with the aroma of smoke and cloves. "You look like the face of hardship itself."

Tuohay took a long drag and seemed to crumple back into his seat. "In these circumstances a midnight exit is far more exhilarating than a morning one, especially when there is a fresh storm afoot." He coughed and wiped his mouth with his sleeve. "And I am visiting Aiden and Rian's apartment in the morning with Eliza, so it is best I get back."

"Yes, the apartment on Kneeland Street where their bodies were found. While I go to visit my mum in Lowell."

"You cannot avoid it?"

"I am afraid not," said Eldredge. "She was not well when I visited last night."

"I am sorry to hear that. Straight from here to Lowell, will it be?"

"It will be simple enough to pay the fare and go straight, yes." Eldredge shrugged. "Besides, mum is an early riser. The earlier I arrive, the earlier I depart to get back here."

Tuohay smiled. "Good man."

Eldredge peered closely at Tuohay's pale countenance. "It seems the case is a little more involved than those we took during our Sleuthhound days. It certainly seems to have done a number on you."

"Uncovering a law exam scandal and who stole the coffer from Grendel's pub were not exactly difficult works of sleuthing."

"They *were*, in fact," protested Eldredge. "You never gave yourself enough credit for our successes."

"Formative collegiate challenges," grumbled Tuohay.

"But look at you now, investigating a proper case. Surely you cannot deny that our early cases played a role in your current profession?"

Tuohay coughed again, specks of red covering his thumb. "Yes, look at me now."

"Are you feeling proper?"

"Sufficiently so, thank you."

Eldredge shifted uncomfortably in his seat. "A train would have had us home by now. But no matter. Did you.... did you get what you intended from Father Donnelly? It was a long trip for such a short interview."

"It was simple enough to obtain, yes."

Eldredge's attempt to moderate the impatience in his voice fell short. "And that was…?"

"To make him nervous, apprehensive. I told him that I had significant evidence in my hands."

"Do you?"

"The letter, for one. And this." Tuohay produced the codex from his leather case. "Take it with you to your mum's."

"Did you have any luck with the invisible ink?"

"I ran some simple experiments in my hotel room, but to no avail. My notes are included for your reference."

Eldredge nodded and put the book aside. "You do realize Father Donnelly will not sit idly by if he believes you have evidence about the Templar Diamond. If he is truly involved, that is."

"Yes. *If* he is involved."

Eldredge asked the question hanging in the air. "So what precisely do you expect him to do?"

"Unfortunately, I am not a man of imagination."

"So… we just wait and see?"

"Presumption, however, I am better at." Tuohay took a long drag on his clove cigarette and closed his eyes. "And I presume we will not have to wait long before we see."

100

Kneeland Street

The morning was stark blue and cold.

Tuohay disembarked from the clatter of the single-horse taxi into the welcoming din of the poor district. Dilapidated tenement buildings stretched the length of Washington and Kneeland Streets in various fades of brown, each building attached to its neighbor by a dizzying array of clotheslines. A vast multitude of garments hung from the lines like a hundred billowing sails, endless in their discolored glory. Windows were thrust open, enabling a vibrant mix of shouting, jeering, and laughing to fall like rain onto the street below.

Tuohay waited on the sidewalk as a silver trolley rolled past him from the building's shadow, the metal gleaming in the sunlight. The whistle of a distant train rose from the alleyways facing South Station, the shrill distraction ignored by the multitude of passersby.

Leaning on his cane, Tuohay set off in the direction of Kneeland Street. The Saturday afternoon folk were out in droves, enjoying their only free day of the week—huddles of lean men in worn coats, cigarettes drooping from thin-lipped mouths; weary-eyed but forcibly energetic women marching with arms linked to the nearby nickel theater; dirt-encrusted boys in roving gangs heading for a dusty lot, a single tattered baseball glove and oil-stained ball between them.

Tuohay passed them by in silence, his eyes missing nothing. Three blocks down Kneeland Street a sagging Gable-house slouched in wait. Tuohay stopped at the dilapidated edifice and read the sign at the front door: *Ivers' Tenements, Rooms for Rent.* Checking his watch, he snapped it shut and stepped to the front door, but paused to take in the sight across the street.

Directly perpendicular from the house was St. James, the neighborhood church. Claiming a handsome gate of wrought iron and a tastefully decorated yard, the great stone building was an island stronghold amidst the wooden tenement buildings and their tangle of discolored sails. *Confessions open Saturday and Sunday* was printed in gold letters along a board out front.

"Jack!"

Eliza appeared from the crowd, standing out in her cranberry brocade bodice and maroon silk skirt. The bodice was highlighted by imprints of majestic gold roses, the skirt chocolate flowers. She clutched her satin hat as she raced over to Tuohay, her boots clattering along the pavement.

Tuohay met her with an anxious frown. "Is everything alright? You look worried. You are not late." He reached into his pocket and flipped open his watch. "Just a quarter past the hour. Time to spare."

Eliza put her hands on her hips. "Do you really think I would be this troubled about making you wait a few extra minutes?" She shook her head before he could reply. "Don't bother answering that."

She took a moment to catch her breath before continuing. "I received a telegraph from Sara Conall this morning." A nervous tension crept into her voice. "She has been contacted by Mr. McBarron, her late uncle's lawyer."

"Yes?"

"He had it on good authority that the Boston police dispatched an inspector for Plymouth this morning to investigate the death of Father Donnelly."

"*What?*"

"Evidently Father Donnelly fell from a balcony early this morning."

Tuohay massaged his forehead. "There is little doubt that the inspector dispatched for Plymouth was Frost. He will want to talk."

Eliza crossed her arms as if against a bitter wind. "Jack. Father Donnelly is *dead*. Possibly murdered, and the morning after you interviewed him. What did you say to the poor man?"

"Nothing that he was not already aware of, I am sure."

"I purchased us two tickets on the next train to Plymouth, 3rd class. We can spend exactly twenty-five minutes investigating Kneeland Street before our train arrives, and then we are taking a look at the scene of Donnelly's death."

"Very good. And I am going to need to see Mary Hart again to discuss what else she knows about her late beau, Father Donnelly."

"One step ahead of you," Eliza replied. "I also purchased two tickets from Plymouth to Medfield via the Boston C-Line exchange, and sent a return telegram to Sara announcing our impromptu visit. The return rail will give us about an hour in Plymouth."

"Medfield, you said?"

"It is where Sara Conall lives. Mary Hart is staying with her, remember? Our schedule is tight. And there is one more thing." She cast a meaningful glance back down the busy street. "I'm pretty sure a man in an olive trench coat is following me."

Tuohay nodded curtly. "Right. Then we best get inside."

Entering the tenement building, Tuohay and Eliza were met by a musty smell and the steady drip of water into a tin pail. A staircase immediately ahead led to the upper floors, a narrow passage beside it trailing into shadow. An open doorway at Tuohay's left housed a small anteroom with a table and several rickety-looking chairs.

An old trolley bell hung by the front door with a thin rope available to ring it by. Tuohay pulled on the rope and the bell clanked unceremoniously. A moment later a narrow-faced man with a beakish nose and balding crown appeared from a side doorway near the stairs. He rubbed his hands on his shirt as he stared at Tuohay and Eliza with cautious interest. His gaze lingered several moments longer on the latter.

"Are you interested in a room to let?"

"Mr. Ivers, I presume?" Tuohay asked.

"Aye, the landlord of this fine establishment." He straightened the lapels of his withered coat with pride. "And you are?"

Tuohay revealed a leather-bound badge marked with the stamp of a delicate but elaborate crown. "Inspector Tuohay of the RIC," he said. "And this is Miss Eliza Wilding."

"Right. Been expecting you, I have. You're here to look at the room on the third floor."

"Precisely. The room in which the Kearney brothers resided."

"Strange pair. Liked fresh air, even in the winter. Always was getting complaints from other tenants about the chill coming from their room. I even painted the fool window while it was open. Priest would have it no other way, even in winter. Liked his fresh air, he did. Not so much now, I suppose."

"No, I suppose not."

Ivers shrugged. "Well, the place has been nearly untouched for three months. A benefactor saw to the rent."

Eliza raised a brow. "Benefactor?"

"The room has been rented since the death of the brothers," said Tuohay. "'By a member of the archdiocese of Boston."

Eliza frowned. "For what purpose?"

"For the reason of unmolested evidence," said Tuohay, dropping his voice. "You see, there are those, even in the Boston archdiocese, who believe the death of Father Kearney needs further review. Or, more to the point, want any clues about the diamond undisturbed."

"You don't say. And they knew enough to keep the room unoccupied by taking up the rent?"

"With some advice from the Irish authorities, yes." Tuohay turned back to Ivers. "If you would lead the way, good man?"

*

Eliza waited until Tuohay had sent Ivers on his way before viewing the third floor. The cramped hallway was quiet, the uncomfortable silence hanging over their heads like a waiting whisper. She pulled a small sketchbook and lead pencil from her purse.

Tuohay nodded appreciatively. "Prepared?"

"Ready when you are, Jack."

The door to the bedroom was a deep burgundy, like old blood. Tuohay took the key that Ivers had given him and slid it into the keyhole. It turned with a reluctant thunk.

Eliza entered the dark chamber one step behind Tuohay, who removed his top hat. The smell of stale fumes filled their nostrils, abrupt but fading in effect. Gray light slid through a sliver in a small curtained window, revealing a one-room affair with a bed in the right corner of the room.

Eliza began a rough sketch of the surroundings. The scene had a sense of fatal permanency that she strained to capture.

"Has anyone been in here since the bodies were found?" she asked, incredulous at the thought. It had been months since the priest and his brother had been found lying in a peaceful repose, dead upon the bed.

"So it appears, though I must assume infrequently. And it does not seem to have been cleaned thoroughly. These walls may speak yet."

The two took separate paths, Tuohay to the right towards the shadowed bed, Eliza to the left where faded light seeped through a curtained window.

"Here is where they were allegedly found by Doctor Kearney," said Tuohay, pointing at the bed. "Cross reference your memory of the newspaper reports for me."

Eliza tapped her chin thoughtfully. "The bodies of the two brothers were found by Doctor Kearney, who visited them on a recurring basis. They were fully clothed above the blankets, serenely side by side. He stated that the air was heavy, the smell of gas prevalent. The furnace door was open, and a lamp was on the table. The one window was closed tightly." She paused in her recollection. "Why didn't you ask the doctor about the details when you interviewed him yesterday morning?"

"I wanted to see the scene for myself first," replied Tuohay. "I plan to have a follow-up interview with our good friend Doctor Sean Kearney in the near future."

"Right." Eliza turned her attention to her half of the room. A cracked basin was sunk into a small wooden protrusion, beside which hung a cupboard and cabinet. The squeaky door on the cupboard revealed nothing but dust, but the cabinet held two glass cups. Eliza took a few quick notes and moved to the basin, from which hung a brittle hand towel. She touched its surface with the end of her pencil, and small flakes fluttered from it into the basin.

Turning to the curtain, she eyed it closely. Scarlet red, it ran from the top of the window frame nearly to the floor, not unlike an evening dress. It had thin lines of dust at the creases, and cobwebs near the corners. A sprinkling of white caught her eye near the floor, and she bent down.

"Paint chips," she murmured. Peering up, she realized that the surrounding walls were a stark white, newly so.

"Jack, did the landlord say when he painted in here?"

There was a pause, and then Tuohay's voice from the other side of the room. "No, except that the brothers were still alive. I would judge it is several months old."

"Several months old," Eliza murmured to herself. She bent closer to the paint chips on the floor, and followed the wall up. Pushing the curtain aside, she watched the yellow glow of day spread across the floor like something holy.

"Paint chips came from the sides of the window," she remarked, taking notes. Putting her forehead to the glass, she peered out the window. There was wooden stair, narrow and rickety, at the base of the window leading down. A fire escape. A busy thoroughfare was some thirty feet below. Across the way the great stone church rose towards heaven, its splendid spires singular against the blue sky.

"I may have something of interest here," said Tuohay, drawing Eliza's attention away. As she turned, her eyes fell to the varnished Victorian oak desk at her right, further from the window than she would have imagined proper, as it was clearly a writing desk with an attached bookshelf pressed against the wall. The shelves were unadorned save a single bible. Her eyes were drawn to the bare surface, as if the spirit of the recluse fallen priest was there now, scribbling madly away.

She shivered, but not before four long scratches along the wall caught her eye.

"Eliza?"

"One moment, Jack." She walked over the desk where it rested against the wall. The scratches were nearly six inches in length running horizontal along the wall, and darker in color.

Tuohay was kneeling by the bed, but looking in Eliza's direction. "What is it?"

Eliza assessed the weight of the desk. "I think...I think this desk was moved. There are scratch marks on the wall from the bookshelf." She put her notepad on the floor and took the end of the desk with her hands. The heavy mahogany barely budged as she pulled.

"What are you doing?"

"Trying to move this thing."

Tuohay stood, leaning heavily on his cane. "I can help."

"Stay put," she directed. "Time for some virtuosity."

"Really, Eliza. It has been years since you've been on the stage."

"So?" Pressing her back to the wall, she lifted one foot and rested it against the far support of the desk. She repeated the feat with her second leg, using the wall as leverage. With a grunt, she pushed with both feet and smiled as the desk and bookshelf pivoted outward with a screech. Catching her balance, she repeated the acrobatics, this time finding purchase on the near leg of the desk. It swiveled out with a tremble.

Tuohay came around just as Eliza slid to the ground on her rump. With a wink, she held out her hand.

Pulling her up, Tuohay's gaze changed from one of bemusement to astonishment as he looked beyond her to the wall. Eliza turned and suppressed a gasp.

Behind the area where the bookcase had been was a scrawling message, etched crudely into the wall: "I AM MY BROTHERS KEEPER."

"Someone moved the desk to cover that up," said Eliza.

"It was written after the paint had been applied," remarked Tuohay, his voice soft. "So it could not have been that long ago."

"There is nothing about it in the papers, as far as I remember." She examined the wall closely, taking a few moments to sketch the message onto her pad. Sighing, she turned to the cockeyed desk. "I need to get this thing moved back."

"I do not think that's possible," replied Tuohay. "No wall for leverage this time."

Eliza was forced to agree. "So we leave it?"

"No use in covering up potential evidence."

She turned to him with a small grin. "So what did *you* find?"

Tuohay cast a sidelong glance at Eliza. "A four foot piece of carpet under the bed. Rectangular, roughly cut and soiled with chunks of dry, crumbling dirt. Strange, that. A shovel, also encrusted with soil. A shuttered lantern beside the bed, along with some tallow candles. No electricity in the place, as to be expected. Gas lamp and gas furnace, also as expected."

"Intriguing, the lamp and the furnace. The alleged devices of suicide. Which we already knew, of course."

"Admittedly, you win this time in the search for clues," Tuohay confessed. "Next time, I go left and you go right."

"Whatever you say."

"Your drawings are complete?"

Eliza reviewed the sketches with a critical eye. "Yes. But Jack..."

"Yes?"

"Are we running two investigations, or one? We are searching for the Templar Diamond *and* investigating the death of Father Kearney. Should we not be focused on one or the other?"

Tuohay leaned against his cane. "I believe the two crimes are threaded together. Working through one will gain us knowledge about the other."

"I'll take your word for it, for now. But I'll want a better explanation soon."

"You and me both." The click of Tuohay's watch-clasp caught Eliza's ears. "Time is up. We have a train for Plymouth to catch."

Fall from Grace

The lingering scent of burnt cedar hung in the air as Tuohay stepped through the pocket doors into the study. Eliza was at his side, notebook and pencil in hand. The late morning light spilled onto Father Donnelly's large mahogany desk from a glass door behind it, the curtains pushed aside to reveal an iron-wrought balcony beyond. Two adjacent sets of curtains remained drawn on either side of the far wall behind the desk, glowing a dark burgundy.

The train to Plymouth *had* been quicker than the express carriage, bolstering Eldredge's former argument for expediency. Departing from the train, Tuohay and Eliza walked the route along the beach to the rectory, where Inspector Frost and a uniformed officer were smoking outside. The Boston inspector greeted Tuohay formally, but was less than professional in his welcome to Eliza. The gracious smile had a poorly hidden leer behind it, but Eliza took it in stride. Ten minutes later they were led to Donnelly's study, the very same spot that Tuohay had interviewed the priest less than twelve hours ago.

Tuohay indicated the balcony beyond the opposite door. "That is the location from which Father Donnelly fell?" His question was directed at the imposing figure of Inspector Frost standing in the hall, a pipe clamped between his teeth.

"Right you are," Frost replied. The Boston official nodded at a uniformed officer positioned at the entrance as he stepped past. "The local constable and I gathered any relevant evidence from the premises early this morning. All the trappings, inspector. The constable is writing up his report, and all signs lead to an accident, pure and simple. Not sure what you expect to find here beyond our record."

"Most likely nothing," Tuohay replied, eyeing the portrait of the young man hanging gloomily over the fireplace, "but I appreciate the opportunity to take a look, nonetheless."

Frost shrugged. "No skin off my nose. You're still brass, even if you're a Queen's man."

"Perhaps we can start with your discoveries," Tuohay offered, "to save time."

"Good, then." Inspector Frost pulled a notepad from the depths of his trench coat. "The rectory is home to Father Donnelly, two curates, and a cook. The curates, Father Bryeth and Father McCallister, are attending a week-long retreat in Vermont. The maid, Miss Newell, arrives promptly at eight o'clock every morning and vacates the premises after dinner at seven in evening. She was not on the premises when the accident occurred."

"Which was?"

"Just after six this morning."

"Based off…?"

"The testimony of the live-in cook, Mr. Dunbar, and the condition of the priest's body under examination." Frost smiled around his pipe. "It will all come out in the wash, inspector. Nothin' will get by us, trust me on that."

"Timeline?"

"Straight forward." Frost squinted at his notebook. "Father Donnelly awoke every morning at four in the morning for prayers. At five, he was known to practice his sermon on the balcony, or verses from Shakespeare. Was a devoted follower of the old bard, evidently." Frost shook his head as if amused by the thought. "He took his breakfast in the study every morning at six, with a cigar afterwards. After that, he was known to spend hours gardening, a passion of his." Frost turned to a new page. "Concerning breakfast: Today being Monday it consisted of hot bread, fried potatoes, cold caraway seed cake, an omelet, and tea."

"And what of Mr. Dunbar?"

"Mr. Dunbar wakes at five every morning, takes a brisk walk, and subsequently makes breakfast for Father Donnelly. This morning it was delivered at five-fifty sharp, no different than any other. He rang that chime there," Frost pointed to a small bell resting on the edge of the mahogany desk, "as he does every morning to indicate that breakfast has arrived."

"Mr. Dunbar leaves breakfast on the desk?"

"Yes. Father Donnelly would have it when he was finished with his sermon."

"And the whereabouts of Father Donnelly when breakfast was delivered?"

110

"Out on the balcony, practicing his sermon, as was normal. He liked to look over his garden when he did so, or the sea, even if Old Man Winter was blowing. Quite a view."

Tuohay walked to the desk and bent over the small bell with a careful eye. "And Mr. Dunbar saw Father Donnelly on the balcony when he delivered the breakfast?"

"The curtain was drawn, as it always is at that time in the morning. Father Donnelly preferred privacy when he was reviewing a sermon."

"No visual contact whatsoever by the cook?"

"Mr. Dunbar stated that he saw the shadow of a figure outlined through the curtains, against the rising sun just so. And the light of a cigar, as well."

Eliza, who had unobtrusively walked up to the glass door to view the balcony beyond, turned to Frost. "I thought you said that he took his cigar *after* breakfast."

Frost smiled wanly at Eliza. "I could use an assistant like you, miss." He made no secret of the prolonged gaze at her figure.

"Maybe I will be available when Inspector Tuohay returns to Belfast," Eliza replied with a coy smile, rolling her eyes the moment Frost turned to Tuohay.

"Hear that, old chum? She prefers red-blooded Americans after all."

"Actually, I prefer men that answer my questions," said Eliza.

"Well then, I shall happily oblige," Frost returned amiably, removing the pipe from his mouth with a flourish. "I asked Mr. Dunbar the same question as yours, and he stated that while it was unusual that the priest would be smoking prior to breakfast, it was not unheard of."

"Indeed." Tuohay limped around the desk, his eyes darting to and fro about the room. "So, the remainder of the timeline?"

"At approximately six-fifteen this morning Mr. Dunbar, while in the kitchen reading last evening's newspaper—"

"No doubt about the search for the Templar Diamond," Eliza interrupted. "It's all over the news. Which of your coppers is spilling the beans, anyhow?"

Frost cleared his throat. "As I was saying, Mr. Dunbar was in the kitchen, at which time he heard a terrified shout from the balcony. He immediately exited the kitchen through the back door to investigate, and coming around to the garden, discovered Father Donnelly in an unconscious state upon the cobblestone terrace two stories beneath the balcony. The priest's position indicated a fall, which was confirmed by the authorities upon arrival."

"May I?" Tuohay opened the glass door at a nod from Frost and stepped out onto the balcony, a sharp sea gust greeting him. Stretching past the balcony, the rectory property, primarily a well-manicured garden and an acre of stunted crabapple trees, spilled onto a stony beach fronting the steel ocean. The sun kissed the gray horizon with the promise of return.

Tuohay's cane clicked against the wooden floorboards as he limped to a circular oak table covering nearly half of the balcony. Two chairs were squeezed between it and the iron grating of the balcony perimeter.

"He fell about here," Frost indicated a spot near the front center of the balcony. "You can see the bloodstains below. The body has been removed, of course."

Tuohay peered over the edge and nodded in confirmation at the dried crimson streaks stamped like veins across the stones. "No signs of a struggle on the balcony?"

"None whatsoever."

"What about possessions? Any indication of theft?"

"So far, none," Frost replied. "There is no indication of any valuables being taken, either from Father Donnelly's person or from the premises. We are continuing to investigate the latter, but everything we have checked on is in its place. Even Father Donnelly's ecclesiastical ring, with its precious ruby, was still on his finger."

"What could have caused him to fall? Did he have any medical issues?"

"We are looking into that," Frost replied.

"Some of his breakfast remains," said Eliza, sidling close to the table. She slipped her notebook into her purse as she regarded the silverware and cold remnants of food scattered on the plate.

"Where is the teacup?" Eliza asked. "You said he took tea this morning."

"Below in a thousand pieces," answered Frost.

"So he was drinking his tea, or holding it, when he fell," remarked Tuohay. He turned to Frost. "Everything we see here is as it was left?"

"We have moved nothing except the body," said Frost, "per your request in the telegram." Frost took off his hat to scratch his head. "Just so you know, I'd appreciate the chance to move on soon. I've been here since nearly the crack of dawn, and walked through this once already with the constable."

"Do not let us keep you," said Tuohay.

Frost chuckled. "Nice try, inspector. I stay for as long as you stay."

"Then we shall quicken our pace for your sake." Tuohay met Eliza's gaze, who nodded in return. They returned to the relative warmth of the study, Eliza pulling her notepad out again. She approached the desk, making note of its sparse contents: a quill pen, a half-full bottle of ink, a blank slate of paper, a worn bible, and a glass ashtray the color of caramel. The ink and pen were to the left of the paper, beside which rested the bible and the empty ashtray.

From there the partners split paths, Eliza to the right towards the grandfather clock, Tuohay to the left in the direction of the fireplace. The pair slowly circled the room in opposite directions, ignoring each other as they crossed paths. Eliza had her pad out and was sketching rapidly, occasionally taking a small knife to sharpen the lead. She was careful to catch the shavings and place them into her pocket.

Frost watched them through the haze of his newly restocked pipe, and finishing that, another. The constable left with Frost's permission as the Boston inspector was stacking his pipe for a third go, the air growing thick with the scent of tobacco.

As Tuohay reached the grandfather clock for a second time he spent a few moments in silent contemplation before turning back towards the room. "What time is our return train?"

"Two forty-five," Eliza replied, looking up from her notes.

"Thirty minutes," Tuohay murmured to himself. "How long was the walk here from the train station?"

"Fifteen minutes," said Eliza. "Yes, good point."

Frost muttered something under his breath about missing lunch, and Tuohay exchanged glances with Eliza. "Shall we move on, then?"

Eliza nodded. "I am ready."

"Finally," Frost declared with relief, tapping the remnants of his pipe into the ashtray on the desk. As they exited the study, he turned to Eliza. "Did you enjoy yourself, miss?"

"How so?"

"Playing copper." He winked roughly. "Looking for dark and dirty deeds, and all that."

"I thought this event was a mere accident. Nothing dark or dirty about it, is there?"

"You know my meaning," he replied sourly.

"Right," was her flat response, "I think I get the gist." They walked on in silence, Frost grinding his pipe with his teeth.

Emerging into the fresh air, Tuohay stopped short only moments after exiting. He held his top hat against a sudden gust of wind. "Inspector Frost, if you do not mind—I would like to take a quick sojourn over to where Father Donnelly's body was found."

Eliza leaned against Tuohay and whispered into his ear. "The train, Jack."

"We have time."

"No, I do not believe so."

Tuohay cast her a puzzled look. "I need to see the courtyard, Eliza. It will be fine."

Frost was already heading towards the back. "This way, Tuohay."

Tuohay flashed a quick glance at Eliza as he followed, who rolled her eyes. At a second glance from Tuohay, she cried out and stumbled awkwardly. "My foot!" She sat down on the steps of the rectory, rubbing her ankle.

Frost halted at the corner. "What is it, Miss Eliza?"

"I turned my ankle on these cobblestones. It's these damn shoes." The pout in her voice drew Frost to her in a few quick strides. "I think it's twisted rather badly."

Frost took a knee. "Here, let me have a look. I'm no stranger to injuries." His inspection in full swing, Frost barely noticed Tuohay as he disappeared around the side of the house.

Frost wrapped his hands around Eliza's ankle, his cold thumbs stroking her ankles and calf. "Does this help, Miss Eliza?"

Eliza smiled weakly, "Yeah, it's really working wonders." She turned away from him and bit her lip to keep from gnashing her teeth.

*

Tuohay and Eliza walked along the shoreline in the calming presence of the thrumming waves, Tuohay's cane sticking in the cold sand as they went. Close by, the town road arched at an elbow to meet the beach, and the train station was just visible beyond the first cluster of cottages. The two strollers watched as the tide slowly rolled in, the furrows in the sand made sleek by the cold rumble of hissing seawater.

"It is a question of ironing out the wrinkles," said Tuohay, indicating the retreating water as it smoothed out the sand. "A smooth surface hides no hills." The tip of an exposed seashell completed the analogy.

"Frost was trying hard to smooth *something* out," said Eliza. "For nearly *ten minutes*, Jack. You owe me."

"I am in your debt," Tuohay agreed.

"And don't think I won't collect." Eliza was walking barefoot, her shoes dangling from one hand, her notepad in the other. There was no indication of any injury from the gait of her step. "He is going to be around more rather than less, isn't he?"

"I believe we have not seen the last of Inspector Frost," Tuohay confirmed. "In fact, I expect the man will *formerly* be wrangling his way into our investigation any day now."

Eliza shook her head. "For the love of Pete."

"In any case," Tuohay resumed, "we were speaking of wrinkles."

"Right. The first wrinkle is the silverware."

"How so?"

"The position the knife and fork were to the right of the plate, indicating use by someone that was right-handed."

"So it appeared."

"But the pen and stationary on the desk indicated otherwise," Eliza continued. "Did you notice any particulars about Father Donnelly when you met with him?"

"He wrote left-handed," Tuohay confirmed. "When I arrived last night there was a work in progress on his desk, and all indications supported that supposition."

Eliza nodded. "That is something."

"Perhaps."

"And then there is the cigar and the tea."

Tuohay pursed his lips with interest. "Go on."

"There are no indications of the remnants of the cigar that I could see, and yet Mr. Dunbar specifically told Frost that he saw Father Donnelly—or someone—smoking a cigar on the balcony."

"Perhaps the water room or the fireplace," Tuohay responded. "The cigar stub could have easily been disposed of in either of those locations. Recall that there was a period of time between when Mr. Dunbar witnessed the shadow behind the curtain smoking the cigar and when he found the body. Ample time for it to be disposed of in a perfectly reasonable manner by Father Donnelly, which would be impossible for us to verify."

"True," Eliza admitted reluctantly. "So I suppose that theory is for naught. Though the fireplace was bare." Her last statement was softly spoken, and had trouble contending with the wind.

"However," Tuohay raised a finger, "there is the fact that I spotted a recently spent cigar stub on the cobblestones under the balcony, near Father Donnelly's garden." There was a twinkle in his eye as he pulled the stub from his pocket.

Eliza gasped. "That is evidence, Jack! I thought you would have learned better at the RIC."

"So I did," he shrugged, slipping it back into his pocket. "But I am in America at the moment."

"Well then," she continued, "let us suppose, for a tickle, that the stub you found represents the cigar that Father Donnelly—or someone—was smoking on the balcony this morning. Do you believe Father Donnelly was the sort of man that would litter his own garden by flicking the stub off the balcony?"

"How am I to know? He very well could have been."

"Come on, Jack."

"Go on," he allowed. But before she could continue, his gaze narrowed at the dunes behind them.

"What is it?" Eliza turned to follow his line of sight. On a distant dune a figure stood, his olive green trench coat flapping in the wind. His hands were thrust in his pockets, and a gray fedora with a pinched brim was adjusted forward over his brow. He seemed to be staring straight at them, unmoving.

Eliza took a step in the man's direction "It's the same fellow that's been trailing me."

"I believe it is a newspaperman named Mountain," said Tuohay, "or a man who *claims* to be."

"He's not acting like any newspaperman I've met," said Eliza. Even as she spoke the words, the man pulled gloved hand free from one of his pockets and offered a faint salute before disappearing back into the dunes. "What does he want?"

"Something tells me we will find out soon enough," said Tuohay, a note of urgency in his voice. "Come on."

They hiked the last fifty feet to the gravel road, and Eliza stopped to put her shoes on. She spent only a few moments rubbing the sand off with her hands before recommencing her walk.

"I lost my train of thought," Eliza complained as the train station came into view.

"Shall I surmise your thoughts for you?" Tuohay offered.

"I will surmise for myself, thank you," said Eliza. "Just give me a minute." She cast a sidelong glance at Tuohay. "Even though it has been ten years, I remember all too well your long-winded sum-ups."

"Pleased to hear I made a lasting impression."

"The bottom line is that the cigar was smoked by someone other than Father Donnelly. That individual carelessly flicked it over the balcony edge into the garden, which does not seem like something a priest with a responsibility to the rectory grounds would do. The broken tea cup on the ground is supposed to indicate that Father Donnelly fell with it in his hand, but that would mean he would have had the cigar in his hand as well as the tea cup, which is unlikely."

"Conjuncture, I am afraid. A merging of circumstances. And perhaps the tea cup was holding alcohol, which goes splendidly with a morning cigar."

Eliza continued unabated. "Put that together with the fact that the silverware indicates a right-handed individual ate breakfast on the balcony, whereas Father Donnelly is left-handed, and we have ourselves a collection of clues demonstrating that something is different than it is meant to appear."

"Unfortunately we cannot ask Eldredge to run statistics on your theory," Tuohay remarked, dry humor in his voice. "At least then we could quantify the probability."

"I do not need statistics to know my hypothesis is conceivable. One must allow for imaginative explanations."

"This is not creating a plot for a play, Eliza," Tuohay admonished. "Granted, creative thought is a component of the puzzle-solving recipe. But it is the *trail of facts* that leads one to the solution, like breadcrumbs through the forest."

"Facts tend to disappear in a case like this, just like breadcrumbs," responded Eliza. "Besides, I *am* using facts."

"Observations," Tuohay argued, but there was a smile on his lips, "though I will admit, they are astute observations."

"Astute?" Eliza laughed. "I suppose I'll take that as a compliment. And what about you? Did you notice anything in particular?"

"The painting of the nephew, Abrams. I swear I have seen his likeness before. But I cannot account for it." He shrugged. "A nagging in my brain for now."

"Well, I've never laid eyes on him. Can't help you there. Anything else?"

"The Adoration of the Magi. There were *eight* paintings of the scene in his study, all from various artists and cultures."

"Sure," Eliza nodded. "They were wonderful, and at least a few are quite valuable. Guess he has a thing for the Nativity." She shrugged.

"That was not the only evident theme."

"Shakespeare." Eliza affirmed. "Yeah, that was abundantly clear. The man has bookcases full of plays and sonnets by the bard, as well as a host of paintings and other knickknacks, even a replica of Yorick's skull from Hamlet. Quite the collection—I'm jealous, to be sure. But I am asking about something of relevance to the case."

"There were numerous architectural journals devoted to the study of religious art. One in particular had pages dedicated to the engineering dimensions of famous pieces, apparently for preservation purposes."

"Uh-huh."

118

Tuohay smiled softly. "I understand not everything can be of relevance to the case, but it is healthy to discuss them to ensure nothing is overlooked."

"Right. So what else was there?"

"Puzzles."

"Puzzles. *Really?*"

"You of course must have noticed the shelves dedicated to books about secret societies, mechanical wonders, strategies of chess, techniques of illusionists and other mystical behaviors, and even famous crimes dating back to the medieval era."

"Sure I did." She shrugged. "And?"

"And...nothing, at this point. But it is good to keep in mind." Tuohay's cane thudded against the wood flooring as they reached the platform of the train station. "Admittedly, part of my concentration was still absorbed with our visit to Kneeland Street. However, it did not distract me completely. I too noticed the details that you have already shared, such as the silverware and such."

Eliza snorted. "Ah, right. So in addition to everything you just listed, you also observed the details that I originally shared with you."

"That is correct, though I am not claiming to have come to the same conclusion that you have."

Eliza smirked. "You're a wonder, Jack."

"There is another detail, of course. The medical diaries."

Eliza rolled her eyes. "Gads. You mean the burgundy collection on the upper shelves to the left of the fireplace?" She brushed a strand of wind-blown hair from her eyes as she recounted her observations. "Thirty four leather-bound journals of various thicknesses. Spines were numbered in black ink and were not in sequential order on the shelves. They were Father Donnelly's collection of medical notes as a practicing physician. Journal number one was dated 1869-1870 on the interior cover, and journal thirty-four was dated 1902 with no closure date."

"Correct," Tuohay said. "But did you notice that journal twenty-eight was missing?"

Eliza arched an eyebrow. "You sure? It wasn't easy to tell the way the books were organized. Or *disorganized*, I should say."

"Yes, I am certain. Based on the dates of the bracketing diaries, the missing book was likely for 1896." Tuohay's cane sank into a sand depression, causing him to pause as he plucked it out. "And there was something else. The ecclesiastical ring."

"The one Frost mentioned?"

"No, the one he did not mention."

Eliza stopped short. "Sorry?"

"When I visited Father Donnelly last night, he had a ring on each hand. I remember how they caught the firelight. A ruby ring, and an emerald ring."

"He could have taken the emerald ring off at any point after your interview last night," said Eliza. "The fact that it was not on his person does not mean it is not on the premises."

"Where it most likely will be found," Tuohay granted, but the tone in his voice held a shadow of doubt.

"By the by, you do remember we are bound for Medfield to meet with Sara Conall and Mary Hart?"

"Yes, of course." Tuohay looked at the platform with a frown. "Where is everyone?"

Eliza responded to Tuohay's look of bewilderment with a sidelong glance. "I *told* you we would miss the train. I assumed we came to the to purchase new tickets. The next train is not for hours."

Tuohay pulled his pocket watch out and clicked it open, murmuring in surprise as he viewed the time. "It took us over thirty minutes to walk here from the rectory? That is nearly twice as long as it took us to get there from here."

"Look—it was 2:45 when we left Father Donnelly's study. At that point, we had just enough time to walk to the station and catch our train, but your ten minute diversion to the courtyard ensured we would miss it. I warned you." Eliza shook her head. "Did you not see the time on the clock in the study?"

"Yes, I saw it," said Tuohay. "But that clock is fifteen minutes fast. It was therefore only 2:30."

"No, it had the right time."

Tuohay turned his gaze to his watch as if the answer resided in its inner workings. His head snapped up. "It was a chain-wound grandfather clock, correct?"

"Yes."

"Where were the weights?"

Eliza stared at Tuohay. "Sorry?"

"The weights. On the chains. That you can see through the glass." He waved his hand as if it would help in the explanation.

"Right. The little gold cylinders, you mean."

"Exactly."

Eliza opened her sketch book and offered Tuohay a glance.

"They are *up*." Tuohay stabbed Eliza's rough sketch of the grandfather clock with a gloved finger. "The clock has been recently wound! Very recently."

"But you said it was fifteen minutes fast? I'm not following."

"The gold cylinders were much lower last night, indicating a winding was due. The clock must have been rewound last night, but whoever wound it also adjusted the minute-hand to the *correct* time."

"Which is why we are fifteen minutes later than you expected."

"Precisely," said Tuohay. "Either Father Donnelly decided to change his clock to the correct time the very morning that he accidently fell off the balcony, or…"

"Or someone noticed the clock had stopped, rewound it, and unknowingly turned it to the *correct* time, because it had stopped ticking for a long enough duration that it was far from the correct time at that point. There was no knowledge that it had been previously set fifteen minutes fast."

"There could be a simple explanation, even for the latter case. The cook, or even Inspector Frost or the constable could have adjusted it," said Tuohay.

Eliza stared into Tuohay's eyes. "Do you believe that?"

"At this point, it is not about belief. It is about probability based on evidence."

"But do you believe that?"

Tuohay hesitated. "To be forthright with you, I admit it is reasonable to entertain the possibility of a nefarious plot against the priest based on our current discoveries."

"*It is reasonable to entertain the possibility.* Wow. You really know how to go out on a limb, Mr. District Inspector, 2nd Class."

"We need *irrefutable* evidence." Tuohay tapped his cane against the ground, brightening as a thought struck him. "And we can obtain it!"

"How?"

"The breakfast, like the cigar, was purportedly consumed by Father Donnelly. If the cigar was smoked by someone else, we can assume the breakfast was as well. And if that is the case, we can prove it."

Eliza snapped her fingers. "Of course. By checking the contents of Father Donnelly's stomach."

Tuohay smiled grimly. "Yes. And now all that remains is getting that information from the autopsy."

"Should we ask Inspector Frost?"

"Let's start with the local constable. We will go to the Plymouth office together. He already knows I am part of the case, and should make allowances for one of us to stay." He gave Eliza an apologetic smile.

"One of us to stay?" Eliza pursed her lips into a small frown. "You want me to remain here."

"It would be best if one of us was present."

"But the autopsy could be as late as tomorrow or the day after."

Tuohay shook his head. "No. Despite Inspector Frost's little act, he is also concerned about the circumstances of Father Donnelly's death. The autopsy will be this evening, at the latest."

"And your visit to Mary and Sara in Medfield?"

"Onward as planned, but we will need to telegram Sara that I will be late." He fumbled in his pocket for a cigarette and propped it in the corner of his mouth. Locating a match, he lit it and quickly transferred the flame. The cherry glow at the end of the rolled paper expanded as he drew the smoke in.

Eliza waited until Tuohay had exhaled before plucking the cigarette from his mouth. "You do realize what it means if Father Donnelly was actually murdered, don't you?"

"It means there is a killer out there who is not only attentive to our activities, but intimately knows our every step and is resorting to deadly violence to fulfill his dark purposes before we can stop him."

Eliza took a long drag of the cigarette and exhaled with a rueful look, wisps of smoke rising past her eyes. "Dramatic, Jack, but not what I was getting at. What it means is that I was right."

An Interested Party

The six o'clock C-line rattled along the tracks at a generous clip, discharging handfuls of white-hot sparks from the wires. Tuohay watched the heavily wooded countryside run past in an olive blur as he gripped the worn leather ceiling-strap in support. The trolley windows were open, allowing a deluge of fresh air to run through the sparsely populated cabin. It carried with it the smell of a recent rain and thin rivulets ran off the top of the trolley, the silver water sheared into spray by the turbulent air.

Tuohay searched the evening scenery for distant, immovable matter. His eyes focused on hills, lakes, fields. These entities passed much slower than the scenery close at hand, creating a sense of permanency. He spotted a red-tailed hawk gliding lazily above a sparsely wooded knoll. The hawk floated gently with the wind, allowing the air to push it higher without straining its faculties. It reached the apex of the draft and began to circle downward again, its wings never varying from their outstretched position. The hawk disappeared from Tuohay's view as the trolley dipped below a line of trees, and he was once again mindful of the hurtling express. A cider mill emerged suddenly, its abundant flock of apple trees blurring past. Beyond the mill a cluster of homes marked the perimeter of Medfield center.

"Medfield ahead! Last stop!" the driver called, ringing the bell. Tuohay gritted his teeth at the clanging of the bell just above his head. The trolley slowed in increments, jerking with each change of speed. The forest melted away as the town center expanded to greet the newcomers. Neighborhoods grew denser, and threads of adjacent tracks appeared from different directions, combining like the center of a web to terminate in front of the clapboard station, the last stop on the line. Several packed dirt roads ran from it in various directions.

The shadows had lengthened considerably by the time the trolley screeched to a stop. Alighting from the electric transport with a handful of commuters, Tuohay leaned on his cane and looked about. Behind him, the grille of a large steam engine smiled with iron teeth, clouds of black smoke belching from its pipe. The sky above was darkening rapidly, with the faint promise of early starlight emerging from the heavenly depths.

A dry tickle in his throat encouraged him to draw out his flask. After taking a quick tug of the warm brandy, he left the train depot and walked towards the center. Coming upon Main Street, he spotted Sara under an old willow tree, its spindly branches hovering over her like a veil. She was wearing the thin white dress and apron of a nurse's uniform, but the traditional cap had been replaced by a more fashionable straw hat. He was struck by the distinctive pose she held, a white spirit hidden beneath the streaming tears of the weeping boughs.

"Miss Conall," he said in greeting as he descended under the hanging branches. He grimaced as the uneven ground caused his bad leg to buckle. "A quaint choice of meeting places, though I would have preferred something indoors."

Sara ran one of the budding leafs through her fingers. "This area is one of seclusion that I use to set my mind at ease after a day at the asylum. But not to worry, Inspector Tuohay. Indoors it shall be." She led him back to the road, her hurried step causing great discomfort for Tuohay as he struggled back up the slope. She took him to North Street, a well-kept road lined with gated residences. In the near distance the white spire of a church rose towards the purple sky.

"Thank you for meeting me," said Tuohay. "I take it you received Miss Eliza's telegram about my delay?"

"Yes. I thought she was coming as well?"

"Unforeseen circumstances prevented it."

Sara slowed her pace. "Is it true that Father Donnelly is dead?"

"It is."

"What does that mean?"

"Perhaps nothing. Perhaps something. That is what I am trying to discern." Tuohay leaned against his cane. "Miss Hart told us that she was staying with you. I believe she has more information about the recently deceased priest."

"Was his death of natural causes?" Doubt dripped thick in Sara's voice.

"I am investigating all possibilities, Miss Conall."

"Call me by Sara, if you please."

"As you wish."

Sara had stopped walking. "Inspector, I am sorry to say that Miss Hart is not currently in Medfield with me. My uncle, Doctor Kearney, had her moved to another one of our trusted friends for safekeeping as soon as we heard of Father Donnelly's death."

Tuohay frowned at the news. "I see."

"However, I will give you the particulars of her current location."

Tuohay coughed lightly into his sleeve. "I would be appreciative of that."

"But first…there is a man who will be meeting with us briefly."

Tuohay's brows raised. "A man?"

Sara stared straight ahead, her face expressionless. "He works for the police, but is ill-intentioned." She began walking again, her brisk pace a struggle for Tuohay to maintain.

"Who is he, if I may ask?"

"Inspector Dennis Frost." Sara noticed her pace and slackened. "He arrived thirty minutes before you did. I have heard from my Uncle Sean that you are familiar with him." Accusation tolled like a bell in her voice.

"Indeed." Tuohay's mood darkened. "I did not anticipate that he would act *this* quickly."

"What do you mean by that?"

"I have brushed shoulders with the inspector several times during the investigation, including this morning in Plymouth. He has made no secret of the fact that he is running an inquiry in parallel with mine."

"Parallel. Are you sure he is not one step ahead?"

"I may walk with a cane but I assure you I am quick to the cut." Tuohay grimaced. "I simply must bear his presence. He works for the Boston brass, who have partnered with me—with who I work for, the RIC."

"*You* must bear his presence?" Sara's face darkened. "He has a wicked tongue, and he'd steal the sugar out of your punch the moment you weren't looking. Three years ago he lied under oath about poor Uncle Aiden—about Aiden taking up with streetwalkers and such lewdness. Inspector Frost claimed that the girls—Mary Hart, Kathryn Dwyer, Susan Lovelace—came running to the authorities with their stories when they heard about Uncle Aiden's lawsuit against the Church. But the truth is that Frost approached *them*. He offered them money to lie on the stand, and then substantiated their claims with his own fallacies."

"So I was told by Mary Hart and your uncle Sean."

Sara's voice dropped as they passed a church, but lost none of its venom. "He made a mockery of everything Uncle Aiden stood for. Inspector Frost lied under the eyes of God and man, and curse him to hell for it. Him and those in the Church who he did it for. Even now he watches us, just as *they* have watched my family since my uncle's trial against the archbishop." Her eyes narrowed as she gazed at the church. Tuohay followed her gaze, but the shadows had lengthened considerably, and little could be discerned.

"He is a dangerous man, Mr. Tuohay," Sara concluded.

The conversation died upon the thin breeze at that, and they walked in silence until coming to a small pond by the side of the road.

"He will meet us here," she said, walking over to the grassy bank.

"How did his arrival come about?"

"He spotted me under the willow tree as I was waiting for you. Showed me his badge as if I needed reminding of who he was." She ground the toe of her shoe into the dirt. "He wanted to know where Miss Hart was, though he would not say why. I told him you were on your way, which seemed not to surprise him at all. He nodded and ordered me to wait by the pond with you upon your arrival."

The stars began to glow in the moonless darkness, casting a pale light off the unbroken surface of the pond. Glancing at the mirror-like sheen of the water, Tuohay pondered the reflection of the glowing sooth-sayers in the sky.

"What do you see?" Sara asked.

"Sorry?"

"The stars. You are looking at their reflection." Her voice softened. "Back in Ireland, my brother Richard and I used to spend long hours looking at them, trying to figure out what messages lay hidden within their glowing patterns. I miss him so," she added with soft but icy bitterness.

"I am afraid there are no hidden messages in the stars, Sara."

Sara blushed. "It was a childhood fancy, is all."

"So it was." Tuohay leaned on his cane as he looked out into the growing darkness. "See there. The inspector approaches from the road."

Sara crossed her arms against the growing chill but said nothing.

Tuohay nodded in the direction of the rapidly approaching Frost. "I must ask you something of importance."

Sara appeared wary. "Yes?"

"The night of our interview at the law firm of McBarronThayer....there was someone there watching us, *listening* to us." His eyes met hers. "Are you being threatened, Miss Conall? Or are you making a game of this? A dangerous game, at that."

Sara clenched her hands into fists. Her eyes narrowed. "I am risking everything just talking to you, so do not make a mockery of my trust."

Tuohay stared at Sara. "Was it him? Inspector Frost?"

"I...cannot say."

"But you do not deny it."

"I am no perjurer, like him." Sara turned away as Frost closed the gap, his hands thrust in his pockets. A scowl was visible as he reached them, despite the fact that his face was hidden by the collar of his trench coat.

"We meet again, inspector," said Frost. "Funny thing, that."

"Quite."

The tension between Sara and Frost was as tight as a noose, strangling any kindness between them into a gasping silence.

"I've been officially assigned to look more closely into the death of Father Donnelly," said Frost, ignoring the daggers in Sara's eyes, "and also been told to keep a closer eye on you, Tuohay, and this Templar Diamond business."

"Looking forward to your company, inspector."

Frost glanced furtively at Tuohay. "Come with me for a minute." He dropped his voice to a harsh whisper as he pulled Tuohay several feet from Sara. "Despite whatever the missus here may have told you, I'm the good guy. No doubt she's relayed quite the tragic tale of the corrupt police investigator in the pocket of the archbishop who hired prostitutes to lie on the stand against her uncle. I've heard it before, and no doubt that Doctor Kearney was waxing your ears with the same. Rubbish, Tuohay! Those prostitutes were tellin' the truth on the stand, and I did my work proper."

"I appreciate your candor," said Tuohay.

"So you're alright with me."

Tuohay drifted back towards Sara, his tone conversational. "You do know that Miss Hart is no longer staying with Miss Conall?"

Frost frowned. "Was I supposed to?"

"I have to be at the asylum before sunrise, Inspector Tuohay," Sara said, her arms crossed against the growing cold. "If you and Inspector Frost have need of me, we should make it a brief meeting at my place. Either way, I am heading back." She started towards the road.

"A nightcap, then?" Frost replied with a smirk.

Sara frowned.

"We will not intrude for long," Tuohay promised, following after her. He removed a clove cigarette from his pocket and lit it, closing his eyes as the promise of tremors in his leg slowly subsided.

"Quite the habit you've got there," Frost remarked. "You were shaking like a Sunday Quaker before you got a draw of those cloves."

"Not just observant, but allegorical."

Sara was walking ahead, and Frost took the opportunity to continue his private conversation with Tuohay. "Keep a sharp eye on that one there. Did you know that she ran away with her sister from her beloved Uncle Aiden after he became their guardian? They were gone for over nine months, disappeared—there were rumors of drunkenness and abuse."

"No, I was not privy to that."

"And you call yourself an investigator," Frost snorted. "It's all in the court documents. I suggest you read them, since it's clear that Sara wasn't sharing of the darker side of their history with you. May open your eyes to the real goings on around here."

The small party continued up North Street in silence. The townhouses, set back behind vine-covered fences, remained hidden from view save for an occasional glow through the hedges. Arising from the trees behind the three companions, the spire of the Universalist Unitarian church struck at the night like a lance.

"Sara, when we were by the pond you mentioned your brother Richard's death," Tuohay said, tilting his face towards her. "Was Father Kearney close at hand during that time?"

"An interesting question," Frost cut in from a few steps behind Sara. "What is the relevance, Tuohay?"

"I know why he is asking," said Sara, her voice a whisper. "And the answer is yes, he was close at hand."

Tuohay dug up a patch of dirt with his cane as he walked. "When I questioned you the first time, Miss Conall, I discovered that your family's relocation to America was your Uncle Aiden's burden. It was he who brought your mother and her children—Richard, Anna, yourself—to America, to follow him to a land where life would be better for you all." A crimson light emphasized his hollow cheeks as he breathed his clove cigarette. He inhaled on the cigarette slowly, a sprinkling of red embers hurtling to the ground like falling stars. "But then again, he *was* a priest, and priests know things that ordinary people do not. Or so his sister—your mother—must have believed."

"You want to know if my family hated him. If we blamed him for Richard's death. For our crippling poverty."

"If I am to uncover the truth in this complicated case, it is imperative for me to understand the nature of all of Father Kearney's relationships." He coughed lightly and took a long drag of his cigarette. "Part of that information rests on how your family fared once they came to America, mainly because of their reliance upon him."

"They fared badly," said Frost.

Tuohay glared at the inspector.

"Inspector Frost is correct," she acknowledged. "And yes, we grew to despise our Uncle Aiden for all the hardship he brought upon the family due to his lawsuit against the archbishop."

"And yet you defend him now."

"Because he was *right*. But my family does not easily forgive, not even me," Sara admitted. "Perhaps it is our terrible tempers, which none of us save Richard were spared from getting."

She stopped and pointed at a small cottage nestled in among a dozen others of its kind. A large iron-wrought fence stood between the road and the spattering of modest abodes. A gate was visible, a flickering Edison lamp playing chase with the surrounding night.

"That is my home, the house closest to the gate. As an asylum nurse, my apartment is on the third floor. Usually, I live with three patients—of similar demeanors—who stay on the second floor. The first floor is where our daily tasks are performed."

"And you can leave them alone?"

"Yes, as long as their rooms are locked," Sara replied. "They are in a better state of mind. And this hospital is not like the others, inspector. It is progressive. Kinder."

"Last time I checked, kindness didn't cure insanity, or anything else for that matter," Frost growled.

Sara ignored his comment. "There is only one patient present tonight, my sister Anna. Miss Hart was a second resident, but she was released by the hospital president this morning based on the professional opinion of my Uncle Sean, as I mentioned."

"You live with your sister?" Tuohay inquired.

"We have lived together as nurse and patient for two years."

"That is all fine and good," Frost interrupted, "but is the door to your house usually left open?"

Surprise registered on Sara's face. "No." Her voice was cautious. "Look there, the first floor window is open as well."

"Are you expecting visitors?" Frost asked.

"Through the window?" Sara said, incredulous. "Uncle Sean told me he was afraid for Mary's safety, which is why he moved her from here this morning. What if he was right? What if—Anna!"

Tuohay dropped his hand to the holster of his Colt Derringer. "And you are certain you did not leave the door or window open?"

"I am *certain* of it!"

"Do you have housekeepers? Guests?"

Panic reached Sara's emerald eyes. "Anna is the only one in there, and she is locked in her room."

"Dangerous business, this is," said Frost, brushing aside his long coat to reveal the barrel of a pistol at his belt. "Shall we, Tuohay?"

"Anna!" Sara swung the iron gate open. "God, please don't let harm have come to her."

"Stay here, Sara," Tuohay ordered.

"I must be certain that she is safe," Sara protested, "it is *my* house! If anything has happened to her…"

The men exchanged quick looks. Tuohay took a step towards the gate. "I'll go in. Watch over Sara."

130

Frost seemed disappointed by the notion. "Why you?"

"I have two weapons to your one," Tuohay replied, indicating his cane and gun. With a dry smile he limped through the gate.

Frost whispered after him. "Are you certain? The intruder may still be in there."

"Precisely the point."

For a brief moment Frost seemed torn, but relented with a grunt.

Tuohay peered over his shoulder at Sara. "I will locate your sister directly."

"Please, hurry," Sara pleaded.

Tuohay limped through the dark yard. Silence descended like a blanket. Gathering his wits, he drew his pistol and held it close as he strode softly towards the front door, his cane sinking noiselessly into the grass with each step.

Reaching the entryway, he gently pulled on the door. It screeched on its hinges. Within, the house was deathly silent.

"And so goes the element of surprise." Holding his breath, Tuohay stepped into the darkness with his gun at the ready.

A Startling Incident

The hall was deathly quiet as Tuohay crept through the inky blackness. A cool breeze filtered warily from an open window, the sound of rustling drapes causing a moment of alarm. Ribbons of moonlight settled like silken webs in the corner of a distant room, their point of entry indistinct.

A shift in the shadows caught Tuohay's attention. He stared in the vicinity of the movement but could make nothing out. Clearing his throat in anticipation of speaking, he was startled at how the simple operation obtruded the silence.

A shadow darted through the broken light.

"You there!" Tuohay shouted. A loud crash shattered the silence. A door slammed.

Suddenly, a gunshot ripped through the darkness like a thunderclap. Plaster exploded in a blinding cloud from the wall near Tuohay's head. He fell to the ground in a heap, blinking debris from his eyes. His head throbbed as the pungent smell of gunpowder filled his nostrils.

His heart hammering in his chest, Tuohay reached for his pistol. A series of crashes shook like an earthquake from the far corner of the room. Like a voice from a fading dream, Tuohay heard Frost call his name from outside.

"I am alright!" Tuohay shouted, choking on the dust. "Stay with Sara!"

Cold sweat beaded against his forehead as silence resettled on the room like a shroud. The creak of a door to his left caused him to twist on his stomach. A doorway gaped in anticipation.

"I am an officer of the law!" Tuohay shouted, keeping his voice as steady as possible. "Put your weapon down and make yourself visible!"

Readying his pistol, Tuohay took a knee and eyed the darkness over an adjacent armchair. White moonbeams spilled in disarray through a barred window to the right, accenting the peculiar shapes of overturned furniture.

A form materialized from the shadows of a nearby chair. The chair was angled towards the cold hearth, partially hiding the entity from view. Tuohay froze, the sweat on his palm making the gun slick in his hands.

"*You there*," he said, "slowly put your hands where I can see them."

Silence met his demand.

"*Hands where I can see them*," Tuohay repeated, but again the shadowed figure remained still in the darkness. Tuohay eyed his cane, just out of reach. Grasping the chair closest to him, he pulled himself into a standing position, his gun trained on the figure.

"I am approaching. I do not want to see any sudden movement from you." With a grimace, Tuohay took a step forward and snatched his cane from the floor with the hand that had been steadying him. His leg buckled but he caught himself on the chair, nearly dropping his pistol in the process. He ignored the sweat dripping into his eyes as he took a second painful step, training his gun once again on the dark figure.

A moonlit face stared back at him with wide eyes.

"Kip Crippen," Tuohay breathed. "By God."

Tuohay took another step closer. Crippen did not move, did not blink. Two smoking bullet holes were burned through his frock coat at chest level, blood spilling from them in streams of violent red.

"Mr. Crippen—"

Crippen lunged at Tuohay, grabbing his arm with an iron grip. Tuohay cried in alarm as Crippen drew him near, his breath metallic blood . "He... said wait six years. But, he...is dead. Nowhere to turn...." Crippen stared at Tuohay with wide, uncomprehending eyes. "I n-needed to... needed.... *betrayed.*"

Crippen gurgled, and his grip grew slack.

"Who did this to you?" Tuohay demanded, but Crippen stared into the darkness with unseeing eyes. "Crippen?"

The shuffle of footsteps in a back hallway was followed quickly by the slamming of a distant door. Stumbling through the darkness, Tuohay followed the direction of the noise. Reaching a door, he pulled it open. Beyond was a small moonlit yard bordered by a tree-laden hill. Movement within the trees caught his eye and he continued the pursuit, his lame leg pulling at him like an anchor.

Grim moonlight spilled across the open ground, ghastly pale.

The ground was soft from a recent rain in the wild brush and undergrowth. Moving through the trees, Tuohay heard Frost shout his name again from the other side of the house, but he continued without response. The direction was taking him away from the hospital grounds and deeper into the surrounding wood.

A small water-filled gulley opened up before him, the banks slick with mud. Hearing the rustle of underbrush ahead, he waded in up to his knees.

The gully brought him to a thicker neck of the forest, the moonlight drawing away as the trees enclosed. Tuohay's sense of direction abandoned him in the wood, but lights from the distant town acted as bearings, mere willow-the-wisps.

A shadow slipped between two trees up a small, tree-laden incline before him.

Dizzied from jagged breathing, he relied on his pistoled hand to steady his ascent. At the top, he came to a wall of thick brush and pushed through. Less than two breaths away a woman with her back to him knelt in the moonlight, her hair ragged and loose.

Tuohay stepped forward and the woman spun on him. Grasping frantically at the ground, she snatched something from the shadows and raised her hands shakily. A pistol trembled in her grasp.

Tuohay held his own weapon steady. "*Put it down*," he ordered. "I am not here to harm you, but I will shoot if I must."

Her eyes flashed with delirium. The woman squeezed her grip on the pistol.

"I say, put it down," Tuohay repeated, side-stepping her slightly. Her pistol followed his path.

"I am taking a step closer," he cautioned. "But I do not wish to harm—"

There was an audible click. She had pulled the trigger.

"Misfire!" Tuohay charged forward, batting the weapon from her hand with his cane. The woman cried in pain and clutched her wrist.

"Who are you?" he demanded, pulling her up by the arm. His breathing came in unnatural breaks as he held her in place. The moonlight played off her features where she stood, and for a confused moment Tuohay thought he was looking upon Sara, though an older and paler rendition. He realized the truth with a start. The woman in his grasp was Sara's sister.

134

"I am not here to harm you, Anna," he said. "Is that your name? Anna?"

"*Harm you. Anna. Anna.*" The woman's gaze dropped to the ground. "Where? Where?"

Tuohay tried to hold her back, but her movements were frantic under his grip. "Please, Anna. Please, calm down."

"*Please calm down. Please calm down.*" She dropped to all fours and looked up at him with a frenzied stare, her eyes filled with tears. Fire danced across her pale green eyes as her fingers closed around a stray object.

Tuohay gritted in pain as he bent towards the ground, his cane sinking into the forest floor. "What is that—"

"No!" Anna snapped at him, the object nestled tight. The gleam of silver faintly caught the moonlight.

"A rattle?" Tuohay's breathing was jagged, but full of surprise.

Anna caressed the child's toy with devotion. It was long, the handle nearly a hand in length, with a rounded head decorated with engravings and script. "My young one's. My young one's." She shook it gently, the whisper of the sifting grains erasing the worried creases of her brow.

Tuohay exhaled slowly. "Anna. I must ask you—did you use a gun…that gun on the ground…to shoot a man in your house tonight?"

Anna did not respond.

"Did you shoot at me in the house?" He indicated the gun on the ground again.

"*Did you shoot at me.*" Her voice was little more than a rasp. "Dark. Terrible sounds. *Terrible sounds.*" A tortured cry rose from her throat, piercing the air.

Kneeling with a grimace, he picked up Anna's gun and examined it. The barrel was warm. He opened the chamber. "This gun has been shot recently."

"I-I don't remember." She clutched her forehead and moaned.

"You do not recall?"

"*You do not recall,*" she mimicked, lashing out with her arms. Abruptly she was huddled and shivering.

Tuohay remained silent, his face impassive. His attention was suddenly diverted by the appearance of scattered lights from the distant road. Voices followed in ghostly echoes.

"Come with me." Tuohay headed back with Anna in tow. They returned to the house and entered through the back door as two uniformed constables entered from the front, Sara and Frost steps behind.

"We are in here," Tuohay called out. Sara rushed to the kitchen, the lantern light from one of the constables bounding to and fro off the walls. Frost entered behind her, but turned towards the parlor.

Sara embraced her sister for a long moment before releasing her. She drew two chairs forward and put Anna in one while taking the second for herself. "*Conas atá tú?*"

Anna broke into an eerie cadence, her eyes fixed on Sara. "*Your lover is dead. What do you know? Anna, Anna. Where did it go?*"

"None of that!" Sara hissed, squeezing Anna's hand roughly. Tuohay watched with growing curiosity until Frost's voice pulled his attention away.

"My God," Frost thundered from the parlor. "It's Crippen!"

Frost barreled into the kitchen, grabbing Tuohay roughly by the arm. The two Medfield officers, who up to that moment had been watching Anna with undisguised interest, rushed past Frost to the parlor.

"What happened, Tuohay?" Frost demanded, his tobacco breath hot against Tuohay's cheek.

A request came from one of the officers. "Sir! If you will."

"Come on." Tuohay led Frost into the parlor where the constables waited. One stayed near the body as the second one approached. The young man was cloaked in a high-collared, dark blue coat lined with wool and silver buttons, and sported a matching navy-blue cylindrical hat. He had his baton at the ready, his curled moustache bristling with nervous tension.

"Who are you, sir?" he asked Tuohay.

"This here is Inspector Jack Tuohay of the Royal Irish Constabulary," Frost replied for him, "he is currently operating locally with the approval of the Massachusetts Police Commissioner." Frost turned to Tuohay. "Did you drop that poor bastard?"

"Crippen was already dying when I found him," said Tuohay. "But just so. The blood was fresh, the smell of gunpowder on his shirt strong. It could only have been minutes."

"Sir. There is a hole in the wall." The second constable raised his lantern to the location of the wall where the bullet had just missed Tuohay's head. The hole was the size of a small fist.

The first constable turned to Tuohay. "Care to explain, sir?"

"I was shot at."

"I thought you said the man was dead when you entered."

"Obviously I was not shot at by him, was I?"

The young constable cleared his throat. "Is that dead man the same Crippen who was mentioned in the papers? The Irish jewel thief who was killed in the 'Boston Wharf Chase', as they're callin' it?"

"The very one," Frost replied. "Though it's clear the chap wasn't killed after all, though I swear I hit him." He looked at Tuohay. "No question of it now, though."

"Sir, there is a crowd forming on the road outside," the second constable said, peering out the window.

"Blast. The press won't be far behind," grumbled Frost. "Damnable leeches."

"Handle it," the first constable ordered. As his partner exited the front door, he turned to Tuohay and Frost, his gaze uncertain.

A sob broke from Anna, diverting their attention. Frost slapped the constable's shoulder. "Come on."

Tuohay took a moment to endure the pins and needles in his leg. Gritting his teeth, he followed them back to the kitchen. Sara was lighting a gas lamp, flooding the room with a hissing white light.

Frost tugged at his moustache as he turned back to Tuohay. "Care to explain what happened?"

"The event was quite extraordinary," Tuohay said. The men were still out of earshot of the women, and Tuohay's account of events was kept to a strong whisper.

"Sara's sister had this." Tuohay produced Anna's pistol. "She pulled the trigger, and I thought it misfired. But it appears it had already been expended."

"A Webley," Frost remarked, eyeing the short-barreled gun.

"It is a British Bulldog Revolver, to be precise," said Tuohay. "A very nice piece for hiding in coat pockets. Crippen was known to carry one."

"What in the blazes was she doing with it?"

"One question of many." In the light of the gas lamp Tuohay's eyes caught the disheveled state of the cottage for the first time. Cabinet doors hung open, furniture was at strange angles, odds and ends lay scattered aimlessly about. Two new officers moved into the parlor with a lantern, one of them kneeling before the body.

"Someone was at it hard," Tuohay remarked.

Frost took in the scene. "Aye. Crippen, I'd say. But for what?"

"He's looking for information on the diamond."

The constable perked up at that. "Diamond? The Templar Diamond?"

Frost ignored the question. "So why would he come here?"

Sara had returned to the bench Anna was sitting at, and Frost approached. He pressed the question to Sara. "Miss Conall, if you know something about all of this, it would be best that you shared it."

"I do not know anything." She held Anna's hand in her own.

"Nothing connected to the diamond? Nothing your Uncle Aiden uncovered that would lure Kip Crippen here, to where you live?"

"No." Sara looked up, her emerald gaze unwavering. She turned to Anna, her brows knitting with concern. "Why is my sister's wrist bruised?"

Tuohay removed his top hat. "I had to take a regrettable course of action against her, I am afraid."

Sara's face colored. "Course of action against her? Of what nature?"

"To be frank, a striking blow with my cane, though the brunt of it was fortunately dealt to this, which was pointed at my chest at the time." Tuohay revealed the pistol to Sara.

Sara stared at it with incomprehension. She spun on Anna. "What were you doing with that? Where did you get it?"

"Perhaps the man in the parlor with two bullets in his chest can tell us," replied Frost. More voices were coming from outside now, and a great collection of lights could be seen through the windows flooding towards the front door.

Sara blinked. There was fear in her eyes. "Anna, *what have you done*? I was gone no longer than thirty minutes, and your door was locked. How....?" She choked on her tears.

Tuohay turned to the constable. "You best help those men protect the crime scene."

The constable hesitated for a moment, but leaped into action as the front door swung open, unleashing a cacophony of new voices.

Tuohay bent close to Sara. "Where is Mary Hart now?"

"Mary Hart?" Sara looked at Tuohay as if the question was incomprehensible.

"I still need to see her, and in a moment we will all be taken for questioning by the Medfield constabulary."

"Do you think she is in danger?"

"I do."

After another moment, she answered in a whisper of her own. "She is being looked after by one of the lawyers, Mr. Stuart Thayer—the same that recently left the firm of McBarronThayer. And by an old friend of Uncle Aiden's, an old war hero. Sergeant Michael McNamara. Both men live in the town of Foxborough. I believe she is staying with the sergeant."

Frost used the moment to address Anna. "Madam, if you would be so kind. My name is Inspector Frost, and I would like to ask just a few questions. For starters, what do you remember about tonight? Did a man break into your room?"

"*Inspector Frost. Inspector Frost. Gets his way at any cost.*" Anna stared blankly ahead.

"I don't have time for this nonsense," Frost spat.

"Leave her be," Sara snapped back. "It is her condition. She cannot control what she says, and has memory lapses. Especially when she is distressed. If that man broke in here and came upon her, and in her fragile state…" Sara's voice trailed away into a sob. She looked up at Frost, her eyes burning. "But she remembers your face well enough, I'd expect. The man who forced those girls to lie under oath about our uncle!"

Frost turned away, his face red. "Damn it all," he muttered. He looked at Tuohay, and then turned back to Sara, anger lining his voice. "You need to realize that I was in the right. For all our sakes."

Sara's eyes were hard. "Do not cast our lot with yours."

One of the constables returned. A small cast of uniformed men were bustling about in the parlor, the room ablaze in their collective lantern light. "We will have to take you all to the precinct," the constable stated. "Especially that one, there." He pointed at Anna.

Tuohay nodded. "Of course." He turned to Sara. "It will be alright."

"Alright?" Sara laughed mockingly. She looked up, and the burden of her sorrow was stripped bare in her fiery glare. "The mills of God grind slowly, but they grind small, they say. Be patient, they say. Justice *will* come. And do you know what *I* say? I say, the mills grind not by God's hands but in the hands of wicked men." Her voice rose with anger. "What proof do I have of redemption in this bleak world? Where can you point me to God's intervention for the sake of the poor, the neglected, the *mistreated*? No, no." She laughed bitterly. "My Uncle Aiden, a *man of God*, used to say that things would be well again someday, that our neighbors would not scorn us like lepers forever. That his bout was not with the Church, but with *bad men* within the Church. That his effort was *pure* in the eyes of God, and God's grace would see us through until the truth was revealed.

"But Uncle Aiden was wrong. There is no truth except the rancid flour that men produce in their mills of lies. Uncle Aiden's actions turned us into lepers, and turned Anna into what she is now. My poor sister…" She turned to Anna, her rage releasing in full. "What did you do, Anna? There is a dead man in our parlor. *What did you do?*"

Sara turned her fury on Frost. "I am done waiting for the mills of justice to grind down the lies. I will use my heel and happily grind the liars myself."

A number of officers appeared at that moment, gently asking Sara and Anna to prepare to come with them. Frost guided Tuohay away by the shoulder. "Come along. She's in a fiery mood."

"Give me a moment." Tuohay limped back to the parlor to attend his attention to the slumped body of Crippen, which was now well lit by several lanterns at its feet. A constable that had been inspecting the body stood at Tuohay's approach, holding a glittering object in his hand.

"You found that in his pocket?" Tuohay asked.

The constable instinctively closed his hand and stepped away, looking for a senior officer. His voice trailed off as he entered the kitchen. "Sir? Sir? Take a look at this…"

The green sparkle had been sufficient for Tuohay. "Father Donnelly's missing emerald ring," he murmured. "What were you doing with that, Crippen?"

Crippen's slouching body remained silent, the once crimson stains at the chest nearly black, the wide eyes staring vacantly into space. Tuohay tore his gaze away, settling it upon Anna in the near distance who was being shuttled out by the constables. In the opposite direction, a man in an olive trench coat with a notepad was at the front door, conversing with another of the Medfield officers.

Tuohay turned his attention back to the corpse. "Kip Crippen. One of the brilliant minds behind the theft of the Templar Diamond. You created quite a stir for me and the Belfast RIC. Yet despite it all, this was not the end you deserved."

Tuohay sensed a presence, a chill along the back of his neck. Turning, he saw Sara glaring at him from the kitchen archway. He made his way back to her, his bad leg nearly buckling from pain and fatigue. She was wearing her coat, her hood drawn. She looked up at him sullenly.

"You are right, Sara," Tuohay said to her. "The mills of justice grind slowly. But they grind fine, and none escape unscathed. Not Father Donnelly, not Kip Crippen. Not any of us, when the time of retribution comes."

Adoration of the Magi

The red of morning spilled into the cramped telegraph office of the train depot through a single window, casting a soft light on the aged man sitting behind the telegraph. The wood-and-metal communication device, positioned at the center of a sturdy table, was well past its prime but well cared for, a cacophony of gleaming copper plates, cylinders, and gears rising from the polished wood like a miniature bastion. A thin piece of white ribbon slid from the copper components, ready to be snatched up by the attentive operator. His fingers rested near a series of black and white keys embedded in the side of the device like those of a piano, each marked with corresponding numbers and letters.

Tuohay collected a telegraph from the operator, who went back to sipping from a tin mug of black coffee.

```
The Western Union Telegraph Company
RECEIVED at Medfield Station Depot    713 AM.
Eldredge returns tomorrow morning. He wires
  "Colin Allotrope born 1883. Parents unknown.
Educated in Lowell convent. Graduated BC
Highschool. Attends Boston College. Possible
benefactor involved in upbringing. "

                  Eliza.


The Western Union Telegraph Company
RECEIVED at Medfield Station Depot    716 AM.

Delay with autopsy until today. I will be
present. What news from Medfield?

                  Eliza.
```

Tuohay handed the operator his response, who took to the keyboard with severity. The room tapped to life with a series of correspondences, each one bracketed by several unobtrusive minutes of coffee and clove cigarettes.

The Western Union Telegraph Company
RECEIVED at BOSTON MA   726 AM.
M. H. not in Medfield. Apparently Foxboro. I. F.
arrived unexpectedly. Crippen also arrived with
a cold demeanor. Late edition will carry it.
Taking 744 train to find M. H. Requesting a place
to breathe for a night.

Jack.

The Western Union Telegraph Company
RECEIVED at Medfield Station Depot   737 AM.
Right. The Cocasset House is good for a
diversion. Stayed there for a performance. Try
it.

Eliza.

The Western Union Telegraph Company
RECEIVED at Medfield Station Depot   742 AM.
Additional request. Need data on Sergeant
Michael McNamara. Foxboro. Repeat wire him
urgent about my visit. Departing now. Send next
correspondence to Foxboro Depot.

Jack.

*

The shrill whistle of the South Framingham express pierced the slumbering hollow like a warning, startling a flock of sparrows into

143

flight. The clap of the tracks reverberated along the forest floor as the train approached, trailing its ever-present coal truck and passenger cabins; a dark blue first-class carriage with white trim led three burgundy second-class carriages and an unornamented tan luggage van.

The four-car express rambled into a leaf-strewn farming community cloven in two by the tracks, the habitants of which greeted the habitual thrice-daily arrival of the express with little fanfare. The early-rising farmers, their cheeks ruddy from hours of work in the fields, took a moment to straighten their backs and peer at the passing fancy.

Seated within the last of the sparsely populated second-class carriages, the two men took little notice of the passing countryside. The train passed with a hollow clatter from firm earth to a vacant bridge.

Tuohay glanced at the paper on his lap and grimaced for the fourth time at the morning's headlines.

A GHOST IN MEDFIELD
BODY OF IRISH JEWEL THIEF FOUND
IN LUNATIC ASYLUM

A DEAD MAN RETURNS. GUNSHOTS FIRED IN ASYLUM. KIP CRIPPEN FOUND WITH TWO BULLET WOUNDS TO THE CHEST. QUESTIONS POSED TO LEAD INVESTIGATORS. SCOTLAND YARD INVOLVED.

"Why do they keep on about Scotland Yard?" Reaching into his pocket, Tuohay pulled out his silver flask, his eyes reverting back to the man across from him. The scent of whiskey rose from the container as he unscrewed the cap. "Would you care to join me, Inspector Frost?"

Frost was humming a tune under his breath, which he immediately ceased. "That flask of yours is a more common sight than the hat on your head," he said brusquely, his square jaw set firm. He nodded towards Tuohay's cane. "I wonder which crutch of yours is the more frequently used."

"Civility is a strong point of yours, I see."

Frost took the flask and downed a mouthful of the liquor. Wiping his mouth with his sleeve, he handed the flask back. "Better? I prefer ginger beer, myself."

"To your health," Tuohay said, taking a taste before slipping the flask back into his pocket. He eyed Frost. "Last night was quite the adventure."

Frost frowned. "Quite." He peered at Tuohay curiously. "Who did you wire this morning from the train station? I saw you pay to have a telegram or two sent."

"A bit inquisitive?"

"A bit, but it's in my blood."

"Mine as well. I was sending a message to my cohorts, Mr. Eldredge and Miss Wilding. With them on the case, it is important that we remain accessible to one another."

"Speakin' of the missus, is that Eliza Wilding overly particular? She's a looker, but should have been snatched up long before now."

"I have not the slightest inkling," said Tuohay.

"Come now. Surely you have inquired, or at least wondered."

Touhay's mouth tightened at the corners. "We have a professional relationship."

Frost laughed. "Right. Well, your loss, if you ask me."

"On the contrary," said Tuohay. "She is charming, yes. But it is her skills of observation that make her valuable to the team."

Frost snorted. "Well she hasn't observed *me*, yet. Not in the way that would benefit her most."

"And let us hope that day never comes."

Frost grunted.

"Read this." Tuohay offered, drawing a piece of paper from his vest pocket. Frost squinted at it, then produced a pair of wire rim glasses to read it by. "It says, *How long ago?*" Frost frowned. "What's the meanin' of that?"

"It means, *how long ago* did you first start spying on me?" Tuohay's eyes remained locked on Frost.

"Why the bloody hell did you have me *read* your question?" Frost boomed.

"Are you avoiding the answer?"

Frost's face was as emotionless as stone. If he was taken off-guard by Tuohay's remark, he hid it well within his sturdy features. "You best explain yourself, and quick-like."

"I recommend that we drop our pretenses."

"My business is entirely professional—"

"I did not state otherwise. It is perfectly reasonable for an inspector to work covertly, including shadowing others. I should know."

"All the same, it is not so."

"*Adoration of the Magi.*"

Frost stared at Tuohay blankly.

"The three Magi discovering Jesus by following the Star of Bethlehem," Tuohay spoke in patient tones. "Do not look so perplexed, Inspector Frost. *Adoration of the Magi* is in reference to an essay I observed in the loft of the law firm of McBarronThayer."

Frost shrugged. "What does that have to do with anything?"

"For starters, I have deduced that the copy I saw was in your possession." Tuohay paused to regard his companion before continuing. "First of all, a pair of wire rim glasses identical to those you are wearing now were resting on the essay."

Frost scoffed and returned the glasses back to his pocket. "Those cheap things? They can be found at any dime store."

"Granted. But the essay was resting open on a desk in the loft of the law firm. Next to a ginger beer, with the scent of perique lingering in the air."

"Perique."

"A peculiar type of tobacco. I noticed that you smoke it in your pipe, but not your cigarettes."

"Me and a thousand others, to be certain."

"Most interestingly, the loft had a peculiar vent through which sound from the drawing room was easily discernable. A strategic point for eavesdropping, I would say."

Frost appeared restless. "I do not see where I come into this."

"You see, the original telegram for the interview stated that it would take place 'in the loft room'. *Loft room*? Does not exactly roll off the tongue. But the Seymore M. *Left room*, otherwise the drawing room at McBarronThayer, is more logical."

"So what? You went to the wrong room, is that the point?"

"You do not have to play coy, Inspector Frost. You know the truth will come out."

The glint of challenge was in Frost's eyes. "Prove it."

"A simple typographical error in our telegram directed Mr. Eldredge and me to the loft, where you were positioned to spy on the interview. As a precaution, there was meant to be a warning of our arrival—the doorbell. However, it never rang, and therefore it was not until the last moment that you heard us unexpectedly coming up the stairs. Enough time to duck out or hide, but not to collect your things."

"There are a hundred other reasonable explanations other than that far-fetched concoction," Frost replied.

"And yet, I just now heard you humming the melancholy tune Sara played on the piano the night of the interview."

"That was not what I was humming," Frost retorted.

"No? How do you know, if you weren't there to hear it?"

The slightest twitch of Frost's lip revealed his surprise.

"I can verify my theory with either Mr. McBarron or Mr. Thayer," said Tuohay, his eyebrow arched. "I am sure the authorities, meaning *you*, would have spoken to them prior to setting up this secret observation in their law firm."

"Perhaps it was the other way around," Frost muttered. "Perhaps the law firm *asked* me to observe."

"Was that the way of it?"

Frost fumbled in his pocket for his pipe, grumbling. "So you have me. Why deny it? I will be frank and admit to being interested in your actions, Inspector Tuohay. There was a reason I was assigned as your liaison to catch Crippen, and why I am here now. As soon as your fellows at the RIC contacted the Boston precinct about your imminent arrival, the local brass got interested in the case." Frost shrugged. "And so they put me on it. I'm a loyal gumshoe. The Boston authorities don't want to be left in the dark on this Templar Diamond business, and I'm carrying the torch for 'em."

"They do not want to be *left behind* on this Templar Diamond business is a more accurate statement. It will be quite a sensation once we find it. The kind of sensation that comes with promotions and acclaim—or embarrassment if it is found by a foreign field agent right under the nose of the local authorities."

"Can you blame 'em? The stone is one of the most valuable treasures in the waking world. There will be headlines for days, weeks even, when it's found."

"It would have been just as simple to let me know," replied Tuohay. "I would not have boxed the local brass out."

"No?" Frost arched an eyebrow. "It's our turf. If the diamond is here, one of our guys needs to find it. Plain and simple. I'm here with you for that reason, and for another. I've got my eye on *you*, inspector. I know about the probation you are on, and why. And unless a gun is pointed at my head, here I stay."

"Fine. So what were you doing with the essay?"

Frost stuck the pipe in his mouth and produced a flame from his lighter. "Can't you tell me, inspector?"

"Adoration of the Magi in Religious Art, Oil on Canvas, Mural, and Stained Glass. How does the essay help?"

Frost eyed Tuohay over a cloud of smoke reeking of spiced tobacco. "The piece itself is meaningless. I'm interested in the author."

"Why?"

"He is the illegitimate child of Father Donnelly's late nephew, Abrams Valentine. Remember the young man in the painting over the mantelpiece in Father Donnelly's study?"

Tuohay murmured, "The nagging in my head."

"What was that?"

"Nothing." Tuohay pulled Eliza's telegram from his pocket and reread it.

> The Western Union Telegraph Company
> RECEIVED at Medfield Station Depot   713 AM.
> Eldredge returns tomorrow morning. He wires
> "Colin Allotrope born 1883. Parents unknown.
> Educated in Lowell convent. Graduated BC
> Highschool. Attends Boston College. Possible
> benefactor involved in upbringing."
>
>
>   Eliza.

"Colin Allotrope is the illegitimate child," Tuohay stated matter-of-factly.

"Yes, that's him. I see you were following the same thread." A smile curled around Frost's pipe. "Interesting that the boy is the grand-nephew of the recently deceased Father Donnelly, yet he grew up in an orphanage not knowing his father or great uncle."

"There is more of interest than just that." Tuohay pocketed the

148

telegram. "Tell me, how did you keep Sara quiet about your presence at the law firm? Surely she was aware."

"She didn't have a choice," replied Frost. "This is an official inquiry by the Boston Police. We told her to keep her trap shut about my presence, or else she would be charged with hindering an investigation."

Tuohay tapped his cane on the train floor. "You testified against Father Kearney, did you not?"

Frost groaned. "So now we're gonna talk about *that*?"

"If you are going to *stay*, as you so convincingly have stated, I would like to know more about you as it relates to that case."

"I was on the side of the *law*, Inspector Tuohay. Surely you understand that. At the time of the trial, Father Kearney was acting *against* the law, and so, I was *not* on his side. I am indifferent to the individual, as is any officer worth his salt. My concern is with the letter of the law."

"Your belief was that Father Kearney was not in the right against the archbishop."

"That, and more. He was not a perfect man or a perfect priest."

"Do you care to elaborate?"

Frost frowned. "He was a whoremonger. There is *proof* of it— proof I discovered and brought to trial."

Tuohay leaned back. "Proof, you say?"

"There were three prostitutes he was involved with—Miss Hart, who you are familiar with, Miss Dwyer, and Miss Lovelace. I do not mean to darken the halo you have placed above the late Father Kearney's head, but that's the truth. His character was flawed. Each of the young women testified on the stand against him, before God and man."

"Worry not about darkening any so-called halo. My search, as you say, is for the truth. Where it takes me is where I will go."

"Good. Then we have an understanding."

"I suppose we do." The conversation lapsed into silence for the remainder of the journey. Neither man attempted to rekindle it, and were lost in the depths of their own thoughts.

Upon arrival, Tuohay visited the telegram office as Frost smoked his pipe on the platform. A few minutes later the two departed together, finding themselves on the packed dirt of Bird Street. It was a widely traveled road budding with large, pleasantly-decorated buildings, increasingly fanciful towards the town common. A black hansom rested in wait nearby but Tuohay declined, saying he would prefer to walk. Picking up a local paper, he studied it for several minutes while Frost waited impatiently. The morning was brisk and cool, the sky a pale blue bespeaking of the cold spell the almanac had predicted.

"Shall we?" asked Tuohay, thrusting the paper under his arm.

"Where to, exactly?"

"To find Miss Hart. I would like to speak to her about Father Donnelly."

"The late Father Donnelly. *Details*, Tuohay."

Tuohay cast Frost a sidelong glance but said nothing. Continuing their sojourn, the men soon reached Foxboro common, the perimeter of which was dominated by two massive white churches.

"They drive like the devil's on their tail," remarked Frost, eyeing the traffic on the rotary before them. Carts thundered past with a clattering of hooves and rattling of wheels; more than one horse-and-buggy rounded the common at a break-neck pace.

"Silly trivialities for the less keen of mind," remarked Tuohay.

"Keen or not, let's make sure to give 'em a wide berth," said Frost, keeping a sharp eye on the road. "So where are we headin'?"

"I would say *that* location looks promising." Tuohay pointed at a two story establishment, its front terrace filled with idling men. A large sign atop the terrace read in bright yellow lettering: *L.E Gray, News Dealer and Variety Store.*

"Short on tobacco?"

"Hardly. An educated guess tells me our man is right up there."

Frost squinted. "And who's our man?"

"Sergeant Michael McNamara."

"You don't say! The old bloodhound. He could pick up a track better than any man in uniform. What's he got to do with Mary Hart?"

"I was told he is her current guardian."

"I'll be," murmured Frost.

Tuohay turned to Frost. "How well do you know him?"

"We crossed paths a few times when he was a copper in Boston. That was years ago at the twilight of his career. Tough as nails, even then." Frost squinted at the porch. "How do you know he's up there?"

Tuohay stopped at the edge of the common where a well-traveled road ran between them and the variety store. "I do not *know*, inspector, I have *deduced*. The front porch of a popular variety store is declared the best spot for discussions of town importance among retired veterans, or so I am aware. And if McNamara is anything like I imagine him, his opinion is greatly valued by his peers and therefore his presence requested at such unofficial gatherings."

"You are putting me on." Frost pointed at Tuohay's pocket. "The location of where to meet him is in the telegram you just received at the station."

"Very good, Inspector Frost," said Tuohay, a glint in his eye. "You are not so easily fooled."

"A test?"

"A measurement."

"Humph. Gotta get up earlier than that to pull one over on me," said Frost.

The two men ascended the steps of the crowded porch, brushing past youths idling on the stairs. The smell of tobacco was thick in the air, and in the far corner a group of well-established men sat in lively conversation.

"I'll be buggered," said Frost, peering at the group. "There's the old gunner himself. Still looks the same."

"Care to introduce me?"

Frost frowned. "Not particularly."

"Then I will save you the trouble." Tuohay's cane clapped against the porch floorboards as he approached the group of men.

Frost crossed his arms from where he watched, murmuring under his breath. "Might be you know something, McNamara. You're always on the scent. And if anyone can get it out of you, it will be this here Inspector Tuohay. He's a promis'n sort of fella, he is." Frost's gaze narrowed. "Promising indeed."

Poisonous Relations

Tuohay cut through the crowd briskly, his cane rattling against the floor. By the time he reached the group, the men on the porch had stilled to a quiet murmur.

"Forgive my interruption," Tuohay began, bowing slightly. "I am looking for Mr. McNamara?"

"I am he," a man with a grainy voice replied. The speaker was seated in a wicker chair, a long-stemmed pipe grasped in his thick fingers. A shock of white hair sprung from the top of a large, perfectly round head. A heavy white moustache and beard filled the man's jaw, and his yellow teeth and wrinkled skin marked his age. But despite his advancement in years, he appeared surprisingly strong. Standing, his muscular frame was to be marveled at. "Who are you?"

"Inspector Jack Tuohay. Did you receive a telegram from my colleague this morning?"

"I did." He looked Tuohay over appraisingly. "Scotland Yard, is it?"

"No, sir. Royal Irish Constabulary, out of Belfast. District Inspector, 2nd class."

"Belfast? You don't say."

"If we could speak in private?"

McNamara nodded and led the way into the variety store. He had a considerable limp but did not use a cane. Tuohay and Frost followed, curious stares at their backs. McNamara brought them through the cramped aisles to a doorway. They entered a back room, wading through piles of old newspapers to a small table at the center.

"A recent injury?" Tuohay inquired to McNamara.

"Hmm? Oh, this damnable thing?" He stared at his leg in disdain. "An old war wound. You?"

"I have had mine nearly all my life," Tuohay remarked. "Accident as a boy."

McNamara grunted in response but made no further comment.

"Does he know what this is about?" Frost hissed to Tuohay.

"If he read the telegram from Eliza, yes."

McNamara sat with his arms crossed. He peered at Frost for several moments.

"My name is Inspector Dennis Frost," Frost said by way of introduction, "from the Boston police force. It's me, Mac. Do you remember?"

"Hell, I remember!" McNamara said, a slight frown creasing his cracked lips. "Inspector Frost. So this is official business between the RIC and the Boston Police?"

Frost nodded. "That's why I'm here. It's on the up and up."

"With you involved? I know how you forced those girls to lie on the stand." McNamara stared at Frost and an uncomfortable silence fell between the two men.

"I apologize for the inconvenience," Tuohay broke in, eyeing the exchange warily, "but we're here to discuss a matter of some importance—"

"Are you a Catholic, Mr. Tuohay?"

Tuohay took a moment to answer. "Yes."

"Practicing?"

"When I can."

"When you can." McNamara considered the words for a moment. "What side were you on in Northern Ireland? The Catholics? Or did you sympathize with the Orangemen?"

Tuohay frowned. "I was on the side of sanity. Reason. Law and order, simply put."

McNamara stared at Tuohay with an even gaze.

"We are here to speak with Miss Hart, who we have been told is in your care. Our questions involve the recent death of a priest named Father Robert Donnelly, and related matters."

McNamara's tone grew somber. "Aye, I heard about the death of the priest from Plymouth." He leaned forward. "You here to ask questions about Father Aiden Kearney as well?"

"We are," replied Tuohay. "You knew him?"

"Of course I knew him," McNamara replied. He glanced at Frost and back again. "He served as pastor here in Foxboro for a period. He Christened my grandson. Best priest we ever had in this town, though his time here was short enough. He came back often to give his Irish Land League speeches, and I got to know 'im well—in fact, I was his bodyguard up until a few months ago." The last phrase was spoken with an edge of challenge to it.

Tuohay exhaled softly. "*Bodyguard*? Forgive me—providing protection at your age?"

"Aye," McNamara said, turning his glare to Frost. "From the likes of *him*."

Frost coughed in surprise. "What do you mean, from the likes of me?"

McNamara glowered broadly. "Before the trial I took the job, mainly when Aiden travelled in public. And especially *during* the trial, once people knew who he was. He even had me up at Boston for a time. Father Aiden was a despised man, taking the archbishop to court."

"But to the point of needing a bodyguard?" Tuohay's doubt still lingered.

"I don't think you rightly understand the devotion of the Catholic following in Boston," said McNamara. "Bringing an archbishop to trial here is like putting King Edward on the stand in Britain. It ain't done. It ain't tolerated. As soon as word of the upcoming trial leaked, Aiden Kearney's life was in danger, very *real* danger."

"Not from me," Frost protested.

"No, you were just a tool used to damage his character," McNamara spat. "Bringing those poor young women to the stand, tellin' 'em to lie. I've got yer scent, Frost."

Frost's face flushed. "*Inspector* Frost, if it pleases you. And you overstep your bounds, Mac. Everything I did during that trial was legitimate. Those streetwalkers warmed Kearney's bed, and when the time came, they sang their tunes. Weren't no fault of mine that I was put on the job to get them to sing."

"It was a setup," McNamara growled. "I known your type, Frost. I known you did it for the money—"

"*Inspector* Frost, if you please. And that is a bold-faced lie—"

"*Enough*," Tuohay interrupted. "Civility is necessary for us to proceed. Rest assured that the truth of the matter, whatever it may be, will come to light soon."

"Not soon enough," grumbled McNamara. "Not for Aiden Kearney, rest his soul."

"Mr. McNamara, if I may," Tuohay continued, "can we speak with Miss Hart?"

McNamara leaned back and crossed his arms. "You're too late, inspector."

154

"Too late?" Tuohay and Frost spoke at the same time.

"I was speaking to the *inspector*," McNamara said to Frost. He turned to Tuohay. "She's not here."

Tuohay propped himself up with his cane. "Where is she, pray tell?"

"On a train to Plymouth for Father Donnelly's wake and funeral. She was all broke up, poor lass."

Frost shook his head, muttering, "A bloody wild goose chase, this is."

Tuohay stood with a grimace. "When did she leave?"

"The better of an hour ago," the old man answered, a rough humor in his voice. "Don't fret, inspector. I already purchased us tickets."

"You were supposed to look after her," Frost said, accusation in his voice. "Just decided to let her go out on her own, is that the way of it? You realize she may be in danger?"

"I'm no fool," McNamara replied darkly. "I sent Mr. Thayer with her. He'll take care that nothing untoward happens." McNamara eyed Frost closely. "Can't say the same about you."

"Who is this man, Thayer?" demanded Frost.

"He was one of Father Kearney's lawyers during the trial," said Tuohay. "He may not have the fondest memories of the alleged role you played with the prostitutes."

"*Right*. That old sot."

"Not McBarron," McNamara growled, "the younger lawyer."

"Ah, yes. The blonde one." Frost shrugged. "I was just do'n my job, gentlemen. Aiden Kearney was in the wrong, and I proved it. I'm not out to make friends, just to expose the truth and see that justice is done."

McNamara snorted with derision. "If you say so." He pulled a faded-gold watch from the pocket of his breeches. "Our train departs in twenty minutes." He looked up. "You may want to get yourself a ticket, Frost."

"*Inspector* Frost, if it pleases you," Frost said. "And I thought you bought us tickets."

"*Us,* yes." McNamara pulled two tickets from the same pocket as the watch. "Two tickets for Plymouth. Inspector Tuohay and I."

"Bloody hell," Frost growled, standing. He stalked off, muttering.

"After what I heard from Sara, I didn't expect you to be working with the likes of him," McNamara said, eyeing Tuohay with distrust.

"I cannot control another man's actions," Tuohay replied, "nor those of the Boston authorities, who have been graceful enough to assist in this endeavor."

"Say it however you like, that man's as crooked as they come."

"You believe he paid the streetwalkers to lie on the stand, then. That Miss Hart and the others were forced to fabricate relations with Father Aiden Kearney in order to destroy his reputation during the trial, thereby ensuring the archbishop's innocence."

McNamara answered unhurriedly, his voice deliberate. "I knew Father Aiden Kearney for a long time, and would swear on my mother's grave in favor of his integrity." He walked to a nearby closet and pulled out a long, black trench coat and bowler cap. Sliding into the garments, he transformed from a surly shopkeeper to a rough-and-tumble gentleman. "But that man Frost, he's another story. Done far worse than what you just mentioned. He's as crooked as a dog's hind leg, and smells the part too. Don't get too cozy in the kennel with that one, inspector. I've tracked the likes of him my entire career."

With that he stalked past Tuohay, his heavy gait reverberating off the thin floorboards.

*

The parish bell tolled under Plymouth's gray sky, carrying the lonely call along the broken shoreline of marsh and silt to where Tuohay and his three companions toiled up a winding path. They paused at the resonating clang, eyeing the parish upon its desolate hill above.

"Not much of a church," Frost announced, his words being carried away by the ocean wind as soon as they left his lips.

"A church need not be judged by its size," McNamara returned gruffly. "God isn't impressed by riches."

"But I am sure He would appreciate *proximity*," Frost muttered. "This parish is a mile out of town. We've been walking for nearly thirty minutes since disembarking from the train."

"Not quite," said Tuohay, gritting his teeth against the bitter wind. "More like a quarter mile." Judging by the lack of pain, the walk was actually doing his leg some good.

Tuohay pulled the telegram he had sent to Eliza from his pocket, and her response. He had gotten word from her mere minutes before the train had left Foxboro station, and spent the last hour contemplating the words. The train itself had been a quiet business, with Frost purchasing a third class ticket and joining them in the carriage. The silent tension between Frost and McNamara had been enough to prevent the three of them from sitting together, and each had taken a separate seat and was left with his own thoughts until arrival.

The Western Union Telegraph Company
RECEIVED at Carriage House, Plymouth   922 AM.
Hope you pick up at 930. M.H. not in Foxboro.
934 train for Plymouth, arrive 1030. Destination is wake for the deceased priest. Meet. Be discreet.

Jack.

The Western Union Telegraph Company
RECEIVED at Foxboro Station Depot   933 AM.
I spotted a distraught M.H. disembarking from train with a gentleman five minutes ago. They hired a carriage.

Also. Stomach contents were empty.

Also. John sent telegram. He says. "Over the first obstacle. The hidden message was on the handkerchief. Second obstacle is a code. What is the significance of 52 or 53?" It has him stumped.

Eliza.

157

"What is the significance of fifty-two or fifty-three?" Tuohay murmured under his breath.

A one-horse carriage rattled past, startling him from his thoughts. The red curtains were drawn, concealing the passengers. The driver sat on his berth at the front, reigns in hand and a pipe jutting from his mouth. Tuohay's gaze followed the progression of the carriage up the rising knoll.

At the top the church awaited, a lean and jagged affair of irregular slate and stone. The gray slabs of its frame rose like intertwined fingers, pressing together at the crest from which a lone bell tower projected.

The old parish overlooked a wide expanse of bogs to the west, a thin shore and steel-gray ocean to the east, and the distant rooftops of Plymouth to the north. The property itself was marked by undulating walls of moss-covered stone, the far end of which broke apart into gray specks. The fragments were revealed to be a collection of crooked tombstones, jutting like rotted teeth at various angles from the earth.

Leading to the summit was a well-worn cart track, peppered with sand and crabgrass. There were other pilgrims on foot as well, men and women draped in the black coats, capes, and gowns of mourning. Every few minutes a carriage rattled by on its way to the parish, adding to the mill of early attendees tramping across the grounds.

"What time did you say the wake started?" Frost asked McNamara.

"One o'clock," was the terse reply.

After a pause, Frost asked, "Is it true what they say you did in the war?"

"And what might that be?"

"You were a gunner in the Union navy, and a few years into the war found yourself on a sinking ship—it had been blown to smithereens by the iron-clad *Merrimac*."

"So. What of it?"

"Legend among the Boston brass is that you were the last man to leave the boat. *The last bloody man*. Waited for all the rest of the men to get off, or as many could ably do so. Then it was into the water for you, for the rescue boat was full."

"I'm no hero, if that's your meaning," McNamara growled.

Frost continued, bringing Tuohay into the telling. "So there he was, good ol' Mac, floating beside entrails and body parts like a man in a flooded cemetery. And not a *scratch* on him. He got through it rightly enough, the old fellow did. And then what's he do? *Re-enlists* as a scout, and became one of the best." Frost's voice grew reverent. "And he showed his mettle more than once on the streets of Boston, he did. Could track a criminal like no one before or since. Not one lost hour of time in twenty years on the beat, either."

"If you think praise is going to change my opinion of you, Frost, you're dead wrong," McNamara said.

"*Inspector* Frost. I earned it rightly enough."

McNamara cast Frost a sidelong glance. "Did you, now?"

Further conversation was cut short by their arrival onto the parish grounds. A crowd was gathered in front of the stone church, waiting for the doors to open. It was a sea of black, a loyal congregation come to pay its respects to the celebrated priest. Tuohay glanced at his companions, but their eyes were riveted on the crowd.

Tuohay sifted through the gathering at the base of the parish, ascending the steps to look for Miss Hart. A gust of icy wind rose from the bluff and spiraled through the courtyard, gnawing at exposed flesh. It wailed like a tormented soul, clawing at Tuohay with frozen fingers.

Tuohay hunkered down, his eyes watering painfully as he scanned the crowd. Catching sight of a red haired woman with a black coat thrown over a matching gown and boots, he grinned, but it was erased a as a man in an olive trench coat caught his attention. The man was at the edge of the crowd, away from most of the gatherers. He seemed to be looking in Tuohay's direction.

"I do not see her," Tuohay called to McNamara and Frost, turning his attention away from the olive-clad stranger.

"Inspector Tuohay?" A handsome man with a friendly smile peered at Tuohay from the bottom of the steps, his sky-blue eyes expectant. He held a silk hat under the crook of his arm, and his rich blonde hair blew freely in the wind. He was attired in the black of mourning, evidenced by his three-piece suit and long coat.

"Yes. And you are?"

The man, closer to thirty than not, reached up and took Tuohay's hand with a firm grip. He was nearly of Tuohay's height, demonstrated as he joined him on the steps. "Vestor Thayer, of McBarronThayer. Pleased to meet you, inspector."

"Pleased as well," Tuohay returned. "How did you locate me?"

"Miss Hart's description of you was more than sufficient," said Thayer. "I accompanied her to Plymouth," he added by way of explanation. A faint lemony musk emanated from his skin.

"Yes, of course. Where is she now?"

Thayer pointed over the crowd to the distant cemetery. A few individuals were roaming about the scattered old gravestones. "There."

"Splendid," said Tuohay. McNamara and Frost closed ranks on the pair, and Thayer met the former with a warm handshake. His demeanor cooled considerably at the sight of Frost, who offered his hand.

"I remember you well enough," Thayer said, ill-concealed repugnance in his voice. He clasped his hands behind his back. "I cannot shake, sir."

"So you're takin' it personally too," Frost muttered, thrusting his hands into his pockets. "It's not my fault that Miss Hart and the others kept Aiden Kearney's bed warm. They was concubines, after all. I merely uncovered the truth of it."

"You *fabricated* the truth and made those poor girls falsely testify at trial," Thayer replied, meeting Frost's gaze. "Why are you here, if I may be so bold as to inquire?"

"My job, which is to investigate," said Frost.

"Investigate what?"

"I don't have to explain it to you, sir," said Frost. "Mary Hart is not your client."

Thayer's blue eyes clouded with anger. "No, but I care for her. And for Sara and Anna as well. Those who march on after the battle has been lost."

Frost turned to Tuohay. "I don't have to listen to this rubbish. We have an investigation to run—"

The clang of the parish bell interrupted Frost's declaration, quieting him and the crowd at large. Again the bell sounded, its eerie, metallic voice settling upon the crowd like a blanket. As it rang, the front doors of the parish opened, and a priest beckoned those gathered to enter.

Tuohay strode towards the graveyard, walking against the crush of people. His companions checked their gaits to stay at his heels, but Thayer pressed forward to speak with him.

"Inspector Frost will make Mary terribly anxious," he said. "She is frightened of the man, and likely has good reason to be."

"She will have to bear it," Tuohay replied. "He is running an investigation, and there is little any of us can do to prevent him from doing so." He glanced at Thayer. "I have to say, I am a bit perplexed by your reaction to Inspector Frost."

"Why is that?"

Tuohay reached into his pocket and pulled out a ring of keys.

"My keys," said Thayer.

"Yes, Sara gave them to me after our interview." He handed them to Thayer. "You are certainly aware that the inspector used your premises, the offices of McBarronThayer, to spy on my recent interview with Sara Conall. In fact, the authorities would have had to obtain permission for him to do so. That seems more like *cooperation* than antagonism to me, Mr. Thayer."

Thayer's face darkened. "I had no part in that. The decision to allow Inspector Frost's surveillance was given by McBarron, not me. I was against it."

"Tell me, what is your interest in this affair?"

They reached a lichgate of black iron and stepped through the archway into the cemetery. A smattering of weather-beaten gravestones lay dispersed on the grounds before them.

Thayer replied, "I have been a part of this since I was signed on as one of Aiden Kearney's lawyers against Archbishop Walsh."

"But the lawsuit was lost in 1897, and the appeal closed with Aiden Kearney's death a few months ago," Tuohay pointed out. "You are separating from the firm of McBarronThayer as well, as I understand it."

"There is truth in that," Thayer admitted. "And the *Thayer* in McBarronThayer is my grandfather, for clarity." He said the last with a rueful smile. "Haven't quite lived up to the old family name, I suppose."

"You have not answered my question, Mr. Thayer." As Tuohay spoke, his eyes fell upon a willowy young woman, elegantly but mournfully attired, in conversation with a stout man. They were hovering beside a marble obelisk decorated with impressive scrawling. "I say, is that Doctor Kearney speaking with Miss Hart?"

"Yes," Thayer said. "He arrived for the wake only minutes after Miss Hart and I did."

"But to answer your question," Thayer continued, "I grew to greatly respect Father Aiden Kearney, and what he stood for. Truth, justice. Right over wrong, even in the face of powerful odds. Reminded me of Teddy Roosevelt's work in New York against Tammany Hall, to be frank." He brushed his wayward hair from his eyes. "I suppose I have always been a terrible optimist, and less of a pragmatist. Even after the trial was lost, I remained in contact with Aiden and his nieces. It had become more than just the case, I suppose. It was about righteousness." He caught Tuohay's eye. "That is what this all means to you as well, is that not true?"

They were coming upon Miss Hart and the doctor, and Tuohay slowed his gait momentarily. "Truer than you know, Mr. Thayer. But tell me this. Did you receive a black letter with silver ink in recent months? It would have had to do with the Templar Diamond."

Thayer shook his head. "No, of course not. Why would such a correspondence be addressed to me? I am aware of what you reference, however. Sara Conall shared the letter she received with me, as did Father Aiden Kearney." Thayer took a moment to regard Tuohay. "Do you think I am somehow tied up with the diamond affair?"

"It is my job to inquire," said Tuohay. "The trial and the diamond should have nothing to do with one another, and yet I cannot disentangle one from the other."

"I cannot help you there, I am afraid."

"Perhaps you can with this—do you have access to the affidavits that Miss Hart and Kathryn Dwyer presented to McBarronThayer? It is my understanding that they contain vital confessions by the women. Confessions damaging to the Church and some of its more prominent members. And to Inspector Frost as well."

"Under normal circumstances, I would not be able to speak of them, even to you. They are sealed."

"Not Kathryn Dwyer's," Tuohay argued. "Her death, and its potential meaning to the case, will allow me to file an injunction."

"Be that as it may, and I would add that I would personally

prefer to see the evidence in your hands, the affidavits are gone."

Tuohay stopped cold. "What do you mean, *gone?*"

"They were discovered to have been stolen from the safe in the law firm the day after your interview with Sara Conall. No sign of forced entry."

"Who had access?"

"To the building, many people. To the safe, only my former mentor McBarron and myself, I am afraid."

Tuohay's face registered disbelief, and it was not until several moments passed that he took stock of his immediate environment. They had reached Miss Hart and Doctor Kearney, and the forming assemblage was no less disquieting than an ocean wave smashing against an immovable bluff, the chaotic spray of its impact reflected in the various faces surrounding him.

Miss Hart's gentle visage was flushed, streaked with dried tears. Her arms were crossed, the apparent argument with the doctor overcome by a look of trepidation at the sight of Inspector Frost. For his part, the inspector had lit a pipe and was eyeing the group with a mixture of dark humor and impatience. McNamara had a permanent scowl on his face, matched only by that of Doctor Kearney, who bettered him with a purpled flush at the cheeks. Even Thayer seemed grim faced, but it was softened by evident remorse for Miss Hart.

"Inspector Tuohay," Miss Hart began, her voice barely a whisper. "What is… what is *he* doing here?"

"I am investigating the death of Father Donnelly," Frost broke in, keeping his pipe tightly clamped in the corner of his mouth as he spoke. "And, when you are ready, I have a few questions for you."

"Of all the damnable business!" Doctor Kearney exploded, taking a step in Frost's direction.

"Doctor, please!" Thayer stepped between them, his hands raised in a placating manner. "Angry words will get us nowhere."

"And where *exactly* is it that we are going?" Doctor Kearney growled. He faced Tuohay. "I thought *you* were working this case. If I had known you were going to partner up with Inspector Frost, I would have—"

"You would have *what*, exactly?" Tuohay's voice was ice. "Would have withheld evidence from me? Would have failed to help me dig for the truth? Would have actively obstructed me?

Would have *what*, Doctor Kearney?"

The doctor took a moment to answer, his voice steady. "I would have reconsidered trusting you and your intentions."

"They remain unchanged." Tuohay turned to Mary. "However, the fact of the matter is that Father Donnelly is dead, and there are questions that I need to ask Mary. Personal questions, I am afraid."

"I understand," Mary whispered, her gaze falling upon the church. "The wake. It has started."

"We can talk afterwards, of course."

"Of course." She stared at the distant church with dread and sorrow in her eyes. "A smoke, anyone? Or better yet, I could use some of the good doctor's laudanum."

"Perhaps you should wait on that," Doctor Kearney suggested.

Mary ignored him and pulled a vial of crimson liquid from her purse. "Joy from a bottle." She swallowed the contents, the alcohol strong on the breeze, and exhaled softly with satisfaction. "Shall we pay our respects?"

"After you, Miss Hart," said Tuohay.

Mary made it three steps before her eyes widened in shock. With abrupt ferocity, her hands grasped at her throat, her fingers ripping her scarf free from her neck. Her breathing grew heavy, her exhalations a shrill wail of obstructed air. The men looked on in astonishment at the sudden transformation, transfixed with horror. Suddenly she crumpled to her knees, a gurgling sound rising from her throat as her face, the slightest tint of blue, contorted in pain.

Tuohay and the others sprang to her assistance as a peal of thunder rumbled above them, marking the coming storm.

Gunshot in the Night

Inspector Dennis Frost slid the white lace curtain aside and peered at the hard gray rain with an impatient sigh. The trees on the front lawn of the Plymouth Brewster House swayed dangerously in the lamenting wind as the remnants of East Street swept by in a mass of chaotic brown. The tempest had made its mark on Plymouth in just four short hours, transforming roads into rushing rivers that seemed better suited for the heights of the White Mountains than here. It was not good for Frost, and his displeasure was etched on his face in deep creases. Tearing his eyes from the depressing scene, he dropped his gaze to the silver buttons of his vest. They needed polishing. He stared at them listlessly until the creak of a floorboard brought him from his tepid thoughts. He looked upon his companion reclining peacefully in a soft-back Renoir armchair.

"How in the blazes can you be calm at a time like this?" Frost snapped.

Lamplight flickered above Tuohay. A glass rested on a table at his elbow. "I am far from calm, inspector. Miss Hart resides in Jordan Hospital." He held up the glass to the light, which held traces of a honey-brown liquid. "A harmless drink, the apparent poisoner."

"Not a drink, an elixir," Frost corrected. "Laudanum concocted by Doctor Kearney, it would seem."

"Or whomever had access to it," Tuohay countered.

"Fair enough," Frost allowed. "Either way, someone wanted to harm that young woman. Silence her for good."

"Not unlike Susan Lovelace and Katy Dwyer."

"The other two prostitutes from Aiden Kearney's trial against the archbishop?" Frost shook his head. "I do not think the circumstances are one and the same, not at all."

Tuohay's face was an immovable mask. "You should return to Boston, inspector."

Frost emitted a throaty laugh. "After Miss Hart's poisoning? No. Where you go, I go. But I would prefer if we were to do something."

"Such as? You took statements from Doctor Kearney,

McNamara and Thayer. You have my statement as well, for what it's worth."

"So we just sit calmly about."

"As I said, what else is there to do?" Tuohay smiled thinly.

Frost glowered at Tuohay and turned back to the window.

Tuohay filled the ensuing silence with a rattling cough, rapid bursts that quickly led to violent heaves. The sudden occurrence left Frost staring uncertainly as Tuohay bent over his knees, loud blasts coming from the depths of his chest. Recovering after several minutes, he dispersed the approaching house manager with a wave and sat up. Reaching into his vest pocket with a shaking hand, he spoke. "It is nothing. I have been dealing with it since I was a boy." His voice was barely a rasp when he finished. He wiped the red splotches from his lips with a stained handkerchief and leaned back with a small groan.

Frost shook his head. "You sound like the death knell itself."

"Surely you have heard worse."

Frost considered for a moment. "Miss Hart gave you a run today with her ghastly reaction to the poison."

"Quite an unnecessary remark, inspector," Tuohay admonished.

"There was another time," Frost continued, unabated. "It was from a man shot in the throat. Came across him on the beat some years ago. I heard the shot in an alley, you see, a little clap it was. I came running, know'n full well I had heard a rounder pop off, and nearly run right past the poor bastard save for his gurgling. He was a goner, but it took some time."

"Another splendid comparison," Tuohay remarked dryly. "I feel the better for it already."

Frost crossed his arms. "You asked."

"Sound advice for the future. By the by, I have taken the liberty of requesting two rooms for the night."

Frost scratched his head. "But we've been together since arriving. When did you have time to check us rooms?"

"You have been glowering out that window for nearly an hour, inspector. I had quite a sufficient amount of time to transact my business without disturbing you and your grumbling in the least." Tuohay pointed to a table beside the cushioned chair. "Your key. It is for room 12, just beside my room, 13. If you do not mind, I will take my leave of you until the morrow."

166

"Tomorrow?" Frost raised his hand hesitantly. "What if Doctor Kearney calls—"

"The clerk knows to wake each of us if the doctor sends word."

"But the cost of the room."

"I covered it," Tuohay waved dismissively.

Frost's lips tightened. "I take no man's charity."

"Sir, I am in no shape to debate your moral compass at the moment. Consider it a regret for your getting wrapped into this affair."

"It won't do. I'll straighten it out with the proprietor."

"As you deem fit."

Frost nodded impatiently. "See you at dawn, Tuohay."

"The morning will bring new tidings, I am sure. Good evening." Tuohay exited the small parlor, his cane clicking against the hollow-sounding floor. He passed another guest of the house who remained buried behind the ink-stained pages of *The Plymouth Sun*. Gold buckles on the reader's boots glinted in the lamp light, catching Frost's eye.

Shrugging it off, he turned to the window once again. "Curse it all," he grumbled, eyeing the storm. It had come on quite suddenly and without warning.

Frost smoked in the parlor for a long, protracted hour, pacing to and fro for the majority. The guest had departed without him noticing. As the sky darkened with the approach of evening he paused to contemplate the great thunderheads, their underbellies glowing electric white. The storm had not let up, and even the Brewster House seemed to be suffering from the prolonged assault, its beams shuddering in the fierce wind.

"Nothin' to do but sleep it out," Frost murmured, snatching up the key Tuohay had left for him. He stalked out of the room and past the desk clerk without a glance. Reaching room 12, he placed the key at the lock and paused. The metal was etched with the number 13. Frowning, he inserted it into the lock but it did not turn.

"Bloody wrong key," said Frost, shaking his head. He thought for a moment. "Or wrong room. Who can be sure what is going through Tuohay's head?" Raising his fist to knock, he refrained. "Ah, the blazes with it." He lowered his fist and proceeded to room 13, which opened with a well-oiled click.

The electricity had been knocked out by the storm and all was dark within the spacious room save a few scattered moments when a flash of lightning sent a faded glow through the rumpled curtains. Fumbling about for a candle or lamp, Frost found neither at hand. Cursing under his breath, he undressed and fell roughly into bed. The storm battered the walls and sleep did not come as easily as he hoped.

A vague amount of time later, Frost was staring at the ceiling, sleep at the tip of his eyelids. The door to his bedroom creaked open.

"Who's there?" he demanded, the sleepiness vanishing.

The dim light of a hallway candle crept into the room and fell past the hidden face of an intruder. Something metallic gleamed in the doorway.

"Who—"

"Just a messenger, mac," was the whispered reply, "And I gots a message for ya." A short burst shattered the stillness, filling the room with the base odor of gunpowder. Frost's ears rang painfully. He blinked with incomprehension as a sharp white light flared to life at the far window. Seemingly angelic, the light moved quickly from the corner of the room towards the door. Trembling where he lay, Frost watched as the light revealed itself as a hooded lamp, which was placed on the bureau by Tuohay.

"Get your things," Tuohay ordered Frost, brushing past the bed. He had a gun in one hand and his cane in the other. The gun, which was still smoking from its charge, was trained on the door where the intruder had been. Swinging the door open, Tuohay gazed down the hall.

"What the devil is going on?" Frost cried.

Tuohay regarded Frost with a frown. "Danger has become deed." He limped out the door in pursuit, leaving Frost gaping after him.

*

"Is that everything, inspector?" asked the grizzled officer. He wiped the pencil shavings from his notepad with the side of his thumb.

Frost sighed irritably. "Yes. We have been over the break-in *three times*." The light from the table lamp flickered in the night-shadows. He tapped the remainder of his pipe into the ashtray with impatience. "I cannot sit here any longer. We need to find Inspector Tuohay."

The officer scratched his silvered beard. "I have a dozen constables on the streets, and another two combing your rooms for clues. But there's no sign of the inspector or the attacker. In the darkness and with this fog off the shore, a man can barely see beyond the length of his arm…"

"He couldn't have just disappeared," Frost growled.

"Stranger things have been known to happen on these streets during a mist."

Frost stood and slid into his trench coat. "Are we done here?"

"It's three in the morning, Inspector Frost."

"So?"

"You're not going to help anything by searching the streets tonight. Leave it to my men."

Frost glared at the Plymouth officer. Collecting his hat, he strode to the door of the hotel, checking under his frock coat that his pistol was unbuckled from the holster.

"You best not have gotten yourself killed, Tuohay," he muttered as he swung the door open. The cold night embraced him with an eerie, billowing fog. "I was just at the point of figuring you out."

Revelations

"Be considerate, it's hot," said Eliza, handing Eldredge a steaming cup of tea on a saucer.

Eldredge accepted the offer with proper caution, setting the ornate cup to his lips. "Good, very good."

His gaze wandered appreciatively about the small parlor. Sunlight streamed through the eastern window in a river of gold, splashing three dark Jiaoyi chairs with the translucent morning light. Eliza perched upon a chair like a dawn angel, though a tired one at that—a wrinkled powder-white gown, bleary eyes, disheveled hair, and bare feet peeking from beneath a crumpled hem all struck an atypically unfashionable yet surprisingly charming figure.

Eldredge was settled more conventionally in a cushioned American armchair and rumpled tweed suit, wisps of cigar vapors still lingering from the shared passage on the 7:15 express from Lowell.

"The morning is kind to you," he remarked to Eliza.

Eliza pushed a stray curl from her eyes with a smile. "I look a fright. But thanks all the same, Johnny." She stirred her tea.

"How is your mum?"

"Brilliant," he replied. "Sharp as a tack, as they say."

"Getting along fine, then."

"Recovering from a cold, but out of the woods." He smiled before taking another sip from the steaming cup. "So, Jack?"

"He's in the next room." She nodded her head in the direction of a closed door. "Were you followed here?"

"No, of course not. I read your telegram about starlight—our old code for staying concealed—why the secrecy?"

"There was an incident last night. I'll wait for Tuohay to share more."

"Whatever is best," said Eldredge. "How is he?"

"I don't think he slept a wink. He's darkly bothered by the poisoning of Miss Hart."

Eldredge sighed with remorse. "Any word?"

"Only that she is being moved to Boston for proper care, with accompaniment. Likely McNamara and Thayer, and the doctor," said Eliza. "The transport alone will be dangerous for her. She's in a fragile state, as I understand it."

"A terrible business," Eldredge said. "Have you seen her?"

"The authorities were not letting anyone near her, not even Jack."

Eldredge frowned. "In your telegram, you said she drank laudanum that Doctor Kearney prescribed, and possibly concocted?"

Eliza exchanged a glance with Eldredge. "He was questioned, but evidently the police have no reason to hold him."

"A terrible thing, the poisoning." Eldredge's face was strained with worry. "With everything going on…I just hope I can be of use."

"It is good to have you back." A brief silence fell, broken only by the small clink of the teaware. "Not exactly like old times, is it?"

"No. Not exactly." Eldredge set his cup down and peered towards the door. "I didn't think I would ever see Jack again when he left Boston to join the RIC."

"The violent, mindless streets of Belfast. The seething tension that never goes away. Fixing the unfixable. It's what he thrives on."

Eldredge considered her words. "He rarely spoke to me of those things."

"He speaks very little of himself at all," Eliza commented. "He needs to help people. Not in the manner of a priest or a doctor. In his own way."

"Should we go see him?"

"Not yet. I am sure he will be out soon, now that it's morning."

Eldredge lifted his briefcase onto his lap. "There is this, in the meantime. I've made progress on the code. Would you like to see?"

Eliza brightened. "Yes!"

"Well, you were spot-on regarding invisible ink as the technique," he said, pulling the leather-bound codex from his case. "The remark about Sympathy, along with the wisdom you and Jack provided, led me to the solution in a rather straight-forward manner. Of all the varying methods that could have been used, one rose to the top during my research. Starch."

"Starch?"

Eldredge released a frustrated sigh. "I should have realized it sooner. It is one of the simplest methods. The thought almost passed me by—until my eye caught the handkerchief."

"You mean…"

"The handkerchief was heavily starched, nearly to the stiffness of a board," Eldredge said. "It acted as a fine bookmark. But also as an excellent medium for the invisible ink, along with nitrate of soda."

Eliza propped her foot on the coffee table, resting her elbow on her raised knee. She dropped her chin onto her fist in the manner of the thinker. "So the hidden message was not in the codex after all, but on the handkerchief."

"Precisely." Eldredge pulled the handkerchief out from the book and laid it flat on the coffee table between them. It was stained through, with a black discoloration in the center. "Iodide of potassium was all I needed to develop the message, which was expertly stenciled."

Eliza bent forward. Close examination revealed a list of faded letters.

ULWVIHVZRUIYFXAFZVRHTEXSVLOAXIJGWZBUKELFPZXNOGMIJ
VBZEKWVIEOTCHTJWJMIXSEKMTBUINWIJVHSEMVIDJLSZI

She looked up with a quizzical frown. "Whoever put this together is mad as hops."

"It is simpler than it seems, I am certain."

"Did you make it any further than this gaggle of letters?"

Eldredge released a long sigh. "Unfortunately, no. There were no simple patterns to speak of. Is it a transposition cypher? A substitution cypher? I looked for repeating letters, employed statistical formulas, created deciphering tables in an attempt to create patterns from a possible random key. All to no avail."

Eliza took the handkerchief and studied it. "Nothing whatsoever?"

"Nothing worth mentioning," he said. He rubbed his hands together with tense energy, his brows furrowed. "I will not be beat, of course. I currently suspect that it is either a random or book key."

"Fascinating," Eliza remarked. "It has the feel of a secret society, doesn't it? Freemasons, that sort of thing. I have always been intrigued by such things. You know, secret societies where nonconformists debate about God, about nature and the universe. It was where rationalists could study mathematics and science, hidden safely away from the repressive eyes of church and state. Freethinkers will find a way. "

"This above all: to thine own self be true," said Eldredge.

Eliza stared at Eldredge. "What did you say?"

Eldredge blinked. "To thine own self be true. You know, Hamlet. Your mention of Freethinkers brought it to mind."

"Shakespeare," Eliza whispered. She stared at the handkerchief. "Let me see that." She took it into her hand. "The embroidery on this handkerchief. *Strawberries.* Strawberries….remember?"

"Remember what?" said Eldredge. "Are the strawberries meaningful?"

Eliza jumped up and began to pace. "Father Donnelly's study was bursting at the seams with Shakespeare paraphernalia."

"I am not following."

"A handkerchief with strawberry embroidery. *Othello*, Johnny. Everyone knows that."

"*Playwrights* may know that," Eldredge said, "and Shakespearean scholars. Of which you are both. But not everyone—"

"*Anyone* who cares at all about the works of the greatest writer of all time knows," Eliza said sternly. Eldredge looked hurt, and she waved the admonishment away. "But in any case, think of it. What if the handkerchief is more than just where the message was hidden? What if it is also a symbol for how to break the code that was written on it? Is there anything Shakespearean that comes to mind in the codes you have looked at? Or Othello? Yes, focus on Othello specifically."

Eldredge scratched his head. "Ah… let me see. Othello…" He extracted his papers from the briefcase and sorted through them. Several pages fluttered to the ground in his haste.

After a minute he looked up with resignation. "I must admit, I do not have the faintest idea what I am looking for."   He pointed at Eliza. "*You* are the expert, however. Perhaps there was an unwritten understanding between the sender and receiver of the code.

Something that would have been triggered by a certain clue, such as the handkerchief's reference to Othello. Are there famous characters in Othello? Famous themes, famous lines? Quotes?"

"There are all of those, and more," said Eliza, her eyes wide with exasperation. "We are talking about one of the most famous plays in history."

"Ah yes, of course." He tapped his fingers on his knee. "So?"

Eliza's initial excitement faded from her face. "Now it's suddenly sounding like a silly thought. No need to send us on a wild goose chase." Doubt lingered in her voice. "Where would we even start?" She looked at the handkerchief as if hoping the answer would materialize on its surface.

"Fifty-two and fifty-three."

Eldredge and Eliza turned to the doorway where Tuohay stood in a wrinkled shirt and breeches, the stub of a clove cigarette in his hand. He leaned against his cane heavily, unshaven and fatigued. But a tireless energy burned in his eyes.

Eldredge stood with a smile. "Jack!" He paused, contemplating Tuohay's words. "Sorry?"

"The pages that the handkerchief marked, you ninny," Eliza scolded Eldredge. "Don't you remember? You even asked about them in your telegram."

"Yes…" said Eldredge. "Pages fifty-two and fifty-three… of the play, perhaps?"

"Pages are not standard," said Eliza, "those depend on the size of the volume."

"But Acts and Scenes are," said Tuohay.

"And so are lines!" Eliza turned to Eldredge, her voice brimming with excitement. "It may be a long shot, but we need a copy of Othello."

*

A plume of green-tinted smoke rose from the interior of the study, the scent of cloves and peppermint heavy in the air. Eliza pushed open a set of windows, breathing deeply as a cool autumn breeze brushed past her face. Tuohay watched from the corner of the room, a freshly lit cigarette in his hand and a small mountain of ashes in a bowl at his side. Papers were strewn about the table and floor, many with markings in ink.

The three companions stretched out at the corners of a squat table cluttered with paper and ink, maps, books, empty wine bottles and plates offering half-eaten baguettes and crumbs of cheese. Tuohay was seated on the floor with his back to the wall, his long legs stretched out before him.

"Well, old boy?" Tuohay asked Eldredge.

"Keep your knickers on, Jack," Eliza said distractedly as she looked over Eldredge's shoulder. "Johnny's almost done."

Eldredge pushed his spectacles up with one hand as he continued to scrawl with the other, referring to the codex often. After a few minutes more his hand relaxed from its maddened scribbling. Exhaling, he wrote a single word and set the pencil down:

revelation

"Revelation?" Eliza exclaimed. "That's *it*?"

Eldredge scratched his jaw. "As far as I can tell."

"Great. *Another* mystery. Or a joke." Eliza crossed her arms. "So how did you come up with it?"

Eldredge pinched the bridge of his nose. "For starters, you got me the key when you retrieved Othello from the library."

"You'd think I wouldn't have to travel twelve blocks to get hold of a work by the greatest author on earth," Eliza complained.

"Fifty-two and fifty-three." Eldredge flipped the codex open to those pages. "Not only was the starched handkerchief found between these pages, but the pages themselves had small hand-sketches of strawberries along the border. Thanks to your cleverness, Eliza, we checked Othello and after some juggling of numbers, found what we were looking for in Scene Five, Act Two, Line Fifty-Three."

"*Therefore confess thee freely of thy sin,*" Eliza recited.

"Precisely. And that phrase is the cipher's key. When the key was run against the garbled letters on the handkerchief, aka the cypher, it gave the following." He pointed to his penciled notes with a smudged finger.

Beseechinsulatingondontoknavebloomingnhabitlatherdisagree advocacyrevelationdeliverpalfreyshook

"A list of words," said Eliza.

"Yes," said Eldredge. "I spent the better part of an hour looking each of these words up in the codex, and writing down the pertaining meanings. I then summarized and reviewed the meanings as a whole—rearranging them, looking for themes, looking for duplicates, looking for indicators, for anomalies. In the short time I spent, everything came up nonsensical. But then it struck me. There was one word that was not in the codex. The only word without a translation. So I thought—perhaps *it* is the answer, plain and simple."

"Revelation," said Eliza. "So that's it, then? You think the entire cryptic message boils down to that? It almost seems…"

"Inane? Based on the analysis so far, it is the lead candidate. I have seen stranger things when working with codes."

Tuohay exhaled a long plume of lavender smoke. "Fine work, both of you. I am sure the cryptic meaning will become clear as the mystery unfolds. " His voice was somber, almost soft.

"I thought we were doing all of this work *to* unfold the mystery," argued Eliza.

"And we are that much closer," Tuohay offered.

"Doesn't feel like it." Eliza frowned. "How about you? You've been locked in this room since last night, doing God knows what. Have any investigative insights to share?"

"Let's hear about Eldredge's review of Father Donnelly's accounting books first."

"Avoiding the question, I see." Eliza gave Tuohay a hard stare.

"Gladly," said Eldredge, missing the exchange between Eliza and Tuohay in his excitement to share his information. "As you all recall, the good doctor and Mary Hart handed these over to us during our meeting at the hotel." He pointed at a pile of leather-bound ledgers arranged neatly in a column on the floor. "I believe it was indicated that they were second copies of the financial records of the parish, which had been obtained by Aiden Kearney during his investigation of Father Donnelly."

"That is correct," said Tuohay, detachment in his voice. He rubbed his eyes with his palms.

"Hold on, Johnny." Eliza stood and stomped over to where Tuohay was slouched. She addressed him with her hands still on her hips. "What's gotten into you, Jack? Huh?" She leaned forward and wrinkled her nose. "You're drunk."

176

"It's not an unusual circumstance for me," he replied. "The spirits enhance my deductive reasoning."

"You need a good kick to the face, you know that?"

"I'll stick to the brandy for my kicks, but cheers all the same," said Tuohay. He reached for his cigarette case with shaking fingers.

"If you've got something on your mind, say it. We're a team, Jack. *Your* team. You owe that to us." She kicked his foot to get his attention. "What's got your goat, huh? The poisoning of Miss Hart? We got rid of Frost, so that can't be it."

Eldredge's brows rose with curiosity. "Got rid of Frost?"

Eliza looked over her shoulder. "Yeah, we haven't told you yet, have we?"

"No, not at all."

Eliza formed a gun with her fingers and whispered in a Brooklyn accent, "I gots a message for ya, Inspector Frost. Blam!" She blew the fictional smoke from her fingers with a wink.

Eldredge jumped up, his notes spilling to the floor. "You *shot* him? You shot Inspector Frost?"

Eliza stared at Eldredge as if he had two heads. "What?"

A moment later, Tuohay burst into a fit of coughing. He tried to stand, and waved away help as he struggled to the windowsill. He stuck his head into the fresh air, his shoulders trembling. When he turned back, tears were in his eyes.

"Are you...*laughing*?" Eldredge cried.

"Bloody hell, John," said Tuohay, his voice barely more than a rasp. A pained smile crossed his face. "As always, you know how to cheer a fellow up."

Eliza rolled her eyes at Tuohay. "Enough already." She turned to Eldredge. "Listen. What I was portraying for you was a *setup*. Jack and I put it together last night for the benefit of Inspector Frost—to get rid of him for a spell, if you catch my drift. We originally planned it for the Cocahasett House in Foxboro, until Miss Hart left unexpectedly for Plymouth. So we set it up at a local hotel here. I came in, threatened Frost, Tuohay chased me... and we escaped into the night."

"Of course! One of your famous Sleuthhound performances, just like the old days," said Eldredge. "If only I had been here to witness it." The wistful smile on his face slowly diminished as a thought struck him. "Though…there is a severity that comes with hoodwinking the authorities."

"We are far beyond *hoodwinking*, old friend," said Tuohay, his smile gone. "Far beyond indeed." He rapped his cane against the floor. "Back to it, then. The financial accounts of Father Donnelly. What did they have to say?"

Eliza stood between Eldredge and Tuohay, her hands on her hip. "No—not until you tell us what's wrong."

Tuohay lifted himself slowly with his cane, grimacing with pain. He turned to Eliza and Eldredge, the look of misery on his face causing a hush to fall upon the room.

"What is it?" Eliza demanded, her voice laced with concern.

"You are right, Eliza," he said. "I have a revelation to share, and I ask for your forgiveness for it."

Eldredge took a tentative step forward. "Jack, are you alright?"

"I have been in contact with a protected source through the RIC. Someone who I have been prohibited to share with you. He has been consulting with me on the matter of the diamond, and on the priests in Boston. He has come to Plymouth and demanded a meeting in secret tonight."

Eldredge's gaze was uncertain. "Protected source?"

Eliza stamped her foot. "You know I detest secrets, Jack. It is why I am so keen on breaking them!"

"I have not meant to deceive you, my friends. But…I am on probation at the RIC. And, more significantly, Scotland Yard has me listed as a suspect for the theft of the Templar Diamond."

Eliza paled. "What?"

"Six years ago, shortly after the diamond was stolen from St. Peter's in Belfast, I was discharged from the RIC—the highest officer removed for the debacle."

Eliza stared at Tuohay. "You were *removed* from the RIC? Because of the diamond theft?"

"Negligent failure to prevent a crime." The words had a bite to them. "A serious charge that carried more penalties than just the loss of my living and reputation. I have been a suspect for the last six years, though the evidence was contrived. After the crime, the RIC brass needed a scapegoat, and I was it. But the administration changed last year, and several months ago, when Father Aiden Kearney contacted me about the new evidence he had uncovered regarding the Templar Diamond, the RIC gave me a second chance."

"Second chance?" Eldredge fidgeted nervously with his ascot.

"I was reinstated as an investigator on a probationary basis," Tuohay replied with a morose smile. "To be fully reinstated, I needed to prove my innocence by solving the crime."

Eliza frowned. "They can do that?"

"Not officially," said Tuohay. "It was a gentleman's agreement of sorts."

Eldredge's voice dropped to a whisper. "You, involved in the theft of the diamond? It's... preposterous."

"I am going to meet with the witness within the hour, if you would like to join me," Tuohay offered. He turned to Eldredge. "And rest assured, old boy, I was *not* involved in the theft. But other than myself, there may be very few who actually believe that—except, I hope, my last two friends." He coughed into his sleeve, and took a moment to catch his breath.

Recovered, he met their gazes with one of resolution. "If there is anything you are still willing to believe, make it this—I am going to find the diamond, and bring the truth to light about any crimes connected to it."

Eliza crossed her arms. "No Jack, I'm sorry to say that you are not going to do that. It's not possible."

Tuohay looked frowned. "Eliza, please—"

"It's not possible on your *own*." She gave Eldredge a wink but continued to glare at Tuohay. "*You're* not going to do anything because *we* are, the three of us, as a team. That alright?"

Relief flooded into Tuohay's voice. "Perfect."

"Hear, hear," Eldredge added.

Eliza twisted her lips into a curious frown. "Jack, is it true that Johnny and I are your only two friends? Anywhere?"

Tuohay nodded slowly. "I would say so, yes."

Eliza whistled. "Jeeze. No wonder the RIC made you the scapegoat for the crime. Mr. Popularity. Maybe the next time you're in Belfast, you should learn how to make a few pals."

"One thing at a time," Tuohay replied.

Eldredge cleared this throat. "And perhaps... ah, not to sound ungracious. But perhaps you should not disappear *entirely* from your only two friends for a decade without a word in between. Just an observation," he added quickly, tugging at his ascot.

Tuohay regarded Eldredge and Eliza with the ghost of a smile crossing his lips. "In truth, the fact that you have not had to put up with me for a decade is probably the only reason you're willing to now."

"You know what they say, *make hay while the sun shines*." Eliza shot a playful smile at Tuohay. "You haven't worn out your welcome yet, Jack. So let's get back to work before you do."

The Contact

A misting rain fell lightly upon the shore, a bouquet of wet caresses transformed into warm tears as they ran down the face. The drizzle swept in from the sea along the waves; occasionally bearing a soft crystal of snow that floated unhurriedly and in no apparent direction on its own, coming to rest upon the shore to dissipate into nothingness.

Tuohay walked along the shoreline, his cane sticking in the cold sand. The waves rolled in at his feet, bringing the salty scent of the sea with them. Opposite, the town of Plymouth was visible beyond the grassy dunes, but the shore itself was shielded by the rigid backs of vacant warehouses. Remnants of a long-forgotten campfire littered the grounds. It was a cold and forgotten strand of beach, with only the squawk of seagulls and the chime of a distant buoy as company.

Somewhere in those dunes Eldredge was perched, watching. Eliza was using the time to take a quick lunch.

A figure appeared on a path between the dunes and approached unhurriedly, his hands clasped before him. Tuohay met him near the water's edge as the waves crashed behind them.

"Inspector Tuohay."

"Your Grace."

Archbishop Patrick J. Walsh was adorned in a black cassock, rippling in the wind. Usually buttoned to the throat, it hung open in a sign of hastiness, beneath which a finely pressed alb was visible, flowing like a black river as he moved. The pectoral cross wetly gleamed.

"I am here for Father Donnelly's service, so our time is short, and we must maintain a low profile."

"Of course."

"Shall we?" Walsh asked.

Tuohay regarded his companion as they walked along the hushed shore. The archbishop's visage was not radiant. Nor bold, or soft. It was something altogether different, something singular. At first glance it appeared preoccupied and worn. Lean with a long nose, framed by a crown of stark white hair brushed back smooth like the head of an eagle, the look was emboldened by bold eyebrows and sharp eyes. Deep within the clerical wisdom that emanated from his being there existed a furtive irony that only age could have wrought; in essence it was a lingering cynicism, a dry humor that seemed to ask how such an enormous task had fallen to one man in one life, and how that one man had become him. A man responsible for the spiritual well-being of thousands upon thousands of devoted Catholic followers.

"You have kept my involvement in your work a secret," Walsh asked.

"As we agreed," said Tuohay.

"But the work itself has not been kept a secret," added the archbishop. "The papers are ablaze with news about the Templar Diamond."

"So they are."

"And Father Donnelly. *Deus misereatur*," murmured the archbishop.

"I pray that God has mercy on him as well, your Grace. And for the Kearney brothers, for that matter."

"Aiden and Rian." A gust of wind blew over the rolling waves as if in response, tugging at the archbishop's cape like an angry hound.

Tuohay grabbed his top hat tightly and the archbishop gathered his cassock and alb as the torrent of wind passed by. "I am going to see this investigation through to the end, despite your request to conclude it now," Tuohay stated.

"I performed my end of the bargain," the archbishop said. "I paid the rent on the Kearney brothers' flat after their death until your arrival so any evidence would remain untouched; I opened the way for you to interview Father Donnelly; I used my influence to the best of my ability with the top Boston brass to minimize interference with your investigation."

"So you did."

"But now...."

"Now?"

"Things have gotten out of hand," the archbishop murmured. "Father Kearney is dead. *Dead*. I wanted him investigated, not harmed. Your main suspect, Kip Crippen, shot in cold blood— silenced. Miss Hart poisoned, on the brink of death. Gunshots in hotels, dead bodies...this is not at all what I signed up for, inspector. I simply wanted the diamond found, and the truth uncovered."

"Nor I," Tuohay admitted. His voice hardened. "But nor did Father Aiden Kearney when he first came to these shores as a priest. Perhaps if you had listened to him from the first, none of this would have come to pass. He discovered wrongdoing with Father Donnelly and others long before any of *this* happened, and he informed you of it. If you had been objective then, and not allowed your misguided opinions to deceive you into blanketing the truth, this all could have been avoided."

"Da Vinci, is it? A man's opinion is his greatest deceiver? Well, perhaps it is." The archbishop cast his gaze across the gray sea. "But you misunderstand me, inspector. I am concerned with *discretion*, not deception. It is deception that I hired you to ferret out. But your life is simplistic, free of politics, free of such demands. Not so for me."

The archbishop clasped his hands behind his back as the rain darkened his cassock. "There are ways that we deal with these things that Aiden did not understand. He wanted to raise these indiscretions directly to Rome. And then to the *civil court*. No, no." The archbishop shook his head. "There are systems within the American Church to deal with imprudence. Effectively, quietly. But he would not listen. He did not understand, could never understand. So he had to be silenced—not in death, mind you—but discredited. Removed from the flock. I had no choice."

"You destroyed his life."

"He would have done that and more to the Church, inspector."

Tuohay coughed into his hand. "To you, you mean."

The archbishop's eyes flashed. "It is not about *me*. It is about maintaining the integrity and authority of the burgeoning Catholic Church in America. But it is not your place to judge. Nor to understand. It is—or *was*—your place to unobtrusively find the diamond and discover the truth behind its disappearance. Instead, you have brought bedlam to my shores."

Tuohay stopped to lean against his cane, wincing as his leg buckled. He grimaced through the pain. "Bedlam, you say? What do you think Mary Hart and Kathryn Dwyer experienced during their time locked up in the Danvers lunacy asylum? How do think it felt to be Aiden Kearney, a promising and honorable priest who uncovered criminal behavior in your diocese, and suffered for years as a pariah only to be *silenced* in the end? No, do not speak to me about bedlam, Your Grace."

The archbishop glared at Tuohay, but there was anguish in his voice as spoke. "I never intended for anyone to suffer."

"Then let me finish my work and put an end to the suffering," Tuohay offered. "I know you came here to tell me to cease my work, but I will not. You *know* I will not."

"I have known that all along." The archbishop reached into a pocket of his cassock and withdrew a small leather booklet. "And so I brought this. Perhaps it will be of help. It is the last I have to offer." He handed the booklet to Tuohay, who arched an eyebrow at the handwritten title on the cover.

CROWN MOUNT

Archbishop Walsh noticed Tuohay's distracted look. "Do you know what *Crown Mount* is?"

"Yes. *Crown Mount* was the codename the RIC in Belfast used for the Templar Diamond operation—to keep it safe and secure at all times."

"This book was given to me under the strictest of confidence by the highest authorities in the RIC," the archbishop said. "It was protocol that the Church and State be aware of the operational details of the diamond's movement."

"But you shared its contents," said Tuohay with sudden realization," with Father Donnelly."

"I did. He was the operational lead for the Church on the American side of things."

"*That* is how Father Donnelly obtained the information needed to know where the diamond would be," said Tuohay. "The very information need to pull off the heist." A furrow appeared in Tuohay's forehead. "Why did you not tell me this before?"

The archbishop glanced at Tuohay. "I wanted to see what you would come across first. I hoped… I hoped it would not be necessary to expose this truth. Sharing Crown Mount with Father Donnelly was a serious oversight. It was for my eyes only."

"Is there anything else you have not told me?"

"No. That is everything. And as far as I am concerned, I have done all I can, inspector. Even putting my own career at risk. I believe my usefulness as a source for the RIC is at an end."

For the first time during their conversation, Tuohay noticed the deep lines of sorrow etched across the archbishop's face. "So you are *not* interested in the uncovering the truth?" Tuohay slapped the booklet against his hand. "This may be the break I have been looking for—after going this far, you would pull back now?"

"Do not patronize me, inspector. I will always be interested in the truth. But I want no further part in what it will *cost*." He turned away from Tuohay to face the sea, his hands once again clasped behind his back. "Do what you must. Find the diamond, if you can. Nothing would please me more. But do not turn to me for further assistance. I can make no more sacrifices."

Tuohay stood beside the archbishop for nearly a minute, watching the waves in silence. Finally, he turned to his companion. "Good evening, your Grace." He departed without another word, his cane sinking into the sand with each laborious step.

In the distance a man in an olive trench coat observed them from the dunes, his coat rippling in the wind.

Reconciliation

Tuohay awoke to hushed voices, quickly discerning them as the familiar laughter of the wind frolicking with the windowsill. Blinking the sleep from his eyes, he was attentive to the crimson light of evening spilling through the open crevices between the curtains of the hotel study. One particular crimson glow caught his attention, and with a start he realized it was a single ember still burning in a half-spent clove cigarette where it rested on the floor, half crushed.

Pulling his watch from his coat, Tuohay checked the time. It had only been an hour since he had left the archbishop. Eldredge was not in the dunes as he had expected, leaving him to hobble back to the hotel as inconspicuously as possible.

After a moment he realized the whispering was not only the wind, but a murmur from beyond the door. Grabbing the cigarette, he had it lit by the time the door creaked open. Eliza stepped through, her curls wet from the weather. Eldredge followed, his countenance soft.

Tuohay regarded them through a bluish haze. "Where did you run off to, John? I checked the dunes and you had disappeared."

"It didn't feel right, spying in that manner. I... spotted the archbishop, and that was enough."

The scent of wet cloves filled the room. "You are a better man than I."

"Tell us something we don't know, Jack," Eliza scoffed.

Eldredge shrugged. "Truth be told, I desperately needed a bite to eat."

Eliza laughed, the musical sound drifting through the taut air like a warm embrace.

Weariness not yet conquered by the brief respite swept over Tuohay, but he forced a smile. "Ten years was too long, my friends."

Eliza crossed her arms defiantly, but gentleness filler her eyes. "*You* left *us*, remember?"

Tuohay offered his cigarette to Eliza, who took it without hesitating. He eyed her critically. "Are we truly fine?"

"We are, Jack," she answered solemnly. "And that's the end of it, I promise."

"I leave it to you."

"Well, there *is* one thing. No more secrets. No matter whether it's for our protection, for your protection, or whatever foolish reason you try to think of." She took a drag of the cigarette to mark her words. Coughing, she pulled it away and made a face as she peered at the burning stub in her hand. "This tastes terrible. What, did you find this on the *floor*? It looks like the one I crushed out."

"No more secrets," Tuohay pledged. "And therefore, yes I did find that on the floor."

Eliza gave him a pitied stare. "You are in desperate need of help."

Eldredge's voice rose from a stack of books near the corner of the room. "Shall we speak briefly of the financial ledgers belonging to Father Donnelly?" He was already transferring the stack of the leather-bound ledgers onto the desk before him.

"By all means," said Tuohay.

Opening the top ledger with one hand, Eldredge removed a loose paper from it as he adjusted his spectacles with the other. "As you both recall, Mary Hart gave these ledgers to us during our interview with her and the doctor. They had been given to *her* by Aiden Kearney shortly before his death. And he, in turn, had found them during his investigation. There is something interesting in their details."

"As was expected," Tuohay said, taking the clove cigarette back from Eliza.

"The ledgers are for the years 1887 to 1898," Eldredge began. "They include detailed parish costs such as church office rent and mortgages, travel costs, education expenses, almshouse expenses, furnishings for the rectory, furnishings for the church, construction and updates to the parish and rectory, pastor miscellaneous expenses…well, you get idea."

"Yeah, we get the idea, Johnny," Eliza sighed, perching herself on the windowsill. A breeze blew in from behind her, tossing strands of hair across her face.

"Well, the long and short of it is—the numbers are fabricated."

"How do you know?" Tuohay asked. The cigarette was little more than ash in his fingers, and he flicked it out the window. "Are there unaccounted for expenses? Anomalies?"

"No, everything is accounted for neatly," replied Eldredge. "Too neatly, in fact. And on pretty much any day of the week the ledgers would easily pass a fiscal audit."

Eliza leaned forward. "But?"

"*But* I am not an auditor," said Eldredge. "I am a statistician. I look at things in a different way." He straightened his ascot with an absent-minded smile. "You see, there is a man I know—an old colleague from my astronomy club days, to be precise—named Simon Newcomb. And he did a fascinating thing with natural numbers."

Tuohay scratched his forehead. "Natural numbers?"

"Numbers generated through natural circumstances. What Newcomb determined was that not all digits—take one through nine as an example—occur with the same frequency at all times."

Tuohay scrabbled in his pocket for his lighter. Locating it, he slipped a new cigarette from the silver case and partnered it with the flame. Inhaling with fervor, he slumped against the wall. "Are you trying to tell me that one number occurs more frequently than another? Say, if I were to roll a die, a one would come up more often than a six? Seems unlikely, old boy." The room was renewed with the scent of wet cloves.

"No, that circumstance is governed by random behavior. But look at this—I brought it as an example." Eldredge pointed at a sheet of paper with numbers in pencil scratched across the surface. "When I was at my mum's, I took the Boston Globe for the last seven days and listed every number printed on the front and back pages, fourteen pages in all. Examples of numbers include '*six* days ago', and '*two* home runs', those types of things. My mum keeps weeks of these papers for the fireplace, which was handy."

Eliza padded over to Tuohay and swiped the cigarette. "Sounds like you need a new hobby, Johnny."

"Just the opposite," said Eldredge, pushing his spectacles up. "This is fascinating subject matter. I classified each number by its first numeral, tallied its occurrences, and determined its overall frequency compared to the others. Here, I made copies." He passed yellowed paper with pencil scratchings across them to Eliza and Tuohay.

Digit	→ Occurrences	→ Frequency
1	→56	→26%
2	→48	→23%
3	→27	→13%
4	→20	→9%
5	→30	→14%
6	→11	→5%
7	→8	→4%
8	→9	→4%
9	→4	→2%

"What does this tell us, exactly?" Tuohay asked.

"This experiment is representative of the actual frequencies, in nature, that these digits occur. My colleague, Mr. Newcomb, discovered the phenomenon years ago when he noticed that the pages of logarithmic tables in a logarithm reference book were more worn than others. The logarithmic tables of smaller digits, such as one and two, were much more worn from use than pages with logarithmic pages for the higher digits, such as eight and nine. He built a fascinating theorem around it, and sent it to several of his colleagues, including me.

"For my part, I tested it over the years on different domains in my spare time," Eldredge continued, "such as the heights of different mountains, the sizes of various populations in the UK, a list of atomic weights in a chemistry handbook, and, as it so happens, the financial accounts of dozens of government businesses spanning a minimum of five years. And, most recently, the pages of *Boston Globe* to use as an example for you."

Tuohay frowned thoughtfully. "Truly?"

"Truly. I captured the frequencies from this massive pool of data, as I will show you in a moment."

Eliza gave Eldredge perplexed look. "Johnny, shouldn't you publish these findings? It sounds like a pretty big deal."

Eldredge waved the question away, blushing slightly. "No, no. This is just the noodling of a semi-recluse. I do not think it's worth pursuing beyond fancy."

"Are you sure?"

"I do not like attention, as you know. In any case," Eldredge continued, tugging at his ascot with anxious fingers, "there is financial data in the Plymouth accounting books that do not follow the expected rate of decimal frequency. Instead, the digits appear at a nearly consistent rate. This occurs in the ledgers between 1892 to 1896, whereas data from 1887 to 1891 and 1897 to 1898 match the expected natural patterns."

"So… the strange patterns in the financial data for the Plymouth parish appear only for a specific period of time," said Tuohay. "How confident are you in these findings?"

"I must grant, the numerical examination will not hold up in court, for the statistics are, shall we say, before their time. But the analysis is solid. Thus, the span from 1892 to 1896 is indicative of fraudulent values, of someone fixing the accounts. Misappropriation of funds, most certainly. You can trust me on this." Eldredge removed his glasses and rubbed the bridge of his nose with his thumb. He passed another set of notes to Tuohay and Eliza.

Digit	→ Frequency of Digit		→ Expected Frequency
	('92-'96)	('87-91,'97-'98)	
1	→11%	→29%	→30%
2	→12%	→19%	→18%
3	→11%	→13%	→12%
4	→10%	→9%	→10%
5	→12%	→9%	→8%
6	→10%	→6%	→7%
7	→11%	→5%	→6%
8	→12%	→5%	→6%
9	→11%	→5%	→5%

"There is a significant amount of data analysis that goes into these numbers," said Eldredge, pointing at a stack of papers rife with mathematical formulas and calculations. "Especially the original data used to create the expected value, such as the various population sizes and atomic weights and so on. If you would like, I would be more than happy to explain further—"

"We trust you, old boy," said Tuohay, raising his hand. "These dates of fraudulent behavior… they appear to be the dates that Miss Hart was Father Donnelly's paramour."

"It fits if he was taking from the church coffers to spend money on her," added Eliza, "bolstering the truth of her claim that he was infatuated with her."

"There is one more bit of information in the ledgers," said Eldredge. "In 1897, a sizable series of expenses appear on the books. The costs are all linked to the relocation of a medieval stained glass window from an abandoned church in Glendalough, Ireland to St. John's seminary in Brighton. Shipping expenses, restoration of the glass, and installation at St. John's are noted for a period of several months. It was evidently quite the feat, based on the margin notes."

"Interesting," agreed Tuohay. "I wonder how Father Donnelly's nephew ties into it."

"Father Abrams?" Eliza mused, exhaling a trail of lavender smoke. "What does he have to do with anything?"

"I am quite sure he was dead by that time," Tuohay continued, "but Father Donnelly mentioned that Abrams was involved in the study of classical stained glass art. And, more compelling yet, he is the father of the young man."

"What young man?" Eliza handed the cigarette back. "Use names, will you? I'm trying to keep track here."

Tuohay peered at the burning embers as if they had awakened him from a thought. "Frost told me that Abrams Valentine was the father of Colin Allotrope—the young man who wrote the essay we found in the loft of the law firm; the same essay Inspector Frost was perusing. Its title mentioned something about the restoration of stained glass art."

"You don't say," Eliza murmured. "A priest with a son who wrote an essay, and the essay was in Inspector Frost's possession. So?"

"If I may," Eldredge interjected, "I looked up Colin Allotrope as you requested, and have information to share."

Tuohay nodded. "Excellent. Go on."

"As I stated in the telegram, Colin Allotrope was an orphan brought up in a Lowell convent, and showed unusual talent by all accounts. He went to Boston College preparatory and Boston College high school, and currently attends Boston College, his skills in oil on canvass and stained glass earning him several accolades in religious and artist circles. To date, he has recently been accepted to seminary at St. John's in Brighton to become a priest. His parents are unknown, but there are strong indications that he has enjoyed the financial support of an anonymous benefactor."

"St. John's in Brighton," Tuohay mused. "Remarkable coincidence. And he seems to have followed his father's path into Christian art."

"And priesthood," added Eldredge.

"There is the anonymous benefactor as well," said Tuohay. "Seems to be a trail worth following."

"Hold on a moment," Eliza protested. "The boy was brought up in a convent, so it's not a stretch that it had an impact on his choice of careers. And he was, what—twelve when the diamond was stolen? Are you forgetting your focus? There are only three of us to do the work, don't forget."

Eldredge scratched his head. "You have point, Eliza. But I don't think Jack is connecting Colin to the diamond crime, he's simply looking for how the background of these individuals fits together."

"But none of them are even suspects," Eliza countered. "What's the point in that?"

"Alright, you two," Tuohay interrupted, "let's take a step back for a moment to review all the facts. Set things in order."

"Good idea." Eliza took her journal out and found a pencil in her pockets. After a moment she began to write.

"Ready?" Tuohay inquired.

Eliza looked up. "What? Oh, sorry. Don't wait for me, Jack. I'm not your scribe. I'm jotting down notes of my own here."

"Right, then." Tuohay straightened his posture as if preparing to give an address. "The Templar Diamond was stolen in 1896 in Belfast," he began. "At the time, Father Donnelly was in charge of the logistics for the Church from the North American side of things. That's his main connection to the affair, which under normal circumstances would be considered minimal. But there is the fact he had access to *Crown Mount*. I would not have thought the RIC would have shared operational information with the Church, but there it is, plain as day."

Eliza and Eldredge looked at Tuohay with puzzled frowns.

"Ah, sorry." Tuohay pulled the booklet from his pocket, the leather cover slightly damp. He tapped his finger on the title. "*Crown Mount*. These pages contain the secret operational details and responsibilities of the RIC task force responsible for keeping the diamond safe during its stay in Belfast. The script is encoded."

"Where did you get it?" Eliza had turned back to her journal and was scribbling as she asked.

"The archbishop gave it to me."

Eliza arched a curious brow but didn't press further. She leapt lightly off the windowsill, her eyes still on her journal. "For some reason I am stuck on the nephew…when did he die?"

"Father Abrams Valentine died in 1896," said Tuohay. "It would have been shortly after the diamond disappeared." Tuohay paused to think. "If I am not mistaken, Father Donnelly told me that his nephew *came home to die*."

"From Belfast?"

"Possibly," said Tuohay. "So if we were to start at the beginning again, and summarize in full—"

"Hold on, Jack," Eliza interrupted. "Before you get into one of your long-winded soliloquies, let's work off of this."

She laid her journal open for Tuohay and Eldredge to see.

Name	Death	Tie to Diamond?	Thoughts
Fr. Robert Donnelly	Recent	Told Mary he was involved in crime. Was the N.American coordinator for logistics	Mastermind of the crime? <u>Access to Crown Mount?</u> Sent Mary to asylum.
'The Nephew' (Fr Abrams Valentine)	1896	? – in Belfast at time of crime? Died shortly thereafter	Connected to the crime?
Archbishop		?	Lost Cardinalship due to Aiden's trial against him,

			embarrassment
Colin Allotrope		? – only 12 at time of crime	Son of 'The Nephew', wrote essay on Adoration of the Magi
Kip Crippen	Recent	Jewel thief... came here to claim diamond?	Killed... why? By who?
Fr. Aiden Kearney	Dec 1901	Mary gave him evidence	Investigative priest... at odds with Archbishop... suicide or murdered?
Dr. Sean Kearney		Aiden gave him evidence	Wants truth revealed for Aiden
Sara (and Anna)			Wants truth revealed for Aiden? ... family history → hardship
Mary Hart		Fr. Donnelly told her of his involvement in diamond theft	Fr. Donnelly's lover? Wrote affidavit against Fr. Donnelly, Archbishop, and Frost. Poisoned.
Katy Dwyer	Oct 1901		Wrote affidavit against Fr. Donnelly, Archbishop, and Frost. Killed on way to visit with Frost...
Susan Lovelace	1897		Died two months after trial
Inspector Frost			Told concubines to lie on the stand? Why is he involved now?

Current date, March 1902
Diamond Theft, Belfast, 1896
Alleged convention of the three diamond criminals, 1902—to get diamond?
Invitations sent with clues to how to find the diamond? Who sent them? Who received them? Why?
Trial against Archbishop, 1897

"Right." Tuohay looked over the journal scratchings with a nod. "Well done. To add to that—"

194

A thunderous knock at the front door reverberated like a threat. It was followed by a gruff voice. "Open up! I know you're in there, inspector!"

Tuohay groaned as if he had been punched in the gut. Looking at his companions, he shook his head as Eldredge began a frantic collection of their things.

"It is not worth it, old boy," said Tuohay. "We cannot run. It seems it is time for me to take my knocks."

"Not alone, you won't," said Eliza. She plucked the last of the cigarette from Tuohay's mouth and finished it with a long drag. Dropping the remnants, she ground it to ash with a twist of her foot. "I'll go see what the ruckus is about."

Tuohay chuckled with dry humor. "You haven't changed a bit, have you?"

"Perhaps I should go instead," Eldredge cut in.

There was a second knock, and Eliza squeezed Eldredge's shoulder reassuringly. "Not this time, Johnny. If anyone's going out there alone, it's me. Be harder for them to enter uninvited if it appears to be a woman's chamber, especially one who seems to be on her own." She fought off the protests of her partners and slipped from the room with a wink.

Eldredge turned to Tuohay. "She's something else."

"That's one way to put it." The two listened to the click of the bolt at the front door, followed by the squeak of the hinges. There was an exchange of muffled words, trailed by a brief silence. Tuohay and Eldredge exchanged glances.

Eldredge stepped towards the office door. "Should I see what is going on?"

At that moment, the uneven clod of heavy boots against the floorboards echoed from the parlor. The door to the office swung open with Eliza in the lead, a giant of man shadowing her. Wet strings of white hair were plastered across his wrinkled forehead wildly. He was cloaked in a heavy trench coat, his collar pulled up. A dripping newspaper was tucked under his arm.

Tuohay's brows raised in puzzlement. "McNamara! What are you doing here? How did you find us?"

McNamara took a long look at Tuohay before responding. "There's a lot of people lookin' for you, inspector. And most don't have pleasantries in mind."

"And you?"

"I ain't bearin' a wreath of goodwill, if that's your question. I come from Boston with information."

Eldredge's surprise registered on his face. "You came all the way back from Boston? Didn't you just arrive there this morning with Miss Hart?"

"So I did," McNamara growled in response. "And now I'm back. There have been grander accomplishments in the world than a roundtrip."

"Information." Tuohay spoke the words with the delicacy of a skater crossing a thinly frozen lake.

"Aye." McNamara turned to Tuohay with a black look. "Mary Hart is dead."

The room stilled.

"Sorry to be the one to give you the news," McNamara continued. "Figured it needed to be told to you in person, 'specially before the papers got a hold of it. It was the poison, of course."

"She didn't make it," said Tuohay, his voice marred with anger. He offered McNamara a composed nod of appreciation. "I am indebted to you, coming as you have."

"I'll get straight to the details." McNamara took on an official business-like tone, setting his newspaper aside. "Doctor Kearney, Mr. Thayer, and I accompanied Miss Hart in an ambulatory wagon from Plymouth to the Boston City Hospital this morning, along with an officer. The ride did not do her well, but the doctor insisted on it. His status on the staff got her immediate treatment by some of the best doctors in the city, the country maybe. But it weren't enough, in the end."

"Will there be an autopsy?" Tuohay asked, trying to control the heat rising in his throat.

"The Boston commissioner wants one of their own to perform it. It's likely to take place in the morning at the BCH, under close supervision."

"And Doctor Kearney?"

"Returned to his apartment after they declared her. I went along with him for a spell, he lives close to the hospital. Him and I go back, you see, so he was willin' to talk. I told him I had heard the Boston brass was lookin' at a getting a warrant against him, and I wanted to feel him out."

Eldredge expressed disbelief. "A warrant?"

"Word is," McNamara said, "some of the coppers think the doctor persuaded Mary Hart and Kathryn Dwyer to fabricate lies so his brother Aiden could have affidavits for his appeal. In exchange, Doctor Kearney signed some papers releasing them from the Danvers lunacy asylum. From what I've heard of the place, anyone would have done that and more just to get free. Poor girls."

McNamara's face darkened. "Then the coppers say the doctor got rid of them—Katy Dwyer, who had second thoughts about the whole thing, and poor Mary Hart with a poisoned tincture of the doctor's making. He did it so the women couldn't speak the truth after the fact 'bout his plan, and all that sort of rubbish."

"Not too convincing," said Eliza.

Eldredge shrugged. "It's as good as any theory I have heard so far. Not saying it's anywhere near right, though."

McNamara reflected. "You know what they say about two evils. Nothing good comes from combining 'em, and that's the truth of it. So if it *were* true about the doctor's intentions, which seems improbable, all he got in the end for his troubles was two dead brothers."

"And what did he say to all of that when you brought it to his attention?" Tuohay asked.

"He said *Frost* is behind the whole thing." McNamara rubbed his eyes, leaving them raw and red. "If I may, I could use a drink—"

"I'll make you some tea," Eliza offered.

"Fine." McNamara's grizzled face expressed a wisp of benevolence at Eliza. It vanished like a snuffed-out candle as he continued with his account. "The doctor claims that Frost has always been to blame, even tracing back to the trial. He says Frost stole Hart and Dwyer's affidavits from the office of McBarronThayer the night of the interview, and that he had been figuring on a way to silence the two girls since they were freed from the asylum. With them out of the way, along with Aiden and Father Donnelly silenced for good, and the affidavits destroyed, *all* possible proof about a staged trial has been destroyed. Frost comes out clean. Doctor Kearney says it's plain as day. As for me, I wouldn't put it past the scoundrel, neither."

Eldredge chewed thoughtfully on an end of bread discovered near his elbow. "That theory is devoid of proof, but maintains a sense of logic, I suppose."

"Frost knows his way around evidence, both how to find it and how to make sure it's never found. In any case, the poor girl is dead." McNamara pulled a rumpled piece of paper from his pocket. "This is Doctor Kearney's address on Washington Street in Boston, adjacent to the Northampton Street El station. Perhaps you should consider payin' him a visit, see what you can gather. You're the inspector, after all."

"Another tragedy," Tuohay muttered, taking the paper from McNamara. His gaze settled out the window on the backdrop of Plymouth, the old houses, cold beaches, and remorseless ocean. A church rose from a distant bluff. "I had hoped to spare Mary Hart from it."

No one spoke as Tuohay continued to stare out the window, the anticipation of further communiqué from him hanging in the air like a silent promise. It finally came in the form of a forced whisper.

"There is a heartless scoundrel behind this affair, playing us in an ingeniously crafted match. Every move he makes, another piece is eliminated from the game. And he is always one move ahead, knowing how the game will play out, furthering his sinister plan closer to conclusion without fail. *But how?*"

The darkening landscape did not respond except with a lonely sigh of wind. If it had answers, it was holding them to itself.

Groundwork

The teapot whistled with the promise of a warm reprieve, and a minute later McNamara was accepting a steaming cup smelling faintly of a floral arrangement from Eliza. He gave her a thankful nod and settled onto a nearby stool, eyeing Tuohay closely as the inspector reviewed a handful of scattered notes.

"How did you find us?" Eliza asked, diverting the old man's attention to her.

"I knew Tuohay'd be holed up 'round here somewhere after cutting out on Frost," he replied with a glint in his eye. "When Thayer and I alighted from the coach in Plymouth, I got straight to work."

Tuohay's attention was roused. "Thayer? He came back from Boston with you?"

McNamara waved impatiently. "Said there was something he needed to look into, but was vague 'bout it. I think he just didn't want me ridin' alone, with everything that's been going on. He was acting peculiar, but that's not unusual for anyone connected to this bloody business."

"When are you supposed to meet back up with him?"

"Tomorrow morning for breakfast. Said he would have something interesting to share by then."

"Strange." Tuohay seemed to ponder it for a few moments before letting it go. "In any case, how was it that you finally tracked me down?"

"Still have some bloodhound in me, for a fact. Figured I'd lurk around the telegraph offices and train stations for starters. Had only completed one circuit when I got hungry, and what do you know—I caught sight of your friend 'ere leaving a café. Easier than it should have been."

Eldredge's face flushed. "Gads. I didn't realize I was being followed."

"No need to feel inadequate," McNamara replied in his gravelly voice. "I've got a lot of years as a beat cop under my hat. I know what I'm do'n when it comes to trailing a suspect."

"You got hungry and lucky," Eliza laughed.

"It's about the timin', miss," McNamara replied without a hint of humor. "More to it than you're aware. Luck don't come to nothin' without setting the proper circumstances. It comes from experience, it does."

Eliza shrugged. "Alright, Mr. McNamara, I won't argue with that." Despite her allowance, she did not seem entirely convinced.

"In any case, it comes down to me." Eldredge's face was dark with guilt.

"It's alright, John," Tuohay stated, his attempt to be sympathetic spoiled by the weakness of his voice. He looked the worse for the wear, his linen Edwardian shirt and frock coat crumpled and slightly askew. Even seated, he leaned heavily on his cane, and death itself would have presented a cheerier disposition.

Eliza regarded Tuohay, finally stepping close enough to draw his attention. She looked as if she was about to ask a delicate question, but changed her course of thought. "Brass tacks, Jack. What does it all *mean*? All of these events, past and present, seem to be connected, but…are they, really?" She mused for a moment. "There is Father Donnelly's death from his fall, Miss Hart's poisoning death, the deaths of Aiden and Rian Kearney….the various clues we found at the crime scenes… remember that scrawling on the wall, *I am my brothers keeper?*"

"Yes, I remember," said Tuohay.

McNamara cleared his throat. "And then there is this." He picked up the newspaper that he had set aside and held it to the light for the others to see. "This came out before Mary Hart's death…that will be in the late edition, no doubt."

DEADLY TIES
BODY DREDGED FROM BOSTON HARBOR
POISON AND GUNSHOTS IN PLYMOUTH
ANSWERS WANTED BY MEDFIELD POLICE
ALL LINKED TO TEMPLAR DIAMOND

UNIDENTIFIED BODY WITH GUNSHOT WOUND DREDGED FROM HARBOR.
BODY SHOWS SIGNS OF ADVANCED CONSUMPTION.

WITHIN HOURS OF EACH OTHER.

**WOMAN ATTENDING FR. DONNELLY'S WAKE POISONED.
SHOTS FIRE IN A PLYMOUTH HOTEL.
SUSPECT AT LARGE.**

**MEDFIELD AUTHORITIES REQUESTING INFORMATION FROM
THE ROYAL IRISH CONSTABULARY
IN MURDER OF KIP CRIPPEN.**

Tuohay started. "Body dredged from the harbor?"

"I was wondering which of those headlines would get your attention first," said McNamara.

Eliza pointed at the paper. "They did a good job on your profile sketch. Add that to your limp and your cane, throw in a few clove cigarettes and they'll have you within the hour."

"At least he is not wanted for a crime," said Eldredge. "The caption just says he is working with the Boston authorities." He squinted. "Why is there a sketch of Father Abrams Valentine next to Jack's?"

"The dead nephew?" Eliza tilted her head to get a better angle. "Where?"

"Just below the fold." He pointed to a drawing on the backside of the paper, below Tuohay's. "It looks nearly identical to the sketch you made of him in your journal, Eliza—when you investigated Father Donnelly's study, you sketched him from a portrait. That's how I recognized him in the paper."

"That *does* look like the man in the painting," Eliza agreed. She handed the paper to Eldredge and scanned the room for her journal. Finding it on a pile of loose papers, she flipped it open to the page with the sketch of the nephew's face from the painting. "Not identical, but certainly close."

McNamara stood and lumbered over for a look, holding his lame leg with a beefy hand. He grunted in agreement.

Tuohay pulled himself up, his eyes riveted on the two pictures. "May I?" Laying the paper and journal on the table side by side, he stared at them for several moments in silence. He broke his reverie with a curse. "Why didn't I see the resemblance before?"

Eldredge shook his head. "I am missing the point."

Eliza pointed at the sketch in the paper. "The point is, that's *not* Father Abrams Valentine in the paper. It is a police sketch of Kip Crippen."

"Kip Crippen? You mean, that's *not* a sketch of the nephew?"

Eliza turned to Tuohay. "Jack, it could be a coincidence. They're just sketches, after all. One looks like the next and all of that."

"No, you are exacting in your work," Tuohay argued. A cold eagerness entered his voice. "Do you recall what we found in the brothers' apartment on Kneeland Street? The shovel, the dirt-covered rug?"

Eliza frowned. "I was afraid you were going to say that."

Eldredge waved his hand for attention. "What are you two talking about?"

"There has been a nagging in my brain ever since I laid eyes on the painting of Father Donnelly's nephew," Tuohay answered.

Eldredge exhaled in frustration. "And?"

"And it is time to address it."

McNamara scowled. "I got a bad feelin' about where this is going."

Eldredge set his pipe down, a note of apprehension in his voice. "How do you plan to address it, Jack?"

"You are going on the first available carriage to Boston. Or by train, if necessary," he added with a dry smile. "I need you to get into the Customs House and look through the 1896 passenger lists to Boston from Britain, primarily Belfast, for Abrams Valentine."

"Not an easy task, but consider it done." Eldredge looked at the others. "Not as dire an errand as I expected, from Tuohay's grave tone."

Eliza gave Eldredge a small smile. "Wait for it, Johnny."

Tuohay turned to Eliza and McNamara. "As for us, we need shovels." His face turned grim. "And we need to locate the nephew's grave and pay it a visit. *Tonight.*"

*

A midnight mist immersed Plymouth in an ethereal river of eddying vapors and undulating wisps beneath the broken moonlight. Tuohay shambled down Church Street, his coat wrapped tightly about him in the chilly haze, the dirt road packed under his feet. The opaque gloom transformed the gable-roofed buildings into desolate hulks with vacant sockets for eyes, death-like in their stillness.

The mist parted as a horse and buggy careened past him from Pond Street, the clatter of the horse's hooves audible long after the fog swallowed them again. Tuohay turned north up an unmarked dirt row, the sprinkling of a new rain cool against his face. The moon had disappeared. After a long sojourn up the row, he paused at the gated entrance to the graveyard, the mist low enough to reveal the tombstones closest by.

A shadow rose from behind the bones of a dying oak tree. The black form was that of a man. "Who goes there?"

"A midnight owl," Tuohay replied, stepping under the gate where the man stood. McNamara glared back at him.

"You are mad, Tuohay. *Mad.*"

"Yet you have come. Does that not make you mad as well?"

McNamara eyed the darkness warily. "If we are caught—"

"Then you will tell them that you accosted me here breaking the law, and I will adhere to the story. You have nothing to fear."

"Lie to the authorities? Who do you take me for? I thought you were a man of truth, Tuohay."

A rough smile broke across Tuohay's face. "A man *seeking* truth. I never claimed to be anything more."

"Is that so?"

Tuohay stared across the twisted grass of the dark graveyard. "It is." He bent close to gate, muttering to himself. "Eldredge said he would leave it here... ah, yes."

"Is that a lamp?"

Tuohay struck his lighter to the wick, and within a moment a dull glow emitted from the shuttered lantern. He allowed only a slight beam to escape, which danced eerily in the fog. "This way."

"And Eldredge?"

"As planned, Eldredge will not be involved with our activities tonight. He's leaving by stage for Boston within the hour—I need him to look into 1896 passenger lists from Belfast, and to work out a coded operations book from the RIC."

"Don't know how you think he'll get a hold of passenger lists at his late hour."

"He's a statistician that consults for the Immigration and Emigration Office, and two dozen other agencies. He has the keys to more lists and data in Boston than the census bureau—of which he also has access to."

"Right." McNamara did not inquire further and the two men struck into the expansive grounds of the graveyard, taking to the headstones rather than the paths. Large, bare trees rose from the darkness like sentinels, glaring down at the men with accusing stares.

McNamara pulled the collar of his coat tight around his throat. "What in high heaven do you hope to accomplish out here?"

"I have to know if Father Abrams Valentine is actually buried in his grave."

McNamara's voice dropped to a hiss as if the graves themselves were listening. "You really believe the death of Father Donnelly's nephew could have been a hoax?"

"I have reason to believe it was, yes."

"What reason?"

"Look—there!" Tuohay pointed to a pinprick of light at the top of a nearby hill. "That would be our man."

With renewed purpose Tuohay marched in the direction of the light, lasting only a few moments more before dissipating into the fog. McNamara kept pace with a grim look, his right hand thrust into his pocket.

"Damnable fog," McNamara muttered, wiping the moisture from his forehead.

"Could not have picked a more appropriate night, in fact," Tuohay replied. "It will shield our activities."

"I don't like the sound of that, Tuohay."

Tuohay grunted as his leg stiffened beneath him. "No one said this was going to be a clean business."

They were greeted by a cold blast of air at the summit of the hill. The scent of the sea was heavy upon it. Tuohay slid the shield back from the lantern's glass and allowed a beacon of light to shine. A moment later a similar beacon responded some fifty feet away.

They approached at a hurried clip and came upon the figure in the center of a row of graves. A large rock stood at the apex, shielding Eliza from the wind. Despite that, her cheeks were ruddy from the cold.

Setting her lantern down, Eliza's usual crooked smile was missing. "You sure about this?"

"You know which is his?"

Eliza led them to a stout marker, the gray stone barely marred by the weather. She kneeled beside it and wiped a crust of dirt from the name. "Here."

Beneath
This stone lie the Remains of

Rev. Abrams Valentine

Late of St. Malachy's Church
Who died March the 1ˢᵗ, 1896
Aged 36

"St. Malachy's," Tuohay whispered. "There is one in Belfast, not far from City Hall."

McNamara frowned. "Why would they bury 'im here, if his work was done in Ireland?"

"That's the entire point of our endeavor tonight," Tuohay replied. He watched as Eliza pointed at the bare dirt before the stone. Thin grass, still struggling against the last vestiges of winter, surrounded it.

"The grave itself should be six years old," she said, standing and brushing the dirt from her black skirt, "but it looks less than even a few months, taking into account the passing of winter."

"We need to get to work," said Tuohay, shivering as a cold wind blew past him. The fog receded as a curtain of slanted rain took its place. Eliza stooped over a rolled carpet and unfurled it flat. Dragging it beside the grave, the lantern light fell upon a pair of shovels, a crowbar, and a cord of rope.

"This is madness," McNamara growled.

"No," replied Tuohay through gritted teeth, "this is us getting to the bottom of the mystery. Literally, I am afraid." He seized one of the shovels with a gloved hand and dropped his cane to the ground. Steadying himself with his good leg, he thrust the shovel into the grave with a crunch. The soil gave way. With a grunt, he heaved the dirt onto the carpet.

"The dirt goes there so it can be easily transferred back when we are done," said Tuohay. He struck again, and the rain lashed down like a whip. "Mr. McNamara?"

McNamara stood with the other shovel in his hand. He remained rooted in place, his eyes wide with anguish. "I can't do it."

"Give it here," Eliza commanded McNamara, holding a gloved hand out for the shovel. The old man hesitated. "Is there a problem with a woman takin' over, Mac?"

McNamara handed the shovel to her with a grunt. "I've seen plenty of women digging graves in my time, Miss Eliza. During the war it was a common thing for the camp women to get to their work after a bloody skirmish. It ain't 'bout that, not at all." He looked at the grave ruefully. "It's… it's just not proper, this course of action."

He met Tuohay's gaze, but the inspector was unswerving. With a soft apology, McNamara departed, the darkness swallowing him.

"So much for him," Eliza said, squaring up to the grave with her shovel. She stabbed it into the earth and buried the spade with a well-place stomp. "Shall we?"

"The dirt is still loose," Tuohay remarked, turning back to the grave. He thrust his spade in and broke out another chunk of wet soil. "The earth is fissured—it seems it was broken recently, and was packed hastily. Good news for us."

"Should be a song, then," Eliza muttered. She scavenged out a chunk of earth and tossed it onto the awaiting carpet.

With shared grimaces, the pair commenced digging, their efforts frustrated by Tuohay's lame leg, and after thirty minutes he was digging from his knees. Eliza's skirt was tucked into her bicycle boots, which were spattered brown in the lantern light.

The hole dependably filled with rainwater, creating a slope of mud that fought to fill the widening gap. Time became less a measure of seconds and minutes, and more a measure of shovel strokes and progress into the hole. Tuohay, his chest rattling, pulled his flask from his pocket and took a long swig. The hole was nearly two feet across and as many deep.

Attempting to stand, he grasped his leg as it buckled beneath him. "Cursed thing," he hissed, using his shovel to prop himself up.

"Take a break, Jack," Eliza said, her face flushed from the strain. "Maybe Johnny is done with that code and could come back and help." From her tone, it was evident she was only half-kidding.

"I cannot leave this to you alone," Tuohay said.

"Nice try, Jack. I'm not made of glass, you know."

Eliza worked methodically, the rain battering down as the wind howled the call of the dead. All was lost to the pair except the small world revealed by the flickering lanterns: Eliza struggling against the grave, her shovel rising and falling, piles of dripping soil transferring in heaps onto the carpet. Her face was red from exertion, but white beneath, displaying a mixture of action and fatigue.

"Dammit all," Eliza muttered on more than on occasion as portions of the hole caved in on themselves, leaving her knee-deep in soil to be re-dug. But she stuck with it, intense to the point of obsession.

The rain had subsided to a shower when Tuohay pulled his pocket-watch out. "Just after two," he said. The hole was nearly four feet deep, but just wide enough for Eliza to stand in.

"I cannot—cannot go on," she gasped, leaning against the side. She managed a weak smile, but there was desperation in her gaze. "We'll never finish this before sunrise."

"Come out of there," ordered Tuohay.

"No, it's hopeless, Jack."

Tuohay peered into the water-filled hole. "I need to finish what I started."

Eliza eyed Tuohay skeptically. "Even in full health it would be nearly impossible. As it is, you are in no condition—"

"Please, Eliza." Tuohay's statement was emphasized by a chest-rattling cough. "Let me down there."

Eliza took a hand up and climbed from the hole. The crunch of soil marked the commencement of Tuohay's efforts as he slid in, and Eliza turned away to stare into the blackness surrounding her. Finding Tuohay's flask, she took a long swallow and huddled in the cold, the rhythm of the digging lulling her into a fatigue-laden sleeplessness.

The thunk of metal on wood awoke Eliza from her doze nearly an hour later.

"Get the lantern over here," ordered Tuohay, his voice little more than a rasp. "In the light, shall our evils be exposed."

Eliza grabbed one of the lanterns and leaned over the side, allowing the light to spill into the hole. The point of the shovel rested against a slat of wood the length of a hand—the first exposure of the coffin.

"Well, you found it," said Eliza. The sight of the coffin gave pause to the affair, and the two stared at the exposed wood in contemplative silence. "Jack...."

"I know."

The silence endured for another few moments until Eliza broke it with a harsh whisper. "What are we *doing*? This is a man's final resting place."

"I need a drink," said Tuohay. He reached up to Eliza who handed him his flask. Taking a long draught, he bent to a knee. The walls of the exposed grave closed in around him as he huddled at the bottom, his eyes on the exposed coffin. He traced it delicately with his fingers, the dirt around him crumbling down to slide over his knees and boots.

"What now?" asked Eliza. "Can we get the rest of it cleared off in time?"

Tuohay did not have a chance to respond before Eliza's eyes widened. "Jack!"

A chill ran down Tuohay's spine. "What is it?"

"Get out. Get out!"

Tuohay froze, the fear in Eliza's voice springing to mind goblins and ghouls. He took hold of his senses and followed her gaze into the darkness. Baubles of lights approached through the fog at a rapid pace.

"We have visitors." Tuohay offered Eliza his hand and she pulled him up, her boots sliding in the wet soil. He was wheezing as he grabbed his cane. "We best get out of here."

"But what about the grave?"

"If we are caught, the grave will be the least of our worries." Tuohay limped in the opposite direction of the approaching lanterns, Eliza jogging at his side. A voice echoed from the mist behind them, followed by another.

"I can barely see out here," Eliza whispered. Gravestones rose from the mist like specters, some tall and looming, others short and crumbling. Tuohay's breaths came in spurts as his face broke into a cold sweat.

Suddenly the voices rose to shouts, and the lanterns convened like distant will-o'-the-wisps on a dark location.

"They've found our work," Eliza said, a tinge of fear in her voice. "Who are they?"

208

"Constables, I believe," replied Tuohay, his voice strained from fatigue. Suddenly he was on the ground, his cane lost to the mist. He swore as he tried to stand, his lame leg tangled with a shin-high gravestone.

"Are you alright?"

A whistle pierced the air, and the distant lanterns scattered directions. Voices called back to one another as they progressed forward.

"I need my cane," Tuohay said.

Eliza searched the darkness frantically, the voices coming closer with each passing moment. "Here it is!"

She handed it to him, helping Tuohay stand. His face was white with exhaustion. "Go, Eliza. Leave me here."

"Not a chance, Jack. Come on."

Tuohay suddenly broke into a coughing fit, his face contorting with pain. He attempted to quiet it, but the force of the attack was overwhelming. A single lantern seemed to suddenly edge in their direction.

"I think someone heard us," Eliza whispered.

Tuohay couldn't speak. Wiping blood form his lips, he waved Eliza away. Declining his gallantry, she pulled Tuohay by the arm further into the mist. The ground sloped down at their feet, the grass slick. An ancient oak materialized from the darkness, its leafless branches a twisted maze of claws scraping at the moon. Reaching the tree, they turned back to see the lantern light less than fifty feet away, the tramping of boots marking its hastened approach.

"He's got us," Tuohay hissed, leaning against the oak. Eliza circled around the tree as the yellow light broke through the mist.

The sound of heavy breathing came from the shadowed form with the lantern. The man stopped his approach and lifted his lantern up so that the light fell directly on Tuohay.

"I should'a known it was you," said Inspector Frost, his voice full of wrath. "What the devil do you think you're doing out here? *Digging up a grave?*"

Tuohay sheltered his eyes against the light. "Running an investigation, just like you."

"Like hell." Frost took a step closer. "What were you lookin' for?"

"How did you know we were out here?"

"I'm the one askin' the questions."

A voice called in the distance. The other lanterns were lost to sight. "I'll answer them after I get some answers from you, Tuohay. I figured out the little attack at the hotel was a *ruse*, probably to get rid of me. No bullet holes. No trace of an attacker, or you. This is some kind of game to you, is that it?"

"I needed some space to work," said Tuohay. "Which, based on current circumstances, it appears you are not willing to give me."

"Where are your friends? I know you weren't working out here alone." Frost carefully made a half circle around the massive tree, exposing the shadows at its base, all the while keeping a strand of light pooled on Tuohay. "Not hidin' behind the tree, anyhow."

"*If* I had friends out here, they would be long gone by now. As you know, I have this slowing me down." He indicated his cane. "But as it turns out, I was alone."

"You? With that leg of yours? And with two shovels?"

"In case one broke. A shovel, that is. Not a leg."

"I don't have time to jest. What are you up to?"

Tuohay leaned against his cane and regarded the shadowed form of Frost hidden behind the lantern. "The coffin of Father Abrams Valentine is empty, inspector. There's no body in there."

"*What?*"

"His death in 1886 was a ruse. A ruse because he was part of the diamond heist. But I need to see inside the coffin to provide evidence for my theory."

"He was part of the diamond heist?" Frost laughed. "Half of the force thinks *you* were in on the heist."

Tuohay wiped the sweat from his brow with a gloved hand, leaving a trace of mud streaked across it. "I need to know that the body is not in there."

"You need to explain."

"Not now, not here."

"You're not calling the shots, Tuohay."

"Inspector, do you care about discovering the truth of the diamond?"

Frost took a moment to answer. When he did, his authoritative stance had changed to a more conspiratorial tone. "Look, Tuohay. You know I do. But do you think I have the authority to dig up a priest's grave? On what basis? I have done some things in my time, sure. But *that*?"

"You are missing the point. From your perspective, the coffin was *already broken into*, and the perpetrators were in the process of re-burying it when your lights scared them off."

"You're a bastard."

"I do not care about the credit, I just need to know."

"I would need to check the contents of the coffin for signs of robbery," said Frost. "That's your tact, is it? Get me to finish what you started. But why on earth would I do that for you?"

"Not for me. You want answers, just like I do. Need I remind you of that?" Tuohay coughed into his sleeve. "And what if the diamond is there? For all I know, it very well could be."

That revelation drew a breath from Frost. It was followed by a look of suspicion, but the initial excitement at the possibility could not be extinguished from his eyes.

A series of calls broke out from the darkness. A lantern appeared in the distance, cresting a nearby hill. "Now you're just playing me," Frost growled.

"I am headed to Doctor Kearney's apartment on Washington Street in Boston," Tuohay said. "There is a carriage leaving here at the break of dawn. My advice is for you to finish the job here— investigate the coffin, get to the truth. If there is a body, collar me at the doctor's and I will not resist. But if there is *no* body, as I suspect—"

"I get your point," Frost snapped. He swore under his breath. "I know I shouldn't do this… but get goin', already. And Tuohay—we never had this conversation." He turned and shouted into the darkness, his call met by another. With a quick pace he headed back in the direction of Father Abrams's grave.

The darkness poured over Tuohay, bringing with it a blanket of silence.

"Lucky thing for him he left when he did." Eliza's voice came from the branches above. "I was ready to drop on him like a stone."

Tuohay wheezed in surprise, a tinge of humor on his lips. "How the blazes did you get up *there*?"

"Beats me," was the shaky reply.

"Can you get down?"

"I'll figure it out." The branches rattled precariously. "That was quick thinking, Jack. But that Frost fella… he's a blackheart. I don't trust him."

"He's got motivations of his own," Tuohay allowed, "and I played off those. It bought us a little time, in any case." His voice softened. "Eliza, things are going to get… more dangerous from here on out. After this incident—I have a bad feeling. You have a career…a good career. An actual *life* outside of this madness I've lured you into."

"*Je-sus*, Jack. You're going to do this *now*?"

"Well—"

"Spare me the sob story, alright? I gotta concentrate on getting down without breaking my neck."

"No, listen for a moment. The danger, the implications. They are real. Very real. You can walk away, and be free of this mess. And I would understand. I'm already eternally grateful for the assistance you have provided."

"Maybe I should drop on *you*," Eliza scolded. "Knock some sense into that head of yours. I sure as *hell* am not walking away now. Especially considering my position in this tree."

There was a sigh from Tuohay, filled by a series of exasperated coughs and then a long silence.

"You still alive down there?"

"Do you own a gun, Eliza?"

There was a pause. "Why? Will it help get me out of this tree?"

"I'm being serious."

Another pause followed.

"I thought as much," Tuohay continued. "When we get to Boston, I want you to get yourself one. Nothing second hand. Riley's is the place. I am sure you know where it is."

"No more trying to talk me into deserting you?"

"You seem quite resolute, so no."

"But do I—do I really need a *gun*?"

"Yes, Eliza. Unfortunately, *now* would have been a preferable time to have it."

"*Now*? I was kidding about needing one to get out of the tree, you know."

Tuohay's voice was solemn. "Not for that. We're breaking into Father Donnelly's study—as soon as you get yourself down."

212

Candlelight

The pervading gloom surrendered to the wind along the shoreline, beneath which a barricade of black clouds momentarily locked away the eye of the moon. The sharp scent of the sea permeated the courtyard, the garden so inundated with the smell of brine it seemed to be drowning in the roiling waters. But the sea was distant, the thudding of the waves an echo in the waning night.

The rectory rose before Tuohay and Eliza like an old acquaintance, familiar yet harboring its own confidences. It seemed to whisper into the silence, to breathe its knowledge of secrets and dark deeds, but in a language that only the wind and memories understood. Eliza's boots clicked softly off the courtyard as she approached the rectory wall directly beneath the fateful balcony. The crimson stains on the rocks were invisible in the darkness, but the presence of the dried blood was as tangible as the rectory itself.

She stopped halfway along the courtyard, Tuohay joining her with the click of his cane. A rectangular wooden trellis was propped against the rectory wall, shadowed ivy climbing up the wooden framework like a fountain of twisting snakes. It rose to the height of the balcony, providing possible access to the study. Eliza studied the wooden lattice with grim determination.

"Think that thing will hold my weight?" She immediately reconsidered her question and turned abruptly to face Tuohay. "Actually, don't answer that."

"We can find another way."

"So are you actually saying that it won't hold my weight?" Eliza put her hands on her hips, pressing her sullied dress close to her figure.

"No, I am not saying that at all." Tuohay sensed that he was drifting into no-man's land, and spoke softly. "I am simply saying that if you have any doubts about this mode of ingress, there are other options to explore."

"If *I* have doubts?"

"You misunderstand." Tuohay tried to remove the tired strain from his voice. "Simply put, I don't want to place you in danger."

"It's a little late for that, Jack." She narrowed her gaze at

Tuohay. "And I appreciate your concern, but let's face it—we don't have time for gentlemanly manners. It's only a few hours before dawn, and we're both on the brink of utter exhaustion."

"I am in earnest. There may be other ways inside that are less fantastic."

Eliza shook her head. "We need access to Father Donnelly's study, and those balcony doors are a direct entry. The climb looks simple enough, and the lock was a flimsy thing, remember? Assuming the doors up there are locked at all."

"But *I* still need to get in there," Tuohay argued, his voice a harsh whisper. "I can't climb, so you'll be forced to navigate your way through the darkness. There is no telling if there are residents within, or what else you may run into."

"What, like goblins?"

"I was leaning towards something real."

"Look, it's simple enough. Tell me what we are searching for. I have sharp eyes and can cover ground quickly. I'll find it if it's there to be found."

Tuohay glared at his cane as if it were an enemy to be loathed. "Cursed thing. If I was not a shambles of a man—"

Eliza cupped Tuohay's chin in her hand, taking him by surprise. Her palm was wet and warm, and smelled faintly of earth. Her fingers pressed gently. "Stop being a ninny, Jack."

"Ninny?"

"Act like a child, get talked to like a child." Eliza smiled and slid her hand from his chin.

"You are right," Tuohay admitted. He took a moment to gather himself. "But there is still a complication. The issue at hand is that I do not know exactly how Father Donnelly would have documented what I am looking for."

"Try."

The moon broke from the clouds, its pale light reflecting off the surviving vestiges of the misty night. Tuohay led Eliza from the silvery eddies to the shadowed wall beneath the balcony. "Do you remember the medical journals?"

"Yes. There was a collection of thirty-four, and you said one of the journals was missing. Number... twenty-eight, I believe."

"Yes, the journal from 1896. The same year the diamond was stolen, and the year Father Abrams Valentine sailed to Plymouth to

214

die in the care of his uncle, Father Donnelly."

"So….the medical journal contains some kind of clue? And that is why it is missing?"

"I believe so."

"And you think I can find that journal?"

"No, I think it is gone," said Tuohay.

"Alright…so then?"

"It is possible what the journal contained may also be detailed in one of the other journals."

Eliza suddenly seemed tired. "In one of the other *thirty-three* journals."

"You said you have sharp eyes."

"Sure. But I didn't think I would need them to sift through thirty years worth of medical jargon while crouched in the dark. That sounds like a job for Johnny."

Tuohay chuckled. "Crouching in any form is not a job for Eldredge, never mind breaking into a rectory in the wee hours of the night."

"It's not exactly my cup of tea, either." Eliza was quiet for a moment. "How sure are you that this information will be in one of Donnelly's remaining journals?"

"A hunch, that is all."

"I figured." The lattice trembled as she tugged on it with her hands. "Seems sturdy enough. Well, no time like the present. What exactly will I be looking for?"

"Are you sure you want to do this on your own?"

Eliza let out a sigh of frustration. "Jack, we'll be arguing until morning if we keep this up. Just tell me the exact details, already."

"As you say," Tuohay relented. "Look for references to research on neurotoxins, especially in any of Donnelly's journals dating thirty years ago or so. Consider citations or inferences to research performed in Haiti as strong indicators that you are on the right track."

"Haiti?" Eliza sounded skeptical. "And neurotoxins. Yeah, that… makes sense."

"It will, in time. There is another term you should look for that will be a telltale clue—if you see the word in any of the journals, take the sources in hand."

"Sure thing. What's the term?"

Silence filled the night, broken only by the distant crash of the waves.

"Jack?"

"Zombi."

Eliza chuckled. "*Zombi?* Sounds like a phony word. What does it mean?"

Tuohay's voice was eerily soft, his tone matching the blackness surrounding them. "It means bringing back the dead from the grave."

*

The ticking of Tuohay's pocket watch stabbed into his ears. It had become the only relevant sound in the still night as he stood alone, the span between one click and the next excruciating. He closed his hand around the metallic counter, but muffling the sound brought no comfort.

Before him, the broken moonlight dappled the courtyard in a drifting white light, mirroring the gaps between the hazy clouds overhead that otherwise thwarted much of the moon's pale glow. The night's shadow, given life by the dance of the moonlight, stretched up the side of the rectory like a twisted hand, clawing its way into windows and the balcony doors.

Tuohay's attention was never parted from the presence of the dark stains that had seeped into the cobblestones, the blood of Father Donnelly black under the glimmer of moonlight.

"Come on, Eliza." It had been over fifteen minutes since she had climbed up the lattice-work onto the balcony and slipped into the study through the unlocked balcony doors. The curtains were drawn save a small crevice she had left open, but even that provided nothing but the darkness of the void.

A light appeared within.

It was dim, the flicker of a candle silhouetted against the heavy curtains. Tuohay caught his breath. He watched with rapt attention as the light floated away from him, carried by the apparition beyond his vision.

"Damn it," he cursed. Indecision wracked his brain as his gaze bore into the balcony doors and the barrier of blackness they represented. The light had diminished into the room, and had almost disappeared, when it came back closer to the doors again. It suddenly stilled, apparently set in one spot.

The curtains were thrust closed. Eliza's sign for trouble.

Tuohay's heart thudded in his chest as he limped with great effort across the courtyard, his cane smacking against the bloodstained stones. Knowing the front door was locked, he headed for a garden path through the hedges that led to a side door. Finding the knob with a trembling hand, he discovered it was locked. Swinging his bad leg in time with the cane, he limped furiously along the perimeter, investigating two more doors until finding a servants entrance that had been forced open.

The mere breath of a moment revealed the unimaginative use of a crowbar to gain entrance. Shouldering his way inside, Tuohay was greeted by a cramped cloakroom as black as the night outside.

The way led into a back pantry and the kitchen, but in the darkness little was discernable except the strange patterns and living forms the motionless objects surrounding him took. He stumbled into something—a chair—and it topped to the floor with a crash. His cane nearly slipped from his grasp as his palms grew slick with nervous sweat.

Somehow he reached a set of narrow stairs. Despite the racket he had created, he was careful in his approach. His leg was dead weight on the narrow steps, and he pulled it up behind him like a sack better left behind. Reaching the top, he tried to gather his bearings as he stared at the dark passageways opening before him.

A ghost flitted past his vision, nearly causing him to cry out. He realized with alarm that it was the candle that had caught his attention. Reaching into his jacket pocket, Tuohay quietly extracted his revolver and began the long approach towards where the light had been.

The candle itself was not visible, but the globe of light slowly materialized like a floating bauble in a black mire. Suddenly his cane clanged against something metal, the sound louder in his ears than any chorus of cathedral bells had ever been.

Knowing his cover was blown, Tuohay used the wall to lead him straight, the crack of his cane against the wooden floorboards an unwanted introduction.

And then he was in the study, crossing the threshold through a narrow doorway near the hearth. The room was large and dark and as quiet as the grave, except for the ticking of the grandfather clock from somewhere across the room.

The grandfather clock that once had been fifteen minutes fast.

"Eliza?" Tuohay's voice sounded like a harbinger in his own ears, an utterance of things gone wrong, of checkmate in three.

"I'm over here." Her voice was meek, strained. It came from a corner of the room.

Relief and dread poured over Tuohay in a toxic combination, causing his breaths to come in rapid bursts. Despite his efforts to prevent it, a wracking cough tore through his lungs and throat.

"Move to the balcony doors and move the curtain aside," a man's voice commanded.

"Who are you?" Tuohay demanded, pressing himself against the wall. His pistol felt heavy in his free hand.

"Get in front of the curtain and pull it open so I can see you!"

"Eliza—"

"It's Thayer," Eliza replied. She tried to sound brave, but there was a tremor in her voice. "He's got a gun, and it's pointed at me."

"I don't want anyone to get hurt," Thayer interjected. "Not you, not her, not me. So just do what I say."

Tuohay complied, walking to balcony doors behind the large mahogany desk and pulling the curtain aside. Moonlight spilled in, silhouetting Tuohay against the shimmering backdrop. There was movement from the darkness in front of him, and Eliza appeared, walking slowly in his direction. She looked disheveled but otherwise healthy. The ticking of the grandfather clock made time with her pace.

"Alright, now just put down that gun," Thayer said.

Tuohay rested his pistol on the desk. "Alright, Vestor. We are all reasonable people."

Thayer appeared on the fringe of the moonlight, his rugged face lined with worry. Wisps of blonde hair fell past his eyes, which were filled with suspicion.

"What are you doing here?" Thayer demanded. A small, snub nosed pistol was in his hand, the metal gleaming in the new light.

Tuohay met his gaze squarely. "I would ask the same of you."

"I'm looking for the affidavits. I'm supposing you may be doing the same."

"Nothing of the kind," Tuohay replied.

Thayer wiped his forehead with a sleeve. He was cloaked in a heavy, black trench coat. A crowbar was clutched in his opposite hand. He used it to point accusingly at Tuohay and Eliza.

"It's been you all along, hasn't it?" The crowbar shook in Thayer's hand. He let the pistol drift down in his other hand, where it pointed at the floor. "Inspector Tuohay. I thought you were one of us. One the good guys."

"I never claimed to be a good man, but my intentions are not criminal."

"Really." Thayer swallowed hard, trying to compose himself. "You are a suspect in the crime. I overheard officers talking about it. So what was it—you, Kip Crippen, and Father Donnelly?"

"Leave the investigating to the experts," said Tuohay.

"Is that supposed to be you? Then explain to me why you were fired from the RIC only weeks after the jewel theft, and yet claim to be an investigator still working for them? And why it is that Father Donnelly was found dead the morning after you interviewed him?" The room itself seemed hush at the mention of the dead priest, as if his spirit were listening.

"And then Kip Crippen found dead, *by you*, after gunshots were heard in Sara's house. You claimed it was who—Anna? And then Miss Hart's poisoning. I'm not sure how you did that, but you were present. And so was she." Thayer pointed at Eliza. "Hidden in the crowd. I recognize her face."

"I was there, that's right," said Eliza. "But as an investigator."

"No, no," said Thayer. "I haven't figured it all out yet, but I know you're behind this—you being here to tonight proves it!" His breathing was short, his nerves on edge. "Father Aiden *trusted* you, Mr. Tuohay. He believed you were a good man. And all along… all along you were betraying his trust, just like all of the other scoundrels he faced."

"You have it wrong, Vestor," said Tuohay. "There is a misunderstanding here."

"I've got to take you to the police. They're looking for you anyway."

"And what will you tell them? That you stumbled across us while you were breaking into a dead man's study?" Tuohay shook his head. "We can talk this through—"

"*No.*" Thayer raised the gun. "I'm not sure what I'll tell the authorities yet, but the fact of the matter is that I have the man responsible for the theft of the Templar Diamond, and for the deaths of at least three people. Step around the desk, if you will—"

A gravelly voice broke from the darkness. "Now just a moment."

It startled the group, and Thayer whirled around, his eyes wide. "Who's there?"

"Just me," was the reply. The voice was both assuring and authoritative.

"Mac," said Thayer, surprise and relief flooding his voice. "What are you doing here?"

The sound of McNamara's limp resounded through the room as he approached. His looming figure broke into the moonlight, and his grizzled face was dark and angry.

"None of you are to blame," he growled. "So just put down the gun, Vestor."

"But—"

"Do it. Tuohay and the woman are on the up and up."

"Hey, I have a name, thank you very much." Eliza's voice rang with defiance.

Thayer seemed confused, but he dropped his arms to his side. A short silence followed. Tuohay took the opportunity to address the old officer. "How in God's name did you find us here?"

"I told you I'm a bloodhound," replied McNamara with a grim smile. "I may not have wanted to help you raid that poor priest's grave, but I wasn't goin' to let you just wander off on your own either. I knew you'd get yourself into trouble soon enough—though this was even sooner than I expected."

"You followed us," said Tuohay.

"And more trouble's coming," McNamara added. Even as he spoke, a light appeared in the courtyard below, accompanied by the hollow echo of voices.

"Constables," Eliza warned, carefully peering out the window.

McNamara nodded as if expecting nothing less. "Time to go."

*

Tuohay peered out the window of the fast-moving carriage with tired eyes, the gray of morning casting a pallor across his face. In the distance the sea glittered like a silver thread, the sun still below the horizon but showering the edge of the world with the promise of new gold. A wind leaned on the high sea-grass, shifting their embodiment of solitude from stillness to a slight ripple.

The companions had escaped their predicament through little more than sheer luck, retreating through the front of the rectory as the Plymouth constables circled around to the smashed door in the back. From there it had been a quick discussion about leaving Plymouth immediately, and Tuohay taking McNamara and a reluctant Thayer on board the carriage awaiting them at the train station.

Eliza was taking an alternate route to avoid being seen together.

Tuohay turned his attention to his cigarette case, and procured a clove cigarette and lighter. A flash emitted from Tuohay's fingertips as the lighter gave birth to flame, startling the darkness into flight for an instant. He lit his cigarette and inhaled, flicking the ash upon the trembling floor.

McNamara and Thayer sat across from him, the former snoring into his scarf. Thayer was slouched on his side of the passenger bench, his arms crossed, his chin pressed against his chest. The spark of Tuohay's cigarette diverted his attention away from the passing landscape.

Tuohay exhaled lightly. "Shall we talk?"

"The only reason I didn't turn you in is because of Mac," said Thayer, glancing at the slumbering form beside him. "If there's anyone I trust, it's him."

"Then I'm glad he came when he did."

"But it still doesn't mean I trust *you* or your intentions," Thayer continued. "I've dealt with a lot of slippery clients in my time as a lawyer, and can sniff out deception."

"And what do you smell now?"

"Other than cloves, you mean?" Thayer straightened his posture, smoothing his long coat as he did so. "I smell the foul scent of a man who dug up a priest's grave. At least according to old Mac here."

"He's right about that," Tuohay acknowledged. "But the point is this—I believe the priest was not in the coffin."

Thayer's visage remained unchanged, almost as if he had expected some kind of outlandish reply. "But I suppose the famous Templar Diamond was?"

"No. More likely there was a pile of heavy stones roughly equal to the weight of a man." Tuohay exhaled a veil of smoke through his nostrils. "Let me ask you something, Mr. Thayer. When did you receive your invitation in silver lettering to the chase?"

Thayer's gaze narrowed. "I told you before that I did not receive one. I was made privy to Sara's and to Father Aiden Kearney's as their legal counsel, but that was the extent of it."

"You are staying with that claim?"

"I am."

"Then I would like to know exactly what you were doing in Father Donnelly's study last night."

"It's simple, really," Thayer responded, more quickly than Tuohay had expected. "I was looking for the missing affidavits— the affidavits given by Mary Hart and Kathryn Dwyer to me and Mr. McBarron at the law firm."

"You shared that with me already. I am more interested in *why*."

"I accompanied Mary Hart from Foxborough to Plymouth on the day she was poisoned," Thayer began. "Despite everything that man had done to her, the way he treated her—"

"Father Donnelly?"

"Yes," said Thayer. "Regardless of that, she was nearly inconsolable when she heard he was dead. And there was nothing Mac or I could say to change her mind about going to the funeral. So we did the only thing we could—we tried to keep her safe during her journey."

"McNamara stayed in Foxborough because he had received a telegram about my impending visit, and meanwhile you accompanied Mary to Plymouth."

"That was the way of it," Thayer acknowledged. "During the passage, she confided in me. More than that, she implored me for help. She was emotional, and perhaps even… frightened."

"What did she tell you?"

"Mary confessed that prior to the interview you had with Sara Conall at the law firm, Sara had inquired to Mary about the location of the affidavits. Mary knew it was a strange question, but Sara simply said she wanted to know that they were safe, so that she would not fret over them. Mary knew we kept them in the safe at the law firm, and told her as much."

"Sara Conall was interested in the affidavits?" Tuohay reached into his jacket for his flask and offered a drink to Thayer, who declined with a motion of his hand. Tuohay took a swig as Thayer continued his account.

"Of course I did not think anything of it at the time, but I recently realized that I had given the keys to the law firm to Sara so she could get in for the interview with you. But the key ring also had the key to the safe on it, and the affidavits were discovered to be missing the morning after the interview."

"But why would Sara have any interest in the affidavits?"

"Mary told me that Sara had recently begun dredging up the years of hardships her family endured because of the trial between Aiden Kearney and Archbishop Walsh, and how it had devastated their wellbeing. Evidently, Sara implored Mary, even before the death of her uncles, to consider the negative impact of an appeal. The mud-slinging press, enduring the scorn of an entire city, and so on. As strange as it may seem to you, I understand Sara's point of view. My own career suffered, as did the law firm of McBarronThayer itself, from that folly of a trial."

Tuohay's gaze narrowed. "You are saying the Mary Hart believed that Sara did not want an appeal to occur."

"That is right. In fact, Mary confided in me on our trip to Plymouth—as I said, the very day she was poisoned—that Sara demanded to know if Mary intended on furthering Aiden's cause for truth. Father Donnelly was now dead, the affidavits were missing, and Aiden Kearney, the very man who had been wronged in the first place, was three months buried. Sara's point to Mary was that it *did not matter anymore*, and it was best to let sleeping dogs lie. Simply put, Sara didn't want any more trouble."

"And Mary's response to her?"

"Mary was *still* intent on finding a way to tell the truth, and she told Sara that. In her account to me, Mary said she felt a chill from Sara after she said that."

Tuohay considered what he had heard for a moment, glancing out the window. Without adjusting his gaze, he inquired, "And how did Mary ask you for help?"

"First of all, she asked me to help in my capacity as a solicitor. She still wanted to expose the archbishop's role in her being forced to lie at the trial, and in her being locked away in the Danvers asylum. But deeper still, she wanted to see justice served for

Inspector Frost in the aforementioned activities and, in her belief, the murder of her friend Kathryn Dwyer. "

Tuohay turned his gaze back to Thayer. Weary though it was, a glimmer burned within. "I see. But what about the affidavits, as you mentioned? How does Sara's involvement connect you to Father Donnelly's study last night?"

"There was one more bit of information Mary shared with me that had come from Sara."

"Yes?"

"Sara told Mary there were other ways to handle those that had betrayed her uncle Aiden. That they could use the affidavits in another manner, as a threat to hang over Father Donnelly's head—"

"Blackmail." Tuohay pondered as he exhaled another cloud of blue-tinted smoke. "Perhaps over the archbishop, and even Inspector Frost as well. It seems a dangerous game for Sara to play."

"Mary would have none of it," said Thayer with a lasting frown, "but Sara told her it had already begun. Sara said that Father Donnelly was a wealthy man, more wealthy than even Mary knew, and that had already paid his first installment to keep Sara from sending the affidavits to the press."

"So you believe Sara sold him... one of the affidavits? And kept the second?"

"I was not certain," Thayer shrugged. "After Mary was poisoned, I was at a loss. I could not let these crimes go unanswered, and... seeing the way she died, it changed me. My resolve. I know it was a long shot, but if I found evidence of the affidavits in Father Donnelly's study, I would have known there was truth to Mary's claims. What else could I do?"

"Stayed out of it, for one. It is not your place to put yourself in the midst of an investigation such as this."

The carriage hit a rut in the road, causing a loud, wet snore to emit from McNamara. The carriage continued to rattle for several seconds before reverting back to a mere trembling.

Thayer glared at Tuohay. "And what about you? What was your reason for being there last night? And with the constables after you, it seems."

"My partner and I were looking for *actual* evidence," Tuohay replied evenly. He tapped the medical journal resting at his side for emphasis.

Thayer raised an inquisitive brow, but Tuohay turned his gaze back to the window, throwing a blanket of silence across them.

"You are not the only one with actual evidence," Thayer said, breaking the silence. The soft tone in his voice caused Tuohay to turn back.

"What do you mean by that?"

"Has your investigation uncovered the existence of a young man by the name of Colin Allotrope?"

"It has," Tuohay replied carefully. "What of him?"

"Then you must know who his father is."

Again Tuohay's response was guarded. "Yes."

"Father Abrams Valentine." Thayer studied Tuohay closely. "But what about the boy's *mother*?"

Tuohay stared at Thayer. "You know who she is?"

Thayer met Tuohay's gaze, wavered, and then grew resolute. "I do. The young man's mother is Anna Conall, Sara's sister."

Tuohay leaned back, astonishment registering on his face. "*Anna?*"

"Eighteen years ago Anna and Sara ran away from Father Aiden Kearney when they discovered that Anna was pregnant, afraid of his reaction. To make matters worse, the father of the unborn child was a priest, Father Abrams Valentine. It seems it was no coincidence on the part of Abrams."

"Meaning?"

Thayer frowned. "If you are Father Abrams, what better way is there to get back at a muckraking, holier-than-thou priest like Father Aiden Kearney than to sleep with the sanctimonious priest's niece?"

Tuohay sighed. "She was just a piece in Abram's game."

"Anna and Sara fled to another uncle, Doctor Kearney, who took them in," Thayer continued. "He delivered the boy, and kept the whole scandal hush-hush. He got Colin set up at the Trinitarians of Mary convent, with help from Valentine's uncle, Father Donnelly. It's been a well-kept secret for eighteen years."

"Why didn't you share this information with me earlier? That ties Doctor Kearney and Anna to Abrams Valentine, as well as Father Donnelly."

"Everyone has secrets. Especially lawyers." Thayer massaged

his temples as if struck by a sudden headache. With a weak smile, he indicated Tuohay's right-hand coat pocket.

"I think I'll take that drink now, inspector."

A Warm Discovery

The seismic rattle of the tracks above the Winthrop Street rooftops of Charlestown did not elicit a response from the man standing in their shadow. To a newcomer the thunderous clanking and groaning would have caused an involuntary shudder as any number of unfortunate scenarios ran through the imagination, the most common that the sky was falling with a metallic roar. But to a true Charlestownian the reverberation was nothing more than the common occurrence of a train passing along the elevated tracks.

Tuohay lit a clove-scented cigarette and peered from his gloomy roost to the snake-like creation above him. The El was an unmistakable intrusion upon the old historic city, meandering through the tight-knit communities like an unwanted guest and arching over the bunkered homes in a wave of skeletal metal. Responsible for an influx of industrial business, including a boom to the previously well-established Naval Yard, the El was looked upon as a mixed blessing by the community. An eyesore in a seaside port with such worldly attractions as the Bunker Hill Memorial and Patrick Keely's masterful St. Mary's Church, it was truly representative of the evolving industrial age.

Tuohay looked upon it with disdain.

Checking his watch, he stood and stretched his leg, leaning on his cane for support as he struck out towards the heart of Charlestown.

He stopped at a crossroads, a thick stream of horse-and-buggy traffic rumbling past. Picking the right moment, he crossed at a brisk clip, despite his sickly complexion and barely concealable limp. He shifted his top hat to deflect the sun shining through the elevated tracks above.

The resounding clatter of the tracks grew in intensity as a train rumbled overhead, drowning out all other sounds. Tuohay muttered under his breath as debris floated down from the tracks like fine snow. Brushing himself off, he continued in the direction of his destination.

A few minutes later, Tuohay was craning his neck, eyeing the three-story brick building before him. "Doctor Kearney's apartment building," he murmured, checking the rumpled note from McNamara. "Third floor."

He stepped back into the shadows and waited. Within fifteen minutes, a woman in a rose-hued tailored blouse and white skirt marched down the sidewalk, the black parasol in her hands nearly leaping from her hands at a strong breeze, but she continued unabated. A fashionable straw hat entwined with roses completed the ensemble, and matched the burgundy curls framing her eyes.

"Miss Eliza." Tuohay stepped from his perch.

"Jack," Eliza nodded. Her lips were painted a soft red, matching the rogue faintly applied to her cheeks.

"We are apart two hours and you return transformed." He shook his head in wonder. "Truly, I never would have guessed that you have barely slept in the last two days."

"A girl's got her methods." She cast a critical eye at Tuohay. "You could have used some help, though. You look a fright."

"Appreciate the opinion."

"It's a *fact*, Jack. Trust me."

"Point taken." He met her gaze. "You did remember to stop at Riley's, of course?"

Eliza patted the black velvet purse hanging at her side. "You bet."

"Oh, I nearly forgot," she continued, her eye catching the end of a newspaper sticking from her purse. "Seen this yet?" She freed the paper from the purse's embrace.

"I am afraid not."

"Take a gander."

Tuohay accepted the paper and stepped into the sunlight for a better view.

GRABBED FROM THE GRAVE

Final Resting Place of Priest Believed to be Hiding Place of Templar Diamond.

Grave Robbers Take Everything, including Remains.

Police Stumble Across the Scene Too Late.

Diamond Still at Large.

"The coffin was empty," Tuohay said, slapping the paper against his leg with enthusiasm. "Just as we suspected."

"Just as *you* suspected," Eliza corrected him. "And the imaginary 'grave robbers' got the wrap for cleaning out the casket, including the Templar Diamond." Eliza smirked. "Quite the leap, even for a newspaper. You should read the rest of the article, it's a dandy."

"Inspector Frost needed a legitimate reason to permit the dig, so there you have it." Tuohay stuffed the paper back into her purse. "I have the information I need, in any case."

"Which is?"

"The death of the Nephew—Father Abrams Valentine—was fabricated, and only someone with medical knowledge could have helped pull it off."

"Doctor Kearney?"

"I am leaning towards Father Donnelly. *Imhotep* himself."

"So Father Robert Donnelly *was* involved in this whole thing?"

"The shadows of deceit are beginning to disperse before the light of truth—ah, there's our man." Tuohay pointed down the street. The rotund form of Eldredge in a dapper gray suit and blue ascot emerged from a small crowd. He strolled about almost aimlessly, looking into storefronts and pausing at various stoops, his course only slightly angled in their direction. Occasionally he bent down as if strangely fascinated with the ground.

"What in high heaven is he doing?" Eliza asked. "Is he drunk?"

"I believe that is his version of acting covertly."

"Hasn't he ever just taken a walk? You know, down the street like a regular joe? The old 'hide in plain sight' routine."

"He does things his own way, as you are well aware."

Eliza smiled at that. "I didn't realize how much I missed you two."

After several minutes Eldredge finally sidled up to them, not addressing either until he was within whispering distance. Even then, he allowed only the slightest nod as he reached into his pocket for a pipe, fumbling about a bit. Finally he extracted it and a lighter.

He cleared his throat and murmured, "Greetings."

Eliza suppressed a laugh. "And a firm and cheery greetings to you, good sir."

Eldredge cast a confused glance at Eliza. "What?"

Getting no response but a smile, he took a step backwards so he could whisper to Tuohay. "I wasn't followed. Sure of it, my good man."

"Splendid." Tuohay regarded his friend. "Did you have any good fortune with your work last night?"

"The RIC code is broken, thanks in part to your recollection of key words. As you anticipated, it was operational details. Times, locations, names. Everything and anything needed to locate the diamond for a heist."

"And the other task?"

"I visited a friend at the customs house this morning; found our man on an 1896 passenger list—the *Carinthia*, Cunard Line. Belfast to Liverpool, from there to Boston."

"What man?" Eliza asked.

"Father Abrams Valentine, sailing to America due his sickness," Tuohay replied. "It appears he was, in fact, near Belfast during the time of the diamond crime." He turned back to Eldredge. "We'll review the RIC information in more detail after our visit to Doctor Kearney. No time now."

Eliza addressed Tuohay. "Jack, was it really necessary to go through this whole rigmarole? Three separate routes to the doctor's apartment? If Inspector Frost wanted, he could just snag us now like three peas in a pod. He knows we're here, remember?"

"He won't interfere," Tuohay replied. "If he plays his cards right, he benefits from our findings. But there are others on the lookout. For your own sake, it's best that you and Eldredge are not seen in public with me."

Eliza rolled her eyes. "Not that again. But I guess I asked for it this time." She looked up at the apartment building. "Can we go in, already?"

"Yes." Tuohay led the way up the stone staircase to the front door of the building, his cane clicking in time with his steps. "It's time to get to the bottom of the good doctor's role, if any, in Mary Hart's death."

"Inspector Tuohay!"

Tuohay, Eliza, and Eldredge turned as one at the voice from the street. They were at the top of the landing, entering the doctor's building. A woman in a slim pea green dress was approaching, her threadbare jacket hunched at the shoulders.

The troubled face of Sara Conall came clearly into view as she reached the building, and she raced up the steps, her cheeks red from hurrying.

"Miss Conall," said Tuohay, wonder registering in his voice, "what are you doing here?"

"Considering this is my uncle's flat, I believe the question is more appropriate pointed at the three of you." She crossed her arms to ward of a sudden breeze. "McNamara visited me this morning and told me of your plans to visit my uncle."

Eliza craned her neck so she could see past Sara. "Is that man with you? A friend of McNamara's, maybe?"

The group shifted their gaze to a man in an olive suit leaning against a post supporting the elevated trolley tracks. One hand was thrust in his coat pocket, a newspaper squeezed to his body by the same arm. He held a burning cigarette in the other hand, which he raised to his lips.

"No, I've never seen him before," Sara replied.

"Well, we have," Eliza muttered.

"Inside, quickly," Tuohay ordered, corralling the group with his free arm and waving them into the dark passageway of the tenement building.

"What's going on?" Sara demanded as the front door closed behind them.

"We are here to pay your uncle a visit," Tuohay said, looking down the narrow passageway. "I was told that the police have him listed as possible suspect in Mary Hart's death. There are details I need to ask him about that."

"He would never hurt her," Sara replied, her voice soft. "He is not that kind of man."

"I understand," said Tuohay. "But I still need to talk to him." He motioned towards a rickety staircase with a grimace. "It appears we will have to take the stairs."

Sara glanced at Tuohay's cane and stopped his forward motion with a touch of her hand. "There is a lift. Follow me."

The three partners followed the woman in the green dress down the narrow hallway, reaching a lobby with several hallways escaping from it. A rectangular exit was established to their left, closed off by a rather fanciful iron gate.

Sara led them to it and pulled the gate open, which folded upon itself with a high-pitched whine. Guiding them through, she followed and closed the gate. They were standing on a small lift, a silver handle protroduing from a gear-works box marked with floor numbers.

Eliza frowned. "There is no operator for the lift?"

"No," Sara replied, "the building is owned by a cooperative who did not deem it necessary to hire an operator to move a lift up and down." For emphasis, she took hold of the gear and shifted it to the marker for '3'. The lift rumbled to life beneath their feet and slowly began its ascent.

Tuohay turned to Sara, raising his voice over the clamor caused by the squealing winch and pulleys. "Care to tell us what you are doing here?"

Sara's frown warned of dark news. "I came to Boston as soon as I received word of Mary's condition, and stayed at a hotel last night. I was at the hospital yesterday when they declared her...declared her dead." She forced the last statement out with a lump in her throat. "I went back to the hospital this morning to meet up with my uncle. As I was waiting, Mr. McNamara appeared, looking haggard. He told me he had recently separated company from you, inspector, and that you were intending to see my uncle. It was at that moment that we heard from a frantic hospital worker that Mary Hart's body had somehow been stolen from the autopsy table."

The statement elicited a round of exclamations from the listeners, accentuated by the grinding halt of the lift as it reached the third floor. Eldredge moved the gate aside, and the group waited in a hush until they were clear of the lift to continue the conversation.

"The body was stolen?" Tuohay peered at Sara with a hard gaze.

"Before the autopsy could be performed," Eliza added. "Meaning the exact cause of death will remain a mystery."

"That is what I heard," Sara confirmed. "I looked for Uncle Sean at the hospital to establish the truth while McNamara went to find Mr. Thayer, but my uncle was nowhere to be found. It was corroborated by several other sources, and eventually the police arrived. That is when I decided to come here."

The group followed Sara's lead in disquieting silence, stopping at a door in the center of a windowless hallway. Sara drew a key from her coat pocket and fit it into the lock. Turning the doorknob, she opened the door a crack.

"Uncle Sean? It's me, Sara. I am with Inspector Tuohay." Her voice faded into the darkness of the apartment without a response. She called again, this time louder, but was met only with silence.

She turned back to Tuohay, concern in her emerald eyes. "He's not here. I have a bad feeling about this."

"I have no authority to enter your uncle's flat, but under the circumstances I deem it the necessary thing to do."

After only a moment Sara nodded in agreement, and fully pushed the door open into the apartment. They entered one at a time, the oppressive heat of the room washing over them like a summer wave.

"Gads, it is stuffy in here," Eldredge remarked, tugging at his collar as he entered. In only a few moments beads of sweat began to form on his forehead.

"You've got that right," Eliza consented, removing her jacket as she looked around.

They were situated in the parlor of a three-room flat consisting of two separate bedrooms and the parlor, which by appearances also functioned as the kitchen. Two windows at either end of the apartment allowed enough light to see by, though it was gray and shadowed.

A cast iron stove with six burners sat in the corner of the room with copper pans arranged upon it, but it was not responsible for the heat. On the wall above, a wooden shelf held a variety of spices and oils, and several iron cooking utensils hung from it in tidy fashion. A basket of pressed laundry sat in a corner.

"There are vents in the floor," Eliza said, pointing at an iron grating in the floor. She bent near it with her hands. "It's like an inferno coming through."

"The furnace is in the basement," said Sara. "The building was renovated a few years ago, which included new piping for heat. I remember my uncle talking about it with great satisfaction when it was installed."

"A centralized heating source for the tenants. Quite the

amenity," commented Eldredge.

"When it is not driving you from your own apartment," Eliza muttered.

"Uncle Sean?" Sara left the group where they stood and wandered towards the bedrooms, calling out her uncle's name.

Tuohay turned to his companions. "Look around."

They got to work quickly, separating their focuses on varying parts of the apartment. They had only begun to look when Sara appeared in the doorway of the one of the bedrooms, her face pale.

"Inspector, you may want to see this."

Tuohay turned to the others. "Keep at it." He limped towards Sara, trying to decipher the gravity of the concern etched across her face. Coming upon her, he was surprised to find her trembling. "What is it?"

Sara pointed into the room beyond. It was a small affair with a single bed and nightstand, a candle perched upon it. The window was closed and curtained, casting a shadow across the chamber. Despite the gloom, the object of Sara's apprehension was clearly distinguishable.

Tuohay entered the bedroom. "A wheelchair?"

"He does not own a wheelchair," said Sara.

A sinking feeling struck Tuohay. "Can one walk here from the hospital?"

"Quite easily," said Sara. "It is only a few blocks away."

Tuohay reached the wheelchair and noticed the white sheet draped across it. It was smeared with blood. "An autopsy sheet," he whispered. His eyes flashed across the room, a sense of urgency filling his senses. Sara raised her hand to her mouth to suppress a gasp.

"Do you think…did he—"

"I do not know what to think just yet," Tuohay responded, checking the closet and brushing the sheets on the bed aside with his cane. Satisfied that the room was otherwise empty, he strode out, his cane clattering against the floor. Sara stood in the corner of the doorway, pale as a ghost.

Eliza was the first to notice Tuohay's perturbed state. "What is it, Jack?"

Tuohay was already in the second bedroom, this one similar but lived in. He rummaged through the closet and bed, discovering nothing. He turned to the doorway where Eliza leaned in, a question on her face.

"There is a wheelchair in the other room—from the hospital. If the body was stolen last night…"

"What better way to sneak a body out of a hospital," Eliza finished, her cheeks flushing—though from the heat or the revelation it was hard to tell. "Doctor Kearney stole the body and wheeled it here under the cover of darkness. But…where is it?"

"Let's not get ahead of ourselves," Tuohay cautioned.

Sara covered her mouth as a sob issued forth. "There must be some other explanation."

"Well, we've found a few things of our own," said Eliza, indicating the common room with a jerk of her thumb.

"Lead the way," Tuohay urged, following Eliza back to where Eldredge was hunched over a table, casting an eye over items that had been unearthed from nearby bookcases and desk drawers.

"What have you got?" said Tuohay, the resolve in his voice unmistakable.

"A few items of note," said Eldredge. "First, there's this." He pointed a pudgy finger at a stack of paper bound by a metal clip. The familiar title read: *Essay for Admission. Adoration of the Magi in Religious Art: Restoration Practices of Oil on Canvas, Mural, and Stained Glass. Authored by Colin Allotrope of Great House, Trinitarians of Mary.*

"The same essay we found in the loft of the law office," said Tuohay.

"Not the exact same. A draft sent by the seminary, addressed to Doctor Kearney. And there is a note in the back." Eldredge flipped to the last page and pointed at a script in flowing handwriting.

Dear Doctor Kearney,
Young Colin Allotrope has been accepted to seminary. Here is a copy of his work, which was received with high praise. Your generosity as a beneficiary for the boy has borne fruit. We are blessed that you remained his supporter, albeit anonymously.
In faith, Sister Agatha.

"Then, quite intriguingly, there are these." Eldredge directed

Tuohay's attention to a small black cardboard container that had been wrapped in a red ribbon. The ribbon was undone, and Eldredge removed the lid to expose a pile of black cardstock with white borders beneath. He lifted one up and handed it to Tuohay.

"This is same paper that the *Invitations to a Chase* were scripted on," Tuohay remarked. "Notice the white border is devoid of the winged serpents, which indicates they were personally added to the invitations by the author."

"But the most compelling is this," said Eliza, picking up a black leather-bound journal. "It was locked in his desk. Easy lock to pick, of course." She fanned through the pages, all of which were chock full of notes and sketches. Nearly halfway into the journal she stopped at a page. The words I AM MY BROTHERS KEEPER were sketched across it, the formatting nearly identical to the etching discovered in the Kearney's apartment.

"There are notes in here about how his brothers' flat looked when Doctor Kearney discovered their bodies. It is not at *all* as he described it on the record." She offered the journal to Tuohay.

Tuohay took it and scanned the contents. "So he lied to us about the state of the scene concerning Aiden and Rian's death."

"If the journal entry is legitimate, he must have."

"Not just that," Eliza added. "He would have physically changed it to what the authorities were shown to what he claimed the scene to look like."

Tuohay was silent for a moment, the discoveries slowly settling in. "I need a minute to sort this out."

"Not sure if that's the best idea in this heat, Jack," Eliza replied, taking one of the black stock cards to fan her face. "Can we close that vent or something?"

"Jack! Look at this." Eldredge's nose was buried in the nativity essay, his spectacles dangling at the edge of his nose. He turned the book around so the others could see it. A sketch of a stained glass window took up most of the page, bracketed on the top and bottom with scrawling verbiage relevant to the drawing's significance, including the date and artist of the stained glass it represented. The colors were done with soft pastel.

It was a replica of the nativity scene, but with alterations. An open faced stable was positioned in the bottom center of the sketch, a warm golden glow emanating from an indistinct light source within. Surrounding the stables were stone buildings with circular roofs and oblong windows, the edifices various shades of blue in the moonlight. Rows of fingernail-shaped trees were presented along the bottom half of the sketch, lending emerald and evergreen hues. Over the village the top half of the sky was filled with stars, cascading white against a black background.

But the stables were empty except for a woman draped in blue. No wise men, shepherds, or Joseph. No child. The light within the stables, though blurry, seemed to emanate from beneath her feet.

Under the drawing in scrawling black letters, was the word *Revelation*.

Eldredge tapped the word with his finger. "That is what caused me to pause on this sketch."

"What does the essay say about it?" Eliza asked.

"Colin Allotrope's essay states that this invaluable stained glass window, called *Revelation*, belonged to an old stone church nestled in the Wicklow Mountains of Glendalough in Northern Ireland, and is over six hundred years old. While it is not a scene of the Nativity, it has been included in his Nativity essay for two reasons. First, the scene *does* signify the birth of the savior, and second, it represents a restoration project that Colin Allotrope was part of."

Tuohay stared at the sketch. "Which was?"

"Rescuing *Revelation* from the crumbling church in Glendalough by transferring the stained glass, piece by piece, to St. John's seminary near Boston, and rebuilding it there. The project ran from 1894-1897. And, believe it or not, it was initiated by Father Abrams Valentine."

"Father Donnelly's nephew," Eliza exclaimed.

"And Colin's father, though we do not know if the boy knew that or not," added Tuohay. "Does it say anything about Father Abrams role in this project?"

"Simply that he brokered the deal behind the scenes with priests in Ireland and America regarding the transfer of this priceless piece of art before sickness took him from the work. He was not alive to witness the completed restoration in 1897."

"He allegedly died before it was completed," Tuohay mused.

"There may be more evidence in the apartment if we look longer," Eldredge added. "It is a small space, and these items were not difficult to find."

"Fellas—I don't think we have that kind of time." Something had caught Eliza's eye out the window, and she leaned close to the glass. "Unless I'm seeing things, I'd say Inspector Frost just got off the El, and he's heading this way with a pair of constables at his side. And by heading this way, I mean they're here."

Tuohay cursed under his breath.

"I know what the serpent means." The statement was soft, almost hollow, and laced with faint sorrow. The others, having forgotten Sara's presence, turned with surprise to face her.

"You'll have to explain it later," said Tuohay. "Leave the evidence for Inspector Frost," he directed Eliza and Eldredge. They gathered their coats as Tuohay nodded to Sara, who opened the door to the hallway. As they stepped quietly out, a flush of cool air washed across them.

Distant voices rose from the staircase down the hallway.

"They are coming up the stairs," Eldredge warned, wiping the perspiration from his face.

"The lift." Tuohay limped towards it, and waited as the others boarded. The voices in the hallway reached a crescendo as Sara brought the lift to life with the gears. It rumbled under their feet and began to slowly descend.

After a moment, Eliza turned to Tuohay. "What about Mary Hart? What about…her body?"

In the same instant, Eldredge wiped his forehead, muttering a complaint about the heat in the apartment.

"My God" Tuohay grabbed the lift's handle and shifted the indicated destination an additional floor down.

Eliza stared at Tuohay. "What are you doing?"

"Taking us to the basement."

A few moments later, the lift shuddered to a halt. The opening beyond the gate was nearly pitch black, with only a distant electric torch providing light in the cavernous space. Tuohay slammed the gate open and limped onto the earthen floor of the basement. As the others exited, Tuohay took a moment to turn over his shoulder. "Send the lift up to the first floor."

Eliza saw to it as Tuohay delved into the darkness, the others close at his heels. The knocking of pipes, creaking of boards, and occasional rush of running water filled the darkness, each whisper and hiss bringing the building to life in their imaginations.

A hollow, groaning whoosh rose from the darkness ahead, and continued to grow louder as they neared. The relative warmth of the basement increased exponentially with the sound until the heat was palpable, dry and crackling like a hot summer's day off their faces.

From the darkness the source of the whooshing heat materialized like a metallic giant. They had entered what appeared to be a small tunnel without realizing it, pipes wrapping like snakes above their heads to disappear into the bowels of the building above. The tunnel was in fact two looming furnaces designed to lean inwards on each other, the heat produced by the fire in their vast rectangular bellies connected by two massive pipes above, from which smaller pipes split off like arteries bearing the edifice's lifeblood.

A light flared to life, creating a small globe around Tuohay's outstretched hand. He held his lighter forth, the light passing by the puzzled faces before him. Eliza had rejoined the group, the rumbling of the ascending lift echoing in the darkness.

"Look there," said Tuohay, pointing at the dirt floor. Two parallel tracks led through the dirt to a circular portal in the furnace to their left. Beside the furnace bins of coal stretched into the darkness.

Eldredge knelt close to the tracks. "What are those?"

"Wheelchair tracks," Eliza whispered in reply.

Without warning, Tuohay grabbed the latch of the metal portal and swung it open with a clank. An inferno of heat and white light flowed over them in a wave, causing all but Tuohay to stumble back. Blinking in the newfound brilliance, they regained their footing and fought against the overwhelming heat to follow Tuohay's gaze.

Within the roaring blaze a long object was barely discernable, blackened by fire. The remnant of a sheet, no bigger than a coin, escaped from the depths of the furnace into the darkness, dancing along the warm currents like a windswept butterfly.

"By thunder," Eldredge said, his voice shaking as he stared deep into the flames, "there's a body in there."

The Final Performance

The rumble of the lift coming to life reverberated through the silence of the basement, the thin screech of metal accompanying it like a forlorn wail. Tuohay stared into the flames like a man possessed, the metal tip of his cane gleaming in the firelight. The sweat of his companions had been baked off by the incessant heat, their clothes feeling starched, almost brittle.

"My God. Mary." Sara grabbed Tuohay's sleeve, the fabric hot to the touch. Her face was as pale as a ghost. "I-Inspector?"

Eliza shouldered in. "Jack, snap out of it—"

Tuohay spun on Sara, his eyes fevered. "Go to Inspector Frost. Tell him about everything we found here, including the body. We cannot stop the blaze, but the bones will remain for some time."

The distant clang of the lift stopping on an upper floor rang through the basement.

"But Frost can't be trusted," Sara protested. "Remember everything I told you about him?"

Tuohay was immovable. "Do it, Sara." He set a hand on her shoulder. "And you said McNamara is nearby? If you can get him, do so as well."

Sara's emerald eyes were shadowed in doubt, but she nodded. "I will. But what do I tell them? Frost and McNamara?"

"Everything you know." Tuohay limped towards a staircase visible in the soft glow from the furnace. He turned to Eldredge as they walked. "I don't want Sara to go alone. Can you get her to Inspector Frost without notice? There is danger afoot."

Eldredge paled at the thought, but quickly composed himself. "Of course."

"We will meet you at the Northampton El in ten minutes."

The gears of the lift screeched to life from one of the upper floors. Eldredge linked Sara's arm with his and led her to the staircase. "This way."

Sara glanced over her shoulder at Tuohay as Eldredge led her up the stairs, the worried lines on her face framed by shadow.

"Good luck, Johnny," Eliza said.

Eldredge tipped his bowler cap. "All will be well. See you

outside."

As Eldredge and Sara disappeared up the stairs, the clank of the lift stopping on the floor above resonated through the basement. The screech of the gate and tramp of boots overhead followed.

Eliza scanned the vast darkness surrounding them, broken only by the flaring glow of the furnace. "Now what?"

"We find a way out."

"Easy enough," said Eliza. She nodded towards the furnace. "That monstrosity consumes a lot of dirty coal—not the type of loads they'd want to bring through the carpeted front entrance. Must be an exit from the basement somewhere. Follow me."

Even in the darkness, it did not take long to discover the faint outline of light indicating a gate. It was comprised of twin doors outlined by slim daylight, faint from a distance but easily discernable upon approach. Up close, the doors looked little different than those for a barn. A wooden beam secured them, which Eliza pushed against with a grunt. It scraped across the metal supports before sliding free. She pulled at one of the doors.

Light spilled over her through the slim egress. Nodding to Tuohay, she led the way out. A gravel ramp led into a small lot buttressed by brick buildings and alleyways. Blinking in the light, they felt the bite of the cold morning air greet them as the clatter of an elevated train thrummed like a beating heart above.

Tuohay grimaced as he walked, Eliza eyeing him with a concerned look. Fatigue was scratched across his face in deep, worrying lines. The vision of the burning body in the furnace was never far from either of their memories, lending to the nearly crippling anxiety coursing through their veins.

"Here we are," said Tuohay, practically gasping as they reached the top of the Northampton elevated platform. It was abuzz with morning commuters, and the pair remained unnoticed as Tuohay dug a clove cigarette from the depths of his pocket with shaking fingers.

"I don't see much down there," Eliza commented, indicating the doctor's apartment building a few blocks away. "You?"

Tuohay shook his head as he lit his cigarette. Coughing fiercely, he twisted away from the crowd as he continued to shudder.

"Wait—there's Frost," Eliza hissed, shielding the sun from her eyes with her hand. "He just left Doctor Kearney's building. Sara is with him, and a few uniformed jacks."

"Eldredge?"

"No." Eliza tapped her foot nervously. "Looks like they're coming this way."

A gust of wind tore through the platform, sending newspapers and the occasional hat swirling into the air. As if in answer, the tracks began to vibrate with the approach of the train.

"Where's Johnny?" Eliza muttered. Frost had broken away from the others and was hurrying towards the El station. "Oh brother. Frost is coming our way."

"Eliza…."

The apprehension in Tuohay's voice caused her to first turn to him, and then follow his gaze to the street below. To her astonishment she watched as a man climbed into a one-horse chaise and took the reins. From the El platform, the roof of the chaise hid the carriage's interior, which was otherwise open in the front. It pulled onto the road with startling speed.

Eliza raised her hand to her mouth. "Was that Eldredge?"

"Yes."

The train pulled into the station in a cacophony of clamoring metal, pausing the conversation. As it squealed to a stop, Eliza grabbed Tuohay. "What do we do?"

"Wait—there!" Tuohay pointed at a different section of Washington Street closer to them.

"Jack?" Eliza could not see what had excited him.

"Come on. And keep an eye on that chaise." Fighting through the crowd, Tuohay led the way down the length of the trolley, his cane cracking against the wooden platform. The train jerked to life as he reached a second stairway descending to the street.

Eliza followed Tuohay down, spotting a wheezing Frost rushing up a parallel staircase to theirs, his trench coat snapping in the wind.

"I can't see the carriage anymore," she said as they reached the ground. It had taken a sharp right three blocks down Washington Street. Above, the elevated tracks rattled with the departure of the train. "Jack, what's going on? Where are we headed?"

Tuohay ignored her as he strode across the street, coughing in the dust of a horse and buggy trotting past. He stopped at a familiar chocolate-brown automobile. The driver, a young boy in a dusty gray sports coat and checkered cap, looked up with surprise.

"I'd rem, emba' that top hat and cane anywheres," the boy said with a mischievous grin.

"I need your auto, Ronald."

The boy looked past Tuohay at Eliza in her rose-hued blouse and white skirt, the black parasol folded in her hands. "Wow." He swept his hat off with a short bow, never taking his eyes from her. "Pleased to meet ya, miss. You've got the face of an angel, you know that?"

Eliza stared at Tuohay. "Who is this?"

"Name's Ronald, ma'am," the boy answered. "Motorist extraordinaire. Bet you've neva' met a more handsome driver than me."

She looked from the boy to the motorized cart. "You drive this thing? What are you, fourteen?"

"It's a Cuh've Dash Olds, miss. And I'm a strappin' twelve. Good age for motorists, see. Quick reflexes and all. Ask yer pal here, he came along once."

"It was intoxicating, Ronald," said Tuohay, casting a sidelong glance at Eliza. "Which is why I have returned."

"I'd offer you a ride, see, but I'm already on the clock with another fella." The boy jerked his thumb at a nearby dime store. "He just went inside for a tonic."

Tuohay climbed onto the left side of the automobile's bench, pulling Eliza up behind him.

"Hey! You can't do that," the boy cried. "There's only room for two!"

Avoiding the steering tiller protruding from the auto's front panel, Eliza slid past Tuohay onto the seat, placing her black parasol across her lap. She patted the sliver of bench real estate remaining on her right. "Guess we'll have to sit close."

"Ronald." Tuohay reached into his pocket and tossed a pair of gold coins to the boy, who snatched them in midair. Whistling in surprise, the boy raced around the front of the auto and jumped onto the remaining bench space beside Eliza.

"Ten dollars! Mister, you must need a ride somethin' fierce."
The boy adjusted two levers beneath his seat with a click, pressed one of two metal pedals with his foot, and spun the crank to his

right like a jack-in-the-box. The engine caught, sputtered, and then roared to life, the seat trembling beneath them. The boy took hold of the steering tiller with his left hand as his right grabbed the gear lever. Pressed tightly against Eliza, he winked at her as he pulled back on the lever. The auto jerked forward with a dull roar, spitting up dirt.

"Where to, sir?" The boy shouted.

"Take a right up there." Tuohay pointed at the intersection the chaise had turned at. "Full speed, Ronald."

"Whateva' you say, boss." The boy pushed the gear forward and the auto picked up speed, passing by an elaborately decorative two-wheeled curricle. A well-dressed gentleman shook his fist in fury as a blanket of dust from the auto settled onto his horse and carriage.

"Sorry, mac," the boy shouted well after they were out of earshot. Turning to Eliza, he smiled wickedly. "Hang on!"

Reaching the intersection, the boy pushed the tiller of the auto to the left, brushing Eliza's bosom with the back of his arm. She caught him smiling as the mechanized cart took a sharp right, sending the passengers skidding left.

Straightening, the auto followed a narrow gravel road for several blocks, passing various shops and tenement buildings. Traffic of all sorts hazarded the road, but the boy navigated the tiller and brake with surprising agility.

"Look!" Eliza pointed. The black chaise Eldredge had entered was several blocks ahead. The horse was at a trot, but maneuvered slowly at the haphazard knots of traffic. The chaise suddenly veered left, and Eliza grabbed Ronald's shoulder. "Follow that carriage."

"You got it, miss!" The car rumbled past pedestrians and carriages, turning left at the appointed street.

Eliza leaned close to Tuohay. "This is Chauncy Street. We're in the theater district."

Tuohay nodded, his gaze fixated on the chaise which was less than fifty yards distant. "It just turned right," he called.

"I see it," replied the boy. Less than a minute later they pulled a hard right, the vast green of the Boston Common in the distance. Closer, the road was snarled with traffic. Two figures emerged from the blocked chaise, the heavy set man leading the way stiffly. They disappeared around a slow moving cart in the obstacle-strewn road.

Eliza stood up, holding Tuohay's shoulder for support. "I see them! They're heading towards the corner of Washington and Boylston. I think Eldredge is being forced to move at gunpoint!"

"Hold on!" the boy shouted, passing a pushcart on the left and suddenly slamming the brake with an oath.

Tuohay pulled Eliza down a moment before they pitched forward, nearly tumbling out of the auto as it slid to a halt. A bespectacled man with a newspaper looked up in shock at the motorized vehicle rumbling mere inches from where he stood.

"Look where yer goin'!" the boy shouted at the pedestrian, who was too surprised to respond.

Tuohay stumbled from the auto, leaning on his cane for support. Eliza pressed her lips against Ronald's cheek. "Thanks for the ride."

The boy's jaw dropped as she slipped past him and leapt from the auto, leaving her parasol in his lap. His joyous whoop followed her into the river of hats and umbrellas washing down the sidewalk.

Tuohay surfaced first, breaking from the crowd at the corner of a newly renovated playhouse. It was as white as snow in the mid-morning sun. Three stories tall, the stone edifice was narrow but elegant, a water-filled fountain stationed before a set of cream colored double doors. A newly planted rose garden, the flowers powder white, filled the space between two arching windows and the white cobblestone walkway. Long curtains hung beyond the glass like shrouds.

"The Alabaster House," said Eliza. "The grand opening is not until early summer."

Tuohay stared at the playhouse. "I saw them enter by a side door down that passage." He pointed to a shadowed alleyway that ran to the back of the playhouse. A newly painted sign hung from a wooden archway framing the alleyway, *Performers Exit Here*.

Eliza exchanged a glance with Tuohay. "Well, there's no time like the present."

"I am going in alone."

Eliza stepped in front of Tuohay, placing her hand on his cane. "You are kidding me, right?"

Tuohay would not meet Eliza's eyes. "I do not know what kind of danger to expect in there, Eliza."

"Eldredge is in there and *he's* in danger. I sure as hell am not waiting out here for you to try to handle it alone." She turned on her heel and strode into the alleyway, the shadows deepening beyond the reach of the white light.

The click of Tuohay's cane followed her as they passed several shuttered windows before reaching a small side door. It was ajar.

"Ladies before gentleman," Eliza said, sliding in before Tuohay could protest. She was in a murky, narrow hallway, a hidden part of the theater that would be thriving in the backstage obscurity during shows, but for now slumbered in silence. Dim shapes rose to teetering heights around her; stacked furniture, mirrors, crates of several shapes and sizes, trunks, coils of rope, piles of sandbags, all one upon the other. The cluttered hallway seemed as if it were going to fall in on her at any moment as she followed it into the darkness.

After several twists and turns the passage opened onto a backstage space with heavy curtains hanging in the distance. Eliza stopped for a moment to listen, waiting for the click of Tuohay's cane to catch up to her. The scent of wet earth and cloves reached her before he did.

"Where are they?" Eliza whispered, her voice frantic.

Before Tuohay could answer, the sound of something heavy being dragged across the stage whispered from the darkness ahead. There was a soft thud, followed by a second dragging sound.

"Eldredge!" Tuohay's voice rang into the darkness.

There was a metallic click and the stage beyond the side curtains blazed to light. The backstage remained shrouded in shadow, but the white light was plainly visible through the gaps in the curtains.

"Stay here," Tuohay ordered, not waiting for Eliza's response. He limped to the curtains and pushed them aside. The stage stretched before him, bathed in a glaring white light. Eldredge sat in a straight back chair, his arms outstretched, a small sandbag clutched in each hand. His arms were quivering from the strain.

"John!"

Sweat beaded on Eldredge's forehead. "Jack, stay there," he gasped. "It's a ruse to capture you." A square table was in front of him, with two empty chairs. Otherwise the stage was empty.

Tuohay's heart pumped in his chest. With his free hand, he reached into his pocket for his pistol.

246

"She said she'll shoot me if I drop one of the bags." Eldredge blinked into the glare.

"Come out, inspector," a soft voice hissed from the darkness across the stage. "If you want your friend to live."

"Who are you?"

"Do it now. And drop the gun."

One of Eldredge's hands slipped and lost a grip on its bag for a moment. Eldredge's groaned in pain as the two weights bore down. "I can't ...hold these."

Tuohay dropped his gun and limped onto the stage. He reached Eldredge in three quick strides and took one of the bags from his hand. Before he could take the other, a shift in the shadows caught his eye.

"That bag is for your other friend. Tell her to get out here, *now*."

Tuohay stared into the dark folds of the curtain from where the voice came. "I came here alone."

"I don't have time for games. Do it!"

Eliza emerged from backstage, her hands up. "I'm here! Don't shoot." She rushed over to Eldredge and took the second sandbag from him.

"Good. Now sit down at the table."

Eliza and Tuohay complied.

"Put your hands where I can see them," the voice commanded.

The three slowly placed their hands on the table, the flesh inhumanly pale in the light.

"I'm sorry," moaned Eldredge. "She came out of nowhere with a pistol—"

A figure in a long, black dress, boots and gray cloak emerged from the curtains. The hood was pulled up, and in one of her hands was a silver pistol pointed at them. She came close enough to be seen within the light, but still too far to reach.

"Who are you?" Eliza demanded.

Tuohay grimaced. "Mary Hart."

Mary laughed, pulling the hood back from her face. Her chestnut eyes were devoid of warmth, the coldly beautiful face domineering, the paleness of her skin like ice.

Eliza gasped. "But you...but you were poisoned. You died. And your body was burned."

"Back from the dead," Mary replied, a cruel smile passing across her lips. "Isn't that right, inspector?"

Tuohay remained stone-faced.

"It must be gut-wrenching to come so close to solving the mystery, to finally see through all of the haze and misdirection, only to have it end like this."

"Don't hurt them," Tuohay said in a soft voice. "All you want is the diamond. You can secure that without causing any more harm."

"No," Mary said. "They've seen too much." She shrugged. "Besides, what's another few deaths at this point in the game?"

"But…who was that burning in the fire?" Eliza demanded.

"Poor Doctor Kearney," laughed Mary. "He never saw it coming—not until it was too late. To be burned alive while your muscles are rigid, your body not responding, but your consciousness ticking along like a clock. He could have taken a bullet to the head, but he chose *zombi*."

Tuohay's gaze turned to ice. "You're a monster."

Anger flared in Mary's eyes. "A monster? *Me*? After all the transgressions you've witnessed, you call *me* the monster! I am *ridding* the world of monsters."

"The doctor? How was he a monster?"

"Your precious doctor was the one who changed the murder scene at his brothers' apartment. He was a *liar*."

Tuohay's eyes hardened. "Yes, after *you* killed them and made it appear like Aiden and Rian Kearney had turned on each other. Doctor Kearney simply panicked for the sake of his brothers' reputations, and foolishly tried to make it appear like a peaceful suicide."

"Doctor Kearney was *a liar*, like the rest of them—"

The slam of the side entrance to the theater echoed through the darkness, followed by the clatter of footsteps. Mary rushed to Eliza and pulled her up, pointing the gun at her head. Slowly she pulled Eliza into the shadows. "If you say anything, she dies."

"Inspector Tuohay!" The grizzled call, recognizable as Frost's voice, came from backstage.

There was a rattle of movement and a few curses from backstage as Frost stumbled through the darkness. "We know you're in here! That auto ride of yours left a trail a blind man could follow. So come on out. We need to talk." Within a few minutes Frost emerged from the side curtains onto the stage, blinking in the light. "Tuohay?"

A man in an olive suit followed closely behind Frost.

"Mountain?" Eldredge whispered in confusion, recognizing the journalist from the *Boston Evening Traveler*.

At the sight of Tuohay, Frost and the man in the olive suit stopped cold.

Frost stood as if transfixed. "Tuohay. What the *hell* is going on?"

"Get out," Tuohay hissed. Eldredge stared at the men imploringly, sweat running down the side of his face.

Suddenly, Mary emerged like a specter from the curtains behind the men, her face etched with venomous anticipation.

"No!" Tuohay cried.

The crack of Mary's gun shattered the silence, and the man in olive collapsed in a heap, a crimson pool spilling beneath him. Eldredge fell backwards from his chair in shock as Frost spun upon Mary, his mouth agape.

"But you're dead," Frost gasped.

"No. You are." The second report from Mary's pistol sent Frost onto his back, his hand clutching his chest. Blood seeped through his fingers as he moaned in pain.

"You deserve far worse than that," she snarled, turning away.

She faced Tuohay, who sat ashen-faced at the table. "You should thank me for killing the Scotland Yard agent." Her eyes flickered to the shivering form of the man in the olive trench coat. "He was here to arrest you, after all."

"No," growled Tuohay. "He was surveillance. I am a suspect, but not a criminal. *You* know that better than anyone."

"And soon I will be the only one alive who knows that." She nodded in Eldredge's direction. "And also the only one alive who knows where the diamond is hidden, thanks to your friend. All it took was for me to point a gun at poor Eldredge's head—or should I call you John?—yes, at poor John's head, and I got the word that I needed. *Revelation*."

Eldredge stood, shaking. His voice was fierce but trembling as he stared at Mary. "What did you do to Eliza?"

Mary raised the grip of her metal pistol to the light, a smear of blood marking it. "I hit her in that pretty little head of hers so I could deal with Inspector Frost. And I took her pistol for good measure. But don't fret, I'll finish her after I deal with you."

"I never should have let you take me here, even at gunpoint," Eldredge lamented, angry desperation in his voice. "I should have let you shoot me!"

"Don't fret. That part is coming up."

From the stage floor, Frost gurgled as he struggled to turn on his side. He coughed once, blood running from his lips.

"God, help him!" Eldredge cried.

"Let it be," said Tuohay, turning to Eldredge with sympathy in his eyes. "There is nothing we can do."

"If I hadn't been kidnapped by her, you wouldn't have followed me, and those men wouldn't have followed you...." Eldredge's voice trailed away into a miserable sob.

"Don't blame yourself, John," said Tuohay softly. "This all comes back to *me*. If only I had put the last few clues together *quicker*, I could have prevented all of this." He turned his gaze to Mary. "But I did not. And so there is nothing left to say."

"No, there is not," Mary agreed. She pointed her gun at Tuohay's head.

Frost gurgled a word, causing Mary to pause. She turned to him with a half-smile. "One last word, Inspector Frost?"

"Blood...hound," Frost croaked, gritting his teeth in a bloodstained smile.

Mary frowned. Before she could act, the barrel of a Winchester rifle emerged from the curtains. It was pointed directly at her chest. A tall, white-haired man followed it out, holding the rifle steady despite the years lining his face.

"Drop the gun, Mary!" McNamara ordered.

Mary screamed in anger but did not move.

"Last warning, lass."

Mary dropped her weapon with a shaking hand and slowly put her hands in the air, angry tears running down her face. "What are you doing here?"

Eldredge scampered up and ran towards the curtains, shouting Eliza's name.

"Inspector Tuohay had the foresight to send Sara to call on me," McNamara answered. "And once I'm on a scent, I never lose it. Just a matter of timin', is all."

Mary snarled. "How could you do this to me? You were supposed to *protect* me!"

"You're ill in the mind, Mary," said McNamara, his voice filled with sorrow. "You had me fooled. You had all of us fooled."

"That's because you *are* fools," Mary cursed. "Sick in the mind, you say? I've known exactly what I have been doing all along. It was all to solve my beloved *Abram's* riddle, and to take back what that coward hid from me!"

"The diamond you stole with him and Kip Crippen," Tuohay finished.

"The Templar Diamond is *mine*. *I* was the mastermind behind the plan to steal it, and the one willing to kill for it."

"In that case, it's your soul that's ill," said Tuohay, standing with pain. "And you best pray that God forgives you that, for the law most assuredly will not."

The Deliverable

John Eldredge looked upon the neighborhoods of Brighton with an appreciative eye as the Allston-Brighton trolley rolled him through the quietly industrious area. The jet black trolley slid almost silently along the rails as a whistling officer in a tall beaters cap walked the aisle with his hands clasped behind his back. Eldredge peered beyond the newspaper-laden commuters to the horizon and saw a maze of thin blue strips winding through the fractured gray clouds like the delta of swollen river.

The air was still heavy with the scent of new-fallen rain, and a slight chill hung in the approach of evening. Eldredge kept his coat fastened tightly about him, his hands thrust in his pockets.

The trolley officer took a quick break from his whistling to announce the next stop. "Chestnut Hill, end of the line!"

The trolley slowed, and many of the passengers hopped off prematurely, but Eldredge waited until the wheels had completed their last rotation, picking up a stray newspaper as he did so. Exiting with as controlled a step as he could muster, he spotted the distant turrets of St. John's Seminary and began his approach. It was a short walk, but Eldredge was already sweating by the time he reached the entrance to the grounds.

A short drive stretched before him to the front of the formidable structure and parted like a cloven river, the left circling the main building while the right climbed a small knoll and disappeared into the midst of the school's secondary structures. Eldredge's gaze remained locked on the front of the main edifice where a tall set of black mahogany doors sat solemnly between two coned towers. An array of stained glass windows filled the brick edifice, several of them glowing with first light as the evening grew closer.

"One of the enduring gems of Archbishop Walsh's tenure," said a voice from behind Eldredge, startling him into a whirl. Eldredge grasped his chest as he looked upon Tuohay's smiling visage.

"I took you for a ghost!" said Eldredge, wiping his brow. "Could you not have announced your presence before scaring the spirit out of me?"

"My apologies, old boy." Tuohay stepped past Eldredge and

peered at the seminary with careful eyes. "All is prepared?"

"Yes. Eliza has seen to it."

"Exactly as I outlined?"

"Precisely so," replied Eldredge.

"The clothing order?"

"Jack, please. It is being handled."

Tuohay nodded. "Right."

A carriage rattled up the main drive of the seminary behind them, its unlit lantern swinging to and fro from the wooden brow. The crimson light of evening was fading rapidly to gray, lengthening the shadows.

"The guests are arriving," said Tuohay.

"The welcoming ceremony for the next class accepted into seminary," remarked Eldredge. "I suppose we are running short on time?"

"The closing of the ceremony is growing near." Slipping another clove cigarette from his jacket, Tuohay drew a disapproving glance from Eldredge as he set his lighter to it.

"Medicinal, you say?"

"You bring that up now?" Taking a long drag, Tuohay cast a sideline glance at his companion. He started again towards the back end of the seminary where the windows were aflame with light. A deep and heavenly chanting suddenly floated from within the great chamber.

Eldredge unfolded the newspaper from the trolley and glanced at the front page. "Evening edition," he said. "Front page story about our endeavors yesterday. Have you seen it?" He handed the paper to Tuohay, who perused it briefly.

STRANGER THAN FICTION
STAGE DRAMA LEADS TO GUNSHOTS AND ARREST
SUSPECT RETURNS FROM THE DEAD
DIAMOND REMAINS AT LARGE

INSPECTOR FROST TO MAKE A FULL RECOVERY
OFFICIAL STATEMENT TO BE FORTHCOMING
SPECIAL AGENT FROM SCOTLAND YARD IN
STABLE CONDITION

"Good," said Tuohay. "I am glad to see our old friend Frost is going to make it."

"And that agent from Scotland Yard that was following you around," added Eldredge.

"Admittedly, he was doing more than that—he *did* break into my hotel room looking for evidence."

"What did he want?"

"Scotland Yard must have sent him to keep an eye on me in case I found the diamond and tried to disappear with it."

"Well, he's fortunate to be alive," said Eldredge. "A little while longer and he as well as Inspector Frost would have bled out."

"A little while longer, and we *all* would have bled out," said Tuohay solemnly. "But let's not ponder on that."

Eldredge shuddered. "Agreed."

The chanting from the seminary was drowned out by the approach of a carriage, the gravel crunching beneath its wheels. The carriage was pulled by a large brown mare, her eyes reflecting off the shining seminary lights. The driver was hooded and remained silent as he drew the carriage to a halt beside Tuohay and Eldredge. The windows were veiled by thick curtains, shielding the inhabitants from view.

"Well done," said Tuohay. "The carriage is precisely on time." He stepped to the carriage and opened the door.

Two women emerged first, their faces hidden by wide-brimmed straw hats. They were adorned in long, sleek blue dresses that hung below rich brown coats and matching scarves. Their hands were gloved in white lace and each carried a fashionable umbrella though the rain had since passed. Eldredge recognized the determined face of Sara immediately, her emerald eyes a mix of relief and sadness. He did not recognize the woman beside her, but her resemblance indicated a close relation.

"We are here, Anna," said Sara in a soft voice. Anna whispered to herself, and it was unclear if she was aware of her circumstances at all.

The third woman to alight was Eliza. A gown of rose velvet with silver bow-knots captured her graceful figure, the lines of the dress severe in their devotion to her. Swan-necked, her soft visage framed by a curled pompadour with soft burgundy coils brushing past her eyes, Eliza looked the part of the classic American darling. A fashionable straw hat was tilted to side, covering the bandage wrapped around the back of her head.

"I'm always looking for a good reason to get dressed up," she smiled, taking Tuohay's hand as she stepped down. "And this one should be a dandy."

"I'm sure it will," Tuohay agreed. He reached past her into the carriage and stepped back with a bulging leather satchel. "It's all in here?"

"Sure is," Eliza replied. "The financial ledgers, Aiden Kearney's investigative notes, the codex, Donnelly's medical journal with the appropriate passages annotated. Even the affidavits are in there."

Tuohay nodded, leaning close to Eliza. "I had a feeling Frost would cooperate, as long as we promised to keep his name out of it."

"You were right. He was quite willing to let me know where the affidavits were hidden as long as we promised to keep quiet about the fact that he stole them from the law firm's safe the night of Sara's interview. He desperately wants to keep his role as a strong-arm in the trial a secret."

"McNamara was right. Frost is as crooked as a dog's hind leg. But enough about him for now."Tuohay turned the conversation to Sara and Anna. "I am honored escort such lovely women to the ceremony. Shall we?"

"Let me take that for you." Eldredge shouldered the heavy satchel.

"Thank you, old boy."

Sara smiled boldly as she took Anna's hand. "We are ready, inspector. Lead the way."

Tuohay did so, bringing them through a quiet garden to a side door. Making a fist, he knocked three times. The sound resonated from within, indicating a cavernous space. Sara and Anna stood a step behind Tuohay, their breathing shallow. Nearly a minute passed before the sound of a latch was heard. The door swung open and light spilled into the gray evening. A young acolyte robed in white stepped aside, and Tuohay entered. Eldredge hesitated for a moment as the women stepped past him. The last to enter, he tried to catch the acolyte's gaze but the boy did not look up.

Tuohay led the way through a maze of airy passageways, his cane echoing off the floor. The sound of a single voice echoed around them—a man giving a speech. The voice grew louder until finally they were at the door from which the voice was coming.

"Come," said Tuohay, pushing the door open. The magnificent arches of St. John's chapel rose above them, a decorum of angels and saints, beneath which hung a dozen long cylindrical lamps shining with pure white light. Two rows of ornate monastic choir stalls faced one another along the length of the chapel, each housing an assortment of fashionably dressed onlookers. A long, polished floor stretched from the door to the far end of the chapel, ending in an arched circular apse with a golden cross hanging from its heights. The archbishop stood in front of a linen-shrouded alter, his rich voice filling the chapel as the gathered observers listened intently. Facing the archbishop were twenty young men garbed in white robes. Tuohay and the others were not noticed as they quietly made their way to the closest pew and sat with the observers.

They listened quietly as the archbishop spoke. The welcoming ceremony was directed towards the young men in the white robes. They were from all around the country, and in a few cases hailed from outside of America. The archbishop spoke warmly to the incoming freshman seminary class, finishing with the following quote from the Bible.

"Remember my young flock that the Lord is with thee, and shall give thee guidance as you begin your journey on the path to priesthood. And as we, the outsiders, look upon you, the future of the Roman Catholic Church, we are reminded of God's enduring words from Ephesians 5:14: *Christ shall give thee light.* Go forward now, young seminarians, and walk into the light." Here he turned to the audience. "All rise."

The congregation rose as the choir began to sing. Archbishop Walsh led the new class towards the exit along the polished nave running through the pews, and parents waved as the new seminarians walked past with pride in their eyes.

Eldredge felt a shiver beside him and turned. Suddenly, as the host of young men walked past, Anna rose.

"Wait," said Sara, reaching for her sister, but Anna did not heed her voice.

The procession slowed to a stop as the onlookers came out to greet their loved ones. Anna emerged ahead of the crowd, stepping from the pews to one of the young men. With trembling hands she touched his face. "Colin. Oh Colin."

"Excuse me?" It was clear that the young seminarian did not know Anna. Sara appeared beside her sister and drew her back, but upon doing so, she touched the young man's hand.

Sara spoke hurriedly. "I am sorry... my sister is confused—"

"Wait." Colin Allotrope took Anna's hand softly in his own, drawing her back to him. "Do I know you?"

"M-my darling son," Anna whispered.

The seminarians around them were receiving congratulations from relations and well-wishers, but Colin noticed none of it as he stared at Anna. "But...I—"

"Your father was Father Abrams Valentine," said Sara in a kind but cautioned voice. "It's alright, Colin. We know."

Colin's cheeks flushed. "He... I mean, I was told my mother died long ago."

"Your father did not want you to know about her," Sara replied softly.

Anna reached into her jacket pocket and pulled out Richard's silver rattle.

He stared in wonder at the rattle and its elaborate designs. "I remember this." His voice was barely a whisper. "How? Is it true?"

"We were only supposed to watch you today," said Sara. She looked at Anna, "we did not intend to surprise you with this revelation."

Colin's smile was one of wonder and benevolence. Kindness shone in his eyes as he embraced Anna.

Tuohay used the opportunity to break away, taking the leather pack from Eldredge. Limping through the crowd, he reached Archbishop Walsh. The archbishop peered at Tuohay with a mixture of solemnity and anger. "What are you doing here?"

"I have something for you," Tuohay said, offering the leather satchel. "A thorough summary of the transgressions within your diocese, many related to the diamond, but not all."

The archbishop glowered at Tuohay. His cheeks red with anger, he took the satchel. The two men's gaze remained locked for several long moments. "But the diamond is still at large," the archbishop said with reproach.

"Not any longer. Follow me, your Grace."

The archbishop's eyes widened, but he said nothing.

Tuohay led the archbishop to the circular apse, the golden cross hanging above gleaming in the fading light. Eldredge and Eliza followed, and the archbishop merely raised a curious brow at their inclusion.

"Well, inspector?"

Tuohay leaned against his cane and pointed at a stained glass window at the back of apse. The archbishop turned to face it. "The Adoration of the Magi."

"No. Notice that the woman is the only figure with color. The others surrounding her are mere shadows."

"It is a restored piece," said the archbishop, "relocated five years ago from a medieval church in Ireland. Some of the pieces are original, and others had to be replaced. It was not a perfect restoration."

"The original only had one figure in it, and that was the woman. The others were added as part of the restoration by Father Abrams Valentine."

The archbishop shook his head. "Inspector Tuohay, Father Abrams died the year before the restoration took place."

"No, in fact, he did not," said Tuohay. "As will be made clear to you when the full details of the case emerge." He drew the archbishop's attention back to the stained glass window. "It was not the scene of the nativity, despite what you may have thought, but an ancient rendition of the rebirth of Jesus to a lone woman standing on the moon." Tuohay pointed at the light emitting from beneath the woman's feet. "It is a clever piece of art, I must say. It was meant to mislead the casual observer."

With the light of evening cast through it, the window glowed in the soft hues of blue, emerald, lavender, and soft gold. These colors filtered through various representations in the scene; the cobalt stone of the buildings, the lines of multi-hued trees, the darker violet shades representing the shadows of night, and the soft gold of the light glowing from beneath the feet of the woman to fill the stables.

But it was the depiction of the night sky that caught the attention of the small audience. A vast array of stars stretched above the stables, floating in the blue and lavender canvas above. They were dazzling in the soft evening light.

"Dragons!" said Eldredge in awe. "Look closely. You can see the images captured within the stars like constellations."

"Precisely," said Tuohay. "The constellations are the multi-headed dragon, the woman has a halo of twelve gleaming points around her head and the moon glowing beneath her feet. This, my friends, is a scene from Revelation 12, which also happens to be a clue for where the diamond would be discovered."

"*Revelation*," Eldredge whispered.

The archbishop exhaled nervously. "Are you saying..."

"Your Grace, each of the hundreds of stars you see before you in the stained glass window above is a diamond in its own right, and was once part of the great Templar Diamond."

"The Star of Bethlehem," Eliza whispered. "Cut into hundreds of sparkling shards and hidden right above the heads of the congregation in plain sight. It's been here all along."

They stared in silence at the stained glass window for a long time.

*

"Hope Cemetery." Eldredge read the sign in the dying light of evening. The carriage they had arrived in departed for Medford with Sara and Anna within.

"Father Aiden Kearney and his brother Rian were interred in pauper's graves," said Tuohay. "Follow me."

Eliza and Eldredge walked beside Tuohay as he made his way along the winding trails of the cemetery. The sun was dropping below the horizon, and it would soon be dark. Tuohay walked at a rapid clip in hopes of reaching the gravesite while there was still light.

"Jack," said Eliza, "why were Father Kearney and his brother killed by Mary?"

Tuohay stopped at the base of a small hill. Along the slope in front of them lay a stretch of grass embedded with hundreds of rectangular stones. The gray stones were marked by number only.

"As you recall, Father Robert Donnelly was known as Imhotep because of his sheer brilliance," said Tuohay. "As it turns out, he sought like-minded geniuses to surround himself with. That is why he chose to become the guardian of Abrams Valentine and Kip Crippen, brothers by a different name many years ago, from the orphanage near Belfast. And that is also why Mary Hart became his paramour so many years later. It was her *mind* that excited him."

Eldredge frowned. "Were they as intelligent as he was?"

"The intellect of each of those individuals is hard for us to comprehend," responded Tuohay.

"Speak for yourself," said Eliza with a smirk.

"In Mary Hart's case, her genius was not wrought by schooling, but remained an untamed birthright," said Tuohay. "Regardless of the circumstances, as great as their minds were, Mary, Abrams, and Crippen were only truly excited by the challenge of manipulating others. In truth, Mary Hart was never in love with Father Donnelly, and enjoyed the charade and her ability to manipulate him."

"She probably got a fine share of expensive gifts from the doting old priest," Eliza remarked. "Most of all, when Father Donnelly was shown *Crown Mount* by the archbishop, Mary Hart must have seen it as well, and memorized its contents."

"She has confessed to as much," confirmed Tuohay. "Mary shared the operational details of the Templar Diamond's visit to Belfast with Abrams Valentine and a plan was hatched. They brought in his brother Kip—the notorious jewel thief—and with that information in hand and their brilliant minds at work, they pulled off one of the largest diamond heists in recent history."

Eliza tapped Tuohay's pocket. "You gonna light another one of your cigarettes?"

"For once, no." He cast her a sidelong glance. "Why, are you interested in one?"

She shrugged. "I probably shouldn't, but those cloves…well, I've taking a liking to them. For the pain in my head, you know." She pressed her lips into a sarcastic smile.

"Right." Tuohay reached into his pocket for his cigarette case.

"About the diamond…Father Abrams never meant to share it, even with Mary," said Eldredge. "At least as I understand things."

"That is what has come to light," said Tuohay, handing Eliza a cigarette and producing his lighter. "He was a con artist at heart, and in his final performance, misled even those closest to him. As Mary misled Father Donnelly, Abrams misled Mary."

"A vicious circle," said Eldredge, shaking his head.

"So Abrams cut the diamond, and hid its pieces in the stained glass window during the restoration stage," said Eliza, taking a drag of the cigarette. She frowned. "Why do I smoke these? They're horrid."

"By that time he had faked his death, and simply must have worked as one of the artists on the job at the old church in Glendalough," Eldredge added. "Ingenious." He frowned thoughtfully. "But... how did he fake his death?"

"Father Donnelly was his accomplice for that," replied Tuohay, watching Eliza take a draw of the clove cigarette before turning to Eldredge. "Father Donnelly used a certain medication—or poison, if that definition suits you better—that he discovered in Haiti, to produce the effect of death. As documented in his medical journals, he developed a chemical hypothesis using a neurotoxin native to, of all things, *pufferfish*, that with the proper application, would in fact create the appearance of death for several hours, even days."

"Gads. That sounds like witchcraft."

"Very much so," said Tuohay. "And it is extraordinarily dangerous, one would imagine. However, Father Donnelly was a man confident in his skills, and he manufactured and used the toxin on his nephew to create the appearance to any who examined him that he had, in fact, died."

"It's the same neurotoxin that Mary Hart used to poison herself," said Eliza, exhaling through ruby lips. "She of course had access to everything of Father Donnelly's, and was a quick learner from the sounds of things."

"It was Mary's death that threw me off her trail," Tuohay admitted.

"You're not gonna beat yourself up over that, are you? She was declared dead."

Tuohay's grim countenance showed that even *that* reason was not a good enough excuse for his oversight. "When I realized it was Abrams Valentine and not Kip Crippen that Inspector Frost shot at the harbor—"

"How?" Eldredge cut in.

"Based on the fact that they were nearly identical as brothers, and that the body in the harbor suffered from a fatal ailment just as Father Abrams did—do you remember the newspaper article mentioning consumption?"

I do," Eldredge confirmed, and Eliza nodded in agreement.

"I realized Abrams had *not* died in 1896. My attention was turned to those close to him, especially Father Donnelly, but *he* was already dead by the time I began to put the pieces together. Mary was the next logical choice, but with her apparently murdered as well, my attention was diverted. Just as she wanted."

"Like I said, I wouldn't beat yourself up over that," Eliza stated. "How were you supposed to know she was going to get off the gurney, visit Doctor Kearney in his apartment, and administer that terrible drug at gunpoint? And then roll him into the furnace, alive."

Eldredge gritted his teeth. "Poor man."

"I could have prevented his death," Tuohay said.
"You're still human, Jack. Like the rest of us." Eliza took out her journal and flipped it open to the back, handing it to Tuohay as she did so. "For posterity's sake, I documented the following details. Take a gander."

Name	Death	Motive
Father Abrams Valentine	Faked— 1896	Allowed him to disappear without a trace after diamond theft, and to hide the diamond.
Susan Lovelace	1897	Ruled natural causes.
Kathryn Dwyer	Oct 1901	Killed by Mary Hart to cast suspicion on Inspector Frost
Father Aiden Kearney, Rian Kearney	Dec 1901	Mary Hart.... Motive ?
Father Abrams Valentine	Mar 1901	Shot by Frost. Abrams likely chose that as his moment to die for the game.
Father Robert Donnelly	Mar 1901	Poisoned by Mary and, still alive, was dropped from the

		balcony. Revenge and to eliminate his chance at the diamond.
Kip Crippen	Mar 1901	Shot by Mary to eliminate him from obtaining the diamond. She knew he would visit Anna. Planted Donnelly's ring on him. Mary planted gun on Anna.
Doctor Kearney	Mar 1901	Poisoned by Mary and, still alive, was thrust into a furnace. A ploy to further suspicion on the doctor for poisoning her.
Mary Hart	Faked— Mar 1901	Elaborate ruse to divert attention away from herself.

Tuohay regarded the journal. "The motives you have captured appear valid, but it is even simpler than that. Mary's fundamental plan was to eliminate anyone she suspected of harboring damaging information about her. She was meticulous, devoid of conscience, and a master at diverting suspicion onto others. In the end, it really *was* a game to her. A game initiated by her former lover and betrayer, Abrams Valentine."

Eliza looked out upon the graves spread before them. She handed the clove cigarette to Tuohay, who glanced at rose lipstick smudged on the cigarette while Eliza spoke. "But why Aiden Kearney, and his brother Rian? What was the point of killing them?"

Tuohay took a drag of the cigarette, savoring the taste. "Remember, the Kearneys got her released from the Danvers asylum based on the promise that she had evidence that could take down Father Donnelly and the archbishop."

"Which, apparently, she did," said Eldredge.

"At some point in her investigation into the whereabouts of the Templar Diamond, Mary realized that Father Abrams' death was a ruse. To prove it to herself, she dug up his grave."

Eldredge furrowed his eyebrows. "How do you know that?"

"There was evidence of it in their flat," Tuohay replied. "Shovels, a rug caked with dry dirt, a hooded lantern, and the like. And the ground was still broken in when Eliza and dug up the grave."

Eldredge shuddered.

"It added up," Tuohay finished.

Eliza whistled. "You mean, Mary Hart had Aiden and Rian dig up the grave? How did she convince them to do that?"

"It was most likely only Rian," said Tuohay. "And probably on the premise that the diamond was hidden there, which would have gone a long way in restoring Aiden's reputation. I am certain it was with goodwill in his mind. In any case, it was done, and Mary's hunch about Abrams faked death was confirmed by a coffin full of stones."

"And when she returned to their flat…" Eliza dropped the cigarette and crushed it out with her boot.

"Sadly, yes," confirmed Tuohay. "She poisoned them, like the others. She would leave no trace of her presence or activities, and even go to the trouble of diverting suspicion onto others by etching 'my brothers' keeper'."

A gust of wind caused a lapse in the conversation, which stretched into a lengthy silence. The numbered graves waited quietly below, and upon reflection seemed to expect the same from those looking upon them.

"I think we've talked enough about the case," said Eliza, her gaze fixated on the gravestones. "The truth is, I'm glad to be standing here, and not residing in my own grave right now."

"Life isn't quite done with us, it seems," said Tuohay.

"So, this is where the brothers are buried?" asked Eldredge. "A pauper's grave…not even consecrated ground for a priest that deserved it above so many others."

"Indeed," said Tuohay, his voice solemn.

"Do you know which markers are theirs?"

Tuohay nodded. "Those two there, side by side." He clasped his hands behind his back and stood against the wind. They gazed silently upon the rows and rows of meagerly marked graves for several more minutes. Breaking the reverence, Tuohay took out his flask and handed it to Eldredge.

"You first, old boy."

Eldredge removed his hat. "As our good Lord says: *for those who honor Me, I will honor*." He raised the flask and took a long drink. Blinking from the strength of the liquor, he handed it to Eliza.

She took a moment, the breeze blowing wayward strands of hair across her face. "In the words of the great bard, *Mine honor is my life, both grow in one. Take honor from me, and my life is done*." She took a swig. "They were honorable to the end, and so it was life that was taken from them instead."

"Well said." There was a distant look in Tuohay's eyes as he accepted the flask from Eliza.

"To my brother Gregory," he said, and he drank the last of it.

Acknowledgements

I am indebted to my father, William Milhomme, for providing the historical content for the novel, and more importantly for being my partner on this journey. Without him, this story would not exist. And to my mother, Donna, for indulging the countless hours spent by her husband on his research.

Additional debts to Cole Confer, who took part when the characters were at their most vulnerable; to Jen, Kent, and Helen Marie, who provided a steady stream of fuel for the imagination; to Tracy, Toby, Matt, and Brandin for their thoughtful and creative insights and contributions; to Jennifer Weltz for her enduring support over the years; and to Danelle McCafferty for her invaluable consultation and editing.

The largest thanks go to my wonderful wife Marcy; without her this and so much more simply would not be, and to Saylor and Hadley, upon whom I will always rely.

CPSIA information can be obtained at www.ICGtesting.com
Printed in the USA
BVOW06s1153090815

412494BV00010B/137/P